THE WITCHES'
HAMMER

JANE STANTON HITCHCOCK

THE WITCHES' HAMMER

A DUTTON BOOK

DUTTON

Published by the Penguin Group
Penguin Books USA Inc., 375 Hudson Street, New York, New York 10014, U.S.A.
Penguin Books Ltd, 27 Wrights Lane, London W8 5TZ, England
Penguin Books Australia Ltd, Ringwood, Victoria, Australia
Penguin Books Canada Ltd, 10 Alcorn Avenue, Toronto, Ontario, Canada M4V 3B2
Penguin Books (N.Z.) Ltd, 182-190 Wairau Road, Auckland 10, New Zealand

Penguin Books Ltd, Registered Offices:
Harmondsworth, Middlesex, England

First published by Dutton, an imprint of Dutton Signet,
a division of Penguin Books USA Inc.
Distributed in Canada by McClelland & Stewart Inc.

First Printing, October, 1994
1   3   5   7   9   10   8   6   4   2

 REGISTERED TRADEMARK—MARCA REGISTRADA

LIBRARY OF CONGRESS CATALOGING IN PUBLICATION DATA
HITCHCOCK, JANE STANTON.
THE WITCHES' HAMMER / JANE STANTON HITCHCOCK.
P. CM.
ISBN 0-525-93641-6
1. RARE BOOKS—COLLECTORS AND COLLECTING—NEW YORK (N.Y.)—FICTION. 2. MAN-
WOMAN RELATIONSHIPS—FICTION. 3. WITCHCRAFT—FICTION. I. TITLE.
PS3558.I82W57 1994
813'.54—DC20   94-17420
CIP

Printed in the United States of America
Set in Caslon 540

Designed by Steven N. Stathakis

For Arnold Cooper

"In much wisdom is much grief: and he that increaseth knowledge increaseth sorrow."

Ecclesiastes 1:18

At the beginning of August 1944, Adolf Hitler, reeling from an unsuccessful attempt on his life, secretly dispatched a courier to Allied-occupied Rome. The courier was transported by a Storch light aircraft, used for such purposes. He made his way to the Vatican disguised as a priest and met with Pope Pius XII, whose secretary noted the brief meeting on his calendar, but not its purpose. Leaving Rome, the courier returned to the field where the Storch was to pick him up at dusk. There, an American patrol spotted him signaling with a flashlight to the circling plane and captured him. The courier's effects were confiscated, and he was sent to an interrogation center for prisoners of war. When the effects were examined, the G-2 captain found they included nothing but his forged identity papers and an old book. . . .

The *Malleus Maleficarum* was published in 1485, accompanied by a papal bull, sanctifying it with supreme Church authority. It was the law of the land in both Catholic and Protestant Christendom for over two hundred years.

THE WITCHES'
HAMMER

 T CAME AS NO SURPRISE TO THOSE WHO KNEW HIM that John O'Connell named his only child for a character in a book. He called her Beatrice, after Dante's guide in *The Divine Comedy*. A surgeon by profession, John O'Connell loved books: they were the passion that shaped his life. His library of rare books and manuscripts was well known to those in the field. Over the years, he had assiduously cultivated what he called his "little garden of knowledge," using expert advice and his own shrewd instincts to form an eclectic but first-rate collection. Even at the beginning of his career, when some purchases were a financial strain on the family, Dr. O'Connell could not resist a book or manuscript that struck his fancy. Unlike most other collectors, who sell their finds or trade them up for rarer, more valuable ones, John O'Connell, having bought a book, never let it out of his possession. To him, books were friends; once acquired, they were his for life.

The man most instrumental in helping O'Connell form his collection was Giuseppe Antonelli, a renowned Italian book dealer, who

sold him some outstanding treasures over the years, including a
Book of Hours illuminated by Del Cherico, Niclaus Jenson's incunabulum of Pliny's *Historia naturalis*, printed on vellum, and a complete set of the *Divina commedia*, with illustrations, published in 1804
by the master printer Giambattista Bodoni.

John O'Connell met Giuseppe Antonelli in Rome in 1954.
O'Connell liked to recall the day he wandered into a tiny rare-book
shop on the Via Monserrato, where a volume of Plutarch's *Lives* on
display in the window caught his eye. He bought the book on the
spot and entered into a lengthy discussion with the proprietor, who
spoke perfect English with a light Italian accent.

"Giuseppe and I recognized each other immediately, like Rosi-
crucians," O'Connell would say later. "We both knew a bookman
when we saw one."

In the ensuing years, the relationship between the two men
evolved into something more than that of client and dealer. They
forged a genuine friendship with each other, based upon their mutual appreciation and love of rare books. Whenever Signor Antonelli
visited New York, he paid a call on Dr. O'Connell in his town house
on Beekman Place, a quiet neighborhood, well away from the bustle
of city life, overlooking the East River. The four-story brownstone
was one of a number of old-fashioned houses on the charming tree-
lined block. Sometimes Antonelli brought with him a parcel of wares
he thought might be of interest to the doctor. O'Connell, in turn,
took pleasure in showing Antonelli his recent acquisitions. On occa-
sion, a curator in the field or another bookman was invited to dine
with the two gentlemen. Afterward, they would sit in the library,
drinking brandy, smoking cigars, trading book stories, until long past
midnight.

Giuseppe Antonelli was a wiry little man. Angular cheekbones,
a prominent nose, and meticulous grooming gave him a striking profile. His beady black eyes, sparkling with inquisitiveness, were forever darting about in search of an object or a person to pin with their
penetrating gaze. John O'Connell, on the other hand, was big and
stocky. His large features and gentle pale-blue eyes were dominated
by a mane of white hair. A ready smile and a shambling, cozy appearance contributed to his aura of strength and intelligence.

Signor Antonelli always wore a starched white shirt, a pin-
striped suit, cut in the English style, and highly polished black
shoes. He sported a cane, the handle of which was a gold hawk's

head with an elongated beak. The sculpted bird had red ruby eyes. Antonelli presented a marked contrast to Dr. O'Connell, whose clothes, casual or formal, never seemed to fit.

Even in their manner, the two men could not have seemed more dissimilar. The Italian maintained a somewhat stiff, formal edge, while the American doctor was naturally outgoing and friendly. However, there was an underlying remoteness in them both, which expressed itself in their obsessive love of books and the solitary life of reading.

In later years, Signor Antonelli, semiretired, made fewer visits to the United States. However, he and Dr. O'Connell continued to correspond. A bachelor, Antonelli filled his days with his studies and the company of a few close friends, while Dr. O'Connell enjoyed the life of a family man. When Elizabeth, O'Connell's wife of thirty-seven years, had died, two years before, Signor Antonelli sent his friend an incunabulum of Latin meditations on the life of Christ as a remembrance. Though the bereaved surgeon took a dim view of religion and its supposed consolations, he appreciated the gesture.

In the wake of his wife's death, John O'Connell grew depressed. Neither his work nor his library seemed to fill the void created by her passing. His daughter, Beatrice, was suffering as well. Beatrice's grief was compounded by the failure of her marriage, which had ended in divorce the previous year, and the frustrations of a stalled career. As is often the case under such circumstances, father and daughter drifted closer together. Eventually, Beatrice gave up her apartment and moved back home. Though she and Dr. O'Connell agreed the arrangement was only temporary, it seemed to suit them both, and no effort was made by either of them to change it.

One day, John O'Connell announced to his daughter that Signor Antonelli was coming to New York, after a four-year hiatus. As the day approached, Beatrice watched her father anticipate his old friend's visit with growing impatience, and was certain that his agitation somehow involved a book. She hadn't seen him quite so jumpy since he'd discovered a copy of the rare and valuable *Bay Psalm Book*, one of the earliest examples of Colonial printing, at a rummage sale outside Boston over fifteen years earlier.

Dr. O'Connell was often secretive about the books he acquired, or was thinking of acquiring, particularly if they had an odd provenance. His late wife had learned early in their marriage not to intrude upon his collector's mind, and she had taught her daughter likewise. When John O'Connell got into one of his moods, he retreated to his library, shutting himself up there for hours after work, barely acknowledging the existence of his wife and daughter. During those periods, Elizabeth O'Connell, who had a wry streak, used to joke that her husband was "away with his mistresses" but that luckily for her, most of them were "several hundred years old."

A few days before Signor Antonelli was scheduled to arrive, Dr. O'Connell began to spend increasingly more time alone in his favorite room. Insisting on an early supper, he didn't linger over coffee, listen to classical music, or discuss the news of the day with Beatrice, as he usually did. He would excuse himself from the table abruptly and retreat to his library for the rest of the evening, with the door closed. When Beatrice asked him why he was being so secretive, he responded evasively. She knew better than to press him. Encroaching old age and the recent sorrows of life had deepened and darkened all her father's moods, and she decided it was best to let this one simply run its course. Beatrice, being independent and solitary by nature, went on about her business—reading, writing, and researching—knowing that sooner or later he would tell her what was going on.

Finally, the day of Antonelli's visit came. Beatrice felt her father's spirits lift when the doorbell rang promptly at seven-thirty that evening and Signor Antonelli, still the dapper dresser, still sporting the same hawk's-head cane, walked through the front door.

"Giuseppe! Welcome, welcome!" John O'Connell cried warmly, shaking hands with the gaunt old gentleman.

"My dear John, how good it is to see you! *E cara Beatrice*," he said with a stiff smile, for he hardly recognized the daughter of his old friend.

Beatrice had greatly changed since the last time he'd seen her. He remembered her as an extremely pretty and lively girl with luxuriant hair, a luminous complexion, and a warm, appealing smile. Now, however, she appeared somber and pinched, like a fruit with all the juice sucked out of it. She had lost weight. Her skin was slightly sallow. Her narrow face was still aristocratic but too thin, and her soft gray-green eyes were rimmed with shadows. An edge of sadness marred all her expressions. She wore her abundant dark hair pulled back in a tight bun. Her clothes, strict and black, concealed her lithe figure. She walked with her shoulders slightly hunched over and her head down, as if she were hiding from the world. Neither age nor infirmity was afflicting her, but rather a profound lack of confidence and energy. Soft responses, weak smiles, and vague irritation at the interruption of routine marked her as a disappointed woman—a woman downtrodden by life.

"Come this way, please," Beatrice said, leading the two men upstairs.

"Giuseppe, I can't tell you how much I've been looking forward to your visit," Dr. O'Connell said. "You haven't changed a bit."

"Nor you, John."

"No? I feel old. We'll have a drink before dinner, shall we?" the doctor said, affectionately patting his old friend on the back as they climbed the stairs in tandem.

In the living room, Beatrice fixed her father and Antonelli Scotches and poured herself a glass of white wine. She sat by silently, only half listening to the two men as they entered into polite small talk. She was more interested in the wine and the dulling effect it had on her nerves. Her mind drifted off during the conversation. She wondered casually if Signor Antonelli had ever had a passionate relationship with anyone. She always wondered that about men.

Signor Antonelli allowed as how New York had changed for the worse since his last trip. He said his regular hotel was under new management, which, not knowing him, took no pains to accord him the special treatment he was used to. Dr. O'Connell, in turn, spoke briefly of the escalating turmoil in the world, touching upon the political situation here and abroad. The four years between the two old friends quickly melted away, however, and the conversation took a more personal turn.

"John," Antonelli said, "please let me say again how sorry I am about Elizabeth. She was a lovely person, very *simpatica*. I remember her with great fondness."

"That's very kind of you, Giuseppe. . . . Yes, it's god-awfully lonely here without her. Thank God for Beatrice," O'Connell said, beaming at his daughter. "She's moved back in with me for a while. Gave up her apartment to be with her old man, didn't you, hon?"

Beatrice looked up distractedly.

"I'm telling Giuseppe how you moved back home to take care of your old man."

"Ah, so you and your husband live here now?" Signor Antonelli asked.

"No . . . I'm divorced," Beatrice said.

"Oh, I am so sorry," Signor Antonelli replied, with an air of concern. "I never met your husband, but he looked like a fine fellow from the little wedding picture your mother so kindly sent me."

Beatrice thought of the small marriage ceremony which had taken place in that very room over five years earlier, remembering it as the happiest day of her life. However, her thoughts quickly tumbled through the dissolution of the union.

"It was for the best . . . I think," she said, fiddling absently with her watch, turning it around and around on her wrist as she spoke. "Anyway, I was looking for another place when Mother died, and Daddy seemed so lonely here in this big house that I thought, well, why not just move back in here for a while until things get a little more settled?"

"She's like the daughter who came for dinner. I can't get rid of her!" the doctor joked.

"I couldn't very well leave you to rattle around here all by yourself," Beatrice said.

"She's a devoted daughter. She's here because she knows I need her."

"Children must be a great comfort in one's old age," Signor Antonelli said, glancing over at Beatrice with a wistful smile. "I do not regret never having married. But I do regret never having had children."

"So what are you up to, Giuseppe? Are you enjoying your retirement?"

"Well, as you know, John, in my profession, one never really retires. It is true I have sold my shop. But I continue to buy and sell privately for a few very special clients—among them you, my dear friend." He toasted the doctor with his glass of Scotch. "In fact, I am very, very anxious to see this mysterious book about which you have written to me."

"I haven't told Beatrice anything about it yet."

"Then it must be very mysterious indeed!" cried Antonelli with mock seriousness.

"Oh, you know Daddy. He's like that about his books sometimes. I'm used to it." Beatrice got up and poured herself another glass of wine.

"Yeah, I've been pretty distracted for the last few days, haven't I, Bea? . . . But she understands me."

O'Connell winked at his daughter with affection. Just then, the clock on the mantelpiece chimed eight.

"Come on, let's eat," the doctor said, putting down his glass decisively. "I'll tell you the whole story at dinner."

Beatrice took another sip of wine. Then she and Signor Antonelli followed Dr. O'Connell downstairs to the dining room, where the round table in front of the bay window facing the tiny back garden was set for supper. The men helped themselves to the cold buffet laid out on the sideboard, while Beatrice lit the candles around the room.

"Please excuse our informality," O'Connell said, pouring his friend a glass of red wine. "I let the cook go when Liz died, so it's a little bit catch-as-catch-can."

"But this is delicious!" Antonelli exclaimed, forking in a bite of *vitello tonnato*. "Who made it?"

"I did," Beatrice said, joining them at the table with a plate of food.

"You are a marvelous cook. This is just the sort of supper I like."

Beatrice was pleased. She enjoyed cooking, though her father seldom noticed the finer points of her efforts.

"I must say, it is lovely to be in a proper house rather than an apartment. What one misses in a city is space." Antonelli sighed, looking out onto the enclosed garden, where twilight was descending. "It is so relaxing and comfortable here—not at all like being in New York."

"It's really too big for me now, even with Bea here. But I can't leave it on account of my library."

"Not just because of the library, Daddy. All your memories are here. You said so yourself. Mother's here."

"Yes, you're right. Liz loved this house. Anyway, it'd be hell to pack up all those years of living. I don't know what you're gonna do when your old man croaks, Bea."

"Daddy, please," Beatrice said with evident pain. "I've told you, you're not to talk like that."

"I'm leaving the library to Beatrice," Dr. O'Connell went on. "She'll decide what she wants to do with it."

"Signor Antonelli, you can see this is a subject I hate," Beatrice said. "But rest assured my father's library will remain intact. It will go to a public library or a university with my father's name on it, so people can know what a wonderful collector he is."

"With one little exception, of course," O'Connell said.

"And what is that?" Signor Antonelli inquired.

"In fact, it's an incunabulum you sold me. The *Roman de la Rose*. She's always fancied it, haven't you, Bea?"

Beatrice nodded.

"Ah, the poem of courtly love," Antonelli said. "A very good choice." He looked more closely at Beatrice, divining for the first time a deep romantic streak in the handsome but disconsolate-looking young woman.

"Now, John," Antonelli continued, "when are you going to tell us about this mysterious book you have acquired?"

"Yes, Daddy. I'm longing to hear about it too."

Dr. O'Connell leaned forward and cleared his throat. He folded his hands in front of him, looking somber. Beatrice poured them all some more wine. She and Signor Antonelli sat back, making themselves comfortable, prepared to listen to the story.

"About a year ago," O'Connell began, "I performed an operation on a referral patient from Oklahoma City. The operation was a success. The man went back to Oklahoma, and I didn't give it any more thought until one day last month, when a package arrived with the following letter." He extracted a piece of white paper from the inside pocket of his jacket, unfolded it, and read aloud:

" 'Dear Dr. O'Connell, I haven't known how to properly thank you for all that you have done for me. I feel I've licked this damn cancer thing thanks to you, and I am forever in your debt. I learned from one of your associates at the hospital that you have a very great book collection. Well, here is something I think you will enjoy. I picked it up during the war and kept it as a souvenir of those terrible and wonderful times.

" 'I don't know if the book is worth much, but its sentimental value is, for me, enormous because it represents a time in my life when I felt I was doing something good for my God and my country. There is no person I would wish to have it more than you, Dr. O'Connell, for I know it will be safe and properly cared for in your fine, capable hands—just as I have been. God bless you.' Et cetera, et cetera."

John O'Connell put down the letter and stared at it for a long moment, having grown somewhat emotional while reading. His eyes moist with tears, he folded it carefully and put it back in his jacket pocket. Beatrice leaned over and touched her father's arm reassuringly.

"A lovely sentiment," Signor Antonelli said.

"Yes, the letter's very fine, very appreciative," O'Connell said, taking a sip of wine. "The book, however, is an altogether different matter."

"Whatever do you mean, John?"

"You'll see," the doctor replied, with an appearance of perturbation.

"Why, Daddy? What on earth is it?"

"I'm not sure."

Antonelli fidgeted with the corners of his linen place mat. "Perhaps I will know," he offered.

"That's exactly why I wrote to you, Giuseppe. Because if anybody's going to know what the hell this thing is, you will."

"Please—may we be allowed to view the book?" Antonelli said.

"Sure, why not? Might as well get it over with." Throwing down his napkin, O'Connell rose from the table. "Let's go on up."

Ever mindful of decorum, Signor Antonelli folded his napkin precisely before following his host upstairs. Beatrice was extremely curious and decided to join them before making the coffee. Reaching the second floor, the doctor opened the thick mahogany doors at the entrance to the library. They swung apart to reveal a double-height room lined floor to ceiling with old volumes and manuscripts. He flicked a switch, which lit up a row of old-fashioned brass light fixtures mounted on the bookcases.

Signor Antonelli looked around, taking a deep breath, relishing the smell of old leather as if it were fresh country air. He was pleased to see that almost nothing in the room had changed. The two large windows facing out onto the garden were still cloaked in heavy dark-green damask curtains, pulled shut to block out all light. The antique furniture was just as he remembered it, grouped away from the walls so as not to impede the locating of any book. He admired once more the old Tiffany lamp on Dr. O'Connell's desk, its domed stained-glass shade dripping azure and emerald leaves. The tall wooden library ladders, which slid on tracks across the vast bookcases, reminded the old gentleman of the mild arthritis in his knees. He noted one new acquisition—a draftman's table, tilting upward, on which a copy of Dr. Johnson's *Dictionary of the English Language* was displayed.

As was his habit, O'Connell checked the thermostat on the wall, making sure the temperature was just right. The doctor then unlocked the top drawer of his desk and took out a small black leather-bound book, measuring about six inches in height, four inches in width, and an inch and a half in thickness.

"This is it," he said, practically throwing the unprepossessing-looking volume down on top of the desk, as if he couldn't wait to get it out of his hands.

Signor Antonelli and Beatrice stepped up to look at it. The dealer reached into his breast pocket and extracted a pair of spectacles, put them on, and picked up the book in order to examine it more closely. Holding the volume close to his face, he sniffed at it and turned it around every which way, gingerly running his fingers along the binding and the top, fore, and bottom edges, which looked brownish in color, as if they had been singed. Then he laid the book back down on the desk and opened it carefully, with a certain ceremony. On the first page, there was a single line of Latin text in dense black Gothic lettering, the capital letters of which were rubricated.

" '*Videmus nunc per speculum in aenigmate, tunc autem facie ad faciem,*' " he read aloud—but more to himself than to the company.

"What does it mean?" Beatrice asked.

"It is a quotation from Saint Paul," Antonelli replied reflectively. "It means, 'For now, we see through a glass darkly; but then face to face.' "

Beatrice and her father stood by while Signor Antonelli gave the work a thorough examination. As he turned one yellowing page after another, his eyes began to flicker with excitement. Periodically, he issued a little cry of delight or recognition or horror—Beatrice wasn't quite sure which. He paused over the center section, then continued on until he reached the last page. Finally, he closed the book and looked up.

"Well?" O'Connell said.

"Please—let us sit down," Antonelli replied.

Dr. O'Connell sat behind his desk, while Signor Antonelli and Beatrice pulled up two chairs and faced him. Beatrice picked up the book and began perusing it, as Antonelli spoke in a slow, measured voice.

10

"Well, my dear John, you have in your possession a grimoire."

"Ah." The doctor nodded.

"What's that?" Beatrice asked.

"Very simply, my dear, it is a book of black magic," Antonelli said.

"I figured it was something like that," Dr. O'Connell said. "Though from the looks of it, I thought it might have been a work of pornography."

Antonelli smiled. "Very often, they are one and the same, John. It is written in French," he went on. "Printed on vellum, published in 1670. Its author signs himself 'Pape Honorius III,' but that is a spurious attribution. No pope wrote this. The illustrator is not mentioned. It was re-bound sometime in the eighteenth century, I would say. The text is accompanied by a series of illustrative woodcuts, as you can see. It has no title page except for the date, written in Roman numerals, and the place, 'A Rome'—a rather humorous location for such a work, no? What is particularly interesting is the quotation from Saint Paul at the beginning. . . . The author was having a little joke, trying to make the reader think he was about to embark on a religious tract, when, in fact, he was about to dabble in the black arts."

As Dr. O'Connell and Signor Antonelli continued their discussion about the book, Beatrice began to leaf through it. Page after page revealed the most macabre sensibility imaginable. Interspersed through the dense French text were occult signs and a series of gruesome woodcuts depicting bizarre sexual acts, frightening supernatural occurrences, and images of demonic animals and people. A particularly disturbing section at the center of the book highlighted a terrifying journey of death and resurrection.

The vignettes first showed a man and a woman coupling in a clearing in the woods. The woman disappears, and the man is murdered by a priest, who stabs him through the head, heart, and groin with a sword, the hilt of which is an upside-down cross. Left to rot, the corpse is assaulted by lions. The beasts then carry the dismembered pieces to the center of a maze and bury them. The flesh rots away, leaving only bones. A full moon rises, and by its eerie light a sorcerer appears, holding a book. He draws a circle on the ground, marking it with crosses, the twelve signs of the zodiac, and seven occult symbols.

Stepping inside the circle, the sorcerer begins to call out strange

words from the book. Soon the woman reappears and tries to seduce
the sorcerer, to no avail. Protected by his magic circle, he is immune
to her advances. Becoming infuriated, she turns into a succubus with
fiery eyes, fangs, and a tail, her mouth dripping with blood. This
hideous creature again tries to get at the sorcerer, but she cannot, for
the magic circle protects him. The sorcerer continues with his incan-
tations. Unable to harm him, the succubus departs. With that, the
bones of the dead man are reassembled, and his skeleton arises from
the center of the maze. The sorcerer lifts the book to the heavens
in praise as the skeleton flies upward toward the moon.

Beatrice felt a strange pull in her gut as she looked at the woodcuts. She stared at the succubus with its bloody fangs, rolling eyes,
and flicking tongue, its hair and breasts blowing wildly in an imag-
inary wind. She couldn't help thinking that this ghastly, sexually voracious being, depicted by the artist with such evident loathing, was
the aspect of women that men fear most. And horrifying as it was,
she felt a disturbing kinship with it.

Dr. O'Connell scanned his daughter's face. "What do you think
of it, Bea?"

"Primitive, but compelling," she replied matter-of-factly.

"The woodcuts deal with the blackest magic there is—namely,
necromancy, the raising of the dead," Antonelli said.

"And who are the dead, Signor Antonelli? Men?" Beatrice said
somewhat facetiously.

"What do you mean, Beatrice?" the old man asked.

"Well, it just seems to me that the artist was quite terrified of
women, judging from this image of the succubus."

"Surely, a succubus is not anyone's image of a woman, my dear
child. A succubus is an image of evil."

"Yes, but choosing to personify evil as a woman is an interesting
choice nonetheless."

"It is in keeping with the imagery of the time."

"Perhaps." Beatrice shrugged.

Antonelli stared at her for a long moment. Beatrice looked away
and closed the grimoire, then put it back on the desk. Taking the
book in his hands, Dr. O'Connell scolded it directly, as if it was a
person.

"Well, we're going to have to give you a shelf all to yourself,
you hear? To prevent you from contaminating my friends! Tell me,
Giuseppe," he went on, "have you seen a lot of these things?"

"A few, yes. I have a client who is interested in such oddities, and occasionally I have located one for him. But they are extremely rare, and this one is in very good condition. Also, the illustrations make it particularly amusing."

"*Amusing?*" Beatrice raised her eyebrows.

"My dear Beatrice, one cannot take it all that seriously. Grimoires are a product of the medieval mind, which was full of superstition, as you know. These are people who believed the earth was flat, after all, and that one would sail off the edge of it."

"How about the Inquisition?" she said. "Not a very amusing time."

"Oh, but that was mainly politics, my dear—the result of the *Malleus Maleficarum.*"

"Ah, yes," Dr. O'Connell said knowingly.

"What's that?" Beatrice inquired.

"The *Malleus Maleficarum* means 'The Witches' Hammer,' " Signor Antonelli said. "It is a tract published in Germany in 1485, written by two fanatics, Jakob Sprenger and Heinrich Krämer. It is important because it elevated witchcraft to the level of heresy, branding it once and for all as the work of the devil rather than the misguided acts of a few disturbed human beings. It offers strict guidelines for ferreting out witches and for conducting the trials of the accused."

John O'Connell was nodding in acknowledgment.

"I've never heard of it," Beatrice said.

"It is nothing—a footnote of history, interesting only because it was legitimized by the famous bull of Pope Innocent VIII, which of course endowed the work with supreme authority," Antonelli continued. "By treating witchcraft in this very serious and organized way, the Vatican cleverly increased its power."

"How?" Beatrice asked, genuinely curious.

"Well, now it had a specific and well-defined enemy in everyday life against which to focus its energies. That is what led to the increased power of the inquisition. It was all politics, as I said."

"A shameful time," Dr. O'Connell said, lighting his pipe.

"Of course, it all seems rather ludicrous today," Signor Antonelli said. "Imagine the idea that there are such things as witches among us—real agents of the devil. And that if a poor unfortunate old woman goes to gather herbs in her garden, it is for nefarious purposes. Or if a husband loses his potency, it is because his wife has put a spell on him and she is a succubus. No, no, no—it is all a grim fairy tale, if you will excuse my little pun!" He laughed.

Antonelli picked up the book and began examining it again. "You know, John," he said, "this client that I spoke of—the one who collects curiosities—I think he would really rather fancy this little orphan. May I contact him and ask him if he might be interested in purchasing it? He will pay you a good price."

Beatrice detected a sense of urgency beneath Signor Antonelli's apparently casual proposal. She thought he was far more interested in this "curiosity" than he was letting on.

"Giuseppe, that's very kind of you. But you know my policy: once a book in my library, always a book in my library."

"Yes, of course, John. I understand. But I thought as you had not acquired it yourself, and it seems to disturb you in some way . . . In other words, it is not a work that you yourself purchased, merely a present, so—"

"Presents are even more precious to me," the doctor interrupted. "I have a little section set aside for them. I still have that Nancy Drew mystery you gave me for my birthday years ago," he said to Beatrice.

"And just *when* did I give you a Nancy Drew mystery for your birthday, Dad?"

"You were around nine or ten, I think." O'Connell addressed Signor Antonelli in that affectionate way parents have of telling stories on their children when they are present. "Her note said she thought I'd like it—and P.S., could she borrow it after I'd finished?"

Antonelli smiled politely, but he seemed preoccupied.

"I give Bea a book every Christmas and birthday, don't I, darling? Greatest present you can give someone—a book."

Beatrice nodded, recalling all the works of literature her father had given her through the years, which she kept lined up neatly in the bookcase stretching the length of one wall in her bedroom. They were not valuable books, except for their contents: Homer and Dante; Chaucer, Shakespeare, and Blake; Eliot and Austen and Dickens; Balzac, Flaubert, and Proust; Tolstoy and Dostoyevsky and Chekhov; Emerson, Thoreau, Melville, Hawthorne, Twain—classics meant to be read and reread—plus the mysteries she so dearly loved, starting with Poe and Wilkie Collins, straight on through to Conan Doyle, Agatha Christie, P. D. James, and Elmore Leonard.

Beatrice noticed that Signor Antonelli was growing increasingly edgy. He caught her looking at him and rose abruptly from his chair.

"I'm afraid you will have to excuse me," he said. "It is quite late for me with the difference of time. Will you forgive me if I bid you both good night?"

"Won't you stay for a little coffee, Giuseppe?" Dr. O'Connell said. "I'm sorry I didn't offer you any, but I was so anxious for you to see the book."

"No, no, I really must make my apologies. I am so pleased to have seen you, John, and Beatrice. And the book, of course, is really very, very interesting—a little treasure."

Beatrice and her father walked Antonelli downstairs, where she removed his hawk's-head cane from the umbrella stand near the front door.

"I remember playing with this cane when I was a little girl," Beatrice said, handing it to him.

"What once was an affectation has now become a necessity," Antonelli replied, leaning on the elegant stick.

"What's your schedule now, Giuseppe?"

"I will call you tomorrow, John, if I may, and we will certainly meet again before I leave."

"And when do you have to go back?"

"I am not sure. It will depend on a few things. In any case, it was lovely to have seen you both, and *mille grazie* for a delightful evening."

"I'll be puttering around here all day." O'Connell opened the front door for his friend. "I look forward to hearing from you."

"I shall telephone you in the morning, John, when I am more certain of my plans."

"Sure, Giuseppe, whatever you like."

"*Buona sera*, then. *A domani.*"

Signor Antonelli walked into the night.

"Be careful, Giuseppe!" O'Connell called out. "This neighborhood isn't as safe as it used to be!"

"Do not worry! I shall take care!" the old man cried back.

Antonelli disappeared down the dark street, the tap-tap-tapping of his cane on the sidewalk fading gradually in the distance. Dr. O'Connell closed the front door.

"There's something he's not telling us," Beatrice said.

"You think so? Like what?"

"I don't know, but did you see the way he was looking at the grimoire? Plus, he couldn't wait to get out of here."

"He was just tired, that's all. You know how jet lag suddenly hits you. Giuseppe's always been very straight with me."

"You mark my words, Daddy."

Dr. O'Connell smiled. "How about making us some coffee?"

Beatrice went into the kitchen to make a pot of the espresso they both loved. She prepared a tray and took it upstairs, joining her father in the library.

"Giuseppe looks older, don't you think? Even though I told him he didn't," Dr. O'Connell remarked, taking little sips of the strong coffee. "I shouldn't lie, but that's what comes of having kissed the Blarney Stone, I guess. Anyway, I'm glad to know what it is for sure. Loathsome things, aren't they, grimoires. But interesting."

"Don't give it to him, Dad."

"You know me. I don't part with my friends, Bea—even if they're a bit unsavory."

"I wonder what it is about this book," Beatrice said, getting up to examine the grimoire, which lay on the desk where her father had left it.

O'Connell poured himself another cup of espresso.

"It's probably worth a few bucks and he thinks he can make some money. He's a dealer, after all."

"No." Beatrice shut the book and paused thoughtfully. "It's something else."

"Like what?"

"I don't know, but something. . . ." She ran her fingers over the black leather cover, colorlessly tooled with the signs of the zodiac and other occult symbols.

"Giuseppe's an honest guy. He's not about to gyp me. Don't forget, I've known him since before you were born, you little pipsqueak."

"Yes, well, I think he's going to try to get it away from you, Dad."

"I doubt it," O'Connell replied nonchalantly. "He understands my policy about the library and respects it. Not that he doesn't occasionally try to buy books back from me—I won't say that. After all, he's sold me some great stuff over the years. But he knows I mean no when I say no. And he never pushes."

"He will this time. Want to make a bet? I bet he calls you about it tomorrow."

"Bet he doesn't."

"How much? A hundred dollars?"

"Ten dollars," the doctor countered. "I'm not as rich as you are."

"Okay, ten. Ten dollars says he calls tomorrow and makes you some amazing offer for it." Beatrice pointed an accusatory finger at him.

Dr. O'Connell shook his head, seemingly amused.

"Don't laugh, Daddy. I have a very uneasy feeling about this little devil. There's something about it he's not telling us. I just know it. I *feel* it."

"Come here and sit down, Sherlock Holmes." O'Connell patted the couch.

Beatrice obeyed, snuggling up against him. Her father sometimes had the effect of making her feel like a little girl.

"You know, ever since you were small, you always loved a mystery," John O'Connell said, stroking his daughter's hair.

"Did I? I suppose I was preparing myself for life."

"Is life a mystery to you, Bea, dear?"

"And how! I can't figure out what the hell I'm doing here."

"I just hope you're not waiting for something that's never going to happen."

"I know . . . like Emma Bovary, ever searching for that sail on the horizon. Or John Marcher and his beast in the jungle. I feel that way sometimes, Daddy. I really do. Like I'm waiting for something or someone to shape my existence, to clarify what the whole damn thing's about, I guess. Do you know what I mean?"

"In a way. But I was lucky. I had a calling. I always knew I wanted to be a doctor, and that shaped my life right there."

"I wish I had a calling," Beatrice said sadly. "I wish I knew for certain what it was I wanted to do."

"What about your novel? Have you abandoned that?"

"I start things. Stop things. I can't seem to finish anything."

"Well, you have your research. You're very well respected there."

"Oh, that's just something I do for other people," she said dismissively. "It's *about* writing, but I'm not really writing myself. It's just a job."

17

"All your authors seem to write good books and win prizes based on your efforts, sweetheart."

Beatrice was a specialist in a little-known area of publishing in which writers hire people to do their historical and sociological detail work for them. The job was well-paying, as people of her competence and academic background were in demand. She prided herself on the investigative work she had done for several best-selling authors, two of whom had won National Book Awards and one a Pulitzer.

Doing research had always given her the illusion of being up on things, in on things, without ever really having to test herself as a writer. She simply supplied the ammunition to soldiers at the front lines of their profession, those willing to risk savaging by the critics. "No guts, no glory," her father used to say in an effort to encourage her to branch out and get more into life as well as write a book of her own.

"I was thinking," Beatrice said. "Maybe I ought to go back to school and try to become a teacher."

"Really? That sounds like a fine idea."

"Oh, Daddy, I don't know." She sighed. "I'm drifting, drifting in the wake of failure. . . . I can't seem to latch onto anything."

"You haven't failed, honey."

"Oh, yes, I have. I've failed miserably in my marriage, my career . . ."

"Those aren't failures. Those are setbacks—nothing to be ashamed of."

"Daddy, forgive me. But you're speaking from the vantage point of a distinguished career and happy marriage. You've had a full life."

"Well, you see, life takes on a different aspect when you confront death, day in, day out. As a surgeon, I've seen people die, and within minutes of their passing, their faces are almost unrecognizable, because the life force has simply gone out of them. In that moment, it all seems very simple: a spirit inhabits a body for a finite length of time and drifts on to somewhere else. There's no intended shape to existence, Bea. Life is only the moment at hand."

Beatrice and her father sat in silence for a time. Beatrice thought back to the grimoire and the figure of the succubus.

"Some moments are too dangerous," she said at last.

Dr. O'Connell looked askance at his daughter. "What do you mean, sweetheart?"

"I'm not sure. But when I was looking at the grimoire, I thought—" She hesitated.

"What?"

"Oh, I don't know." She shook her head, knowing she couldn't tell her father what had really crossed her mind, so she made light of the thought. "Do you think I'm missing my moment, Daddy?"

"I don't know, sweetheart. But you seem reclusive and unhappy. And much as I love having you here with me night after night, I can't help feeling you ought to get out more with people your own age and have some fun."

"I have friends."

"But you don't get out with them much anymore. I've noticed that."

"Maybe. I don't seem able to break into my life. It's as if there's an invisible shield between me and it. I can't quite feel anything."

"Ah, my little *Beatrice.*" He gave her name the Italian pronunciation. "I wish with all my heart that you were happier."

Beatrice shrugged. "What does 'happy' mean?"

"I'm very sorry you don't know. I worry about you after I'm gone."

She flinched. "I've asked you not to talk like that."

"I think about it a lot, particularly now that you're divorced. By the way, have you had any news of Stephen?"

The mere mention of her ex-husband's name always sent a little jolt of pain through Beatrice. She leaned over and opened the cigarette box on the coffee table. It was empty.

"What'd you do with all the cigarettes, Dad?"

"Are you smoking again?"

"No—just occasionally."

"Do you still think about him as much as you used to?"

"Yeah, I guess so." She got up and began pacing around the room like a caged cheetah. "But it's hopeless. You know how he is. He can resist anything except female temptation."

"Darlin', I know how *men* are."

Stopping, she glared at him. "Not all men, Dad."

"Find me the one that isn't, and I'll give him a medal."

"You were never like that," Beatrice said confidently.

"Settle down, honey. Come on back here."

"I'll tell you something," she said, sitting down. "When things were really bad with Stephen, I used to think of you and Mom and how great your marriage was. It's hard to explain, but it was knowing in the back of my mind that it's possible to have a good marriage that made me want something better for myself."

"You know, Bea," Dr. O'Connell said slowly, "no marriage is a steady course. There are always storms along the way."

"Oh, I know that," she said impatiently. "But I guess it just depends on the type of storm. Some of them are too damn hard to get through."

"Look, if you really love someone, you can get through anything. Love has to be greater than the sum of its parts, or it can't survive."

"Daddy, you don't know the half of what happened between me and Stephen."

"No, I don't. And it's none of my business. But I do know what happens in relationships, Bea. They all have twists and turns in common. It's their nature."

"Yes, but you never betrayed Mommy the way Stephen betrayed me. I couldn't forgive him after that. I just couldn't. Oh, I don't want to talk about it." She sighed. "I'm sick of thinking about it. It's over. Finished."

O'Connell was pained by the regret in his daughter's voice. He blamed himself for having failed her in some way he could not quite fathom.

"Men are vain creatures, Bea. Some of us respond a little too easily to flattery. Women are better able to resist temptation, I think."

"I doubt you would ever have done to Mom what Stephen did to me," she said.

"Well, I never would have left her, that's true. Even for a time. But you mustn't be too judgmental about people, Bea. They can't live up to it. They'll always disappoint you in the end if there's no forgiveness in your soul."

"I'd rather live alone for the rest of my life than put up with a man who was unfaithful to me."

"Even if he was sorry and wanted desperately to come back?"

"Stephen was sorry and he wanted to come back. But I don't think you ever get over it," Beatrice said. "Anyway, I didn't."

John O'Connell looked closely at his daughter. He saw in her a combination of opposites that disturbed him more now that she was growing older. On one hand, she was proud and strong, and on the other, she was timid and fragile. Her idealism about him and his marriage was touching, but far from her own best interests. He watched her wipe a tear surreptitiously from the corner of her eye. In that moment, he made up his mind to open himself up to her as he never had before.

"Bea, darlin'," he said, shaking his head, "just as there's a lot I don't know about you and Stephen, there's a lot you don't know about your mother and me."

"Like what, for instance?"

"A lot. And I'm worried that you're going to spend your life adhering to a standard that ..." His voice trailed off.

"That what?"

"Nothing ... Just that your mother understood me. And I understood her. We loved each other very much, but more important, we were friends."

"Friends don't betray each other."

Dr. O'Connell shifted uncomfortably on the couch, edging away from his daughter. "That depends on what you mean by betrayal."

"You were never unfaithful to Mom, were you?"

The doctor lowered his eyes.

"Daddy ... ?" Beatrice said hesitantly. "Were you?"

"Was I what?"

"Unfaithful to Mom?"

He avoided her gaze. "I guess I made some mistakes," he said at last.

Beatrice stared at her father in disbelief. She heard his words but could not quite comprehend them. "You were unfaithful to Mom?"

He suddenly looked up at her with a pleading expression on his face.

"You betrayed her?" Beatrice said, incredulous.

"Betrayal is the wrong word. I loved your mother deeply. But I confess to one or two missteps. One in particular."

Beatrice felt her chest constrict. "What do you mean?"

"I once fell in love with someone else."

"Who?"

"A nurse at the hospital."

"You fell in love?"

"I thought I did. But it passed after a time, and Liz understood."

Beatrice was at a loss for words.

"Your mother accepted me, Bea," he continued, looking hard into his daughter's eyes. "She accepted me the way I am, not the way she wanted me to be."

Shaking her head, Beatrice rose from the couch, unable to believe what her father had just told her. She felt as if all these years, she'd idealized a lie. The thought was unbearable. Dr. O'Connell held his breath, for he knew this was a turning point between them.

"What was she like?" Beatrice said.

The doctor cleared his throat. "She was a younger woman. Much younger than I was. A very decent and good person. It was very difficult for both of us."

"When did this happen?"

"About, oh, thirteen, fourteen years ago."

"Really?" Beatrice said, thinking. "That was right around the time Mom got sick."

"One thing had nothing to do with the other."

"No?" she said curtly. "How do you know?"

"I know."

Feeling her anger rising, Beatrice shook her head from side to side, while her father sat immobile.

"So that's where I got it from," she said at last, with great bitterness.

"What?"

"My attraction to bastards."

O'Connell winced. "Your mother didn't think I was a bastard, Bea."

"Stephen was a bastard."

"Maybe. But I'm not Stephen."

"And I'm not my mother."

Dr. O'Connell slumped down on the couch, feeling utterly defeated. "I shouldn't have told you," he said at last.

"No. Probably not. It's better when people don't tell each other things."

Beatrice left the room and returned moments later with a lighted cigarette in her hand. She leaned back against the desk.

"I'm not sure why this comes as such a shock to me," she said. "You and Mom are the last people in the world that I ever thought anything like this could happen to. Was I blind? Was that it? There must have been signs I just didn't see."

"Children sometimes put their parents up on pedestals. They don't want to see things."

"Yes, but they feel them, don't they? I must have felt something—some tension between you two I didn't recognize. There must have been some climate that prepared me for the pain of my own marriage." Beatrice's manner was edgy and full of recrimination as she puffed anxiously on her cigarette.

"You shouldn't smoke," her father said.

"I shouldn't do a lot of things," she replied coldly. "But what the hell?"

"Did you ever think of forgiving him, Bea?" Dr. O'Connell asked her after a time.

"Tell me, are you trying to justify your own behavior? Are women always supposed to forgive? Is that our role?"

O'Connell began kneading the fingers of his left hand with his right hand, cracking the knuckles, one of his nervous habits. "Believe me, I'm not trying to justify anything to you, darlin'," he said without anger.

"So," she said, shifting her body so that her weight rested on one leg. "You said once or twice. Who's the other one?"

"That was nothing. Just a dalliance at the beginning of our marriage."

"A dalliance," Beatrice said sarcastically. "Did Mom know about that?"

"Bea, it was all a long time ago."

"No, I'm curious. I'm really curious. You started this."

"All right, yes," the doctor said. "She found out."

"You told her?"

"No. A friend told her."

"Some friend."

"It meant nothing. It was a kind of . . . I don't know . . . Look, your mother and I were married. We had you. We had a life together. I only told you this because—"

"And what about Mom?" she interrupted him. "Did she ever retaliate?"

"I . . . I don't know."

"I wonder."

"I don't want to know."

"Why not? Are you afraid?"

"Of what?" The doctor cocked his head to one side.

"That her drives might have been as ungovernable as yours?"

He paused for a moment. "I should never have said anything. But I thought, if you go on thinking people are perfect—"

"I think people are far from perfect, Dad. I think most of us, with some very rare exceptions, are tormented and neurotic and buffeted by forces we don't understand."

"Bea," he said, "all of us are human and vulnerable, even you, darlin'. I'm afraid you're going to be so lonely if you hold people to such high standards."

"Are fidelity and loyalty such high standards?" She stubbed out her cigarette with ferocity.

"They're different things, Bea. You can have one without the other."

"Can you?"

O'Connell saw a wave of blackness sweeping over his daughter's face. He rose from the couch and walked over to comfort her. She waved him away.

"Bea, honey, please—please don't be so upset. I'm sorry for you, sweetheart. You don't know how sorry I am."

"Be sorry for yourself and for poor Mommy, God rest her soul." Beatrice picked up the grimoire and brandished it in front of her father like a weapon. "I love the way men portray us," she said angrily. "We're all witches and temptresses, creatures of the devil. Tell me what you criticize, and I'll tell you who you are. It's you guys who can't keep your goddamn pants on. I bet Mommy got sick because of what you did to her!"

John O'Connell froze, looking utterly stricken. "My God, Bea. Don't say that."

"Why? Because it might be true?" She glared at him, feeling no pity.

"There's a lot you don't understand—"

"Me? What about you? You never stopped to think, did you? She counted on your love, and you betrayed her. You betrayed her just like Stephen betrayed me!"

With that, Beatrice turned on her heel and strode out of the library. She went upstairs to her bedroom, slamming the door behind her. Leaning against the dresser, taking deep breaths, she wondered if her mother had experienced the same sense of loneliness and abandonment she herself had known during her brief, tempestuous marriage. For Beatrice, infidelity had been the most damaging, ego-bruising treason imaginable. There was no hurt in her life to compare with it. She looked down at the bureau and stared at the idyllic photograph she had taken of her mother and father on the beach years before. Feeling nothing but contempt now for the hypocrisy it seemed to represent, she turned it facedown.

A few moments later, she heard a soft knocking on her door.

"Bea ... ?" she heard her father say.

She remained silent.

"Open up, will you?"

"No."

"Come on, darlin', talk to your old man, please?"

"Go away."

"Please try to understand."

"Go *away*," she said emphatically.

After a minute or so, she heard her father retreating wearily down the hall. Beatrice cracked open her door and watched him enter his bedroom at the end of the corridor. Stooped over, he looked old and frail, utterly defeated. She felt too raw to say that she understood, to tell him that if her mother could have forgiven him, so should she. The self-righteous, indignant daughter wasn't ready to grant pity or charity. She wanted nothing more than to seethe over the failure and disappointment of her own life.

As Beatrice undressed for bed, she brooded about this new-found knowledge. Her relationship with her ex-husband now seemed less like an unlucky choice and more like an inevitable extension of her parents' marriage, except theirs had lasted and hers had split apart. All night long, she lay awake in a fury of regret and rage.

A little before eight, she heard her father stirring about in his room, and for one brief moment she thought of knocking on his door to tell him she loved him. But instead she hurried past his bedroom, walked downstairs, and slipped quietly out of the house.

2

EATRICE HAD AN APPOINTMENT IN HARLEM, TO gather information for a well-known writer working on a book about black and Hispanic immigrants. The writer was interested in what he called the "love boutiques" that were flourishing around the city. Her contact was a social worker named Luis Diaz. Diaz, the writer had told her, knew all about the little shops catering to those seeking power over romance through the charms of the cult of Santeria.

Beatrice had phoned Diaz earlier in the week to ask some general questions and to set up a meeting. He had sounded quite businesslike. When she asked specifically about the love boutiques, Diaz had told her that most of the potions and powders sold in such establishments were ineffective and harmless.

"For five dollars, you can buy an amulet guaranteed to attract a mate," he explained, with his slight Hispanic accent. "For ten, you can get a powder and sprinkle it on your lover's food to make him faithful. Mostly they're kind of seedy places run by bodega owners who want to make a quick buck off the lovesick. But I'm going to take you somewhere special," he assured her. "A place of power."

Beatrice, with her innate skepticism about such things, had dismissed Diaz's claim. But now, having seen the grimoire and having reacted to it so unexpectedly, she was more intrigued with the concept of dark, mystical sexuality and with magic itself. She had arranged to meet Diaz at 9:00 A.M. in front of Sister Marleu's shop, on Second Avenue at 113th Street.

"How will I recognize you?" Beatrice had asked him.

"I'll recognize you," Diaz said, and hung up.

Two things were on Beatrice's mind as she left the house that morning: the argument with her father, and the grimoire. Though they were seemingly unrelated, the knowledge of her father's infidelities and the horrific image of the book's female succubus kept preying on her mind, coiling around each other, inexorably linked. She tried hard to concentrate on other things as she boarded the uptown subway, but she felt an uncontrollable anger switching this way and that between her father and, to her surprise, herself.

Beatrice got off the train at 116th Street and began walking. Holding her handbag close, she paid close attention to the life around her. The neighborhood was a combination of poverty and vitality. As distant strains of rap and salsa music wafted through the air, a group of children played on the cracked sidewalk, splashing one another with water spewing from a broken fire hydrant. Exotic cooking smells mingled with the stench of garbage. She passed a homeless man camped inside the carcass of a stripped car. People loitered on stoops and grouped in the doorways of the dilapidated brownstones, talking among themselves or watching the street life with passing interest. Beatrice felt some of them eyeing her as she made her way up the block. She walked straight ahead, eyes front, though occasionally she glanced down, and at one point noticed a syringe and a used condom.

A young couple was walking ahead of her, holding hands. The girl was light-skinned and blandly pretty. She wore a uniform such as Beatrice had worn when she attended Catholic school. The boy was wearing chinos and a sweater. His face was beautiful in the way that the faces of adolescent boys can be beautiful—that is to say, almost feminine—with a delicate nose and a full-lipped mouth. Gazing into each other's eyes, they looked dreamily romantic.

They stopped abruptly, and Beatrice halted too. She watched as the girl suddenly grabbed the young man's head with both her hands and insinuated her tongue into his mouth. He cupped his hands over her breasts and began massaging them so fervently that her blouse wrenched free of its prim pleated harbor. Grinding their bodies together, they kissed and fondled each other, oblivious to the life of the street. Beatrice stood mesmerized, impaled on a blade of longing. The young girl slid her eyes onto Beatrice and stared at her impassively as she continued to roll her tongue in and out of the young man's mouth. Beatrice walked past them, unsure if what she felt was distaste or simple jealousy.

She came to a tiny storefront wedged between a cheap clothing shop and a convenience store. A short flight of steps led to the entrance below, the door of which was partially open. A reddish glow radiated from within. There was a hand-painted sign nailed above the doorway, spelling out the name SISTER MARLEU in uneven red letters. As Beatrice peered down, wondering if she should wait for her contact on the street or venture into the shop, she felt a light tap on her shoulder. Whirling around, she found herself staring at a man who stood slightly too near her.

"Did I frighten you? Forgive me," he said in a low, lightly accented voice. "I am Luis Diaz. Hello."

The man in front of her was of medium height and extraordinarily handsome. He had a smooth, tan complexion and wavy black hair, slicked back in long, comb-marked strands. His watery brown eyes were rimmed with thick black lashes. He was dressed in khaki pants and a brown shirt, open one button too many at the neck. His sleeves were rolled up, revealing the strong, well-articulated muscles of his arms. He moved gracefully, never taking his eyes off Beatrice, almost as if he were stalking her.

There was something distinctly feral about Diaz. Beatrice felt uneasy in his presence and drawn to him at the same time. He was like a sleek jungle cat she had the urge to reach out and pet. His mouth, she noted, was slightly crooked and did not seem kind, even when he smiled. She could not tell if she was unsettled by him or by the couple she had just seen.

"This way," he said, heading down the stairs.

Beatrice followed. He took her arm when she hesitated at the entrance.

"Come," he said.

She felt the extreme warmth of his hand through her sweater.

Diaz stared at Beatrice for a moment as they stood in front of the long curtain of red beads hanging directly behind the door.

"Don't be afraid," he said, waving aside a handful of the plastic strands so she could pass through.

"I'm not." She walked inside.

Beatrice found herself in a small space, lit with red and white candles of all shapes and sizes. When her eyes became accustomed to the sparkle, she began to make out shelves and wooden stands, upon which a variety of bottles, jars, and amulets glinted in the candlelight.

On a low pedestal at the far end of the room was a three-foot-tall plaster statue of a young woman, surrounded by candles and robed in a white cloth tunic and a crimson velvet cape trimmed with gold. The white angelic face of the figurine was saccharine with simplistic features, like a cartoon. Perched atop her head was a gold filigree crown. In her right hand, she held a chalice encrusted with faceted red glass jewels; in her left, a wooden sword, painted gold and silver. A small plaster tower completed the display. Amid the offerings of bead necklaces and other cheap jewelry strewn at the feet of the image was a glass of copper-colored liquid and a cigar.

"That's Santa Barbara, isn't it?" Beatrice said, walking over to take a closer look.

"So you know something about Santeria."

"A little. I did some research. I was interested in how the African deities have mixed with Catholic saints and become dual personalities. Though the idols take on the physical aspects of the saints, they still possess the magic of the old Yoruba gods."

"Very good," Diaz said.

"She's wearing her colors, red and white. And there's the tower, her symbol."

"I'm really impressed."

"And you make an offering to Santa Barbara if you want love or . . ." Beatrice hesitated.

"Revenge."

"That's right, revenge. So all these little trinkets are from people who want passion or revenge," Beatrice said, plucking one of the cheap necklaces out of the pile.

"Love or revenge," Diaz corrected her.

"Love, of course. What did I say?"

"Passion. You said passion or revenge."

"Well, perhaps they're one and the same."

"What? Passion and love, or love and revenge?" he said.

"You're teasing me." Beatrice laughed, twirling the necklace around her finger. "What's in the glass?"

"Rum. The rum and the cigar are for Chango, her other aspect—the god of fire, thunder, and lightning."

"I wish I had something to offer her," Beatrice said, putting the necklace back.

"Why?" Diaz said. "Are you after love or revenge, or both?"

Just then, a low, musical voice came from the opposite end of the room. "Welcome! Welcome to Sister Marloo."

Beatrice turned and beheld, sauntering toward her, a short, plump woman of indeterminate age, with skin the color of milk chocolate. She was wearing a long tented dress and intertwining necklaces made of red and white beads, which swayed from side to side as she walked. Gleaming jet-black hair, plaited in a hundred snakelike braids, gave her round, friendly face a certain ominousness.

"Sister, meet Beatrice O'Connell," Diaz said.

Sister Marleu stood motionless for a moment, appraising Beatrice with slow-moving eyes. She gripped Beatrice's hand and held it for a long moment in both of hers, as an inscrutable expression crept over her face.

"We know each other," Sister Marleu said in a suggestive, sing-song voice.

Beatrice returned the woman's gaze, more amused than intimidated. "Oh, I don't think so," she said.

"Yes, yes," Sister Marleu insisted, squinting at Beatrice. "I know you. We know each other very well."

"Forgive me, but I don't think we've ever met."

"No," Sister Marleu said in a sly tone. "We have never met. But sisters know each other."

Beatrice withdrew her hand from Sister Marleu's clasp, noticing that the woman's short fingers were studded with rings. Then Sister Marleu held her own hands up in front of her nose and turned them over once or twice, sniffing at them, as if she were trying to inhale traces of Beatrice's scent. A performance, Beatrice thought, but not a bad one. She glanced at Diaz, who was regarding the proceedings with a bemused look on his face.

"Why have you come to Sister Marleu?" the woman asked.

"I'm doing research for the writer Nathan Markham. He won a Pulitzer Prize several years ago."

Sister Marleu looked at Beatrice with interest. "Research? About what?"

"Love boutiques, such as this one. I wanted to know something about Santeria."

"That is the reason you have come to Sister Marleu?"

"Why, yes," Beatrice replied, nonplussed.

The woman shook her head. "And you think that is the real reason?"

"Yes. What other reason could there be?" Beatrice said, fascinated by the strong energy emanating from this odd little woman.

"The gods. Fate. Destiny, maybe," the woman said.

"Whatever. Mr. Diaz here said you'd be willing to help me."

"Luis may want to help you himself," Sister Marleu said, flashing Diaz a brilliant, toothy grin.

"I've already helped her, Sister. I've brought her to you," Diaz said.

At that, Sister Marleu let out a great musical laugh. Flinging her arms into the air, she cried, "Sister Marleu can help you for sure! Sister Marleu helps everyone! What is it that you seek?"

Beatrice pulled out her notebook. "I'd like to learn about Santeria," she repeated. "I understand that drug dealers use it sometimes to keep their soldiers in line."

"Sometimes," Sister Marleu said.

"How?"

"Are you a drug dealer?"

"No." Beatrice laughed self-consciously.

"Then you have no business to know that."

"All right, then. Tell me about the animal sacrifices and the potions you sell. Who are your customers? Who comes to consult you?"

Sister Marleu looked directly into Beatrice's eyes and was silent. Then: "That is not what you need to know."

"Well, it is for a start."

"No." Sister Marleu shook her head. "You have trouble. Love trouble."

"Doesn't everyone?" Beatrice said. "But I don't want to buy anything, if that's what you mean. I just need some information."

"You need answers, yes. But first you must learn the right questions." Sister Marleu waved her hand impatiently. "You come back to see Sister Marleu when you've found them." She started walking away.

"Wait! Please. I don't understand. I thought you'd agreed to talk to me. I thought Mr. Diaz had explained . . ." Beatrice flashed Diaz a look of consternation.

Sister Marleu stopped walking, faced Beatrice, and stood with her hands on her hips. She paused for dramatic effect, then said, "He cannot give you Sister Marleu's answers. Maybe he can give you your questions."

Beatrice closed her notebook. "Can you help me here, Mr. Diaz?"

"Sister, I told Miss O'Connell that this was a place of power and that you were someone worth talking to."

Sister Marleu was growing impatient. "She doesn't want to talk to me. She wants me to talk to her. I do not talk to those who do not talk to me."

"Listen, I'm happy to talk to you," Beatrice said. "What do you want me to talk to you about?"

"Chango," Sister Marleu shot back.

"What the hell do I know about Chango?" Beatrice said, deciding that a flash of temper might be a smart journalistic move. "You know more about Chango than I do—I hope. You're the expert."

"That is right. I am the expert," Sister Marleu said. "Chango is desire. Sister Marleu will only talk to your desire."

"I'm sorry, but I think my desire's on vacation at the moment," Beatrice said.

"That is not what I am getting." Sister Marleu narrowed her eyes. "I see a wolf." With that, the little woman turned on her heel and disappeared into the back room. Beatrice looked at Diaz. "What the hell was that all about?"

"You tell me," he said with a laugh. "What do I know about your desire?"

"I guess she doesn't believe in small talk. Just baring of the soul, right? . . . Well, now what? You have any other great ideas? Know any other people who can help me?"

"We're here. Why not take a look around?"

"Might as well, I suppose." Beatrice shrugged. She began to wander around the shop. "I suppose it's too much to ask what I'm looking at, or for." She picked up a vial filled with brown liquid. "What do you suppose this is?"

"I don't know. Drink it and find out. Your wolf may be thirsty."

"Sure," Beatrice said sarcastically, holding the small bottle up to a candle and examining the contents. "It's green when you hold it up to the light. It looks revolting."

"Give it to me."

Beatrice handed Diaz the vial. He uncorked it and swallowed the filmy liquid in one gulp. Beatrice looked at him incredulously.

"I don't believe you did that! You don't have any idea what was in there."

"No, but now it's in me. And you're right. It was revolting."

"It could be anything. Could be poison, for all you know."

"Could be." He put the vial down. "We'll find out soon."

"I guess it was *your* wolf that was thirsty," Beatrice said.

"My wolf is always thirsty."

"Mr. Diaz, what are you trying to prove?"

"Nothing. Just let me know if I start howling."

"I'll be sure to."

Beatrice scanned a couple of the other shelves. "What do you suppose she meant by that?"

"What?"

"All that business about my *wolf*." She pronounced the word with disdain. "And that she knew why I'd come here."

"Oh, that's Sister's way. She's a *santera*, you see."

"I thought a *santera* was a sorceress. But now I know—it's a pain in the ass."

"Oh, don't underestimate Sister. She's the real thing. A great *santera*, and a *madrina* too."

"A *madrina?*"

"A godmother—someone who helps initiates."

"Maybe she saw me as an infidel, since I don't believe in any of that stuff. Too bad. I really wanted to talk to her."

"You might not have liked what she had to say."

"Why not?"

"She only talks to people's other side."

"What do you mean?"

"The hidden side. The side they don't show. The side they don't let on they have. The side they may not even know they have. She talks to that side and makes it talk to her."

"I'm sorry to disappoint you, but some of us are pretty straightforward," Beatrice said.

34

"Some are, yes . . . but not you."

"Look, I'm *very* straightforward. What makes you say I'm not?"

"It's obvious," Diaz said.

"If you ask me, people like her just want to make you think they have power. A lot of posturing to sway the weak mind."

"Are you feeling weak in the mind?"

"No, definitely not. I have a logical mind. And my logical mind tells me that Sister Marleu, or whatever she calls herself, is a con artist with a good scam going."

"Didn't you feel her magic? Honestly?"

"I don't believe in magic."

"Some of the most logical minds in the world have believed in magic."

"The psychological power of magic, maybe. But there is no actual power. Magic doesn't exist."

"For a smart girl, you don't know very much," Diaz said.

"All right—now you be honest. Have you ever seen any real magic?"

"Maybe." He edged closer to her.

"Are you a believer, Mr. Diaz?"

"Luis."

"Luis. Are you?"

"I am a believer, yes."

"Really? Do you believe in Santeria—the power of the thing itself, without the help of the believer? Do you believe that having drunk that potion, you'll become more potent or whatever it's supposed to do for you?"

"Is that what you think it was supposed to do for me?"

"What?"

"Make me more potent?"

"I don't know." She sighed, wishing to end the verbal sparring. "I just said that because it's probably a love potion, and that's what love potions are supposed to do, aren't they?"

"Your other side is jumping out."

"Oh, give me a break, will you?" Beatrice was growing irritated. "It was just a passing comment. I have one side, and you're looking at it."

"And a nice side it is too." A smile crept over Diaz's face. "So what is it you think Sister saw in you, Beatrice?"

"Stupidity for ever coming here," she said, and began meandering around the shop again, feeling Diaz's eyes on her. She picked up a bean-shaped brown amulet attached to a string of wooden beads and began running her fingers absently over the rough-edged little charm. Diaz approached her from behind and insinuated his body against hers. Her first instinct was to move away, but she did not.

"A very nice side," he emphasized.

She felt his breath on the back of her neck. It was hot and musky. Beatrice breathed in deeply. She had always suspected that the smell of another person was the real aphrodisiac—above looks, above personality, above anything. And she found Diaz's smell delicious.

Diaz reached down and lightly touched the back of Beatrice's hand with his fingers. Her skin bristled with goose bumps. Rhythmically, they stroked the charm together. Then Diaz pressed down hard on Beatrice's hand. The little bean cut into her palm.

"Ow," she said softly, turning to confront him.

They were face-to-face. The scent of him overwhelmed her. She felt light-headed.

"You're hurting me," she said weakly.

"I know."

He pressed down harder, squeezing his hand around hers.

"I know what she saw in you, Beatrice," he said. "And so do you."

"What?"

"Hunger."

"No."

"Yes."

Diaz put his hands up to Beatrice's hair. She flinched.

"Hold still," he said.

Gently, he pulled out the pins securing her bun. Her thick dark hair fell to her shoulders, framing her face in softness.

"Magic!" he exclaimed, his eyes lighting up.

They stared at each other for a long moment. Diaz leaned forward and kissed her gently on the lips. Beatrice opened her mouth slightly. Diaz wedged his tongue inside, deeper and deeper into her mouth. She curled her tongue around his as he reached down and rubbed the tip of her right nipple.

"Don't . . . ," she breathed through the kiss, unable to pull herself away.

He cupped her breast in his hand, massaging it hard. With that, she broke free, feeling embarrassed and flushed. Diaz grabbed her hand and wrenched her back. They stood facing each other. Diaz turned her palm upward.

"You're branded," he said, examining the faint red outline where the bean had marked her.

He lifted her hand up and pressed it against his mouth. She felt his tongue licking the little wound.

"Let me go. Please."

Diaz loosened his grip. Beatrice leaned against the table to get her balance.

"Are you all right?" he said.

"I feel a bit dizzy."

"I'm sorry."

"No, you're not." Beatrice could barely breathe. She touched her palm. It was still wet where Diaz had licked it. As she rubbed it dry with two fingers, her arm brushed against the amulet, knocking it to the floor. Beatrice and Diaz bent down simultaneously to pick it up. Once again, their hands met over the charm.

"Listen," Diaz said, grabbing the bean. "It's got something inside it. Listen . . . The wolf is hungry, hungry, hungry . . . ," he said, rhythmically shaking the amulet around her head. His words were like an incantation, punctuated by the soft hiss of the rattle.

"Stop it . . . please!" Beatrice begged, feeling the immense power of his attraction.

Diaz smiled and helped her up. He replaced the trinket on the table and walked to the front of the shop.

"What if we don't know what we're hungry for?" Beatrice called after him. "Do we starve?"

He turned to look at her. "We search."

"What if we don't know where to search?"

"Then we find someone who does," Diaz said. "And let that person guide us."

"Yes, but finding the right person . . ." Her voice trailed off.

"Why not take a chance?"

Beatrice experienced the same strange pull in her gut that she had felt when looking at the succubus in the grimoire. She was both attracted and repelled by Diaz's raw sensuality.

"My apartment isn't far from here," he said.

Beatrice hesitated. "I'm not sure I'm ready. I've never done anything like this."

"Good."

"Why good?"

"Because first times are memorable. Trust me to be your guide. When the student is ready, the master will come. Trust me."

Beatrice stood immobile and took a deep breath. Diaz strode over to her and gripped her hand. She offered no resistance as he led her out of the shop and onto the noisy street. They began walking together—Beatrice unsure, unsteady, but infused with desire; Diaz confident and determined, a jungle cat cleverly leading his prey.

Nothing in Beatrice's background had prepared her for this encounter. The danger of it, the recklessness of it, struck her with full force as she climbed the dark stairs to Diaz's tenement apartment. Unlocking the door and swinging it open, Diaz put his arm around her waist, cementing her to his side as he led her inside. He slammed the door shut with his foot and, jamming Beatrice up against the wall, began kissing her all over. He fell to his knees in front of her and ran his hands up under her skirt, up the backs of her thighs and inside her underpants, over her buttocks, massaging her firmly as he nestled his head into her belly, kissing her abdomen and crotch.

Beatrice gazed down at him, plowing her fingers through his thick hair. She squeezed her eyes shut, shocked by her own impulsiveness, shocked by her reckless desire and her powerlessness to fight it.

Diaz rose to his feet and led her into the bedroom, where a single small window faced out onto an alley, devoid of sunlight. The only furniture was a reading lamp and a large mattress on the floor, haphazardly covered with sheets and a blanket. A men's magazine and some manila file folders containing papers were scattered on the bed—as well as a pair of black Velcro wrist restraints.

As Diaz pulled her down to the mattress, Beatrice smiled to herself, for she understood this to be the very moment that all the safeguards of her sheltered upbringing had conspired to prevent. Her prim, privileged, upper-middle-class background of private girls' schools, genteel vacations, carefully orchestrated meetings with "the right sort of boys," was meant to protect her from just such an anonymous sexual encounter, which might, if she was unlucky, lead to disease, violence, or even death. In other words, she had been brought up to remain forever shielded from a certain corner of herself. Here at last was an experience destined to reveal another aspect of her nature—her succubus side, or perhaps her wolf. Beatrice took a deep breath, knowing she had no choice but to surrender to the wildness of it, and the danger.

It was beginning to get dark when Beatrice and Diaz emerged from his building. They walked to the corner side by side without looking at each other and stood waiting for a taxi.

"Your blouse is ripped," Diaz observed.

Beatrice ran her fingers along the frayed seam on the shoulder, remembering the moment when it had occurred. After he had thrown her down on his bed, she herself had torn the blouse in her haste to get it off. Embarrassed by the memory of her own passion, Beatrice started to put on her sweater. Diaz tried to help her, but she pulled away, hugging the sweater close around her to hide the tear.

"Are you okay?" he said.

"I don't know," she answered in a barely audible voice.

"You haven't done anything wrong."

She looked up at him with tears in her eyes. "Why do I feel as if I have?"

"Because you've just met your wolf," Diaz said, putting his arms around her. "And you don't know her well yet. She frightens you."

"That wasn't me."

"It's part of you."

Beatrice's mouth was quivering. She didn't want him to see her cry. "Can I blame my wolf?" she said.

"If you like. But she's nothing to be ashamed of."

"I am ashamed." She started to weep. "I'm so ashamed."

"Don't be," Diaz said, kissing her tears away.

"You don't understand. It's not just about me."

"Who is it about?"

"My father. I've been a fool, Luis—such a fool."

"No. You've only been asleep. And now Sleeping Beauty has awakened. And she's a wolf. There's no going back. Call me if you need me. I'm here."

In the taxi on her way home, Beatrice couldn't get Diaz or his words out of her mind: "Sleeping Beauty has awakened. And she's a wolf. There's no going back." She pulled her compact from her bag but kept it cupped in her hand, afraid to look in it, fearing it would reflect the wild, dark side of herself that had sprung full-blown, like a sexual Athena, that afternoon. As the cab weaved its way through the traffic, Beatrice slowly raised the small round mirror to her face and studied her reflection. Something about her had changed, but only she would see it, she thought. There was a wild clarity in her eyes that had never been there before—or that she had never noticed.

Beatrice recalled the grimoire, picturing herself as the craven image of the succubus. That afternoon in bed with Diaz, she had tracked wild passion down to its lair in the deepest groove of her soul—a place she hadn't known existed. Now she understood that the powers of darkness—whether the harmless charms of Santeria or the evil raising of the dead through necromancy—could not be so easily dismissed as the vestiges of bygone, unenlightened societies and less sophisticated minds, as Signor Antonelli had implied. They were just beneath the surface of modern life. They were within her.

As she examined her face in the glass, the fury she'd felt toward her father vanished. She was desperately ashamed of herself for having been so judgmental. Who was she to condemn anyone for the way he reconciled the paradoxes of the heart? Least of all her father, who, despite the cravings of his own "wolf," had been a loving, caring man. The mask she had torn from herself that day had revealed more to Beatrice than simply her own dark side; it had revealed her father to her in a way she would never have thought possible. For the first time, she understood his longing.

Beatrice could barely sit still as the taxi lurched toward its destination. She wanted desperately to beg her father's forgiveness, to apologize to him for her stupid anger over the matter of his infidelity. She had to remove the wedge between them, particularly at this time, when each was all the family the other had left in the world. They were now part of one another in more ways than she could have imagined before that afternoon.

Beatrice asked the cabbie to let her out a couple of blocks from her house, so she could get some fresh air. She began to walk. The evening air felt chilly. She reached up and massaged her bare skin through the tear in her blouse, then pulled her sweater close around her as she walked down the darkening street toward home.

Rounding the corner, she saw two police cars parked outside her house. She made her way through a small crowd of onlookers craning their necks. Ducking under a yellow tape cordoning off the area, she was stopped by a young officer standing guard at the door.

"Sorry, lady, you'll have to stay back," he said, motioning her away.

"But I live here!" she cried, feeling a growing sense of panic.

His expression changed to one of concern. "What's your name?"

"Beatrice O'Connell. This is my house. What's happened? What's going on?"

Without answering, he let her pass. She ran up the steps to the front door and barged into the foyer. There she saw several more men, most of them in police uniforms, all of them looking grim and purposeful. Barely acknowledging her, they seemed to be going about some work she didn't yet understand. She approached a sergeant.

"Excuse me," she said, trying to remain calm. "I live here. Will somebody please tell me what's going on?"

"You the daughter?" he said.

"Yes."

"Frank!" the sergeant cried out, never taking his eyes off her.

"Yo!" she heard a voice call down from upstairs.

"Frank—the daughter's here!"

A balding, heavyset man in a rumpled gray suit appeared at the top of the stairs. He stopped for a moment.

"Miss O'Connell?" he said softly.

"Please—what's happened?"

He trotted downstairs and introduced himself.

"I'm Detective Monahan," he said, shaking her hand somberly.

"Beatrice O'Connell." She could barely breathe.

He led Beatrice into the dining room. She gasped as she entered. The room had been ransacked. The detective helped her to a chair and sat down beside her.

"Miss O'Connell . . . ," he said hesitantly. "It's my painful duty to inform you that your father is dead."

The simple sentence unfurled like a black ribbon. Unable or unwilling to grasp its full meaning at first, she suddenly felt cold and leaden.

"Wait—no, no!" she heard herself say. "There's been a mistake!"

"I'm sorry, Miss O'Connell. I'm so sorry."

"Oh my God. How?"

"He was shot in an apparent robbery attempt."

"Shot! Oh my God ... my God ..."

Hot tears sprang into her eyes. She began to reel.

"Burke!" the detective cried as he rose to steady her. "A glass of water! Quick!"

Beatrice felt a terrible dizziness, followed by a blast of air that gathered force and shot up through her body, straight out the top of her skull. Then she was looking up at four strangers, who stared down at her as if they were peering into a well.

"Where's my father?" she cried out. "I want to see my father!"

A rough hand was stroking her forehead. She recognized Detective Monahan as he leaned over her.

"Take it easy, Miss O'Connell," he said. "Just take it real easy, now."

At that moment, she realized that this was not some nightmare, from which she was going to awaken. Her father was dead. . . . Shot. . . . Shot dead.

Detective Monahan helped her back to the chair. She was shuddering all over. It was the first time she'd ever fainted.

"Where is he?" she asked weakly.

"Upstairs."

"Take me to him."

"Give yourself a minute. Here—drink this." The detective handed her the glass of water.

She pushed it aside.

"I want to go now."

Monahan led Beatrice upstairs to the library. The door was closed.

"I should warn you—" he said.

"Please," she said, shrugging his hand off her arm. "Let me go."

ETECTIVE MONAHAN OPENED THE LIBRARY DOOR,
allowing Beatrice to pass in front of him. Enter-
ing the room, she beheld a battlefield. Precious
books covered the floor like stiff little soldiers,
their spines broken, covers detached, pages torn.
The locked, gold-grated cases in which the most
valuable manuscripts were kept had been pried
open, their priceless contents carelessly strewn in every direction.
All the drawers of her father's desk had been wrenched out and
thrown to the floor. Spidery blobs of black ink from an overturned
inkwell stained the Persian carpet. The Tiffany lampshade was in
smithereens. Shards of the delicate glass crunched beneath
Beatrice's shoes as she proceeded slowly through the wreckage. The
once orderly, elegant "little garden of knowledge" was in chaos.

Several men were at work in the room—taking photographs,
dusting for fingerprints, hunting for evidence—but Beatrice was
hardly aware of their presence. Her concentration was focused on
the far end of the library, for it was there that her father lay, on the
floor in front of the curtained window. As she walked toward him

like an automaton, the men, one by one, stopped what they were doing in order to watch her. Detective Monahan followed at a courteous distance.

Beatrice stared at her father's body. He looked like a broken mannequin—his torso twisted, his legs zigzagged one on top of the other, his arms extended in a macabre gesture of welcome, as if he had been mowed down in the middle of an embrace. A urine stain had seeped through the front of his trousers. There was a strong stench of feces.

Beatrice stood over this grim spectacle, in a trance. She hardly recognized the man at her feet. Dried blood bearded her father's ashen cheeks and streaked his white hair. His right eye had been shot clean out, leaving a deep hole caked with black blood. The left eye was glazed and lifeless under a drooping lid. A livid, swollen tongue peeked out from the corner of his mouth.

In the room's deepening silence, the men stood motionless, looking at Beatrice, awaiting her reaction. After a few seconds, she sank to her knees in front of the body and let out a wail of grief.

"Oh, Daddy, Daddy, Daddy!" Rocking back and forth, she thrust her fist into her mouth and bit down hard to keep from screaming. Moments passed. Finally, Beatrice lowered her hands and looked back at Detective Monahan.

"Can I touch him?" she asked.

The detective nodded.

Beatrice gently caressed her father's face and hair with the tips of her fingers. Fresh teeth marks were visible on the back of her hand. Sobbing softly, she stared at her father, as her tears dropped one by one, mingling with his blood. Then she leaned over and kissed his cheek, allowing her lips to linger on his icy flesh.

"Forgive me, Daddy . . . Please forgive me," she said. "I love you . . . I love you. Forgive me . . ."

Beatrice stumbled to her feet. Detective Monahan supported her as she rose. He led her to the couch and sat her down, signaling the men to go on about their business.

"Are you all right?"

"I can't believe it," Beatrice wept. "I just can't believe it. How did this happen?"

She looked at the detective with a pleading, bewildered expression on her face, like a frightened little girl.

"Who did this?" she said tearfully. "Who would do this to my father? He was the sweetest, dearest, kindest man. He was so good. He was. He really was."

"We're going to try and find out," Monahan said. "Do you feel up to answering some questions?"

Beatrice nodded. The detective handed her a tissue. She blew her nose and wiped away her tears. Extracting a small notebook and a pencil from his jacket pocket, Monahan began a gentle interrogation.

"Where were you today, Miss O'Connell?"

The question stung her, and she hesitated. "I was up in Harlem, doing research."

"Were you with anybody?"

"Yes," she said, flushing. "A social worker named Luis Diaz."

"You were with him all day?"

"Yes." She lowered her eyes.

"You'll tell us where we can get in touch with him, of course."

She nodded as the detective jotted down notes.

"Did your father have any enemies that you know of?"

"No! Everyone loved him, I told you. He was a doctor. A healer. Who could have done this? Who?"

Beatrice broke down again. Monahan waited patiently for her to recover. He continued questioning her. Sometimes the detective's words blurred in her mind and lost their meaning, as if he'd lapsed into a foreign language. She couldn't help glancing over at her father's body every once in a while, half expecting him to jump up, take off that hideous mask, and announce it was all a joke.

Presently, the plump old housekeeper, Nellie Riley, entered the room, supported by an officer. Nellie's kind, open face, usually as fresh as a colleen's despite her years, looked as if it had been trampled. Her rat-red eyes, quivering lips, and tear-glazed cheeks painted a picture of anguish. Beatrice sprang from the couch to embrace the stricken woman.

"Oh, Miss Beatrice!" she cried. "Forgive me, forgive me. I didn't know, I didn't know!"

Clinging hard, Nellie buried her head in Beatrice's chest and sobbed inconsolably.

"It's all right, Nellie, dear. It's all right," Beatrice said, patting the old woman's head. She turned to Detective Monahan. "What happened?"

"It was Miss Riley here who found your father and telephoned us," Monahan replied.

"Oh, Nellie, how awful for you," Beatrice said.

"I didn't understand," the housekeeper said, a dazed expression on her face. "You must believe me. *I didn't know!*"

"I believe you, Nellie, dear. How *could* you have known?" Beatrice said, thinking the old woman was in a state of shock.

"Please, Miss Beatrice, you mustn't blame me." She looked at Beatrice with fear in her eyes.

"Blame you? Of course I don't blame you, Nellie."

As Beatrice hugged the old woman close, two men hoisted Dr. O'Connell's body onto a gurney and covered it with a sheet. Locked together in anguish, Beatrice and Nellie watched the corpse being wheeled out of the room. Nellie shrank back and blessed herself as the body passed by her. Beatrice tried to say a silent prayer, but the words turned to ashes in her mouth.

O dear God in heaven, she thought, how could you have let this happen to such a man?

After the body was gone, Detective Monahan tried to continue his questioning of the two women. Nellie's answers were incoherent. She kept begging Beatrice to forgive her. Finally, at Beatrice's insistence, the poor housekeeper was given a sedative from the medicine cabinet, and Monahan sent her home, accompanied by an officer.

"She's taking it harder than I am," Beatrice said when Nellie had gone.

"It was a terrible shock," Monahan replied. "I think we must give her a few days to recover."

"Recover?" Beatrice looked at him blankly. "We'll never recover from this. Never."

The police left late in the evening. Monahan requested that Beatrice go through all the rooms of the ransacked house when she felt up to it, listing anything she found missing. He posted a guard outside the house.

"I'll be back in the morning, around nine," he assured her. "Make sure you lock all the doors and put the alarm on." He paused at the door. "Oh, and Miss O'Connell. Allow me to say again how deeply sorry I am."

"Thank you for your concern," Beatrice mumbled disconsolately, closing the door behind him.

Alone at last, Beatrice felt the full weight of the day descending upon her like a shroud. Sinking to the floor, she curled herself into a ball and wept. When finally she managed to pull herself together and head upstairs, it was past midnight. Leaden-legged from grief and exhaustion, she gripped the banister to steady herself as she proceeded one step at a time.

Reaching her bedroom, she undressed and got into the shower, where she washed her hair and scrubbed herself with a soapy wash-cloth, scourging her flesh. As the steaming water rinsed the lather from her body, she looked down and saw little red welts, love bites, and bruises emerging on her skin. The sight sickened her, and she scrubbed at herself again, even more furiously, desperate to expunge the memory of Luis Diaz, who, despite all her efforts, remained a constant specter behind the cataclysmic event that had befallen her. Thoughts of Diaz spawned a wave of irrational guilt over her father's death. Could she have saved him had she returned home earlier? Was his death a consequence of her lustful misdeed? Or, worse, of her having wished her father ill the night before because of a force she was just now beginning to understand? Try as she might to dis-pel it, the connection between her "wolf" and her father's murder was now firmly established in her mind.

Beatrice took a sedative and tried to sleep. It was no use. She cursed herself over and over, as his last words echoed in her mind: "Talk to your old man, please? . . . Please try to understand." If only she had understood! She wondered if she would ever eradicate the image of that dear, good man trudging down the hall to his room, without the comfort of her forgiveness. She did forgive him now. She forgave him everything. But he would never know it. This thought was almost as unbearable as his death.

After a while, Beatrice got out of bed and went downstairs to the library. The house was dark and still. Switching on the lights, she gazed once more at the wreckage in that grand room and walked over to the spot near the window where her father had been slain. She stared at the crude white tape outline of his body on the floor—a cartoon of a fallen man. Kneeling, she touched the space in-side the jagged enclosure as if it were hallowed ground.

"Daddy," she said, folding her hands and bowing her head. "Forgive me for not understanding you. I understand you now . . . I understand. And I shall find out who did this to you and avenge you. I swear it." She whispered the Lord's Prayer, and when she had finished, she blessed herself, "in the name of the Father, the Son, and the Holy Ghost. Amen." She was choked with tears.

Beatrice rose to her feet. At that precise moment, it dawned on her that she was completely alone in the world.

She wandered, distraught, around the library, wondering how on earth she could ever hope to put it back in order. How could anyone have mistreated such treasures? For what purpose? She started to gather up the least damaged books, one at a time, and replace them in their appropriate shelves. At first, the task seemed daunting. But as she lingered over her father's favorite volumes—stroking their bindings, reading snippets of their contents—she began to experience a sense of comfort and relief. In handling the little "friends" her father had so dearly loved, she felt close to him once more.

Beatrice worked through the night, occasionally stopping to stare at the spot where her father had been shot. Her efforts proved therapeutic. The hours flew by. Before she knew it, it was dawn. She drew open the heavy damask curtains to let in the light.

Taking a cursory inventory, she found nothing missing—none of the most valuable books, not even the priceless fourteenth- and fifteenth-century illuminated manuscripts. One thing seemed certain: whoever had done this terrible thing hadn't been after any precious volumes. Beatrice was on her way to check the silver and her mother's jewelry, which was stashed away in her bedroom, when a thought occurred to her: the grimoire. Where was the grimoire?

Beatrice ran back into the library and began a frantic search for the mysterious book. No luck. She raced upstairs to her father's room, thinking perhaps he had taken it there. But no. She went through the rest of the house, looking in all the rooms. Though they had been ransacked, nothing appeared to be stolen—not the silver, the jewelry, or any of the valuable objects. But the grimoire was nowhere to be found.

Her heart pounding, Beatrice sat down in the library and tried to calm herself. One thought kept whirling through her mind. If the grimoire was the only thing missing, then Signor Antonelli must have had a hand in her father's murder! With that, she telephoned the old book dealer's hotel, only to find that he had checked out the previous afternoon. She then tried to get in touch with Detective Monahan, but he was not in his office yet. Dressing, she went out for the morning papers, and bringing them home, she anxiously awaited Monahan's arrival at nine.

Dr. O'Connell's murder was a shocking event in the quiet, respectable neighborhood. The tabloid headlines screamed the news: TOP SURGEON BRUTALLY SLAIN . . . SOCIETY DOC SHOT . . . MURDER ON BEEKMAN PLACE. The *New York Times* offered a sedate description of the crime, along with an obituary of the prominent doctor, a large part of which was devoted to his book collection. The account mentioned that Dr. O'Connell had won a Bronze Star for bravery during World War II and detailed his pioneering efforts in the field of thoracic surgery. The last line read: "Dr. O'Connell is survived by a daughter, Beatrice."

Beatrice was in the kitchen, poring over the newspapers, when Monahan rang the doorbell. She ran to admit him.

"Detective Monahan," she said breathlessly, barely able to contain herself. "I think I know who might have been involved in my father's murder!"

They went to the library. Beatrice described in detail the meeting between Giuseppe Antonelli and her father two days before, when Antonelli came for dinner and was shown the grimoire.

"You say that's the only book missing?"

"Yes, as far as I can see."

"And what kind of book did you say it was?"

"A grimoire."

"What's that?"

"A book of black magic."

Monahan raised his eyebrows. He asked her to spell it and jotted down the word in his notebook.

"So you think there's a connection?"

"I certainly do. Don't you?" Beatrice said impatiently. "Signor Antonelli was fascinated by the book. He offered to buy it from my father. He told us he had a client who collected them. An 'oddity,' he called it. Naturally, Daddy refused to sell it to him."

"Why?"

"That's—that was his policy. My father would never part with any of the books in his library. I wish to God he'd parted with this one."

"Run this by me again," Monahan said. "Why, exactly, do you think your father's murder is connected with this book?"

"I told you—it's the only thing missing. My mother's jewelry, the silver, all the valuable objects, the televisions, VCRs, my computer—anything an ordinary thief might want—they're all here. Everything except the grimoire."

"Uh huh. Interesting . . ."

"And I called Antonelli's hotel early this morning," Beatrice said. "He checked out yesterday afternoon."

This revelation seemed to have less of an impact on Monahan than Beatrice had hoped.

"Any chance your father could have put this, uh, grimoire somewhere else?"

"I checked his room. But it was here in the library. He wouldn't have put it anywhere else. He didn't put books that were meant for the library anywhere else."

"You're sure?"

"I am positive!" she snapped.

"Have you looked around?"

"Yes—I told you. I've been through all the rooms to see if anything else was missing. It's the only thing that's gone."

"Maybe you should check again."

"All right, I'll check again." She sighed. Monahan's plodding was beginning to grate on her nerves. "But I won't find it—I'll bet you anything. That's what he was after, whoever killed my father. I know it. I feel it. Antonelli was desperate to have it. I told my father at the time. You've got to get hold of him. He's probably back in Rome by now."

"Tell me, how old a man is this Antonelli?" Monahan said.

"Around my father's age, I guess. In his seventies. Why?"

"Nothing. I'm just trying to get the picture. And he's a book dealer, you say?"

"Yes, yes. He's a book dealer. He's sold things to my father for years. If he is in Rome, can you extradite him?"

"Hold on, just hold on," Monahan said evenly. "I'm trying to get the facts here. And this book isn't as valuable as the others?"

"God, no. There's a Book of Hours that's worth about half a million dollars. But there was something about that grimoire— something he wasn't telling us. It didn't have anything to do with money."

"If he didn't tell you, how do you know?"

"I was there, okay? I saw the guy drooling over the goddamn thing. I even made a bet with Daddy that Antonelli was going to call him back and offer him some astronomical amount of money for it. Look, if you don't want to do something about this, then I will."

"Please, Miss O'Connell, I know you're upset. Let me ask you something. Did Antonelli call him back the next day?"

"Well, I don't know, because . . ." She hesitated.

"Because . . . ?"

"Because I never saw my father again." Beatrice swallowed hard. Her eyes filled with tears.

"I'm sorry," Monahan said, offering her a tissue. "I'm going to call the hotel and find out exactly what time he checked out."

"Yesterday, they said. Yesterday afternoon."

"I'll get on this, Miss O'Connell. Don't you worry."

Beatrice wondered if Monahan was just being patronizing. He pulled a Danish wrapped in soft, transparent plastic from his pocket.

"Breakfast," he said, holding up the unappetizing-looking sweet roll.

Beatrice gazed into his weary eyes. He seemed to her like a man who had stopped expecting very much from life, who stubbornly, with cheerless resignation, made do with whatever came his way. She decided to give him a break.

"So what do you think?" Beatrice said. "Do you think I'm right?"

"I think it deserves to be looked into."

"How are you going to track him down in Rome?"

"Don't worry. If it's necessary, we'll do it."

"But it *is* necessary!" she cried. "Don't you see? That damn book is the only thing missing, and Antonelli wanted it. Put two and two together, okay? Do you have to be Sherlock Holmes?"

"Do you know his address in Rome?" Monahan mumbled, his mouth half full.

"I know his old address. I'm sure he can be located."

An officer came into the room. "Hey, Frank, there's a guy downstairs wants to see Miss O'Connell."

"Did you get a shot at the name?" Monahan said sarcastically.

"Some Italian name. Monelli or—"

"Antonelli?" Monahan interrupted him.

"Yeah, that's it."

Beatrice and the detective looked at each other.

"Send him up."

The officer left the room.

"I don't believe it!" Beatrice said.

"Saves us a trip to Rome. Too bad."

Beatrice felt a bit sheepish. "Well, I *know* he's involved."

"Innocent until proven guilty, remember?"

"In this case, it's the other way around," Beatrice asserted. "I never liked him."

Presently, the officer ushered Signor Antonelli into the library. The old Italian froze for a moment, surveying the wreckage.

"*Dio mio!*" he cried out, gesticulating with his hands. "What have they done to this beautiful place? *E cara Beatrice ...*" He walked toward her, arms outstretched. "I am reading the newspapers this morning and I cannot believe it. My dear old friend—shot! How is it possible?"

Beatrice rose from the couch and, her hands at her sides, let the old man embrace her. "Signor Antonelli," she said coldly, "this is Detective Monahan, the officer in charge of the investigation."

"Giuseppe Antonelli." The dealer bowed slightly as the two men shook hands.

"Monahan. Please sit down."

Signor Antonelli propped himself up stiffly on a chair opposite the couch. He shook his head. "Only the day before yesterday, I was sitting here in this room with John. And now ..."

"Mr. Antonelli, I have to ask you a few questions."

"*Certo.* I am here to help you in any way I can." He smiled sympathetically at Beatrice, who looked away.

"Where were you between the hours of twelve and three yesterday afternoon?"

"Yesterday I had lunch with an old friend."

"Who?"

"Father Morton from Saint Xavier's Church."

"Father Morton?" Monahan said.

"Do you know him?"

"Everybody knows Father Morton. He's one of the city's fixtures."

"We had much to discuss. We have not seen one another in several years, since my last visit to New York."

"And you were with him until when?"

"It was close to three-thirty."

Monahan glanced at Beatrice, who had been studying the old gentleman carefully.

"And Father Morton will verify that?"

"I am sure that he will."

"Just a couple more questions, Mr. Antonelli. Miss O'Connell here says you were interested in a book Dr. O'Connell showed you."

Antonelli paused as if he had to think for a moment.

"Ah yes, of course—the grimoire. It completely slipped my mind."

"Wasn't that the reason for your trip to New York?" Beatrice said.

"No, my dear. I had other things to do as well."

"You wanna tell me a little about this book?" Monahan asked.

"I will tell you what I know," Antonelli said with a hollow smile. "John had written to me about a special book, wishing very much that I would come over to have a look at it. I was not about to make a trip just for that. But as I have said, I had some other business here, with Father Morton among others. So the night before last, I came here for dinner, and John showed me the grimoire. Beatrice was here. We all examined it together."

As he spoke, Beatrice studied the old man, hoping he might betray a sign of guilt. However, she could not help thinking that he seemed genuinely distraught and without guile.

"I understand from Miss O'Connell that you became very interested in it once you saw it," Monahan said.

Antonelli shrugged. "Yes . . . well, it is a rare thing, very interesting to certain collectors."

"And you offered to buy it from him?"

"No, not exactly. What I said was, I have a client who collects these oddities. I thought I would telephone him and ask him if it would be of interest to him."

"Uh huh. And who might he be?" Monahan was poised to make a note.

Antonelli demurred. "I'm afraid I cannot say. My client prefers to remain anonymous."

"So did you?"

"What?"

"Telephone him?"

"Yes. As a matter of fact, I did."

"And was he interested?"

"Very much so. He authorized me to make John quite a sizable offer for it."

"And . . . ?"

"And I did—even though I told my client it would probably be useless."

"Why?"

"Because, as Beatrice will tell you, it was her father's policy never to sell a book that entered his library. When John said no, he meant no. And he had said no the previous evening. Still, in this case, as the book was a gift, and as he didn't seem to care very much for it, I saw no harm in presenting the offer. Particularly as it was an extremely generous one."

"How much, if I may ask?"

"Fifty thousand dollars."

Monahan seemed impressed. "And what did Dr. O'Connell say to that?"

"Exactly what I thought he would say: no. He declined very politely. You see, Detective Monahan, John O'Connell with his books was like a father with his children," Signor Antonelli said with apparent fondness. "He would not give them up for anything."

"And what time did you speak to him to make this offer?"

"I telephoned him from my hotel at about, oh, about eleven o'clock yesterday morning."

"You checked out of your hotel," Beatrice said, unable to contain herself any longer.

Antonelli looked startled by her accusatory tone. "Yes, my dear," he replied evenly. "I believe I told you and John that I was extremely disappointed with the service in my old hotel, because it had changed management. I checked out and went to another."

"Which one?" Monahan asked.

"I am at the Carlyle. On Seventy-sixth Street."

Beatrice had to admit that Signor Antonelli's explanation seemed entirely plausible. And, more than that, his manner was relaxed, if sad. He didn't act like a guilty man.

"Okay, so when you spoke to Dr. O'Connell, did you set up another meeting with him?"

"Yes. I promised I would come by this morning and say goodbye. Then at breakfast I read in the newspaper that my dear friend was shot to death." Antonelli wiped away an invisible tear with the back of his hand. "Forgive me, but I still cannot believe it. Beatrice, my dear, is there anything I can do for you? I was going to go back to Rome today, but I am delighted to stay longer if you would like."

She looked him straight in the eye. "Do you still want the grimoire?"

"Well, yes, of course," he replied, perking up. "Do you wish to sell it?"

"I don't have it."

A look of concern swept over the old man's face. "No? Who does?"

"It's been stolen," she replied.

The old man's eyes widened. "Really?"

"That surprise you?" she said.

"What else has been taken?"

"Nothing. Just the grimoire."

"How extraordinary."

"Why?" Monahan asked.

"My dear fellow," Signor Antonelli replied condescendingly. "If you knew anything about books, you would not ask that."

"So educate me."

"Rare and interesting as the grimoire is, it has not nearly the value of some of the other books in this library. Either the thief took it merely because he fancied it, or he mistakenly thought it was worth more than it is."

"Fifty thousand dollars ain't hay," Monahan pointed out.

"Ah, no—but that is for a special client, whom the thief could not possibly know. Intrinsically, the grimoire is not worth much more than two, maybe three thousand dollars—as compared to the Book of Hours, which is worth several hundred thousand, perhaps even more."

"Miss O'Connell mentioned that."

"In any case," Antonelli continued, "if the thief tries to sell it, I shall surely hear about it. My client in Italy is the largest collector of such books. All of them come to his attention sooner or later."

"Oh, come on. Tell us the name of this mysterious client of yours," Monahan said.

"As I have told you." Antonelli smiled, holding a finger up in protest. "Like a priest or a lawyer or even a psychoanalyst, I am not at liberty to divulge the names of my clients. Otherwise they would not remain my clients for very long. But rest assured, he is a serious collector."

"I don't doubt it," Monahan said, acknowledging the old gentleman's courtliness. "I assume you have no objections if I call Father Morton?"

"No, none at all. But surely I am not a suspect?"

"You are until you ain't, as they say."

"In that case, Father Morton will certainly confirm everything I have told you."

"Please don't leave the city until you hear from me."

"Of course not. . . . Am I free to go?"

Monahan nodded. Signor Antonelli reached inside his breast pocket and pulled out a slim gold case, from which he extracted two calling cards, handing one to Beatrice and one to Detective Monahan.

"Please, both of you, do not hesitate to get in touch with me if I may be of the slightest service."

Beatrice looked at the elegant white card, on which Giuseppe Antonelli's name and his address in Rome were embossed in black.

"My dear, dear Beatrice," he said, rising from his chair. "I cannot begin to express my sorrow at your loss. Your father was a great man. I will miss him more than I can say. My only consolation is that I shall probably be joining him shortly, for I am getting old and rather fed up with life."

Beatrice got up from the couch to bid the old gentleman goodbye. She accompanied him downstairs. At the door, he took both her hands in his.

"If you should find yourself in need of a sympathetic ear, please go and see my old friend Father Morton. He is a very fine priest, and he will help you. You may trust him." He kissed her on both cheeks.

Beatrice trudged back up to the library. "So I was wrong," she said to Monahan, who was finishing his Danish.

"Looks that way. Father Morton's a pretty impressive alibi. Nice card," Monahan said, flicking its pristine edge before inserting it into his notebook.

"Now what?" Beatrice asked glumly, feeling let down that her hunch about Signor Antonelli had proved worthless.

"Now I go and question people in the neighborhood, to see if anybody saw anything or anyone. We wait for the results of the forensic tests and the autopsy. And maybe we get lucky. Miss O'Connell, could I have your father's address book and his diary and a list of the people who knew him best—like the doctors he worked with?"

Beatrice nodded.

"Here's *my* card," he said. "Not as elegant as your friend's, but it's got my direct line at the precinct. I'll give you my home phone." He jotted down a number on the back. "You can call me anytime. I'll be in touch if there's any news."

ONAHAN DEPARTED, LEAVING SEVERAL OF HIS men to search the house for clues. Nellie called to say that she was sick with grief. Beatrice gave her the day off and took the telephone off the hook to avoid condolence calls and inquiries from reporters. She shut herself inside the library and continued the work she'd started the night before, stacking the volumes in separate piles according to the amount of damage they had incurred.

As Beatrice worked, she pictured some of her happiest childhood moments with her parents—the Christmas Eves, when she was permitted to taste her father's famous eggnog and stay up late to trim the tree with the exquisite antique ornaments her mother had collected from all over the world; the Easter Sundays, when she and her mother dyed eggs together for her father to hide all over the house—except in the library, which he said was "no place for little search bunnies"; Thanksgiving and Saint Paddy's Day, as her father called it, when he would take her to view the parades, hoisting her up on his shoulders so she could see over the crowd; the school nights when she would sneak down to the library after her mother had tucked her in bed and make her father read to her until she fell asleep and he carried her back upstairs in his arms.

She had been happy, sheltered and coddled by two adoring parents, or so she had told herself until the failure of her marriage stained the idyllic landscape. But she had somehow managed to shrug it off, explaining the divorce as a bad choice of a man and her inadequacy as a mate.

Now, however, in the wake of her father's revelation about another woman, she began to excavate the terrain of daily life with her parents. She wondered if her mother's apparent piety had been nothing more than a mask for disappointment. Had her father's long retreats to his library been a simple need to get away from the family for a while, or was it an expression of impatience with a false front?

Beatrice began to dig up other, more disquieting moments—the slamming of doors late at night, and then, in the morning, awaking to find her father asleep in the guest room. She recalled her father's brief, but violent, outbursts of temper for no apparent cause. He would stalk off, leaving her mother with a pinched expression on her face and the eternal sigh of "Jesus, Mary, and Joseph" under her breath.

There were the dinners when her parents hardly said a word to each other and she sat quietly between them, worried that they were angry at each other, or, worse, at her. She grew up with the feeling that she had to amuse her parents and their friends with her intelligence in order to allay the tension that existed in the house when they were alone together. But whatever she did never seemed to be enough. They were always setting new standards for her, and she never felt wholly approved of.

Sometimes silence reigned for days in the house, while her father read obsessively and her mother sat in her bedroom, addressing envelopes and organizing benefits for ever more prestigious Catholic charities. Beatrice was acutely aware of her mother's social ambitions, which required the appearance, if not necessarily the reality, of a family life that was stage-set perfect. Beatrice knew she was part of the cast, and she had been a willing player.

Beatrice remembered her mother's snide, disparaging remarks about her friends' husbands and then, later, about the various boyfriends Beatrice brought home. It was as if Liz O'Connell secretly viewed all men with disdain and suspicion. And though her mother had smiled through Beatrice's wedding to Stephen, Beatrice knew that she deeply disapproved of the maverick reporter who was not Catholic and who was slightly offbeat, with his liberal views and his strong attraction to danger.

"I don't trust him," her mother had told her. And much to Beatrice's chagrin, Stephen had proved her mother right.

Beatrice knew, too, that her parents had secrets from her, though she never could have guessed the existence of another woman. But she was just now beginning to fathom the deeper secret her mother kept: Elizabeth O'Connell—staunch Catholic, pillar of the community, good mother, and exemplary hostess—disliked sex, feared men, and was angry at herself and at her daughter for being female.

By four o'clock, Beatrice was utterly exhausted. Everyone had left. She dragged herself upstairs to her bedroom, where she lay down and fell asleep instantaneously.

Sometime later, Beatrice became aware that the front doorbell was ringing. She glanced groggily at her watch. It was nearly seven. A marked stillness gripped the air. Beatrice looked out her bedroom window. The sky had turned dark and silvery, as if a storm might be coming. She leaned over to see if she could catch a glimpse of whoever was calling on her at this hour. The person was obscured from view by the lintel. Smoothing her rumpled clothes, she hurried downstairs.

Through the peephole in the front door, Beatrice saw the face of a man she didn't recognize. She kept the chain on and cracked the door open.

"Who is it?" she said warily.

"Simon Lovelock," the stranger replied.

"What do you want?"

"I have an appointment with Dr. O'Connell," he said in a refined but raspy voice.

Beatrice's heart skipped a beat. Who is this person who doesn't know my father's dead? she wondered. The stranger fished inside his trousers and extracted a ragged business card, which he slipped through the crack in the door. It read simply:

SIMON LOVELOCK
LOVELOCK RARE BOOKS

An address and telephone number were underneath. Beatrice examined the card, then peered out at him again. Thin and of medium height, he had straight lips, an aquiline nose, and a long, somber face, the color of aged vellum. His black hair was flecked with silver strands and his dark eyes, full of inquiry, sparkled with intelligence. Dressed in black from head to foot, he looked slightly shabby but presentable. Beatrice noticed that the collar of his jacket was fraying around the edges. His fingers were stained yellow with tobacco, his nails slightly ragged. He took a final drag of the cigarette he was puffing on nervously and flicked the butt away.

"What business do you have with Dr. O'Connell?"

"I don't know," the stranger said, squinting at her through the crack.

"What do you mean, you don't know?"

"He telephoned me yesterday to set up an appointment. I told him I wouldn't be able to meet him until six-thirty, because my shop stays open until six. I'm sorry if I'm a bit late, but the subway was delayed."

Distant thunder rumbled through the air, then faded. It was beginning to drizzle. Mr. Lovelock hovered closer to the door.

"Uh—is he in, please?" he said, brushing raindrops from his head.

"No."

"Oh. Well, if you'd be so kind as to give him my card. He can call me tomorrow if he wants to set up a more convenient time." He started to walk away. Then, as if he'd had an afterthought, he turned and said, "Please tell him how much I'm looking forward to meeting him, won't you?"

Beatrice didn't answer. She was trying to assess the situation. Why, she wondered, had her father made an appointment with a book dealer? Who was he, really? She closed the door and watched him through the peephole.

Lovelock lit another cigarette and started down the street, pulling his collar up around his neck and hugging himself, an effort at protection from the steadily increasing rain. Feeling a wave of pity for the man, but mainly wishing to satisfy her curiosity, Beatrice ignored caution and flung open the front door to call the stranger back.

"Mr. Lovelock!" she cried. "Wait!"

Lovelock turned around and stared at her, a perplexed expression on his face.

"Won't you come inside, please?" She beckoned to him. "At least until it stops raining?"

"With pleasure!" he replied. Trotting up the front steps, he hastened inside the door. "It's getting nasty out there." He took a handkerchief from his pocket and wiped the rain off his head and shoulders.

Lovelock smiled at Beatrice, revealing a row of tobacco-stained teeth. His smile immediately lightened the dour aspects of his face, lending him a soft, sweet expression.

"I'm Beatrice O'Connell," she said, extending her hand. "Dr. O'Connell's daughter."

Lovelock lowered his eyes. "I'm honored to meet you," he said, shaking her hand with a tepid grip.

"My father won't be keeping his appointment with you," she said.

Lovelock raised his bushy black eyebrows and cocked his head to one side. He seemed disappointed. "Why not?"

"My father is dead."

"Dead?" he repeated dully.

"He was shot yesterday afternoon during a robbery attempt, here in this house," Beatrice said in a halting voice.

Lovelock blinked a couple of times, as if he was trying to digest the news. "Dear God, how terrible!"

"It's been in all the newspapers. I'm surprised you didn't see it."

"I'm afraid I don't keep up with the newspapers," Lovelock replied apologetically. "I had no idea.... Please forgive my intrusion.... I'm so sorry ... so very, very sorry."

"Thank you," Beatrice said, touched by his response.

"I think perhaps I should be going." Nervously, he put his hand on the doorknob.

"No, please. Please stay," Beatrice said. "At least until the rain lets up a little."

"Well, if you're quite sure ..."

"Come into the kitchen, won't you? We could both use a cup of tea, don't you think?"

"Well ..." He hesitated. "If you're sure I'm not intruding ... ?"

"Follow me."

"Very kind of you. Very kind indeed."

Lovelock seemed a sympathetic person, and furthermore,

Beatrice was anxious to find out why her father had summoned him. She led him down the hall and into the kitchen. Sitting at the small table, he watched her as she prepared the tea.

"Let me ask you something," she said, as she filled the kettle. "Do you remember what time it was when my father called you yesterday?"

Lovelock kneaded the lobe of his right ear with his fingers. "I think it was a little after twelve. . . . Yes. It was about twelve-fifteen. I was just going to lunch."

Twelve-fifteen, Beatrice thought. In other words, very shortly before his murder.

"And you don't have any idea what it was he wanted to see you about?"

"No, not really. . . . Well, I assume it was about a book. That's my business."

"But he didn't say what book it was?"

Lovelock shook his head. "No, I'm afraid not."

They lapsed into a long silence, which was interrupted by the whistle of the kettle.

Beatrice busied herself with the teapot.

"Do you take milk, lemon, sugar?"

"Just plain, thanks."

She poured the brewed tea into china cups. Lovelock took a few sips, savoring the smoky blend.

"Ah, that's grand. Thank you," he said.

"You say you didn't know my father?"

"No. I never had the privilege."

"Do you have any idea how he got your name?"

"I'm afraid not."

"Why did you agree to come here?" she asked.

"Well, I didn't know your father personally, but I knew *of* him, of course. Most people in the rare-book trade know the name O'Connell."

Beatrice got up and fetched a copy of the *New York Times* for Lovelock to see. He studied Dr. O'Connell's obituary, shaking his head as he read.

"Oh, dear God . . . dear God . . . ," he kept muttering. When he'd finished, he looked up and gazed at Beatrice with real compassion. "A terrible thing . . . terrible. And they haven't caught the culprit?"

"Not yet. But they will—or I will."

"What a world." He sighed ruefully, putting the paper down.

They listened to the steady patter of the rain. Looking at her father's picture in the newspaper, Beatrice tried to resist the urge to cry. But it was no use. She broke down.

"I'm sorry. Forgive me," she said, wiping her tears with a napkin.

" 'Heaven knows we need never be ashamed of our tears, for they are rain upon the blinding dust of earth . . . ,' " he said kindly.

"That's lovely."

"Mr. Dickens. . . . He could always turn a phrase."

"When I was a little girl and I cried, I used to say I was raining," Beatrice said, forcing a wan smile. "Tell me, Mr. Lovelock, have you ever wished that you could take back the last moments you had with someone and see them one more time?"

"Perhaps not only the last ones," he said, looking away. His obvious pain discouraged further inquiry. "Perhaps I should be going."

"Please have some more tea," Beatrice urged. She liked his quiet manner.

"Oh, thanks . . . ," he replied gratefully.

Beatrice refilled his cup.

"I think the rain's stopped," he said, clearing his throat.

Partially on impulse and partially because she felt him to be a kindred spirit in grief, Beatrice asked Lovelock if he cared to see her father's library before he left. His sad face lit up with delight, as if he'd been given a present.

"Are you sure?" he said eagerly. "I wouldn't want to intrude."

"I'm sure," she said firmly, rising from the table. "However, I must warn you—the room's been ransacked. I've been trying to straighten it up, but it's still in a mess. It's difficult to explain," Beatrice said as she led him upstairs, "but it makes me feel close to my father to show his library to someone who'll appreciate it."

They reached the landing. "Prepare yourself for a shock," Beatrice said, facing Lovelock, before she swung open the heavy mahogany doors.

Lovelock gasped in horror at the terrible disarray of the great room. "Jesus, Mary, and Joseph!" he cried. "What in the name of God has happened here?"

"This is where—where he was shot."

They both entered the room slowly. The look of horror on

Lovelock's face quickly melted into one of sorrow. He knelt down and picked up a book, cradling it in his hands, stroking it as if it were a wounded animal.

"Oh, dear, dear, dear," he said, addressing the tattered volume. "You poor thing. Who did this to you?"

As she witnessed Lovelock's tenderness and concern for the bruised volume, Beatrice was reminded of her father, who would have viewed the desecration of his precious library as an act of attempted mass murder. "He loved his books so much," she said. "They were his friends."

Lovelock got up, still holding the book. "This can be mended," he said.

"It can. I can't."

"No," he replied softly. "But the old adage about time, you know . . ."

Beatrice handed him another book—the *Roman de la Rose*.

"This is my favorite book in this library," she said. "It was the only one I wanted out of my father's whole collection."

"She's a lovely little thing," he said, examining it. "But see here, she's been very badly wounded. She will certainly split apart if she's not tended to shortly—see?" He pointed to the spine, which was dangerously cracked.

"Yes, I know."

"I'd be honored to repair it for you," he offered. "I do some bookbinding in my spare time."

"That's very kind of you. Perhaps you'll let me think about it."

"Oh, of course," he said, flushing with embarrassment. "I just thought that, well, she's such a pretty little volume, and she doesn't need very much—just some stitching and gluing. But I don't mean to impose."

"No, please—you're very nice to offer."

"I'd like to do something," he said, looking around at the wreckage.

His eye was arrested by the partially visible white outline of Dr. O'Connell's slain body on the floor at the far end of the room. He walked over to it. Beatrice followed close behind him. When they reached the spot, they both stood in silence, looking down at the jagged tape.

"That's where it happened," Beatrice said after a time. There were still dark vestiges of blood on the wood floor.

Lovelock lit a cigarette. "Oh, forgive me. I hope it's all right if I smoke," he said as an afterthought.

"Of course; go right ahead. I do myself sometimes."

He exhaled a long plume of smoke, offering her a cigarette from the crumpled pack.

"No, thanks. I won't just now," she said.

"Do they have any idea who did it, or why?"

"No." Anxious to get away from the spot, Beatrice walked toward the door. "I need a drink," she said. "Will you join me in a glass of brandy?"

"With pleasure."

She left Lovelock alone in the library and walked down the hall to the living room, where she poured generous amounts of her father's good brandy into two large snifters. When she returned, Lovelock was perched on the couch, perusing the Del Cherico Book of Hours, which he had laid on the coffee table in front of him.

"Well, the motive certainly couldn't have been robbery," he said, looking up at Beatrice. "This volume is priceless."

"I'm not so sure. There's one book I can't find."

She handed him a glass of brandy and sat down beside him. Lovelock popped another cigarette into his mouth, lighting it with the burning butt of the one he'd just smoked.

"Well, nothing could be more valuable than this." He indicated the tome in front of him. "What illustrations!" With the tips of his fingers, he touched the outline of a delicately painted white lamb in a circle of gold leaf in the center of the large page. "The sweetness of it . . . ," he said. "The beauty of faith and, I suppose, the horrors of it never cease to amaze me."

"The book that I can't find is a grimoire. Do you know what that is?"

"Indeed I do," he said, perking up. "I happen to specialize in occult books."

"Ah!" Beatrice cried. "That's it, then. That's why he wanted to see you."

Lovelock narrowed his eyes. "That's not the type of thing I'd have imagined your father would go in for, judging from what I see of the collection. It's rather a unique field, and I know just about everyone in it."

"It was a present from a patient. He'd just been sent it, only about three weeks ago. It was a terrifying thing. I saw it."

"You saw it? Can you tell me about it?"

She described the book as best she could, drawing on her researcher's memory for detail. She told him of the pornographic woodcuts and the vivid section on necromancy. Lovelock listened attentively. It seemed to Beatrice that his eyes lit up when she recited the Latin inscription at the beginning by rote: *Videmus nunc per speculum in aenigmate, tunc autem facie ad faciem.*

"It sounds interesting," he said flatly.

"Tell me something. Would something like that be of enormous value?"

"Oh, it's difficult to say. I'd have to see it. In monetary terms, it isn't worth anything like some of the other books here. Did anyone else have a look at it?"

"Just Signor Antonelli, an Italian book dealer my father's dealt with for years."

"Giuseppe Antonelli?"

"Yes! You know him?"

Lovelock hesitated. "Again, by reputation only. He lives in Rome."

"Right. He's an old friend of my father's."

"Is he?"

"He was fascinated with it."

"Was he indeed?"

Beatrice detected something ominous in Lovelock's tone.

"Look, between us, Mr. Lovelock, I don't trust Signor Antonelli. I never really warmed to him, and last night, when I discovered the grimoire was missing, I thought maybe . . ."

"What?"

"I thought maybe he was involved."

"Ah . . . But now you don't?"

"I don't know. I honestly don't know," Beatrice said thoughtfully. "He came over here this morning. And he seemed genuinely upset. If he is involved, he should win an Academy Award. So I sort of changed my mind. But still . . . he was just fixated on the grimoire when he saw it. He immediately offered to buy it. Said he had a client who collected things like that. But of course, Daddy wouldn't sell it to him."

"No? Why not?"

"My father would never part with a single book in his library. He was famous for that. If you'd known him, you'd have understood. Parting with a book would have been like parting with a friend," Beatrice said. "I did, however, bet Daddy ten dollars that Signor Antonelli would call him again and make another offer."

"And did he?"

"As a matter of fact, he did. He told me and the detective in charge of the case that his client authorized him to pay fifty thousand dollars for it. But apparently my father turned him down."

"And the grimoire—you're sure it's gone?"

"Oh, it's gone, all right. I've checked every book here. It's just disappeared. As I said, it's the only thing missing. I'll tell you a secret. I tried to trick Signor Antonelli when he was here this morning. I asked him if he still wanted it. He leapt at the idea, so I knew he hadn't taken it. Unless that was an act too."

"So you think that whoever killed your father took it?"

"I can't think of another explanation for its disappearance, can you? Maybe whoever killed my father just took the grimoire because it's so bizarre. That was Antonelli's theory, anyway. Like you, he said that anyone who knew anything about books wouldn't have bothered with it. There are so many other things to take. On the other hand, a person who commits murder might like something like that. You know, something dealing with the occult. What do you think?"

"I think it's just as well to let sleeping dogs lie," Lovelock said.

"What do you mean?"

"Oh, nothing, nothing. . . . I really should be going."

"Obviously, my father wanted you to have a look at it, or he wouldn't have called you. From what I've described, do you think it's worth anything?"

"Again, I'd have to see it."

"Ballpark figure?"

"It all depends on the buyer. It's a different sort of market."

"What do you mean?"

Lovelock shifted uncomfortably in his seat. "Well, there are people who take grimoires quite literally," he said.

"You mean they believe in them—believe in black magic?"

"Uh—yes. You might say that."

"And what would the book I've described to you be worth to a believer? Roughly."

"In monetary terms—oh, say, two to three thousand dollars."

"And in other terms?" Beatrice pressed him.

"A true believer might think it priceless."

"Might pay anything for it?"

"Yes."

Beatrice pinned him with her eyes. "Might kill for it?"

"Might," he said somberly.

Beatrice heaved a mighty sigh and sat back in her chair, contemplating this thought. Lovelock lit another cigarette.

"Listen, Mr. Lovelock, if you think there's a connection between my father's death and this book—"

"I never said that."

"Not in so many words, no. But I can see it in your eyes. You know there's a connection, don't you?"

"I know no such thing."

"I don't know you, but I have a feeling you're a kind man."

Lovelock lowered his eyes.

"This is my father we're talking about," she continued. "I loved him very much, and I want—I *need*—to find out who did this. For all the obvious reasons and for one, maybe, unobvious one. Can you understand that?"

Lovelock nodded, exhaling a fine plume of smoke.

"Now, as I understand it, this world of the occult is fairly small. Specialized. You seem to know everybody, or know of them." She paused. "Do you have any idea—any hunch—who might have done this?"

Lovelock continued puffing on his cigarette. The smoke drifted over his face. He seemed to Beatrice to be in the throes of a decision. He waited before he answered, then spoke in a measured tone of voice.

"I'd like to help you, Miss O'Connell. Honestly, I would. But . . ."

"But?" Beatrice said anxiously.

"I cannot get involved."

"Why not? Are you afraid?"

"It's not a question of that."

"What is it a question of? Please—please help me."

"I have to go. I'm sorry." Lovelock got up from the table and started for the hall.

"Wait!" Beatrice cried, hurrying after him. "I apologize if I've upset you. But I have to know what you know."

Lovelock walked downstairs and paused at the front door. He

looked at her sympathetically. "It would be a different thing if you actually had the grimoire," he said.

"Why?"

"It just would. Don't ask me to explain."

"But I *am* asking you."

"I can't say any more. Really I can't." He opened the front door.

"Can I at least come and talk to you some more?"

"My shop is open from ten to six. You would be most welcome."

He stepped outside. The rain had let up, but there was still a misty drizzle in the air.

"You're sure Antonelli knows you don't have the grimoire?" he said.

"Yes—positive. What? What? Tell me what you're thinking."

"I'm not thinking anything," he said, with a dismissive wave of his hand. "It's late. Thank you for showing me the library and for the tea and brandy. It was very nice to meet you, Miss O'Connell. I wish it could have been under happier circumstances."

"Would you like to borrow an umbrella?"

"You're very kind, but I'll be fine, thanks."

"Well, then, good night," Beatrice said reluctantly.

"Good night."

Lovelock started to walk away, then stopped abruptly. Wheeling around, he stood poised on the steps, clasping the railing to steady himself. He looked up at Beatrice.

"Forget about the grimoire," he said, his eyes sparkling and intense.

"I can't, Mr. Lovelock. You know I can't." She smiled ruefully. "That's like telling me to forget about my father's murder."

"You must try to understand that some things are better left alone."

With that, Lovelock turned away, raising his collar to shield himself from the rain. Beatrice watched him as he hunched over and scurried down the block, a lone black figure fading into the twilight. She closed the door behind him, swearing on the soul of her father that she would somehow learn what he knew.

5

WO WEEKS LATER, A SERVICE WAS HELD FOR JOHN O'Connell at Saint Thomas More's, a small church tucked away in the middle of a block of apartment buildings on Manhattan's Upper East Side. Despite her father's aversion to organized religion, Beatrice felt the necessity of memorializing him in the Catholic faith into which he had been born. She remembered his oft-spoken words to her that the Catholic Church, for all its political problems, "christens, marries, and buries people better than any other institution."

Organ music by Bach and Mozart, John O'Connell's favorite composers, played softly as well over three hundred mourners filed into the dusky little house of worship to pay their last respects. A huge black-and-white photograph of Dr. O'Connell in his younger days, mounted on pasteboard, was placed on a pedestal to the right side of the altar.

Monsignor Regan, a white-haired cleric, conducted the solemn mass with immense dignity and obvious compassion. Beatrice and Nellie sat side by side in the front pew, holding hands, as the monsignor spoke of death being, in some sense, a joyous time, for it was nothing more than a transition from this earth to the glorious world of life everlasting through Jesus Christ.

To her surprise, Beatrice became caught up in the wonder and beauty of the ceremony—the blessing of the cup and the wafer, the soft rhythm of the priest's voice as he recited the moving liturgy, the pungent fumes from the censer. Monsignor Regan's humble piety and simplicity of manner soothed her in an unexpected way. She had tried to follow her father's scientific rationalist's path but had always known in her heart that human beings need more than a mere logical explanation can provide, particularly in moments of grief. The memorial provided that intangible comfort of faith, with the kindly prelate giving her a new respect for the goodness inherent in the Church, and she was grateful.

During the eulogies, by six colleagues and friends of Dr. O'Connell, Beatrice reflected on many things. Disparate images of her father swept across her mind in the pastel colors of memory—his quirky facial expressions as he read aloud to her in front of a blazing fire in the library on cold winter nights, his strong arms holding her tight in the rough, bracing waters of the Atlantic, where he taught her to swim during long, lazy summers in East Hampton, his slow, loping gait, the sadness behind his eyes, his animation when he talked about books.

John O'Connell hated television, calling it "the scourge of the modern age." Determined to instill an appreciation and reverence for the written word in Beatrice, he rarely allowed his daughter to watch it. She smiled to herself, remembering how her schoolmates had teased her for never being up on the latest shows. But now she was indebted to him, for she had learned to love books as he did; they were her lasting friends.

As the service progressed, however, Beatrice's mind took a darker turn, to the day of her graduation from Barnard College, when she saw him reach out affectionately for her mother's hand, whereupon her mother abruptly turned away. This fleeting rebuff had struck Beatrice as odd at the time, but she denied its import until this moment. Now, in the wake of her father's recent revelations, she realized that the encounter had taken place around the time he said he fell in love with the nurse at the hospital. Was her father's gesture toward her mother an attempt at reconciliation or an expression of guilt—or both? Did her mother know of his infatuation? Was she expressing her anger toward him, or was Liz O'Connell simply uncomfortable with displays of affection?

In contrast to her husband, who barely concealed his contempt for the Church, Elizabeth O'Connell had always been deeply religious. Her faith made her seem kind, but passive, as if she viewed life as something to be accepted rather than challenged. Beatrice had never quite been able to get a grip on her mother, who, wrapped in the mantle of her conviction that everything was God's will, seemed oddly untouched by experience. She wondered if her parents' clash of beliefs had led to the breakdown of their marriage and her father's need for another woman. But the marriage had lasted. So in the end, perhaps, their opposing views had bonded them together in some strange way.

She thought of Stephen. She had not heard from him since her father's death, and his silence plagued her. Was he consciously staying away, or did he just not know what had happened? She found herself hoping to see him among the mourners when she left the church. But she doubted he was there. She was convinced she would have sensed his presence, for she still felt deeply connected to him, even after all this time. Her mind drifted back to the baby they almost had—and with that terrible thought, the loss of her father crashed down upon her like an ocean wave.

Weeping, she felt as if she were drowning in a sea of grief and fought back an almost uncontrollable urge to cry out for help in the middle of the service. But just then, her heart veered onto another surprising course. Much to her chagrin, she thought of Luis Diaz. Scenes of their afternoon together spun uncontrollably through her mind. Over the past two weeks, she had been filled with a need to call him. Once or twice, she had picked up the phone but stopped herself before completing the call. Now she was sorely ashamed that the moment of her deepest sorrow was somehow polluted with desire.

The service concluded, Beatrice dried her tears and stood outside the church with Monsignor Regan, accepting condolences from friends. She knew most of the people there, and a small receiving line formed spontaneously in front of her and the monsignor. Presently, a heavyset priest with a round, friendly face marched up to her, wiping his brow from the heat.

"Beatrice," he said, extending his hand in a forthright manner. "I'm Father Morton, Giuseppe Antonelli's friend."

Beatrice was slightly taken aback to see him there.

"Giuseppe asked me to come and pay my respects on his be-half. I'm deeply sorry for your loss. I hope you will feel free to come and visit me at Saint Xavier's at any time. Or if you wish, I can call on you."

At that moment, Nellie came up beside Beatrice with a look of awe on her face. Beatrice introduced her to Father Morton, who smiled and said a few comforting words to the old housekeeper be-fore moving on.

"That was Father Morton," Nellie whispered excitedly to Beatrice. "It's an honor he came here."

"Do you know him?"

"Oh, no, not personally," Nellie said with reverence. "Will you be wanting me for anything this afternoon, Miss Beatrice?"

"No, thanks, Nellie. You take the day off."

"God bless," the old woman said, as she left the church.

The crowd thinned, and Beatrice started walking down the block, anxious to go home and rest from her ordeal. Just as she was about to hail a taxi, she felt a light tap on her arm. She whirled around, hoping it might be Stephen at last. But instead she saw a pretty, middle-aged woman in a brown dress, its white lace collar wilting from the heat.

"Miss O'Connell," she said. "My name is Mary O'Shaunessy. I was a friend of your father's. I just wanted to express my deepest sympathy to you. Dr. O'Connell was a very great man." The woman wiped away fresh tears with a handkerchief.

"Thank you," Beatrice said, looking at her with interest. "How did you know my father?"

"I was a nurse at the hospital. I assisted him on many occasions. He was a remarkable surgeon. He had God-given hands—the hands of an angel."

Beatrice noticed a striking physical similarity between Mary O'Shaunessy and her mother in her mother's younger days.

"You were a friend of my father's?" Beatrice said, probing the woman's face.

"Yes," she replied shyly. "That's all I wanted to say. I'm sorry to disturb you."

"No, no," Beatrice said. "You're not disturbing me. Miss O'Shaunessy, is it?"

"Mary, please."

"Mary," Beatrice said softly, "you knew my father very well, didn't you?"

The woman lowered her eyes. "Quite well."

Beatrice paused. "You were the one, weren't you?"

Mary O'Shaunessy's eyes widened. "I . . . I don't know what you mean."

"My father told me everything before he died," Beatrice said. "Everything?"

"You're the one he fell in love with, aren't you?"

The woman looked away, seemingly at a loss for words.

"Please," Beatrice said. "It's all right. I don't blame you. And I don't blame him. I just wish I could have told him that before he died. I'd give anything for him to know that I understand and that I love him." Beatrice began to cry.

Mary O'Shaunessy touched Beatrice's arm. "He loved you," she said with great feeling. "He loved you more than anything else in the world."

"I was so judgmental," Beatrice said through her tears. "Please forgive me. Somehow, if you forgive me, it would be like him forgiving me, in a way."

"There's nothing to forgive. Your father and I—we loved each other very much. But we knew that it could never be."

"Why? If you loved each other . . . ?"

"Because of who he was. He had a deep sense of loyalty to you and your mother. I was just a moment when he needed to recapture his youth. But you and Liz were his history. He always told me he could never leave you both, and I accepted that. It was enough to be with him for whatever time he allowed me. He was the greatest man I ever knew."

"Tell me something . . . did my mother make him give you up?"

"Oh, no; quite the contrary. . . . Your mother offered him his freedom, even though the idea of divorce was against everything she believed in. She was a kind and generous woman. And she wanted what was best for him. I don't know if I could have done what she did. . . ." She paused, as if the memory haunted her. "It was when he saw the great sacrifice your mother was willing to make for him that he gave me up voluntarily. I think he realized then how much he loved her and how much she loved him—how much they meant to each other."

"My mother became ill around that time, with a heart condition. Did you know about that?"

"Beatrice, I don't know if I should tell you this . . . I don't know if your father would have wanted me to, but . . ."

"What? Please, you must tell me."

"Your mother was ill for a long time before your father and I . . ."

"No, she wasn't."

"Yes . . . but they kept it from you. In a way, your mother welcomed your father's relationship with me. Things were very difficult for her. It's just that . . . well, no one expected that we would fall in love."

Beatrice took a moment to digest this news. "You mean my mother knew about you and my father for a long time?"

"I think so, yes. Anyway, that was my understanding."

"And did you ever meet my mother?"

"I met her once when she came to visit your father at the hospital. We shook hands and she smiled at me. . . . She knew."

"God." Beatrice sighed. "I had no idea any of this was going on."

"Your father wanted to protect you. They both did. We all did."

"After he gave you up, did you ever see him again?"

The woman shook her head. "Oh, no. I left the hospital and moved up to Hartford. We spoke on the phone once or twice, but it was only to say hello, see how the other was getting on. I'm married now," she said, trying to be more cheerful. "To a doctor. I have stepchildren but no children of my own." She smiled sadly.

"I'm sorry."

"Please, don't be. Your father was the love of my life, Beatrice. I wouldn't have traded one second with him for anything in the world. Few people had what I had with him, and I'm very grateful. I couldn't believe it when I read about . . ." Her voice trailed off. "And—forgive me, but I just had to meet you, Beatrice. I had to meet his only child, even after all these years."

Beatrice, profoundly moved, reached out to Mary O'Shaunessy and hugged her close. "Thank you, Mary," she said. "You have no idea what this has meant to me."

"God be with you, Beatrice. If there's anything I can ever do . . ."

"You've done it," Beatrice said. "I feel my father sent you to me."

"Yes," Mary O'Shaunessy said with conviction. "I feel that too. . . . Well, I'll be going now. I have to catch my train."

"God be with you, Mary O'Shaunessy," Beatrice said to herself as the woman turned the corner and disappeared from sight.

After the memorial service, the enormity of her loss attacked Beatrice like a beast. This beast of longing and regret was a brutal, unpredictable taskmaster, exercising its power over her in successive, ever-intensifying assaults. Sudden blows of sadness would leave her feeling helpless and abandoned. She thought every day of her touching encounter with Mary O'Shaunessy and wondered how different her own life might have been had her father followed his heart and left his family. She had a different picture of her mother now, as well as of her father. Perhaps Beatrice should have taken Stephen back when he had begged her forgiveness. But that was the past. Their lives had moved on.

The business of death helped somewhat in alleviating Beatrice's pain. The will was read. Beatrice inherited everything— the house, a modest portfolio of securities, and the magnificent book collection, which, with the one exception of the *Roman de la Rose*, she intended to donate to a university within the year. Her father had always insisted on cremation for himself, and Beatrice had followed his wishes. His ashes reposed in a small silver urn on the library mantelpiece.

Putting aside her researching jobs, Beatrice concentrated her energies on getting the house straightened up and the library back in order. She farmed out the most damaged volumes to her father's regular bookbinders, an elderly couple on Lexington Avenue, saving the *Roman de la Rose* for Mr. Lovelock to repair. His visit preyed on her mind, and she intended to use the incunabulum as an excuse to get in touch with him.

Detective Monahan's visits to the house tapered off. He gave Beatrice little hope the perpetrator would be found, though he assured her he'd taken a personal interest in the case and was following every lead, however insignificant. No one in the neighborhood seemed to have heard or seen anything unusual on the day of her father's death. John O'Connell's murder was beginning to look more

and more like a random break-in that had ended in gratuitous violence.

Signor Antonelli telephoned Beatrice from Rome a few times to
find out how she was getting on. She told him that she was grateful
Father Morton had attended the memorial service on his behalf and
that she had entered a period of mourning, staying close to home,
accepting only a few invitations from close friends. He urged her to
seek out Father Morton if she needed counseling. She assured him
politely that she would, though she had no intention of doing so. At
the end of each conversation, Signor Antonelli asked her, seemingly
as an afterthought, if she had found the grimoire. The old man's in-
quiries rearoused her suspicions, and Beatrice found herself unable
to shake a feeling of dread.

Meanwhile, she had other things to occupy her. Nellie was becoming a problem. The grieving housekeeper missed work continu-
ally, saying she had to go to church and pray. Beatrice began to feel
ill at ease in the house. The sweet memories it harbored were poisoned by the murder. She could not strike the image of her father's
body from her mind. Her most innocent daydreams would suddenly
mutate into terrifying reruns of the crime. She locked her bedroom
door at night. Lying awake, she listened for creaks and other indica-
tions of an intruder. She imagined ghosts. The ticking of the old
grandfather clock sounded more and more like a heartbeat. What
had once been a home now seemed a place of evil, filled with shadows and dark corners. The situation became intolerable. She reached
a painful decision: she had to give up the house or lose her sanity.

"Nellie," Beatrice said over the phone on one of the many occasions when the housekeeper called in sick. "I'm putting the house
on the market. You must come back and help me get things sorted
out as soon as you can."

That afternoon, Beatrice telephoned real estate brokers and arranged for them to see the house. The next day, Beatrice received
a call from Father Morton.

"I wonder if you remember me," he said in a deep, friendly
voice.

"Yes, of course I do," Beatrice said. "You came to my father's
memorial. It was very kind of you."

"I'm calling because I've just spoken to Giuseppe, and he tells
me you're very serious about donating your father's library to a nonprofit institution."

"Yes?" Beatrice said warily.

"I have a proposition I would like to make to you. Would you consider coming down to Saint Xavier's to discuss it with me?"

"Father Morton, I'm sure Signor Antonelli has told you that my father wasn't very religious. I'm really thinking more in terms of a university or a library."

"Yes, yes, my dear. I understand that. But I think what I am offering you will fit that criterion. From what Giuseppe tells me about you and your father, his books might be happy with us," he said. "We never met your father, but he was serious about the preservation and dissemination of knowledge, and so are we."

When Beatrice hesitated, he was charmingly insistent, and Beatrice thought that perhaps he could be helpful, after all. With the house now on the market, she realized, somewhat to her own surprise, that she was ready to think about placing her father's library in caring hands. And Father Morton sounded caring. He seemed concerned both for her spirit and for the great books her father had amassed over the years. Partly on account of this, but more out of curiosity, Beatrice agreed to the meeting.

Having made the appointment with Father Morton, Beatrice decided to take the *Roman de la Rose* down to Mr. Lovelock, as his shop, on West Fourth Street, was in the neighborhood of Saint Xavier's.

The incunabulum in hand, Beatrice headed downtown in the subway early the next day. The summer heat was rising as she got off at Astor Place and walked over to Fifth Avenue. Seeing the old church looming up ahead, its dark spires piercing the morning sunshine, Beatrice stopped momentarily, struck by the building's beauty.

She went around the back to the rectory, whose architecture was in keeping with the Gothic style of the church. Entering, she found herself in a stark white reception room. The sounds of the outside world melted away as Beatrice closed the great oak door behind her. A prim-looking elderly woman, wearing a white blouse and a black skirt, with a pencil spearing the tight bun near the nape of her neck, was sitting bolt upright at a desk, typing. She looked up and squinted at Beatrice through a pair of horn-rimmed glasses.

"Miss O'Connell?"

"Yes."

"Father Morton is expecting you. Just one moment, please,"

she said crisply. She picked up the receiver of an intercom. "Miss O'Connell is here, Father," she announced, then put down the phone. "Be seated, won't you? Father Morton will be with you in a moment." She resumed typing.

Beatrice sat down on a long wooden bench resembling a pew—the only other piece of furniture in the room. Looking around, she noticed a romantic oval portrait of the Virgin Mary, carved out of ivory, hanging alone on the slim space of wall between the front door and the window. The words *Defensores Fidei* were engraved on an ivory ribbon at the bottom.

A few moments later, the intercom buzzed.

"You may go in now," the secretary said, nodding at an inner door.

Father Morton's office was in striking contrast to the reception area. A large, wood-paneled room with carved moldings, it had criss-crossing mahogany beams supporting the high ceiling. Two stunning tapestries, both depicting the unicorn, the symbol of the Virgin Mary, faced each other on opposite walls. Heavy and dark-framed furniture was upholstered in red velvet. Two picture windows curtained in thick blue damask faced out onto a lush back garden.

Father Morton, a fat, pink man with thinning white hair and a ready grin, was seated behind an ornate desk at the far end of the room. He was holding a pair of binoculars.

"Beatrice, my child, welcome," he said, rising. "I was just doing a little spying on the birds."

Putting down the binoculars, he strode across the room. Little beads of sweat dotted his forehead. His black priest's garb was wilted from the humidity. Beatrice noticed that his bulk did not interfere with a marked agility. He clasped her hand enthusiastically. His palm was damp.

"How very, very good of you to come. Have a seat and make yourself comfortable," he commanded in a deep, robust voice—effective in sermons, Beatrice imagined.

She took one of the two chairs across from his desk and crossed her legs, burying the *Roman de la Rose,* in its brown paper bag, under the pocketbook in her lap.

Father Morton returned to the desk and collapsed into his large leather chair, dabbing his brow with an oversized white handkerchief.

"I'm afraid these humid summer days are the very devil to a

man my size," he said. "I'll have Maddy bring us some iced tea, shall I?"

"Sounds good to me. Thanks."

Father Morton picked up the receiver of an advanced telephone system, which looked incongruous in this nineteenth-century setting. Beatrice was arrested by a medieval gauntlet on his desk fashioned out of steel mesh and attached to an iron cuff. It looked like a severed hand.

"Maddy, be so kind as to bring us some iced tea with lots of ice." Father Morton put down the phone and addressed himself to the object of Beatrice's attention. "Marvelous thing, that, isn't it? It was worn by Frederick the Second during the sixth crusade, in 1228—the same year Francis of Assisi was canonized," he said.

"There's a wonderful book on armor in my father's collection. The Germans always made the best armor. As my father liked to say: 'Even then they knew.' "

Father Morton chuckled. "See over there." He pointed to the far corner of the room, in which a full suit of armor was displayed.

"God, that looks uncomfortable," Beatrice said. "Actually, I've always had this theory that if women could have peed from the saddle of a horse, the history of the world would have been different."

Father Morton's eyes widened, and Beatrice clapped her hand over her mouth.

"Oh, dear—I don't know what made me say that." She flushed with embarrassment.

He smiled. "It's an interesting hypothesis."

"I must say, this is quite a spectacular place," Beatrice said, relaxing into her chair. "One doesn't think of the Church as being so rich these days."

"Saint Xavier's is fortunate to have the support of friends. Beatrice, may I say what a lovely memorial service I thought that was."

"Thank you for coming."

"Well, Giuseppe has spoken so fondly of you and your dear father over the years. And again, let me express my condolences."

"That's very kind of you. Do you mind if I smoke?"

"No, no. Go right ahead. I'm a slave to the after-dinner cigar myself." He pushed forward a large glass ashtray.

"Have you known Signor Antonelli a long time?" she inquired, lighting a cigarette.

"I've known Giuseppe for, oh, let's see now. . . . We became friends when I was a student in Rome, so that would be nearly forty years ago. . . . My, has it been that long?" he reflected. "Yes, yes, it has . . . forty years. The wink of an eye, and yet a lifetime."

As he spoke, Beatrice studied him more closely. His ruddy, jovial face was large, with droopy features. The fold of his double chin hung over his white clerical collar band, which was partially obscured. The nervous habit he had of licking his lips occasionally, combined with his easy and ingratiating manner, reminded her of a friendly hound.

Father Morton folded his thick hands on the desk and looked at Beatrice intently. "Your father's death must have been a terrible shock for you."

"To say the least."

"I could hardly believe it myself. A terrible tragedy."

"Yes, it was—is." She took a long drag.

"Giuseppe told me the library was torn apart. Was there much damage?"

"Nothing that can't be repaired, I hope. I've got his regular bookbinders working on some of the volumes now. It'll take some time."

"Yes, a terrible tragedy from all points of view. And how are you getting on?"

"Well, up and down—you know."

"That's to be expected, of course."

"So I'm told," she said without conviction. "You mentioned on the telephone that you wanted to talk about my father's library?" She nervously rubbed the tip of her cigarette in the ashtray.

"Yes." Father Morton leaned back and, looking thoughtful, pressed his palms together as if in prayer. "You mentioned you wished to donate it intact to a nonprofit institution."

"That's my plan. I'm considering several places at the moment. I'm under a certain amount of pressure because I've put the house up for sale."

"Have you indeed?" Father Morton said with interest. "Why is that?"

"It's too difficult for me to stay there now—with what's happened."

"Yes, I can well understand that." He sighed, then cleared his throat. "I don't know whether or not Giuseppe has told you, but I'm affiliated with a foundation—the Duarte Institute. Do you know it?"

"No." Beatrice shook her head. "I'm afraid not."

"It's an interesting place, specializing in philosophical studies. It supports students and researchers around the world. We have a magnificent property in upstate New York, with several buildings on it. One of them is a library, housing several extremely valuable book collections. There's space for expansion, and what I was wondering is if you would consider donating your father's library to us. We would like nothing better than to memorialize him in a suitable manner."

"As I told you on the phone, my father wasn't very religious."

"I'm aware of that. But as I said, the institute is dedicated to philosophical studies. It's nondenominational."

"And your connection with it is . . . ?"

"Purely as an interested party. I'm one of the governors. I wear many hats."

"Well, look, Father Morton, I don't know what to say. I'd be glad to take a look at any literature you have on it," Beatrice said politely.

"Better still, you must come up one day and visit. It's a fascinating place. These tapestries were woven there." Father Morton pointed to the unicorn tapestries on the wall.

"Really? They look very authentic."

"We have a crafts program and instruct students in the old ways of doing things."

"They're wonderful."

"In fact, the Duarte Institute is a little haven from the modern world. You'll see what I mean when you go up there."

"Perhaps when I have a little more time." Beatrice shifted in her chair, and the *Roman de la Rose* slipped out of its bag and dropped to the floor. She bent down to pick it up.

"What is that book you have there?" Father Morton said with sudden interest.

"This?" She held up the little incunabulum. "It's from my father's library. I'm taking it to be repaired."

"May I see it?" Father Morton said eagerly.

Beatrice was just about to give it to him, when there was a knock at the door.

"Enter!" Father Morton cried, obviously irritated at the interruption.

The secretary came in, carrying a small silver tray, which she placed on the desk. It held two glasses of iced tea. "Father, don't forget the bishop at eleven," she said, and closed the door behind her.

"Help yourself." Father Morton indicated the tray. As Beatrice reached for a glass, he said, "You were going to show me your book," and extended his hand.

"Please be careful," Beatrice cautioned him as he took up the little volume. "It's about to fall apart."

"The *Roman de la Rose*," he said, sounding disappointed. He gave it a cursory look. "It's from your father's library?"

"Yes. It's the only thing I'm keeping."

Father Morton handed the book back to her, then picked up his iced tea and proceeded to drink it down in one long swallow.

"Ah!" he said, licking his lips. "Forgive me, but I can't abide this heat.... Tell me," he asked nonchalantly. "Did you ever find that grimoire?"

Beatrice paused in mid-sip and looked up. "Who told you about the grimoire?"

"Giuseppe. Why? Shouldn't he have? Is it a secret?" Father Morton said innocently.

"No. I just wonder why he'd bother telling you about it."

"Well, I'm an amateur bibliophile. Giuseppe and I often discuss books. He said it was a fascinating little thing. He was going on and on about it."

"I see."

"So—has it turned up?"

"No."

"You've looked for it?"

"Yes."

"Everywhere in the house?"

"Pretty much."

"Perhaps it's in a safety-deposit box?"

"No, I've looked there too. It was obviously stolen."

"Well, if it does turn up—"

"I doubt if it's going to," she interrupted him.

"Well, if it does, I'd love to see it."

"Apparently, so would everyone else."

"Who else?" he said, narrowing his eyes.

Her suspicions aroused, she was not about to mention Mr. Lovelock.

"Well, Signor Antonelli and his secret client," she said. "You must know about his secret client if you've been a friend of his for so many years."

"Ah, yes. He's told me he has someone who collects occult books."

"He's very mysterious about it." Beatrice set her glass of tea on the tray. "Perhaps that secret client is you, Father," she said, with a tight little smile.

Father Morton burst out laughing. "Would that I were!"

"Do you have any idea who it is?"

"Giuseppe's client? Heavens, no. Giuseppe's a tomb about such things. He'd never tell me. He'd never tell anyone."

"I suppose not."

"You're suspicious of me, aren't you?" he said playfully.

"No, I'm not," she said, lying. "I just find all this interest in the grimoire a little weird."

"Things are bound to upset you more now," he said solicitously.

"Maybe." Beatrice shrugged.

"You know what I've found to be very helpful after one has experienced a great loss?"

"What's that?"

"Going to a museum."

"Why a museum, particularly?"

"Stepping out into the world a little at a time, at your own pace, in a soothing environment that promotes contemplation and reflection, is good for the soul in trying times. Museums offer us a silent sense of history and beauty, and in so doing, they tell us we are not alone in our struggle to understand what this life is all about." He paused. "And of course, there's always the Church."

"I'm willing to try a museum, but I'm afraid I've inherited my father's skepticism about the Church."

"You and so many others," he said ruefully.

"I did find comfort in the memorial service, though. I like Monsignor Regan very much."

"Yes, he's a good man," Father Morton said. "Rather progressive in his views ... Of course, one needn't go to church to believe in God and find comfort in faith. The Church doesn't exist in a building or a mass or a sermon. The Church is the totality of one's faith."

"And what if one doesn't have any faith?"

"Oh, everyone has faith in something, I find, don't you? Even if it's not in God. It's been my experience that if you take the kernel of that faith—whatever it is, however inconsequential it seems—and you try and apply it to something larger than yourself, eventually you come around to God."

"Really? How so?"

"Well, I'll give you an example. What is it that you have the most faith in?"

"Books," Beatrice replied without hesitation.

"A good answer. You are definitely your father's daughter. Now, may I ask what way you have faith in them?"

"They're sources of knowledge and comfort," Beatrice replied, as if the answer were obvious.

"All right, then, let's take this faith you have in books. What does it consist of? The power to restore and invigorate you; the power to know another person's mind, another universe, perhaps. But what is that mind? What is that universe? And who created it? And why do you want to connect with it? 'Only connect,' as E. M. Forster said. You see, that little silver thread of connection to the world, which in your case starts with a book and in someone else's may start with painting a picture or having a child or just getting a square meal—that little silver thread of connection can stretch all the way to heaven, if you let it."

"My mother used to say that faith was like a gift: you can't buy it, you can't work for it; it just comes." Beatrice glanced at her watch.

"Oh, I think you can work for it a little. After all, if I didn't, I'd be out of a job," he said with a wink.

"That's a good point."

"I believe that when the mind opens fully, it receives God, like a flower opening itself to the sun."

"I wish it were that simple." She rose from her chair. "I'm sorry, Father, but I really must be going."

He escorted her to the door. "Life needn't be such a lonely business," he said.

"Unfortunately, it feels just that way at the moment."

Father Morton took her hand as they reached the door.

"Beatrice, if you need me, you know where to find me. Don't hesitate to call. And please, do think seriously about my proposal regarding your father's library."

He let go of her hand and opened the door, standing aside so she could pass.

"Thank you," she said, walking out into the reception area. "I will."

Father Morton gave Beatrice a little wave, to which she responded self-consciously by inclining her head slightly. He watched her leave.

Outside in the open air, Beatrice took a deep breath, experiencing a great sense of relief as she walked hurriedly away from the splendid, stifling rectory. The interview had left her wary and disconcerted. She was suspicious of Father Morton. He wears his kindness as a disguise, she thought, under which he's hiding something sinister. What was he really after? Not simply her father's collection. And why all the interest in the grimoire?

Clutching the little incunabulum in her hand, she threaded her way through the sunny, tree-lined streets of the Village, dogged by apprehension.

6

IMON LOVELOCK'S SHOP WAS LOCATED IN A DI-
lapidated building, above an abandoned store-
front. A small sign near a separate entrance
read, in shaky black calligraphy: *Lovelock Rare
Books, Second Floor. Please Ring.* Beatrice
pressed the black button beneath the sign several times, but got no response. She stepped
backward, shading her eyes from the sun with her hand, and
peered up at the picture window with LOVELOCK RARE BOOKS
painted in large black letters across the center. It looked dark inside. She tried the button again. There was still no answer. Just as
she was about to give up, a sharp buzzer sounded, unlocking the
shabby gray door.

Entering, Beatrice walked into a dingy, dimly lit corridor, at the
end of which was a flight of stairs. A slim, dark figure loomed above,
barely visible in the gloom.

"Come in, come in," the figure called down to her.

"Mr. Lovelock?" she said. "It's Beatrice O'Connell. Do you remember me?"

"Indeed I do, Miss O'Connell," Lovelock said, holding the door to his shop open for her. "Come up, please."

She ascended the flight of narrow steps, holding on to the rickety railing. Lovelock stood on the landing, dressed all in black, as he had been on their first meeting. His shirtsleeves were rolled up. A cigarette dangled from the corner of his mouth, and he squinted as the smoke occasionally curled into his eyes.

"I'm sorry I took so long to answer," he said as she reached the top. "But you caught me in the middle of a delicate operation. It's very, very nice to see you."

"I hope I'm not interrupting you," she said, following him into the bookstore.

"No, no, no, please," he said nervously. "But if you don't mind, I'll just go finish up what I'm doing, and then I'll be right with you, right with you." He smiled at her, and she could not help noticing that his eyes lingered on her face. Then, flushing slightly, he seemed to catch himself. "Please feel free to have a look around. I won't be a moment."

Lovelock quickly retreated to a back room, leaving Beatrice in the front of the shop. The walls were covered with built-in bookcases filled with every imaginable size and shape of volume, some new, but most of them old and worn. A long wooden reading table surrounded by a few chairs was set up near the picture window facing out onto the street. Though fairly cool, the atmosphere was musty. This place definitely needs a good airing, Beatrice thought as she browsed.

The books appeared to be extremely well organized, despite a layer of dust on some of them. There were various sections, delineated by little white cards Scotch-taped to the bookcases; the headings appeared to be written in the same hand as the sign downstairs. Beatrice perused the numerous volumes, lined up neatly under a large array of alphabetically ordered topics, ranging from *Africa, Alchemy, America, Angels, Animism, Anti-Christ, Apparitions, Aquinas, Arabs, Arithmancy, Assassins, Astral World, Astrology, Atlantis* . . . to *Visions, Werewolves, West Indian Islands, Wild Women, Witchcraft, Yoga, Ziito, Zoroaster,* and *Zodiac.*

Noting the appearance of Thomas Aquinas in this curious lineup, Beatrice speculated upon the venerable saint's connection with the occult. She removed a secondhand copy of G. K. Chesterton's biography, *St. Thomas Aquinas,* published in 1933, and took it over to the reading table. She was leafing through it when she heard a loud crash and then a thump, coming from the back of the shop.

Beatrice grabbed the *Roman de la Rose*, shot up from the table, and hurried through the shop, knocking on the back-room door. Receiving no answer, she opened the door and peered inside. Lovelock was down on all fours in front of a stack of overturned boxes, picking up a handful of instruments.

"Mr. Lovelock, are you all right?"

"Fine, fine, thanks," he said, snaking his head around and seeming embarrassed. "Just clumsy, that's all."

"Can I help you?"

"No, no. All's well." He rose to his feet and dusted himself off.

Looking about, Beatrice recognized the trappings of a rudimentary bookbindery. In the middle of the cramped and cluttered space was a wooden paper press and a frosted-glass table, lit from below. Vials of colored liquid dotted the shelves, and a damp, crinkly sheet of an old manuscript was clamped in a pair of clothespins suspended from strings stapled to the ceiling.

"Welcome to my little hospital," he said with some pride. "Every week I make a vow to clean it up, and every week it gets worse . . . just like life, eh? I suppose I'll get around to it one of these days—like quitting smoking. I was just performing an operation on one of my more ancient patients."

"May I watch?"

"Oh, be my guest, please. . . . Sorry it's so crowded. If you stand there by the door, you won't be in the way. I'm trying to patch up this little fragment of Saint Augustine's *Confessions*. Thirteenth century."

He pointed to a withered leaf of parchment resting on top of the underlit glass table. The dense black Latin text was rubricated throughout, with touches of silver and gold on some of the lettering.

"That's beautiful," Beatrice said.

"Will be, will be. See this break?" He pointed to an ominous tear at the center. "This is the infection. If we're not careful, it will spread. He's a sad little man now, but wait. . . ."

Crushing out his cigarette in a coffee tin filled with butts and ashes, Lovelock selected a sheet of new parchment from a thin stack lying on the one clean shelf in the cramped space. Comparing it to the original, he did not seem content with the choice and proceeded to try three more sheets, until he found one to match the color, thickness, and finish of the fragment almost exactly.

Centering the old leaf on the glass table, directly above the electric lights, he skillfully traced the outline of the tear and cut out a matching piece from the new parchment with a razor blade. His movements were precise and economical, like those of a skilled surgeon. He dipped a wooden stick, half the width of a tongue depressor, into a small glass vial nearby.

"What's that?" Beatrice inquired.

"A solution of gelatin and pure acid of vinegar," he replied slowly, concentrating hard as he applied the glutinous mixture to the fragment. "It's an excellent adhesive for this type of work."

He carefully glued the newly cut piece directly onto the ripped portion of the old page.

"There!" he said, with evident satisfaction. "Now we'll let him dry on top of the lights, and then we'll press him. You won't be able to tell he was ever wounded. All healed!"

Beatrice was amused and touched. Having watched him perform the delicate task with such concern and sureness of hand, she was pleased to give him her little book.

"Here," she said, handing it to him. "I'd like you to repair it for me."

"Ah, the *Roman de la Rose* . . . I'm honored. We'll take good care of you, my lady," he said, clearing a space for the volume on one of the less encumbered shelves.

"Where did you learn this art, Mr. Lovelock?"

"Oh, here and there," he said, lighting a new cigarette. "Patching parchment is relatively simple. It's when you get into the handmade paper that things can be really difficult. Like that old gentleman there."

He pointed to the still-damp sheet of paper hanging from the clothespins. "A rotting Pliny fragment. I had quite a time of it yesterday with him—transferring the text onto fresh paper. Luckily, the ink on these old pages is so durable, it doesn't run."

Lovelock pulled his black jacket from a thick nail on the back of the door and, throwing it over his arm, accompanied Beatrice to the front of the shop. "So—find anything that interests you?"

"Well, now that you mention it, I was wondering about the section on Saint Thomas Aquinas. . . ."

"You mean, what's a nice saint like him doing in a place like this?" he said, grinning.

"I guess so." Beatrice laughed. "I'm interested in Aquinas because he appears in *The Divine Comedy* and I was named after Beatrice."

"Ah—a literary namesake. Well, he's quite a fascinating case, our 'Angelic Doctor,' as the Church refers to him. Historically, he's had his brush with the occult."

"No! Aquinas? The founding father of Catholic Doctrine? I don't believe it."

"Oh, yes indeed." Lovelock's dark eyes glinted impishly beneath his bushy eyebrows. "His tutor was reputed to be a man called Albertus Magnus, a renowned alchemist. Magnus spent thirty years fabricating a man made entirely of brass, which he endowed with magical powers, one of which was the gift of speech. It was reported that Thomas, who had a horror of noise, dashed the effigy to pieces because it wouldn't stop talking!" He giggled, self-consciously covering his mouth with his hand, as if to hide his tobacco-stained teeth.

"Oh, come now!" Beatrice cried.

"I'm only telling you the legend. And it was further said that Thomas himself, having learned certain alchemical powers from his master, made a small brass horse, which he buried under the road in front of his house. The effect of this was that no real horses would go near the place, no matter how hard they were spurred on by their riders, thus ensuring him total peace and quiet. This little legend, plus the fact that books on alchemy were once attributed to him, have gained him a place in my shop."

"Do you believe all that?" she asked warily.

"No, no, of course I don't. Actually, it's been proven that the magical books Thomas Aquinas supposedly authored were falsely attributed to him by those seeking to discredit his position in the Church. But the occult isn't about objective truth," he went on. "It's about mystery, personal perception, and belief. The word itself, as you might know, comes from the Latin *occulere*, to conceal. I make no claims for the veracity of what's in my stock. I simply present it as part of the literature of a fascinating subject, for those who are interested to enjoy."

"And just how did you become interested in all this, Mr. Lovelock?"

"Oh, that's a long story," he said evasively.

"Well, it's a great bookstore. But you should get someone to come in and dust it for you."

"It's all I can do to keep my little apartment upstairs clean. Anyway, I think dust adds to the atmosphere, so to speak."

"How long do you think it will take you to repair my book?"

"I'll examine her and let you know, if I may. It may not be for some time, if that's all right."

"I'm in no hurry." Beatrice scribbled her telephone number on one of the shop's cards and handed it to him. "You can call me when it's ready."

He stuffed the card in his trouser pocket. "Would you care for some coffee, perhaps, or tea?"

"No, thanks. I should be going."

Lovelock seemed disappointed.

"You're getting on all right, I hope?" he asked, walking her toward the door.

"Oh, well, you know. . . ."

"I'm sorry you had to come all the way down here. I would gladly have come to pick up the book."

"I was in the neighborhood, anyway," Beatrice said. "I was visiting Father Morton over at Saint Xavier's."

Lovelock stopped dead. "Father Morton?"

"Yes. Do you know him?"

"Of him," he said. "May I inquire why you were visiting with him?" Beatrice noticed a marked agitation in his manner.

"He wanted to discuss my father's library. Why?"

"How did you happen to come into contact with him, if I may ask?"

"He's very close to my father's friend Signor Antonelli, and he's affiliated with something called the Duarte Institute. He wants me to consider donating the library there."

"Does he indeed?" Lovelock said.

"Yes. Why? What's the matter?"

"Oh, nothing, nothing . . ."

"Do you know about this place? Father Morton says it specializes in philosophical studies. I'd never heard of it. Have you?"

"Yes, I've heard of it," he said.

"Mr. Lovelock? What is it? What's the matter?"

"Nothing, nothing . . . Come. I don't want to keep you." He shook his head and continued toward the door.

Beatrice held her ground. "Wait a minute. I know there's something. Please tell me what you're thinking."

He hesitated. "Well, it's just that . . ."

"That what? What?"

"Well, I wouldn't trust him, if I were you," he said finally.

"Why not?"

"Just wouldn't, that's all. I really can't say any more."

"Look, I'm asking you. Please." A look passed between them. "Was the library the only thing he wanted to discuss?" Lovelock said.

"Okay—to tell you the truth, I think the real reason he asked me down there was to see whether or not I'd found the grimoire."

"You haven't found it, have you?" he said with alarm.

"No."

Lovelock seemed relieved. "That's all right, then."

Beatrice grabbed his sleeve. He shuddered slightly.

"Look, what is it about that goddamn book?" she cried impatiently. "We've been through this before—that evening at the house. If you know something, why don't you tell me?"

Lovelock lowered his eyes and gazed at her hand. She let him go.

"It's better not to get involved with that thing," he said. "Let's leave it at that."

"I don't want to leave it at that."

"Well, I'm afraid I do."

Beatrice sighed, seeing she was going to get nothing further from him. "I suppose we'll have to, then."

They reached the door.

"I'll call you about your little friend in a day or so." Lovelock edged into the corridor, holding the door open for Beatrice to pass.

"Good-bye, Mr. Lovelock," she said.

Lovelock shook her hand and held it for a long moment, looking into her eyes. "Take care," he said with feeling.

"I will, thank you. I look forward to hearing from you."

Beatrice decided to walk home. Beekman Place was a long way from the Village, but she felt she needed the exercise, and she wanted to think. She mulled over her meeting with Father Morton. Aside from the obvious questions she had about his interest in the grimoire and his pushing the Duarte Institute on her, she wondered what had possessed her to make that comment about women peeing from the saddle of a horse. You didn't talk that way to a priest. Yet the remark had leapt out of her mouth, like an imp.

What she had not said was that she had sat there wondering what it was like to go through life without ever having known sexual relations. Had he ever known a woman? Or a man, perhaps? She wondered that about Simon Lovelock. Lovelock had seemed dry and introverted during their first meeting, at the house. But just now, when he shook her hand and held it, she felt the murmurings of an attraction between them. Or maybe it was just her.

What was this newfound preoccupation she had with sex? Had it to do with Luis Diaz? With the image of the succubus in the grimoire? With her father's hidden lust for Mary O'Shaunessy? With her mother's passivity and fear of men? She wondered if she had unconsciously tried to emulate her mother in rejecting Stephen. But now that she felt certain that her mother's piety was imbued with real faith, her own stance in Stephen's infidelity seemed more like blind self-righteousness or, worse, the tantrum of a schoolgirl. Had her mother ever known real passion? No, probably not. The one thing she was certain of was that there was a dark force inside her, itching to jump out.

Passing by a store window, Beatrice paused to look at her reflection. Ever since her encounter with Diaz, she'd imagined herself as fuller somehow, more voluptuous, wilder in the eye. She wasn't pregnant, she was sure of that. Diaz had used a condom—she'd insisted on that because of all the sexual hazards of the modern age. It was more as if her body had swollen up with desire and that desire had remained inside her, swirling around like a noxious vapor. But it was escaping through her mouth, in words, and through her thoughts.

She reached up and removed the pins from her bun, shaking her head from side to side, watching in the glass as her hair cascaded around her shoulders. She remembered the moment when Luis Diaz had unfastened it in the "love boutique." She knew it was just a matter of time before she would be unable to resist seeing him again. She walked home, feeling freer than she had in years.

Nellie was bustling around her father's bedroom, in the midst of packing up his clothes and putting them into shopping bags to give to Goodwill.

"Nellie, I thought you were taking the week off."

"Miss Beatrice, you startled me," the old housekeeper said, whirling around. "I thought I should come in to help you. Did you see Father Morton?"

"Yes, I did." Beatrice thought for a moment. "Did I tell you I was going to see him?"

"Well, you said you'd be out this morning because you were going to Saint Xavier's."

"Oh . . . Well, I went."

"What do you think of Father Morton?"

"He seems quite nice," Beatrice said cautiously, picking up the beige cashmere sweater she had given her father for his birthday the year before. "Remember this, Nellie? How Daddy used to wear it even in the summer?"

"He loved that sweater because you gave it to him. He loved everything you gave him, Miss Beatrice."

"Well, I hope the next person who wears it will appreciate it." Beatrice folded the sweater and put it into one of the shopping bags. "On second thought, I don't think I'll give it away," she said, removing it and slinging it over her shoulders. "I like having it near me."

"I'm sure Father Morton was a comfort to you."

"Why are you so interested in him, Nellie?"

"Oh, I don't know. . . . I go down to Saint Xavier's sometimes to hear him give a sermon. He's a great man of God, you know. All my friends think so."

Beatrice had met some of Nellie's friends. They were a little network of Irish-Catholic working women who, like the old housekeeper, were single and devoutly religious.

"He says he wants to help me with the dispensation of Daddy's library."

"Well, you should listen to him."

"You think I'm a little heathen, don't you, Nellie?" Beatrice said, teasing the old woman.

"Well, I wouldn't be so proud of it, if I were you. You take after your father, you do—God rest his soul. But it was your blessed mother you should've taken after, Miss Beatrice, if you ask me. Now, she was a saint, your mother—a real saint. She believed in the Church, she did." For Nellie, the world was divided into only two types of people—saints and heathens—according to how much faith they had in Catholicism.

The two women continued packing. Somehow, it was the more insignificant articles that affected Beatrice most—her father's toothbrush, an odd sock, his razor, a nail clipper, bifocals. She saved his watch, his pipe, his diplomas and citations, and the pile of old prescription pads he used for scrap paper, putting them into a separate box.

In the midst of their efforts, the doorbell rang. Nellie went downstairs to answer it. When she came back up to announce who it was, her face had a beatific expression that made Beatrice suspect that the caller was a member of the clergy. But she was wrong.

"You have a visitor."

"Who is it, Nellie? You know I don't want to see anyone."

"You'll be wanting to see this person," Nellie said with a grin, refusing to identify the caller.

Nellie had shown the mystery guest into the library. When Beatrice saw who it was, she froze for a moment. The visitor was standing on the spot where her father had been slain.

"Hello, Bea," he said softly.

"Stephen . . . ," she whispered, swallowing hard.

He walked over and put his arms around her, holding her tight for a long time. "How's my little sorceress?"

Beatrice began to weep, for the sight of her ex-husband filled her with sorrow and regret. Stephen hadn't changed. He was still appealingly casual looking, dressed in his usual blue jeans, blazer, open shirt, and worn-out moccasins with no socks—an overgrown preppy. Like her father, he had a ready smile and an easy manner. And like her father, he was adept at gaining people's confidence. Stephen, however, used his charm as a tool to extract information for whatever story he was working on. Beatrice wiped her eyes with the tissue he offered her.

"I just heard the news," he said. "I was away."

"Where were you?"

"Colombia, Peru . . ."

"What were you doing there?"

"A new book."

"On?"

"Drug dealers."

"Something safe for a change," she said.

"Listen, everything's a risk these days—including staying at home."

Stephen viewed the world as an intricate lock he could pick through persistence. He was inquisitive and attracted to danger. During his career as a reporter, he covered the Kurdish revolt in northern Iraq, lived with the rebels in Afghanistan, and infiltrated a contra arms-smuggling ring in south Florida. Then he withdrew from the mind-numbing demands of newsweekly journalism to write books. He had hired Beatrice to do the historical research for his prize-winning book on the ideological and tribal struggles of the Persian Gulf and Middle East, and they had fallen in love.

"Let me look at you," Stephen said, studying her face. "Still gorgeous."

"Oh, I am not, and you know it. But you haven't changed."

"Well, I have, but maybe not physically."

"So—how's life?"

"Tell me what happened, Bea."

"What have you heard?"

"That he was shot by a burglar."

"Yes ... well, that's what they think. It was right over there," she said, pointing to the spot in front of the window. "Where you were just standing."

"Do they have any make on the guy?"

"No."

"Any leads at all?"

"Nope," she said, biting at the corner of her fingernail.

"Who's been assigned to the case?"

"A Detective Frank Monahan. He seems competent, but he hasn't turned up anything yet."

"Are you still mad at me?"

"Oh, it's so complicated." She sighed. "Let me just get used to seeing you again. It's a shock."

"Come over here and sit down." He led her over to the couch and sat down next to her. "Jesus, what a blow. I know how close you were to your dad. I loved him too. He was a terrific guy. Just one helluva guy."

"So," Beatrice said. "How've you been? What have you been up to, aside from trying to get yourself killed?"

"Here," he said, gently turning her face toward him. "I have something for you." He kissed her lightly on the mouth.

Beatrice stared at him. "What'd you do that for?"

"I don't know. I felt like it."

"We haven't seen each other in . . . God, what's it been? Three years?"

"You haven't changed that much, but you look . . ."

"What?"

"I don't know. Disheveled. That's not like you."

"Disheveled? How do you mean?"

"I don't know," he said again. "You looked different, that's all."

Beatrice knew what he meant, but she could not confide in him.

"I'm just worn out. Worn out. Grief is exhausting. This is the worst thing that's ever happened to me. . . . Why did you come here?"

"Did you really think I wouldn't?" He seemed surprised.

"You weren't at the memorial."

"I didn't *know* about it," he reminded her. "I was in fucking Lima, for Christ's sake, trying to trace a shipment of cocaine to a CIA man. I just got back last night, and a friend of mine told me at lunch today. I rushed over here as soon as I could. Bea, for God's sake," he said, grabbing her and holding her close. "Don't you know that I love you? And I always have."

Beatrice buried her head in his chest and was silent for a time, hoping to experience the comfort she had once felt in his arms. But the embrace felt oddly shapeless. She looked up at him. "You left me, Stephen."

"Haven't we been over this a million times?"

"I was pregnant, remember?"

"Okay, I'm a shit," he said, disheartened. "I've admitted that. I admit it now."

"Stephen, just because you say you're a shit doesn't mean you're not one."

"I'm going to say this again, and either you're going to choose to listen to it or you're not. I was a shit. I was scared of being married. Scared of having a family. Scared of being tied down. And I'm sorry."

"You're not scared of getting shot at."

"It's a quicker death."

"Very funny."

He raked his fingers through his hair. "You want your revenge?" he said. "Here it is: not a day goes by when I don't think about what a destructive, despicable asshole I was. You blame me for the miscarriage. But believe me, you can't blame me more than I blame my-self."

"Well, it's all in the past now," Beatrice said. "Like everything else."

"Is it?" He looked at her intently. "You don't think you could ever find it in your heart to forgive me? Even after all this time?"

Hearing her father's last words to her echoing in her mind, Beatrice extracted herself from his arms, got up, and began pacing around the room. "You know what I found out?"

"What?"

"Daddy was unfaithful to Mom during their marriage. And at one point, he fell in love with another woman."

"Really?" Stephen said, watching her. "Who told you that?"

"Daddy did. The night before he died."

"You're kidding."

"No. . . . I was so hard on him. I just hated him for it."

"Why did he tell you?"

Beatrice reflected. "He said he was worried about me—worried that I was wasting my life because I had some notion that relation-ships had to be perfect. I'd always idealized my parents' marriage. And I think that finally he just decided to remove the rose-colored glasses from my eyes. He did it as a kindness to me, really. He took a big chance—and I threw it back in his face."

"Did he tell you who he fell in love with?"

"He just said it was a nurse at the hospital and that my mother understood. But then, Stephen, something amazing happened."

"What?"

"I met her. She came to the memorial, and after the service, she introduced herself to me. The minute she said she'd worked with my father at the hospital, I knew exactly who she was. And the most remarkable thing was that she looked just like Mommy used to look when she was younger. She was such a lovely woman, Stephen. She told me that my father was the love of her life and that my mother had offered to give him up, but he couldn't leave us. . . . I feel like such a self-righteous fool. I'd give anything—anything in the world—to see Daddy again and tell him that I understand. Oh, well." She shrugged sadly. "That's life, isn't it? You don't get second chances."

"Sometimes you do. You could give me one, for example."

"It was slightly different with us, wasn't it? We weren't exactly married for years before you ran off. And besides, I suspect my mother hated sex."

"You weren't so fond of it yourself."

"What?" Beatrice said, taken aback.

"You weren't, Bea."

"Go on," she said, interested.

"You tolerated it. I sometimes felt as if I was forcing you."

"If you felt that, why did you marry me?"

"That's complicated. After we broke up, I went into therapy and talked about it a lot with my shrink. Basically, I think I needed to marry a 'good' girl—you know, the old 'madonna-whore' syndrome. I was very attracted to you for obvious reasons. You were pretty and bright and fun. I loved working with you. And you fit the bill—nice Catholic girl, carefully brought up, fairly innocent. I thought after we were married that you would open up more—"

"Open up?" she interrupted him. "What do you mean?"

"In the bedroom . . ."

"Go on."

"You were, um—how can I put this tactfully?—always a little, uh, reserved."

"You mean frigid," she said matter-of-factly.

"Well, a little chilly, maybe."

"Always?"

"Pretty much, yeah."

Beatrice looked at him, shrugged, and said, "Maybe I was at that," thinking of Diaz.

"And," Stephen went on, "I guess I felt rejected by you a lot of the time."

"Did you really?" she said with genuine interest. He nodded. "And so that was why you ran off with her?"

"It was a lot of things—the baby, the commitment, the marriage. But you're right: basically, I couldn't see spending my life with a woman who didn't really get off on me sexually."

"That's fascinating," Beatrice said reflectively. She was silent for a long moment. "So why are you here, Stephen? You say you're still in love with me. I mean, what's changed? If you still think I'm frigid—"

"I also know from therapy that I didn't give you—us—a chance. You know how dogged I am when it comes to my work? Well, I'm just the opposite in relationships. I'm ready to chuck them over-board if they don't work out right away. It's my pattern."

"And why is that?"

"Well, the shrink and I were beginning to work on that when I quit."

"Why'd you quit?"

"I was away a lot, working. And anyway, I'd pretty much de-cided what I really want in life."

"And what's that?" Beatrice asked.

Stephen looked deep into her eyes. "You," he said with emo-tion. "It's you that I love, Bea, and it was my own pathology that prevented me from sticking with you. I never really gave the mar-riage a real shot. I know that now. . . . Not a day goes by when I don't think about what I threw away."

"So you think you could have made me open up eventually?" Beatrice inquired, somewhat flirtatiously.

"Oh, yeah. I know I could—*can.*"

"Well, this is very interesting, Stephen. This is very, very inter-esting." She considered. "You're right, I didn't see myself clearly."

"Sex does have a way of screwing things up. Everyone goes to their pathological battle stations. It's war. . . . Let me ask you some-thing, Bea," Stephen said after a time. "Do you still love me?"

"I don't know. I don't know anything anymore. . . . Except one thing," she said with conviction. "One thing I know for sure. I'm go-ing to get the bastard who murdered my father if it takes me the rest of my life."

"Will you let me help you?"

"What about this new book you're doing?"

"It can wait. This is more important."

"I could sure use some help," she said. "I have to know one thing, though."

"What's that?"

"Are you seeing anyone?"

"No."

"Are you sure?" she said skeptically. "I've never known you not to be seeing someone."

"I assume the question is am I *involved* with anyone? And I am not involved with anyone. Yeah, I see women, but there's no one special."

"Has there been anyone special?"

"Why do you want to know?" he said.

"I just do, that's all."

"Okay, there was a reporter in Boston. But we broke up about a year and a half ago. I haven't seen her since."

"Why'd you break up?"

"You want the truth?"

"Yes, please."

"She told me I was still in love with you," he said, laughing slightly.

"Really? That's sweet."

"How about you?"

Again Beatrice thought of Diaz. "Me?"

"Who else?"

"No ... I'm not seeing anyone."

"Have you been seeing anyone?"

"No."

"Bea, I know you so well. What are you not telling me?"

"Nothing. I'm not seeing anyone."

"Well, I'm not sure I believe you, but I'll take your word for it—for the moment. I said I'd help you, and I mean it. Maybe I can make amends somehow. So what happened, exactly?"

"Okay," she said, taking a deep breath. "Do you know what a grimoire is?"

"A book of black magic."

"You always know the most obscure stuff," Beatrice said, impressed. "How do you know what a grimoire is? I didn't."

"I probably came across one in a story once."

"That computer brain of yours just files away everything, doesn't it? Is there anything you don't know?"

"I don't know how to live without you," he said.

"Now let's get one thing straight. This offer of help can't have any strings attached. We're not necessarily going to start up our relationship again, okay?"

"Fine." Stephen nodded. "I'm just here to serve."

Beatrice reviewed the whole story, starting with Signor Antonelli's visit. She told Stephen about her disturbing encounters with Simon Lovelock and Father Morton. When she mentioned the Duarte Institute, she saw a quizzical look pass over his face.

"The Duarte Institute?" he said reflectively.

"Have you heard of it?"

"Yeah, I'm just trying to think where. Somebody mentioned it to me just recently. I'll think of who it was. Go on."

"Anyway, I have a weird feeling about Father Morton. His ostensible reason for inviting me down to Saint Xavier's was to talk about donating my father's library, but I think his real reason was to find out if I had the grimoire."

"He knows about the grimoire?"

"Antonelli told him. I told you, they're old friends."

"Yeah, well, you know: Catholicism—black magic. Flip sides of the same coin. As an intellectual, he's probably interested."

"Lovelock doesn't like him," she said.

"How do you know? Did he say so?"

"No, but I could tell. I mentioned Father Morton's name, and he froze."

"Okay, but what do we know about Lovelock? He's a dealer in occult books. Talk about weird. If you ask me, the jury's out on Lovelock too."

"I don't know. I kind of like him. He's such a strange bird. I can't really tell how old he is. He's got one of those ageless faces. There's something quite gentle and eccentric about him. He calls the books he repairs his 'patients' and refers to them as 'he' or 'she.' I'm inclined to trust him."

"I wish I could think of who it was who was telling me about the Duarte Institute. Well, anyway . . ."

"Do you mind if we go outside? I need some air," Beatrice said.

Beatrice and Stephen strolled side by side along the esplanade by the East River, watching the boats go by. Stephen stared at a huge garbage scow fighting the current on its journey out to sea.

"See all that crap?" He shook his head in disgust. "They're just going to dump it all in the ocean until they can figure out a way to shoot it into outer space. Man is, without doubt, the most wasteful, wanton, destructive animal God ever created. . . . I wonder what this country was like before garbage. Imagine coming up this river for the first time. That's what I loved about Afghanistan. You felt you were in another century. Times have changed."

"Maybe, maybe not," Beatrice said. "I wonder if times really do change or if it's just the same old themes in new packaging."

"New packaging, right. . . . Soon we're all going to be able to sit at home and have the world come to us via computer. We're probably going to be able to have sex by computer."

"I think I've had sex with one or two computers." Beatrice smiled.

"I hope they were IBM compatible."

"You know, seriously, I responded to that grimoire in a very strange way, Stephen," Beatrice admitted. "It made me think how much men really fear women deep down. And, maybe, how much women fear themselves."

"What do you mean?"

"Oh, I don't know. Maybe sex with computers is the answer. . . ." Beatrice leaned against the railing, gazing out at the sun-spangled water. "I used to walk along here with my father when I was a little girl," she said wistfully.

Stephen reached out and gently turned her toward him, smudging a tear at the corner of her eye with his finger. "I know . . . ," he said. "I wish I could make you feel better."

"I put the house on the market."

"Good. Move in with me."

"What? Into that rattrap of yours? No, thanks. I always thought it was a bad sign you never gave it up, even when we were married."

"It's my office."

"An office to have affairs in," she said.

"Truce, okay? White flag?"

"Sure," she said wearily. "Well, I guess I'd better get back and help Nellie. We're packing up Daddy's things to send to Goodwill. It's the little things that break your heart, the stuff he used every day—glasses, pipe, pen . . ."

"You want me to help you?"

"No, you go on home. And try to remember who was talking to you about the Duarte Institute. Call me."

Stephen kissed her gently on the cheek. "There's a nice chaste kiss for you."

"Thanks. It's nice to see you."

"Is it?"

"Yeah, God help me, it is." She smiled and patted him on the cheek.

"Bea," he said seriously. "Give me another chance, will you? You won't be sorry this time."

"We'll see."

7

OW'S MR. STEPHEN?" NELLIE INQUIRED.

"He's fine."

"You're happy he came, aren't you?"

"Maybe."

"He never changes. He's a good-looking boy."

"I think he's lost a little weight, actually," Beatrice said.

"Pining away over you, no doubt. He still loves you, you know. And you love him."

"Nellie . . . ," Beatrice warned.

"You ought to marry him again and have a baby, Miss Beatrice. It's no good for you to be alone. You need a husband and a family. Your mother always said so, and your father said so too. We're none of us getting any younger, you know."

"Thanks for reminding me."

Having no relatives of her own, Nellie had always attached herself to the families she worked for, freely offering her views on the conduct of their lives. This trait was both endearing and irritating.

Nellie never spoke much about her own life. All Beatrice knew about the housekeeper's past was that her parents had died when she was young and that she and an older brother had been raised by nuns in a Catholic orphanage near Cork. Her brother, whom she worshiped, had joined the Irish Guards when he was eighteen and was killed in a hunting accident at the age of twenty-one. Nellie had come to the United States when she was twenty-four.

Nellie folded up the last of Dr. O'Connell's shirts and placed it on top of the pile in a shopping bag.

"There," she said. "That's done. I don't know how you can stand to stay in this house all by yourself."

"That's why I'm selling it, Nellie. Have you been through all his suit pockets?"

"Indeed I have. You should move out now. There's ghosts here. The banshees'll soon be wailing."

Beatrice knew that her father's death must have been almost as hard on the old housekeeper as it had been on her. Nellie now seemed as if she was beginning to accept it, however, as she accepted all the sorrows of life, tucking it under the comforting blanket of "God's will." Now in her sixties, Nellie had worked for the O'Connells a little over seven years, living in a tiny, rent-controlled apartment on Ninety-third Street off Second Avenue. Beatrice and her father had viewed her as a member of the family. Nellie, who liked to look back nostalgically on the days of the Latin mass, went to church every day, ate fish on Friday out of habit, thought Vatican II too liberal, and feared for the souls of all non-Catholics.

Now she brought in the bathroom hamper, still filled with Dr. O'Connell's soiled shirts, socks, and underwear. "Shall I wash these before we give them away, or just let them go to the Goodwill like this?"

"I think it would be nicer to wash them, don't you?"

"Huh!" Nellie sneered. "As if most of them would know the difference, or care."

"Don't be such a snob, Nellie. Remember, 'But for the grace of God . . .' "

"The grace of God comes with an honest day's work," Nellie retorted.

"Well, you don't have to do it today. Why don't you just leave it and go home? Tomorrow's plenty of time."

"Are you sure, Miss Beatrice? I would like to go to church this afternoon. I'm going to have another novena said for your father."

"You go on, then. I'll sort the laundry out."

Nellie paused at the door. "It was God's will, Miss Beatrice. You've got to believe that."

"Thank you, Nellie. I'll try."

When the old woman left, Beatrice, heaving a great sigh, lifted up the large woven hamper and emptied the contents onto the floor. As she did so, she perceived a flash of black and heard a light thump. Digging through the heap of shirts, socks, and underwear, she retrieved the object. She held it up in front of her. Her hands were shaking.

"My God!" Beatrice exclaimed softly. "The grimoire!"

She stared at the book in disbelief. Opening it, she found the letter from the patient who had sent it to her father, plus a ten-dollar bill. And here's the payment on my bet, Beatrice thought, taking out the money.

Beatrice telephoned Stephen to tell him the news. His machine switched on, and she urgently asked him to call her. Then, carrying the grimoire to her bedroom, she took a bath, put on a nightgown, and, early as it was, got into bed.

Beatrice began perusing the grimoire, page by page, trying to look at it objectively. The book struck her as much less threatening than she had remembered. The thought that her father might have been killed for this "curiosity," as Antonelli had referred to it, seemed farfetched. However, she found that the crude woodcuts at the center of the book retained their disturbing power. She studied them closely—in particular, those depicting the transformation of a beautiful, enticing woman into a voracious and bloody succubus, images that had so arrested her when she first encountered them in her father's library.

Beatrice interpreted the metamorphosis as a visual representation of the primal fear men have of a woman's sexuality: Sexual Woman equals Woman the Temptress equals Woman the Devourer equals Evil Woman Incarnate. She thought back to Stephen's comment about her not liking sex all that much and his own somewhat blithe reference to the "madonna-whore" complex. In the midst of these ruminations, she was jarred by the phone ringing.

"Stephen?" she said hopefully.

"Yeah. I just got your message. What's up?"

"Guess what I'm looking at, at this very moment?"

"Uh—a triple-X-rated movie, and you want company."

"Sort of, sort of. A triple-X-rated movie of a few centuries ago."

"Sounds interesting. I'm available for voyeurism, participation, and a variety of other services."

"Seriously, Stephen, I've got the grimoire right here in my hot little hands."

"You're kidding. You found it?"

"I did."

"Where?"

"In my father's hamper, of all places, mixed in with the laundry. He must have hidden it. There's the letter from the guy who sent it to him, plus a ten-dollar bill. That was the bet we made. So that means he hid it after he'd spoken to Signor Antonelli."

"I'm coming over."

"I'm in bed."

"Good. That eliminates the middleman. Anyway, I have some news for you myself."

"What?"

"I'll tell you when I get there."

"No, listen, I'm exhausted. I'm not even bothering with dinner. Please tell me now."

"Well, it's about your friend Simon Lovelock."

"What about him?"

"I asked my old buddy Fred Viner about him."

"Who's Fred Viner?"

"Viner Books, you know? They're right around the corner from me, on Columbus Avenue. They serve espresso at night and play chess in the back?"

"Oh, that place," she said. "So?"

"I stopped by on my way home this evening, and Fred and I got to schmoozing. He knows Lovelock. Says he's a real character. A former Jesuit."

"Really!"

"They either expelled him or he quit the order. Fred didn't know. Oh, and you'll love this: Lovelock used to work in the Vatican Library."

"No kidding!" Beatrice said with delight. "You just gave me a chill."

"That's how Fred first heard of him. Apparently, Lovelock was there for a number of years, in charge of publishing mega-expensive facsimiles of the Vatican's most famous books for the American and English markets. Books of Hours and illustrated Bibles—that kind of thing. Fred used to special-order them for a good customer of his. Anyway, Lovelock moved back to New York and opened his occult bookshop about six years ago. According to Fred, he's *the* man in the occult field—the dealer's dealer. That's probably why your dad got in touch with him. So what do you think of them apples, baby?"

"I think we ought to go down to Lovelock's shop tomorrow morning and ask him to take a look at it."

"Why won't you let me come over now?"

"Because I just won't, that's all. Please respect my wishes."

"Okay." He sounded despondent. "But tomorrow morning, first thing, I'll be there."

"Stephen . . . "

"Yeah?"

"Who was the whore?"

"What?"

"If I was the madonna, who was the whore? The girl you ran off with?"

"Well, she wasn't literally a whore," he said uncomfortably. "It's just a figure of speech, the madonna-whore thing, a catchall explanation of a syndrome, you know—"

"No, Stephen, I'm not sure I do know. I'm not sure you do, either."

"What do you mean?"

"Never mind. I'm just thinking about things, that's all. Let's get some sleep. I'll see you tomorrow." She hung up.

Beatrice wedged the grimoire into a pile of other books on her night table. She fell instantly asleep.

The next morning, for the first time in years, Beatrice paid close attention to her appearance. She applied a light layer of makeup to her face, just enough to make her skin glow, but not enough to be noticeable. She didn't want Stephen to think she was making a special effort for him, even though she was. She sprayed herself with eau de cologne and pulled one of her older, more revealing dresses from the closet. She was pleased to note that it still fit. Having let herself go in other ways since the divorce, she had retained her youthful figure. She swept her hair around her face the way Stephen liked it.

When the doorbell rang, Beatrice was already on her way downstairs, grimoire in hand. Opening the door, she saw Stephen standing there, his face obscured by a straggly bunch of flowers.

"Madame, these are for you." He held out the ragged bouquet.

"Oh, weeds!" Beatrice exclaimed. "My favorite. How did you know?" She kissed him coquettishly on the cheek.

"Sorry, but it's all they had at the fruit stand."

"Here, you take this and I'll take these." She handed him the grimoire, and he handed her the flowers. "Come on in. I'll just go put these in a vase."

"So this is the famous grimoire." He followed Beatrice into the kitchen.

"What do you think?" She put down the flowers while she searched for a vase.

"I think I should have brought you strawberries. They looked a lot fresher than those do."

"Not about the flowers, idiot!"

"I know, I know. . . ." Stephen sat at the kitchen table and gave the grimoire a cursory look. "Too bad my French is so lousy."

Beatrice began arranging the flowers in a small glass vase. "I was looking at it yesterday before I went to bed. It seemed much less ominous than I'd remembered it. There," she said, standing back to assess her handiwork. "These don't look so bad. A little wilted, maybe, but aren't we all?"

"Spooky little thing, isn't it?" Stephen said, thumbing through the pages. "You got any coffee?"

"I'll make some. Then we've got to get going. I want to show it to Lovelock."

Beatrice bustled around the kitchen as Stephen studied the grimoire.

"Okay, down to business," Stephen said. Propping up the book on the table, he held it firmly with both hands. "Let's start at the beginning." He opened it and read aloud. "Page one. How's your Latin? *'Videmus nunc per—'* "

" 'For now, we see through a glass darkly; but then face to face,' " Beatrice interjected, as she put six large teaspoonfuls of coffee into the espresso pot. "It's from Saint Paul. Signor Antonelli explained that it was probably a little joke of the author's, to make you think you were about to read a religious tract."

"Uh huh." Stephen nodded. "Remember when we saw that Bergman film *Through a Glass Darkly* and you freaked out?"

"I did not freak out, thanks very much!" Beatrice said indignantly.

"Yes, you did. You got really upset at the helicopter that looked like the spider, and then we went home and had what was possibly the best sex of our entire lives."

"According to you, that wouldn't have been difficult," she said.

"You're not going to let me off the hook about that, are you?"

"I just keep wondering if it's true."

"Why don't we find out?"

Beatrice rolled her eyes heavenward. "Stick to the grimoire, please." She lit the burner and put the coffee on.

"Can't we flirt a little?"

"Stephen, turn the page, will you?"

"You look as if you might enjoy sex this morning," he said, teasing her. "I see you put on makeup and you smell delicious. What's the name of that perfume?"

"Eau Contraire," Beatrice said deadpan.

"Very funny. 'Age cannot wither, nor custom stale her infinite sarcasm.' "

"Shut up and turn the page!" she cried.

"Okay, okay," he said, obeying. "Now, let's see, what have we here?"

Stephen read aloud slowly from the Old French text in a fractured accent. " *'Gremoire du Pape Honorius avec un recveil des plus rares secrets. A Rome. MDCLXX.'* Well, that's not too difficult. Even I understand that. 'The grimoire of Pope Honorius with a something of the rarest secrets.' "

" 'Collection,' " Beatrice said. "Want some toast?"

"Thank you. 'With a collection of the rarest secrets. Rome, 1670.' Then there's this weird little design with a circle and a half-moon and a pentacle, some lions. Wonder what that means. Who knows? Okay. Moving on . . ."

Again, Stephen began to read aloud from the book in a halting voice. Unable to stand his stilted delivery, Beatrice walked over and took the book from him, flawlessly reciting the opening paragraph of the text. " *'Conſtitutions du Pape Honorius le Grand, ou ſe trouvent les conjurations ſecrettes qui'l faut faire contre les Eſprits de tenebres—'* "

Stephen interrupted her. "Just hit me with the translation, please."

Beatrice ran her finger over the sentences, one by one. "Okay," she began. "It's something like this: 'Constitutions of Pope Honorius the Great, where one finds the secret conjurings which are necessary to use against the Spirits of Darkness . . . The Apostolic Throne'—I think that means throne—'to whom the keys of the Kingdom of Heaven have been given by these words of Jesus Christ to Saint Peter: "I give you the keys to the Kingdom of Heaven," the sole power to command the Prince of Darkness and his Angels, which, like the servants of their master, owe honor, glory, and obeisance, by the other words of Jesus Christ: "You will serve your only master"; by the power of the keys of the church you have been made the lord of hell.' "

"What's that supposed to mean?" Stephen exclaimed. "That the Pope's been made the lord of hell with the help of this book?"

"I haven't the vaguest idea. Take a look at this part." Beatrice showed Stephen the woodcuts.

"Crude but effective," he said when he'd finished. "I like my succubuses a little more succulent, however."

"Oh, shut up." Beatrice poked him in the stomach.

"Ow! That hurt."

"It was meant to. Go on."

"Moving right along . . ." Stephen turned to the back of the book where the word *"Table"* was written in bold black type. A pair of grinning demons cavorted on the arms of the *T.* " '*Table*' . . . Table of contents, right?"

Beatrice nodded. She took the book from him. "Page one is the Constitution of Pope Honorius III. Page Two says: *'Bulle du meme Pape, ou ſe trouvera la maniere de donner a cet Ouvrage la force de contraindres les Eſprits & les faire obeir.'* Roughly translated, that means: 'The Bull of the same Pope, which gives the work the power to invoke the spirits and make them obey.' "

"A papal bull—whaddaya know?" Stephen said, amused. "So, basically, it's kind of an evil parody of Church conventions."

"Looks like it. I wonder who Pope Honorius III was. I mean, I wonder if it has any significance."

"They probably just picked on one they didn't like."

"Okay. Skipping a bit," Beatrice continued, "here we have a list of things: *'Conjuration universelle'*—universal conjuring; *'Conjurations des Demons'*—conjuring of demons; *'Conjurations des Mortes'*— conjuring the dead; *'Conjuration du Livre'*—conjuring of the book—' "

"Wait," Stephen said. "What page is that?"

"Twenty-one."

"Read it."

Beatrice turned to page twenty-one and began to read the text aloud: " *'Conjuration du Livre . . . Je te conjure, Livre, d'etre utile & profitable a tous ceux qui te liront pour la reuſſite de leurs affaires—'* "

"Quit showing off," Stephen said, irritated. "Let's save a little time here."

"You just hate that I can speak French and you can't, don't you?" Beatrice said playfully.

"Oui, Madam. Now *donnez-moi un* break and read, please!"

"Okay. 'Conjuring of the Book.' "

"Wait a minute. Can I just tell you something?"

"What?"

"You're beautiful, you know that?" He stared at her admiringly. "It makes me happy to be near you. 'Here's looking at *you,* kid,' " he said, toasting her with his coffee cup.

Beatrice smiled shyly and looked down, slightly embarrassed. She noticed there was something slightly sophomoric about Stephen—a tone, an attitude, she couldn't quite put her finger on. She didn't remember him quite this way, and it disconcerted her. She continued reading.

" 'I conjure you, Book, to be useful and profitable to all who read you for the success of their affairs. . . . I conjure you immediately by the virtue of the blood of Jesus Christ contained every day in the chalice to be useful to all who will read you. I exorcise you in the name of the Holy Trinity.' "

"Is that it?" Stephen sounded disappointed.

"That's it."

"Back to the table of contents," he ordered.

Beatrice returned to the end of the book. "Here we have conjuring for the days of the week: Monday, Tuesday, Wednesday, et cetera."

"I guess a day without conjuring was like a day without sunshine for these folks."

"Stephen, you're not taking this at all seriously, are you?"

"No, I am," he said, straightening up. "I really am. *Continue, s'il te plaît.*"

Beatrice turned the page. "Okay. Then we have conjuring for sore throats, conjuring for headaches, conjuring for buried treasure—"

"Read that one."

Beatrice found the appropriate page and scanned the text. "Oh, you're going to love this," she said. " 'Take the brain of a rooster, powder from the dust of a human grave—*c'est-à-dire* the powder in the coffin itself—oil from nuts, and wax from a candle. Mix them all together and wrap them in a virgin parchment, in which the words *"Trinitas, Omnipotens, Deus, Aeternus, Summum bonum infinitas, Amen"* are written with the following caricature—' There's a little sketch here—look."

Stephen examined the odd drawing of a triangle, a pentacle, and an eye, unevenly juxtaposed in a circle. He shrugged. "Go on."

" 'Burn the mixture, and prodigious things will be revealed to you. But caution: this may not be done by fearful people.' "

"Or intelligent people. Speaking of burning . . ." He sniffed the air.

"Christ!" Beatrice flew to the smoking toaster and removed the charred bread from the slots. "Sorry."

"I think the devil is trying to tell us something."

She poured coffee and sat down again.

"Go back to the table of contents," Stephen said, sipping the strong brew.

"I'm just looking through it. There's nothing much more than some spells. There's a spell to make a naked girl dance, if that's of any interest."

"Really?" Stephen leaned in.

"Yes, here it is," she said, pointing it out to him. " *'Conjuration pour faire danser une fille nue.'* "

"That sounds promising. Read it."

Beatrice shook her head, glancing at him out of the corner of her eye. " 'Write on a virgin piece of parchment the first letter of the girl's name with the tooth of a wild beast dipped in bat's blood,' " she read. " 'Then wrap it around a stone which has been blessed and put the stone on top of a copy of a mass. Bury the stone under the door where the person will pass. . . . *A peine aura-t-elle fait ce trajet, que vous la verrez entrer en fureur, fe desabillant toute nue, & dansera jusqu'a la mort, fi l'on n'ote pas le caractere, avec des grimaces & contorsions qui font plus de pitie que d'envie.'* I'm not quite sure what that means— something about seeing her entering a fury, becoming naked, and dancing herself to death, and regarding her with more pity than envy."

"Right! Well, we get the gist of it. I tell you what. I'll get some parchment, a stone, and a bat. You strip naked, and we'll see if it works." Stephen grinned.

"I repeat: you're not taking this at all seriously, are you?"

"Sure I am, sure I am! Aren't you? This is scary goddamn stuff. Girls dancing naked, spells for sore throats and days of the week."

"But just look at the woodcuts," Beatrice said, losing patience. "See how hideous they are? The really interesting part here is the figure of the woman. At first, she's the beautiful temptress, then she turns into a succubus. The evil seductress."

Stephen shrugged. "Sounds like life to me."

"Men really think that about women, don't they?" she said reflectively.

"I suppose there's a cartoon form of that going on sometimes. We're all children, as you have so often pointed out." Stephen took the grimoire from Beatrice's hand, closed it, and placed it ceremoniously on the table. He put his arm around her and addressed her in a kind, patronizing way.

"Bea, honey," he said. "This grimoire of yours looks like a major contender for the *Guinness Book of Records'* Most Ridiculous Book Ever Written category. However, in deference to the number of apparently intelligent people who seem to be interested in it, I'm willing to reserve judgment until I know more about it. Since neither of us is qualified to assess this thing properly, you know what I think?"

"What?"

"Lovelock's the man."

"I know. But do you think we can trust him?"

"Who knows? But I think he's our best shot at the moment. Unless you want to call Signor Antonelli."

"God, no. I really don't trust him. And look, we know my father called Lovelock, so Daddy obviously trusted him."

"So Lovelock says, anyway."

"What do you mean?"

"Just that. We only have his word for it."

"But why would he have made that up?"

"I don't know. Look, you know me. Everyone's guilty until proven innocent."

Beatrice sighed. "I don't know who to trust anymore."

"You can trust me."

She looked at him askance. "I wish."

Stephen got up from the table and began pacing the floor, his hands shoved down into the pockets of his blue jeans, his shoulders hunched up.

"Truth?" he said.

"Sure. What about?" she said, eyeing him.

"Okay. The truth is, man is not a monogamous animal," he said at last.

"At least we know you're not," Beatrice retorted.

"I'm not atypical, Bea."

"Really?"

"Most men are like me. You're not a guy. You just don't know what happens when a guy has female temptation put in front of him. We don't think of sex like women do."

"No? And how do women think of sex?"

"Differently from guys. You can take my word for it."

"How so?" Beatrice said sweetly.

Stephen hesitated. "The truth is, under the right circumstances, most guys will lay someone they find attractive. Now, not every guy will admit this," he said, facing her.

"The smart ones won't, that's true," she responded wryly.

"The smart ones will. I just did."

"Well, under the right circumstances, the same might be true for most women."

"Some, not most."

"Are you saying that most men in long-term relationships can't be trusted to be faithful?"

"I guess there are some guys who are definitely less driven by their libidos than others. But for those of us who are pretty sexually motivated, the world is one big garden of temptation."

"I see," Beatrice said, nodding. "With women as the fruit."

"Actually, that's about right. The question for those of us who are libido driven is not *if* we'll fall but *when*—under what conditions."

Beatrice sipped her coffee. "I wonder how people can be married, then? How can you live with someone and not trust him? Even putting the obvious health risks aside."

Stephen shook his head. "Beats me. It's a real problem. Even guys with the best intentions are fair game. I guess, with some people, they go off the track once, maybe twice, and they feel so guilty about it, they never get themselves in a situation where it can happen again. Others just shut up about it. They're discreet. I know people who lead total double lives, and it seems to agree with them. I couldn't do that. But I don't know if I could be completely faithful for the rest of my life, either—even to you. Daily life—routine— puts a real damper on passion. Do you hate me for saying that?"

"No; I understand it. I really understand it."

He looked at her intently. "That's a real switch for you, isn't it?"

"Yes, I suppose it is."

"Did some of your research finally lead you into a greater understanding of male sexuality?"

"No; female sexuality."

"But they're different. I told you."

"Maybe not so different," Beatrice said.

"Sure they are. I don't think most women, given the opportunity, would screw a complete stranger."

"Well, you just never know." Beatrice sighed and leaned back.

"Would you do it? Honestly, now. A complete stranger?"

Beatrice paused for a very long time. Stephen watched her with growing anxiety.

"Bea . . . ?"

"I might. Under the right circumstances, as you said."

"Come on, Bea. Be honest. You would not. I know you so well. . . ."

"I doubt it, Stephen, because the point is, I never really knew myself."

"Are you telling me that you, uh, did something like that?"

"Maybe."

Stephen blinked in disbelief. "Who with?" he said, trying to sound dispassionate.

"A social worker I met, doing some research on Santeria. His name was Luis Diaz."

"You're kidding."

She shook her head. "Are you shocked?"

"Yeah. I kind of am." He stared at her in disbelief.

121

"Me too. In fact, Luis Diaz was my window into a very dark part of myself, Stephen. A part that you and I never explored, for some reason. You say it's because I wasn't interested. But maybe it's because *you* weren't interested."

"What do you mean?"

"Maybe 'good girls' aren't supposed to have certain kinds of feelings. Maybe you were afraid of me. Who knows?"

Stephen cleared his throat. "So—what was he like?"

"He was sexy. . . . Violent."

"Violent? Jesus. Did he hurt you?"

"Yes."

"God, Bea—" Stephen frowned.

"Don't look so disconcerted. Maybe I wanted him to."

"You *wanted* him to?"

"Yes. As a matter of fact, I did." She knew she was goading him a little. "But that's not even the most interesting part."

"What is?" he asked, barely audible.

She paused. "That I hurt him," she said finally.

"What do you mean, you hurt him?"

Beatrice stared down at the ground. "I'm a violent woman, Stephen."

"You?" he said incredulously. "Come off it."

"You can't even imagine that part of me, can you?" she snapped, looking up at him.

Stephen seemed taken aback. "Frankly, no."

"I'll tell you a little secret. You want to know who I really am?"

"Who?"

"I'm her." She pointed to the succubus in the grimoire.

Stephen gave out a little inadvertent laugh. "You're prettier than she is," he said nervously.

"Maybe she's not so hideous, really. Maybe that's just how men see women who have the same impulses they do. When men have those impulses, it's normal. When women have them, we become devourers and demons. We threaten you. And you depict us as monsters."

"Well, now I'll tell you something," Stephen said. "I didn't have an affair out of lust. I had an affair because I had to deny my need for you in some way. I felt trapped by our love, if you can understand that. I felt emasculated by it. You see, I don't think women realize the kind of power they have over men."

"I'm beginning to, Stephen. But it's finite—a finite power. Guys can go on forever. You can start a family again at seventy. Women, on the other hand, have relatively short romantic lives. Maybe that's why we feel betrayal so acutely."

"But you're so much stronger than we are."

"You think so?" Beatrice asked.

"Definitely. You're more mysterious, for one thing. Women are magic. Your bodies are magic. You bleed with no wound. You're tied to the cycles of the moon. You give life. You're full of power."

"You fear we'll take away your sexual prowess?"

"On some level, I think that's true."

"Well, Stephen, that's what these woodcuts are about." She traced the figure of the succubus with her finger. "This is the crudest version of a man's fears: the woman who turns into a succubus and zaps him of his powers, his potency."

"Okay, we fear you. Why shouldn't we?"

"The *vagina dentata*, you mean," Beatrice said.

"Exactly. The vagina with teeth. A perfect image."

"So what it boils down to is this: men fear women and women envy men, and it's no wonder that most relationships are hell!" Beatrice laughed.

"Come here." Stephen beckoned.

Beatrice put down the grimoire and got up from the table. Stephen enfolded her in his arms.

"I'm sorry I hurt you, Bea. God knows, I'm sorry."

"I'm sorry too," she said. "Sorry about the baby most of all . . ."

He cupped her face in his hands and gave her a lingering kiss. She felt a stirring inside her, but it was something soft and gentle, a feeling imbued with history and familiarity—a soothing cruise as opposed to the raging sea of desire. Stephen did not seem able to summon her wolf the way Diaz had, and it troubled her.

"Let's make love," he whispered.

Beatrice looked deep into his eyes, trying to feel the passion. She wanted to feel it. She cared for Stephen. But he was almost too . . . What was the word she was looking for? Too tame. That was it. She craved another kind of excitement now.

"No," she said, pulling away abruptly. "Let's go down to see Mr. Lovelock."

 WANT TO KNOW MORE ABOUT THIS GUY DIAZ,"
Stephen said, as he and Beatrice stood on the
sidewalk in front of Lovelock's second-floor
bookshop.

"Why? Does it turn you on?"

"Maybe I want to get to you the way he
did."

"I don't want to talk about him," Beatrice replied.

Stephen looked at her intently. "I want you back, Bea. How can
I get you back?"

"Just give me some time," she said, patting him affectionately
on the cheek.

They were interrupted by the buzzer that unlocked the door.
Stephen followed her into the dark hallway. Lovelock was waiting
for them at the landing upstairs, dressed, as usual, in black.

"Good morning, Mr. Lovelock," Beatrice greeted him. "I'd like
you to meet a friend of mine, Stephen Carson. Stephen, this is Simon Lovelock."

As the two men shook hands, Beatrice perceived a slight irritation in Lovelock's attitude. He showed them into the shop. Beatrice could see Stephen's interest growing as he looked around the musty premises.

"I'm afraid I haven't had a chance to examine your little *Roman de la Rose* yet," Lovelock said.

"We didn't come about that," Beatrice replied.

"Oh? What may I do for you, then?"

"Mr. Lovelock, I've found the grimoire," she said simply.

Lovelock betrayed no emotion, but he was silent for a moment. "Where?"

"My father had tossed it in with some of his dirty laundry. He was obviously trying to hide it."

"We thought you might like to take a look at it," Stephen said.

Lovelock hesitated. "Do you have it here?"

Beatrice opened her purse and extracted the book, which she had wrapped in tissue paper. She handed it to Lovelock, who walked over to the long reading table by the window and sat down. Stephen and Beatrice watched him as he unwrapped the book and pored over it for several minutes.

When he'd finished, he looked up at them. "What is it, exactly, that you wish to know about it?"

"Everything. What's the deal?" Stephen said.

"Mr. Lovelock," Beatrice said, "the day you came to see my father and I told you about the grimoire, you seemed hesitant, as if you wanted to tell me something about it but decided not to. Then, when I came to see you again to give you the *Roman* to repair, you seemed disturbed that I'd been to see Father Morton and that he'd asked about the grimoire. I get the feeling you know a lot more than you're letting on. Am I wrong?"

Lovelock squeezed his eyes shut for a brief moment, as if he were in pain. "No. You're not wrong."

"Then please, tell us what you know," Beatrice begged.

Lighting a cigarette from the crumpled pack he took out of his jacket pocket, he stared at Beatrice and Stephen through strings of blue smoke. He beckoned them to join him at the table. They sat down opposite him.

"All right," Lovelock said. "I will tell you some things. After that, you'll have to make your own decision about what to do." He leaned toward them and began to speak quietly, as if he were in danger of being overheard. His manner was extremely grave. "First of all, how much do you know about grimoires?"

"Nothing, really," Beatrice said. "Except what Signor Antonelli told me."

"Then let me explain a little bit about them. They are essentially textbooks of black magic. The three most famous grimoires in existence are the *Grimorium Verum,* published in 1517, translated from the Hebrew and supposedly based on the Key of Solomon; the *Grand Grimoire,* edited by Antonia del Rabina, also supposedly based on the writings of King Solomon; and the *Grimoire of Pope Honorius III*—the heretical Pope—which purports to give papal sanction to sorcerers, conjurers, and necromancers."

"Our grimoire," Beatrice said.

"Please." Lovelock held up his hand. "Please let me finish. . . . Aside from these three, there are many others. Their object is to invoke devils and demons and then to trick them—usually into finding buried treasure, which the practitioner will then use to fund good works. Before you can properly use a grimoire, you must fast and pray and practice the rites of the Church. That's why many of them have the appearance of being religious books in the opening pages. It's difficult for the rational mind to take them seriously, because they seem quite silly when you examine them."

"I'll say," Stephen said, smirking.

"Make no mistake, however," Lovelock warned. "There are those who do take them seriously. Very seriously indeed."

"Who, for instance?" Stephen said skeptically.

"I'm coming to that," Lovelock assured him. "Recently, that is, within the past fifty years—since the war, in fact—interest in grimoires has been growing steadily, along with interest in the occult in general. The important ones have been very difficult to find. Only one or two have come up at auction during the last ten years, but the prices have been so high, it's been impossible for ordinary dealers like me to obtain them. Now, the rumor is—just so you know—that your friend Giuseppe Antonelli has cornered the market on them for a special client."

"Yes, that mysterious special client," Beatrice said with contempt.

"As you know, when dealers can't afford to buy at auction, we must seek out private sources. About seven years ago, I heard about an important grimoire in a collection of rare books in France. I went

to France and contacted the man who was thinking of selling it. . . .
Unfortunately, I was too late." Lovelock paused.

"Someone had already bought it?" Beatrice volunteered.

"Not exactly. The owner of the grimoire had died under what
I understood were rather cloudy circumstances, and the book had
been stolen."

Beatrice shuddered and put her hand on Stephen's arm. She
noticed that Lovelock seemed to wince at this gesture, and for a moment he grew distracted.

"Go on," Stephen said.

Lovelock cleared his throat and continued, his eyes darting between the two of them as he spoke.

"I didn't give it a great deal of thought until, oh, about three
years later, when a friend of mine—an occult-book dealer named
Jeffreys—came to me and told me a similar story. He'd gone to England to try to buy a grimoire from an old noble family, and when he
got there, the owner had died and the grimoire had been stolen."

Beatrice let out an inadvertent gasp.

"Jeffreys and I did business together on and off," Lovelock continued. "One day, he called me up and told me he'd purchased a
very important grimoire in Pennsylvania. He asked me if I would
put it on consignment in the shop. As it was quite expensive, I told
him I'd have to see it first. We made an appointment for a viewing.
He never showed up."

"What happened?" Stephen said.

"Apparently, his car went off a bridge, into a swamp. They
didn't find him for a month."

"I don't even have to ask about the grimoire," Beatrice said.

"Vanished, of course. It wasn't with the rest of his stock, some
of which I bought. In fact, it didn't even appear on the inventory."

Beatrice swallowed hard. Lovelock took out a fresh cigarette,
used the glowing tip of the old one to light it.

"So when my father called you and asked you to come and see
him that day—"

"I had no idea what he wanted," Lovelock interrupted. "But
when you told me of his murder and that a grimoire was missing, I
recognized the pattern."

"So what does it mean?" Beatrice asked. "Who's responsible?"

"Let me finish. Your grimoire," he went on, tapping the cover
of the little black book on the table, "is one of the most important

grimoires of all—if not *the* most important. In fact, it's a legend in the occult trade."

Beatrice and Stephen glanced at each other.

"Rumors have circulated about it for years," Lovelock continued. "I first heard about it in the sixties, when I was working in Rome. I was told by a friend in a position to know that Pope Pius XII had been in possession of a grimoire. The book had been seen by several people and was described to me in detail by my friend. Sometime during the war, the grimoire disappeared."

"Yes!" Beatrice exclaimed. "It was sent to my father by a man in Oklahoma, who said he'd gotten it during the war. Here—I have his letter."

Beatrice took the letter from her purse, unfolded it, and handed it to Lovelock.

Reading the document carefully, holding it close to his face, Lovelock then gave it back to her. "Yes. Just as I thought."

"But why is this grimoire so important?" Beatrice asked.

"Well, there are two schools of thought on that," Lovelock said, opening the book. "They depend on what you believe."

"What do you mean?" Stephen said.

"Those who sincerely believe in the occult think that the book contains Solomon's own long-lost spell for the most profound sorcery of all—namely, the raising of the dead, otherwise known as necromancy: *nekros* being the Greek word for dead, and *manteia* the word for divination," he added in the swift patter of a scholar. "Those who are more pragmatic and less magically minded, if you will, believe that it contains the key to a vast fortune."

"What fortune?" Beatrice said.

"Well, the common theory is that it harbors Jacques de Molay's coded map to the lost treasure of the Knights Templar, who, as you may know, were a great military and commercial organization in the Middle Ages."

"I knew about the military, but a great commercial organization . . . ? That's certainly a novel way to refer to them," Stephen chided him.

"Well, yes, the crusades and all that," Lovelock said dismissively. "Basically, however, they *were* a huge commercial enterprise, with branches in most of Western Europe. Christianity was big business in those days."

" 'In those days'?" Stephen repeated, raising his eyebrows.

Lovelock smiled. "Point taken."

"Who's Jacques de Molay?" Beatrice asked.

"He was the Grand Master of the order in the early fourteenth century," Lovelock said. "As such, he was in charge of the organization's treasury, to which all the knights contributed every year. It constituted a vast fortune, which the Templars used to propagate their faith and work. De Molay, however, had two extremely dangerous and powerful enemies: Philip IV of France, who was jealous of the Templars' power and wealth, and Pope Clement V, who feared them as a competitive force. Clement was anxious to bring them under the jurisdiction of the Church, so he and King Philip conspired to bring down de Molay and thus dilute the Templars' power. De Molay was denounced by the Inquisition. He was arrested, accused of heresy, tortured, and eventually burned at the stake in Paris. His followers in France and in virtually every other country where the Templars were active were rounded up, tortured, and killed. Their individual fortunes were confiscated, divided up, and sent in equal measure to King Philip and Pope Clement.

"De Molay, before he died, however, managed to send orders to have the great treasure of the Knights Templar hidden. For centuries, that treasure has been the subject of legend."

"Oh, come on. After six hundred years? It can't really exist," Beatrice said.

"I can't say. No one can. But just remember, the *Iliad* was believed to be a work of fiction until Schliemann took it seriously and discovered Troy. And Machu Picchu was only a legend until Hiram Bingham searched for it and found it. Just because a notion is fantastic doesn't mean it isn't true. And these ancient legends are, perhaps, more often valid than one imagines."

"So let me get this straight," Stephen said. "This grimoire is meant to contain a map to the treasure of the Knights Templar."

"That's what they say. If you look at the woodcuts closely, you will see the inverted sword as a recurrent theme. That is the symbol of the Knights Templar. Their gravestones are marked with it and only it—no names."

Stephen picked up the book and turned to the woodcuts. "Yes, here it is." He pointed out the inverted sword to Beatrice. "And here it is again."

"As I said, it recurs throughout."

"But surely that's not the only copy," Beatrice said. "After all, if it's one of the three most famous grimoires, there must be others."

"Very few," Lovelock said. "And in any case, no two grimoires are exactly alike. The binders made sure of that. They would often insert pages or keep pages out, or else add words by hand to the printed text here and there, so that each grimoire would be unique. Yours is the only Honorius III grimoire with the quotation from Saint Paul up front. That is the immediate clue that it contains a secret code of some sort."

" 'For now we see through a glass, darkly; but then face to face . . . ,' " Beatrice mused aloud.

"So," Lovelock said, "now that you know its history, what are you going to do with it?"

"Wait." Beatrice held up her hand. "What about the first reason—the spell? Are there people who really believe in it?"

"Certainly," Lovelock replied.

"Come on, Bea," Stephen said.

"Wait, Stephen. Do you, Mr. Lovelock?" Beatrice asked. "Do *you* believe in it?"

Lovelock paused. "Shall I say, 'There are more things in heaven and earth than are dreamt of in your philosophy'? I don't dismiss it as a possibility. But may I be presumptuous and say that you're both missing the point, as nearly everyone who thinks about this book does."

"What do you mean?" Beatrice said.

"Yeah, what *do* you mean?" Stephen echoed.

"Ask yourselves this," Lovelock began slowly. "The real question here isn't whether this particular grimoire contains a magic spell or a map for the treasure of the Knights Templar, or even whether men have been killed for it."

"What is it, then?" Beatrice asked.

"The real question is this: What was Pope Pius XII doing with a grimoire in the first place? Why was a pope—the spiritual leader of the Catholic Church, and God's word on earth—in possession of a book of black magic?"

Beatrice felt a chill go through her. Stephen cocked his head. And Lovelock puffed on his cigarette, the smoke drifting up his skull-like face and fading into the air.

"Well," Stephen said after a time. "The history of the Catholic Church is intertwined with black magic. Obviously, it was in his collection."

"It's a rather odd thing for a pope to have in his personal collection, isn't it?" Lovelock said, shaking his head in amusement. "A grimoire—a manual of the Enemy?"

"The Enemy?" Beatrice said.

"The *Enemy*," Lovelock stated emphatically.

"I don't understand."

"Grimoires are supposedly the work of the devil, God's Enemy on earth. The Church has spent more than a thousand years ferreting out such books, not to mention their authors. It has always sought to destroy such nefarious works and their devotees and practitioners. As Mr. Carson pointed out, there's a profound relationship between the Church and black magic. You have, I take it, heard of the Inquisition?"

"But that was centuries ago," Beatrice said.

"Was it?" Lovelock smiled wryly. "What about Salem?"

"Granted, there have been witch hunts through the ages," Stephen admitted.

"And what makes you think that this age is any different from all the others? Do you really think there's no more evil left in the world?"

"Yes, of course there is," Beatrice said. "But civilized people don't think of evil in the same way."

"No? And how do civilized people think of it?" Lovelock stared at her.

"Well," she said, growing uncomfortable, "evil is more of a concept than a reality now. You can't reduce things to such black-and-white terms as good and evil."

"Can't you?" he said facetiously.

"What Bea means, I think, is that things which were once considered evil are now viewed as, well, different ways of thought and alternative lifestyles, to use the vernacular," Stephen said. "Isn't that what you mean, Bea?"

Beatrice nodded. "Right. Life's much too complex these days. There's no such thing as good and evil per se."

Lovelock laughed. "Oh, isn't there? Perhaps not to you. You see, one tends to forget the soul in this chaotic age of telecommunications and mass media. But make no mistake. Daily life presents a perilous spiritual journey. And the only real purpose of the Church is to save souls—to make it possible for each person to attain eternal life after death. Churchmen view themselves as soldiers in an ongoing war, the war against God's sworn enemy on earth."

"Sworn enemy?" Beatrice asked.

"Satan," Lovelock pronounced grimly.

"But surely, for most people, Satan's just a kind of metaphor now," Beatrice said.

Lovelock seemed irritated. "Metaphor? Metaphor, you say? No, no . . . evil is no metaphor. It's as tangible as this table," he said, stroking the wooden surface. "The struggle between God and Satan for the souls of humankind is no metaphor, but a war as bloody and destructive as any ever fought on the face of this planet. And," he added, "many feel that we are losing that war."

"What kind of evil are you talking about?" Stephen interjected.

"As far as the Church is concerned?" Lovelock replied. "Well, witches, for one thing."

"Witches?" Beatrice said. "There are no witches anymore—not like there were, at any rate. Or like society thought there were. In fact, witchcraft nowadays is just a euphemism for feminism."

Lovelock shook his head wearily. "If you really believe that, then you are sorely mistaken. There are real witches, and there is real witchcraft. For many in the Church, evil exists just as it did all those centuries ago. Time in that particular realm is frozen. The war for the souls of men is still going on full force between God and the opposing general."

"Could I bum one of your cigarettes?" Stephen asked.

"Of course—forgive me. It's so unfashionable to smoke these days, I never think of offering one to anybody." Lovelock handed him the ragged pack.

It was a brand Stephen didn't recognize. "What kind are these?" he asked, turning a filterless cigarette around in his hand.

"The cheapest kind, I'm afraid," Lovelock apologized. "They're generic. I buy them by the gross. Smoking as much as I do, I'd be bankrupt if I bought good cigarettes. Sorry."

"That's fine by me. I can't tell the difference, anyway." Inhaling deeply as he lit the strong-scented cigarette, Stephen felt a slight rush of dizziness, the effect of which was heady. "So," he continued, "what was Pius XII doing with a grimoire, in your opinion?"

"I wonder," Lovelock mused.

"You must have some theory," Beatrice said.

"I do." Lovelock nodded.

"What is it?"

"Do you know that the Vatican Library is supposed to have a huge collection of pornography?" Lovelock asked.

"That's quite well known," replied Stephen.

"Really?" Beatrice said. "I didn't know it."

"Oh, yeah," Stephen affirmed. "They don't admit to it—not publicly, at any rate. But it's there. Isn't that right, Mr. Lovelock?"

"That's quite right. In fact, I myself have seen part of it. The eighteenth century was a particularly fertile time for such works."

"Pornography through the ages?" Beatrice smiled. "Why would the Church have that sort of collection?"

"Perhaps for edification, but also for amusement. After all, celibacy has its limits." Lovelock's eyes sparkled. "Now, it's my belief," he continued, more seriously, "that the Vatican had, at one time, another collection they never admitted to—one dealing with black magic and the black arts."

"Really?" Stephen appeared fascinated.

"Well, when you think about it, it stands to reason, doesn't it? Don't forget, the Church has spent centuries ferreting out and confiscating such books in order to burn them. But I have good reason to believe that these works were not burned. Or that if they were, copies were made and hidden."

"Buy why?" Stephen asked. "Why would they bother?"

"Oh, it's very simple, really. Would Wellington have destroyed Napoleon's charts and maps had he captured them?" Lovelock said with a slight smile. "Would Mr. Roosevelt have burned Hitler's secret papers? On the contrary. Enemy documents, should they come into one's possession, are carefully studied."

"So you're saying that the Catholic Church treats grimoires and the like as enemy documents?"

"They certainly did at one time," Lovelock replied.

"Isn't that a little farfetched?" Beatrice said.

" 'Extreme' is the word I would use, Miss O'Connell," Lovelock said. "It betrays an extreme point of view about the nature of evil in the modern world."

"So the Church has a collection of books of black magic. So what?" Stephen pressed.

Lovelock shook his head. "What if these books are taken seriously by serious men?"

"What if they are?"

"I don't think you realize the implications of that, Mr. Carson."

"The implications are that they're taken seriously. Again, so what?"

"Yes, but if you take a disease seriously, don't you try to cure it, or at least fight it?" Lovelock asked.

"Well, sure."

Lovelock looked at Stephen as if he now expected him to make the connection.

"And do you agree with me that the antidote to cancer is very often as deadly as the disease itself?" Lovelock said. "In trying to cure the cancer, a doctor may wind up killing the patient."

"I don't understand," Beatrice said.

"Look, the men who take these books seriously are as dangerous to their fellow human beings as the very evil they are purporting to fight. For they have taken it upon themselves to be the judges, juries, and executioners of all those whom they believe to be a threat to the sovereignty of the Church. They believe in fighting fire with fire."

"But where are these men?" Beatrice asked. "And who takes *them* seriously?"

"You might think of taking them quite seriously yourself, Miss O'Connell."

"Are you saying that these men, whoever they are, killed my father?"

Lovelock was silent for a long moment, then: "Or, perhaps, had him killed."

Beatrice sprang up from the table. "Oh my God!"

"Calm down, Bea," Stephen said gently. He took her hand and guided her back to her seat. "Mr. Lovelock," he continued, "what do you know about Father Morton?"

"He's the priest of Saint Xavier's," Lovelock said noncommittally.

"The last time I was here, you told me not to trust him," Beatrice said, still agitated. "Is he one of your 'serious men'?"

"And what about this Duarte Institute? You must know about that," Stephen said.

"They want my father's library. Remember, I told you."

Lovelock looked at his watch. "I'm afraid I have an appointment."

"No—wait a minute, please. What is that institute, exactly?" Stephen asked.

"It's an evil place. You must stay away from it at all costs."

"Evil? In what way?"

Lovelock closed his eyes and rubbed the bridge of his nose. "Just stay away from it, that's all."

"Do you think Father Morton is involved in my father's murder?" Beatrice said.

Lovelock got up from the table and began pacing back and forth, his head lowered, as if he were deep in thought. "I don't think either of you realizes exactly what it is you're up against," he said at last. "You're dealing with extremely dangerous people."

Stephen nodded in agreement. "We're beginning to get the picture."

"No, you have no idea!" Lovelock said angrily. "You have absolutely no idea!"

Beatrice was taken aback by this flash of temper. "Why won't you tell us what you know, Mr. Lovelock?" she pleaded.

"Come on, Lovelock. What's the story with Morton and the Duarte Institute?" Stephen said. "Obviously, you know a lot more than you're letting on."

"I'll tell you this," Lovelock said, taking a deep breath in order to calm himself. "What they say they are, and what they are in fact, are two different things."

"What do they say they are?" Stephen asked.

"An institute for philosophical studies, I believe."

"And what are they really?" Beatrice said.

Lovelock hesitated. "I can't tell you any more than that," he said with some anguish. "I'm not a disinterested party. I'm sorry."

"Does that mean you're involved with them?" Stephen asked, trying to fathom Lovelock's reaction.

Lovelock glared at him.

"Mr. Lovelock, I beg of you. If they've had something to do with my father's murder, you must tell us what you know. You *must!*" Beatrice said.

"That's all I care to say," Lovelock replied coldly. "Now I must go. I have an appointment."

"Mr. Lovelock," Beatrice said, "what are you so afraid of?"

"I *am* afraid; you're right." He looked at her. "But it's not just fear, believe me. Think of your own father and how much he meant to you. Then think of me."

"What do you mean?"

"I cannot express it to you in any other way, except to say that the bonds of family are ones we can never free ourselves from, no matter how hard we try. Perhaps one day you will understand."

"So you won't help us?"

"I've helped you all I can for the moment. I've told you a great deal more than I should have."

"Come on, Stephen," Beatrice said abruptly. "Let's go." She picked up the grimoire and put it back in her purse.

As they were leaving, Lovelock stopped them. "Miss O'Connell, a word of advice. Don't let Father Morton find out you have the grimoire unless you plan to give it to him."

"Why not?"

"Because if he knows you have it, he will certainly get it from you—one way or another."

"He's not going to find out unless you tell him," Beatrice asserted.

"Me! Me tell Father Morton!" Lovelock laughed so hard he began to cough. Beatrice stared at him defiantly as he hacked away.

"Oh, forgive me, forgive me," he said, wiping tears from his eyes. He cleared his throat. "I'm sorry. It's just that the idea is so preposterous. Well, anyway," he went on, taking out a handkerchief and wiping his mouth. "Do be careful."

"Thanks. You've been a big help," Stephen said sarcastically.

Beatrice and Stephen started to walk downstairs.

Lovelock, hovering close to the door of his shop like a black shadow, called after them. "I'll do this for you. If you find out more things, and you want to check your facts, you know where to find me."

When they hit the pavement, Stephen exploded with irritation. "Who the fuck does he think he is—Deep Throat?"

"I think he's frightened, Stephen. Really frightened. And what was all that business about the bonds of family?"

"Bullshit. He's on a weird power trip. I've seen it before on stories. You interview these guys who want to make you think they know the secret of life just so they can feel important. The hell with him. We don't need him." He put his arm around her and hugged her tight. "I think we ought to go up and see this infamous Duarte Institute."

"But Lovelock told us to stay away."

"All the more reason to go."

9

EATRICE, MY DEAR, I'M SIMPLY DELIGHTED THAT you've called," Father Morton said on the telephone. "I couldn't be more pleased. When were you contemplating a visit to our little institute?"

"Well, as soon as possible," Beatrice said, eyeing Stephen through the open doorway; he was listening in on the extension in the library. "How about the day after tomorrow? No time like the present."

"Saturday? That's great," Beatrice said. "I'll drive up there with a friend of mine, and we'll see you then."

"A friend? What friend?"

"Stephen Carson, my ex-husband."

"I see." Father Morton sounded hesitant.

"Is that a problem?"

"No, no, not at all. I'm pleased he can join us. It takes about two hours to drive up. What time do you think you might arrive?"

"Oh, say, around . . ." Beatrice looked at Stephen, who held up ten fingers and then one. "Around eleven o'clock, if that's okay."

"That's lovely—in time for a little tour before lunch. When you get to Milbern, just go through the town and follow the signs. You can't miss us. And besides, everyone knows where we are, if you should get lost."

"Thank you, Father Morton."

"See you Saturday," the priest said brightly.

Beatrice hung up the phone and looked at Stephen. " '*Iacta alea est,*' " she said.

Stephen picked up Beatrice in a rented car at nine on Saturday morning, and they headed for the Taconic Parkway. Milbern turned out to be a picturesque little town surrounding a miniature park with colorful flower borders and grand old shade trees. The main street was flanked by a white clapboard church at one end and a red-brick courthouse at the other, with cheerful, well-groomed shops and houses in between. Everything seemed tranquil and ordered.

Beatrice was struck by the comforting clarity of rural life. "What a pretty place!"

They reached the end of the main street, and there, as Father Morton had said, was a small hand-painted sign: THE DUARTE INSTITUTE, with an arrow. Leaving town on a wooded country road, they followed several like signs until they reached an almost imperceptible break in the foliage.

"Slow down," Beatrice said, for the ultimate sign was not easy to see. " 'The Duarte Institute.' That's it there."

Stephen turned left into a narrow path cutting through the dense vegetation and straggly trees.

About an eighth of a mile later, the winding dirt trail became a wide, gleaming white gravel road that led to the entrance of what looked like a sprawling farm. A high wooden fence surrounded the property. Not far beyond it was a massive nineteenth-century barn, solemn against the radiant blue midmorning sky. A magnificent weather vane in the shape of a cow was perched atop its sloping copper roof, keeping vigil over the horses and cattle grazing in their separate pastures. The long open fields were surrounded by verdant woodlands, stretching to the horizon.

Beatrice and Stephen pulled up to a locked metal gate.

"Now what?" Stephen said.

"I'll go see if I can unlock it."

Just as Beatrice was about to get out of the car, the gate clicked open and swung back slowly, allowing room for them to pass.

"Electric eye," Stephen said, pointing to a small camera concealed cleverly in one of the fence posts.

Driving down through the fields into the surrounding forest once more, Beatrice and Stephen eventually found themselves traveling along more tended grounds. Tucked into the woods and along the side of the road were various weatherworn examples of the stonemason's art—low walls, fountains, benches, and small classical statues of Pan and other sylvan creatures, peeking out of the foliage here and there. They crossed over an arched stone bridge, spanning a clear little stream, drove past what appeared to be some abandoned kennels, and came upon a fork in the road. A small sign nailed to a tree read: TO THE INSTITUTE, with an arrow pointing to the left, and TO THE COTTAGES, with an arrow pointing right.

Just as Stephen was about to turn right, a figure in the distance caught Beatrice's eye.

"Whoa!" she cried. "Stop!"

Stephen jammed his foot on the brake.

"What?"

"You see that man walking over there—just beyond those trees?" She nodded in the direction of the cottages.

Stephen craned his neck in order to peer out the passenger-side window. "No," he said at last. "I don't see anything."

"He's gone now," Beatrice said, her face troubled.

"So what? It was just a man walking, wasn't it?"

"He looked like he was wearing one of those long black old-fashioned cassocks that Roman Catholic priests used to wear. What are they called?"

"A soutane, you mean?"

"Yes. That's right, a soutane."

"They still wear them in Europe sometimes. Here, too, in some of the orders."

"Quite an arresting sight—a figure like that walking in the woods," Beatrice said. "Like something out of another century."

"Well, it's nearly eleven-thirty," Stephen said, stepping on the accelerator. "Father Morton's going to wonder what the hell happened to us."

Presently, they pulled into a circular driveway and up to a huge Palladian-style villa made of limestone, shaded by giant elms and maples. Father Morton was standing in front of the grand double-door entrance, looking at his watch. As Beatrice and Stephen got out of the car, he waved and started down the wide crescent-shaped steps to greet them.

"Welcome, welcome!" he said, clasping Beatrice's hand in both his palms. His hands felt clammy.

"Hello, Father Morton. I'm sorry we're late."

"Not to worry, as they say in England. And this is your friend, Mr. . . . ?"

"Steve Carson," Stephen said, shaking hands with the portly priest.

"Mr. Carson, very nice to meet you."

"Father Morton, Stephen is my ex-husband. I don't know if I mentioned that."

"How nice that you've remained on such friendly terms," Father Morton said. "Now, if you'll both come inside, I'll take you on a little tour, and then we'll have some lunch. How does that suit you?"

"Fine," Beatrice said. Stephen nodded in agreement.

They followed Father Morton up the steps.

"Tell me, Mr. Carson—"

"Call me Steve, please."

"Thank you. Tell me, Steve, how much do you know about the institute?" Father Morton said, pausing midway up the stairs.

"Nothing much, really. Just that you want Bea to donate her dad's library here. So naturally I wanted to come up and check it out."

"Very thoughtful of you. Well, basically, we are a nondenominational institute for philosophical studies. Scholars come here from around the world to avail themselves of the materials we are fortunate enough to have at our disposal."

"What materials are those?" Stephen said with interest.

Father Morton continued on up the steps, talking as he led the way. "Over the years, we have acquired many outstanding book collections, like that of your father, Beatrice. And we keep them and care for them here in our library, which we will visit, for the benefit of visiting scholars and other interested parties—students, researchers, whomever."

He held open one of the double doors. "We call this 'The Bungalow,' " Father Morton said as they entered the foyer. "It was built in 1914 by the daughter of the man who built the original estate. We've converted it into administrative offices."

The foyer was painted white and was starkly furnished. There were no decorations except a square bronze plaque over the empty fireplace. On it was a head cast in relief, and the inscription "Inigo Duarte, 1890–1968." Father Morton escorted them to a large reception desk, behind which a pockmarked young man wearing a black suit and tie stood stiffly at attention.

"This is where our visiting scholars register," Father Morton said. "We're very high-tech now," he said, pointing to a computer. "So, for example, when the scholar is assigned a room, he fills out a card listing his main areas of interest. We feed that information into this computer, which is hooked up to a larger computer. And then we are able to supply him with a list of the books and materials that we have pertaining to his subject. It speeds everything up, you see, so that by the time he goes down to the library, he knows exactly what's available and what to ask for."

As Father Morton was speaking, Beatrice caught the eye of the young man behind the desk. She smiled at him, but he quickly looked away and continued staring straight ahead.

"How many scholars can you accommodate at one time?" Stephen asked.

"Only twenty at the moment. But we're in the process of expanding our facilities. Let's take your car, and we'll go for a quick tour of the property. Inform Central," Father Morton said to the young man behind the desk.

"That sounds very spylike, Father Morton," Beatrice said lightly.

"We have quite an elaborate security system here. Because of the value of the books and because the property is so large, we must protect ourselves."

"How big is it?" Beatrice said.

"It's over three thousand acres, in a contained area—like a little island," Father Morton replied. "It's a rather interesting story, the story of this estate. I'll tell it to you on the way."

They walked outside to the car. Stephen got behind the wheel and Father Morton took the front passenger seat; Beatrice sat in the back.

"Just go around the driveway and follow that road to the left," Father Morton said. He sat sideways, so that Beatrice could hear him as he spoke.

"This entire estate was built in the nineteenth century by a

German immigrant named Wilhelm Dieter. He invented some sort of gas valve that made him a millionaire, and he bought this property around 1880. He imported stonemasons from Italy to indulge his fantasies."

"We saw a lot of stonework coming in," Beatrice said.

"Oh, yes; he built fountains and bridges and little follies all over the property. There are root cellars underneath the ground as well. Thanks to Dieter, the town of Milbern has a large Italian community to this day, many of them descended from the original masons. Anyway, he built a number of houses on the property, along with kennels, barns, a riding stable, and several greenhouses. His daughter inherited it when he died in 1912, and she built The Bungalow—the building we were just in. Dieter, as you will see, had rather heavy-handed taste, and the daughter apparently couldn't stand living in his old house, so she had it boarded up and built her own.

"In the thirties, the daughter went bankrupt and was forced to sell the property to a Texas oilman by the name of Walters. He hardly ever used it, and it got very run-down. Then, just after the war, Inigo Duarte happened to be visiting in this area, and he heard about the estate. It was exactly what he was looking for to start his institute. Fortunately, he was able to arrange its purchase through friends who believed in his work. Of course, there have been improvements over the years. We try and keep things up to date."

Just as Father Morton said this, they passed a large satellite dish nesting in the middle of a wildflower field. Stephen glanced at Beatrice in the rearview mirror.

"And how do scholars apply to come here?" Stephen asked.

"We work only through referrals," Father Morton said firmly. "A scholar must be recommended by someone who has been here or by a member of the board. Take a right just up here, if you will."

They turned into a driveway, at the end of which was an ugly stone cottage.

"Dieter built this for the gatekeeper," Father Morton said as they stopped. "You see what I mean about his taste."

"*Tales of Hoffmann* meets Stonehenge," Beatrice said, referring to the strange house built of huge cobblestones, with ornate wooden eaves.

Father Morton chuckled. "I'll have to remember that," he said, hauling himself out of the car. "We've converted it into workrooms. Come and see."

The cottage had been gutted inside and divided into three large rooms. In the first room were several old-fashioned wood looms.

"You remember the tapestries in my office, Beatrice?" Father Morton said. "Both were woven right here."

"By whom?" she said, noting the absence of any workers.

"We have special courses for those who are interested in learning the old ways of doing things. . . . This may amuse you," he said, leading them into the second room. "We make all our own soap and candles."

Beatrice and Stephen glanced around at the large vats filled with tallow and the array of metal candle and soap molds hanging from hooks on the walls.

"Why do you bother?" Beatrice said, absently fingering some loose wicks lying on a worktable.

"So many arts and crafts get lost over time. It's such a pity. You see, the Duarte Institute is interested in preserving many forms of past knowledge, not just the knowledge that is contained in books. . . . And here is our smithy," he said, leading them into the final room. "We shoe the horses here and mend tack. We even make some rudimentary farm implements and cooking utensils, as an exercise. Many of our scholars come here to watch or to participate. They enjoy getting a small sense of what life was once like."

Beatrice bent down and picked up something that caught her eye near the cold forge.

"What sort of farm implement is this?" She held up an iron shackle attached to a chain.

Father Morton squinted in the dim light. "Oh, that's a hobble for the animals, I suppose," he said indifferently. "Let's move on, shall we? I want to show you the library before we go to lunch."

The three of them got into the car and headed down the road once more, until they reached a large clearing. There, on the right, elevated on a little hill, was a fussy Queen Anne Revival house with pointy turrets, elaborate moldings, and stained-glass windows overlooking a large formal garden, at the center of which was a round classical marble fountain spewing dainty jets of water into the air.

"This was Wilhelm Dieter's residence back in the 1880s," Father Morton said, as they pulled into the parking lot on the side of the house. "It has over fifty rooms. It is now our library."

"I see why his daughter hated it," Beatrice declared, looking up at the ersatz castle.

"Yes, it's certainly a monstrosity, but extremely useful for our purposes—all those rooms, you see. We use the old servants' rooms as cubicles for the scholars. We had quite a time restoring it," Father Morton said, as they climbed the front steps to the entrance.

The foyer of the house was wood-paneled. Another ascetic-looking man dressed in black suit and black tie sat behind a desk at the far end. Father Morton nodded to him in passing and then led Beatrice and Stephen up a flight of stairs. Each of the rooms they entered was lined from floor to ceiling with books. Some had long tables in the center and comfortable chairs for reading. Sometimes a plaque on the wall commemorated the donor of the collection on display. Other rooms were simply filled with a selection of books, all duly numbered and catalogued in the conventional Dewey decimal system. All the windows were sealed and locked.

They went up another flight of stairs.

"Here are the studies I mentioned." Father Morton pointed to a long corridor with doors on either side. "The old servants' rooms."

They walked down the hall and reached a much larger room, outfitted with rows of chairs and desks.

"And here is our scriptorium, where the scholars are allowed to examine some of the more fragile works—the ones that cannot be checked out for the night."

"Where are all these scholars?" Beatrice asked, regarding the empty room.

"Oh, around and about, I suppose."

"I thought I saw a priest walking in the woods as we drove up."

"Did you?" Father Morton said with interest.

"He looked as if he was wearing a soutane," she said.

"That's quite possible. We have visitors from all over the world."

"Priests?"

"Some," he said, leading them back down the hall.

Stephen grabbed hold of Beatrice's hand and squeezed it tight, giving her a look that warned her not to pursue that line of inquiry. They continued on in silence.

After their tour of the upstairs, Father Morton took Beatrice and Stephen down into the bowels of the basement. There, amid the pipes and the climate-control system, was an enormous black Cray computer.

"This is our main computer," Father Morton announced with

pride. "Every book, every incunabulum, folio, and fragment, is entered here." He patted the purring black machine. "Along with its history and when it was acquired."

"That's one powerful baby," Stephen said admiringly.

"Yes, well, as I said, the Duarte Institute likes to keep up with the latest technology."

Beatrice noticed a black door at the far end of the basement. A large sign on it read: DANGER—NO ADMITTANCE. "What's behind that door?" she inquired.

"Oh, machinery, the power supply," Father Morton said. "Come, please."

They walked back upstairs to the foyer. Just as they were leaving, Beatrice noticed a book in a glass case on one side of the room. "What's that?" She walked over to it.

Father Morton sidled up behind her. "Ah, that is the pride and joy of our collection. It is an original edition of the *Malleus Maleficarum—The Witches' Hammer*—a magnificent fifteenth-century work by two Dominican monks, Jakob Sprenger and Heinrich Krämer. It's the only one in the United States. Do you know it?"

"No," Beatrice said, lying, for she remembered Signor Antonelli's mentioning it to her and her father. "What is it?"

"It is the single most authoritative study of witchcraft ever written: a thorough examination of witches and their nefarious practices, as well as a practical guide to hunting them down and ridding the earth of them." The cleric's face grew flushed; he spoke with unmistakable reverence.

Beatrice read aloud the small gold plaque on the front of the case. " 'The *Malleus Maleficarum* . . . Gift of Desmond Crowley.'" She tried to catch Stephen's eye, but he was focused on the case and its contents. "Who's Desmond Crowley?" she asked Father Morton.

"He is a member of our board of directors, a very great book collector and scholar. Your father's collection—if you decide it should have a home here—would occupy the room next to Mr. Crowley's collection upstairs. That is not, if I may say so, undistinguished company."

Father Morton took Beatrice and Stephen to lunch in a pristine white dining room in the back of The Bungalow. A large picture window framed a dramatic view of sloping hills and a distant valley of pines. The three of them dined alone at a long refectory table;

seated on uncomfortable wooden benches, they were served by a grim-looking woman in a severe black dress.

"And what, exactly, do you do, Stephen?" Father Morton said, helping himself to a hefty portion of boiled beef and cabbage.

"I'm a writer," Stephen said.

Father Morton stiffened slightly. "A reporter?"

"Used to be. Now I write books."

Father Morton seemed relieved. "Would I know any of them?"

"Probably not, unless you're interested in the Kurds or the Afghans or the Middle East."

"He's being extremely modest, Father Morton. He's a marvelous writer. He won a National Book Award."

"Congratulations. Sounds fascinating. Politics is not my field, exactly, but I shall look out for your work. . . . I must say, we don't encourage publicity."

"Oh? Why not? This is a fascinating place," Stephen said.

"Reporters have a way of twisting facts—pardon me for saying so. There was a man from the *New York Times* up here a few months ago who wanted to do a story on us. I'm afraid we gave him short shrift. We are a scholarly institution, and we don't think it's necessary for the world to know about us—not yet, at any rate."

Beatrice saw Stephen's eyes light up. "Who pays for all this?" she asked.

"Private contributions. We have a few extremely generous benefactors, I'm pleased to say—people who feel that the preservation of the past's great knowledge through books is man's key to understanding the future."

"And woman's," Beatrice said sweetly.

"Of course," Father Morton said, acknowledging her with a courtly nod.

They continued to chat amicably, their voices reverberating in the oak-floored room. The priest punctuated his worldly conversation with amusing literary and ecclesiastical anecdotes, pointedly steering clear of any more talk on the institute. Nevertheless, halfway through the spartan meal, Beatrice began to feel uneasy in the bleak surroundings, and she longed for the lunch to end.

"I understand your house is on the market," Father Morton said, as the waitress passed a dessert of cut fruit in a glass bowl.

"Yes. How did you know?" Beatrice said, picking out some orange and grapefruit slices.

"I think I saw an advertisement for it in some magazine or other. I hope that means we may have a decision about your father's library shortly?"

"Oh, well, I'm working on it." She gave him a tepid smile.

"The grimoire, I take it, has never turned up?"

"No," she said, glancing surreptitiously at Stephen. "Tell me, Father, do you have any grimoires up here?"

"Oh, no, certainly not. . . . Although we almost acquired a collection of witchcraft once, but the board members felt it wasn't a useful addition to our canon. It tends to attract the wrong sorts of people, you know."

After lunch, Father Morton escorted them to their car. "It feels like rain," he said, as they were getting in.

"Yes," Beatrice said, looking up at the gathering clouds.

"Well—drive carefully. And thank you for coming up to see us," Father Morton said. "I hope we've answered some of your questions and that you'll consider us seriously."

"Thank you for having us. It's been very enlightening," Beatrice said, shaking his hand.

As soon as they had driven off the property, Beatrice sat back and let out a sigh of relief. "That's quite a little spread they have there. There's something really sinister about it, don't you think?"

"Bea, he handed it to me. God bless him, he handed it to me," Stephen said excitedly.

"What are you talking about?"

"You remember I said someone had told me about the Duarte Institute and I couldn't think who it was?"

"Yeah?"

"The reporter from the *Times* trying to do a story on them that Father Morton mentioned at lunch? That's my friend Cap Goldman. He's the religion editor. We had dinner right before I left for South America, and he said something about them in passing. That's where I heard about them."

"Let's go see him," Beatrice said, lighting two cigarettes and handing one to Stephen.

"You bet we will. . . . Do you realize"—Stephen took a deep drag—"that a Cray is one of the most powerful computers in the world? You could store a hundred thousand books on that thing and still have plenty of room for a complete dossier on everyone in the country."

"So what do they need it for? Is that what you're saying?"

"That's what I'm saying."

"Yeah, and where are all these scholars he was talking about? We hardly saw a soul in that whole place. . . . Oh, and how about that so-called farm implement?" Beatrice said derisively. "Those cows must have pretty dainty ankles. . . . What a day!"

"Well, I'm glad we went up there. Listen, if they are on the level, maybe your father's library would be well served. It's a pretty impressive place. Well organized."

"Stephen, they're *not* on the level. You can feel it."

"Yeah, you can. I must say, he's a helluva salesman, old Father Morton. I bet Cap will have an interesting take on it. I'll call him to-night. . . . So, interesting day," he said, turning to her. "We got through it. I held your hand. It's over."

"No, Stephen." Beatrice sighed uneasily, staring out the car window. "I have a feeling it's just beginning."

10

TEPHEN PICKED UP THE HOUSE PHONE IN THE lobby of the *New York Times*'s executive offices and dialed Cap Goldman's extension.

"Cap—it's Steve Carson. I'm down here with Beatrice O'Connell. Can we come up?"

"Sure. Put the guard on."

The security guard murmured something into the phone and hung up. He handed Beatrice and Stephen blue tin identity badges and directed them to a bank of elevators. Beatrice affixed the little button to the collar of her dress.

They rode up to the newsroom on the third floor. Cap Goldman, a beefy, bespectacled man in bow tie and suspenders, his shirtsleeves rolled up, was sitting at the computer in his cubicle.

"Hey, Steve," he said in a harried voice, rising to greet them. "How're you?"

"Good. You?"

"Oh, you know. Plugging along. Trying to manage a byline and a life at the same time. What's up?"

"I'd like you to meet Beatrice O'Connell. I think you guys met once when we were married."

"I didn't know we'd ever been married, Steve. Oh, that's right—you proposed and I declined," Cap said, grinning. "Sorry, dumb joke." He shook Beatrice's hand. "Pleased to meet you. . . . Sit, sit."

Stephen pulled up some swivel chairs from a neighboring cubicle, and he and Beatrice sat down.

"Listen, I heard about your dad, and I'm very sorry," Cap said.

"Thank you."

"This is what happens when there's anarchy in the world, right?" He pointed to his desk, littered with clippings bearing such headlines as: "Pope's Sex Stand Has 'Em Hot & Bothered"; "Catholics Torn on Strict New Edict"; "Wake-up Call: The Religious Right"; "Rattling the Pope's Roost"; "Cardinal Vows to Clean Up Dissidents"; "Christian Conservatives Counting Hundreds of Gains in Local Votes." A *Time* magazine cover proclaimed: "God and Women: A Second Reformation Sweeps Christianity."

"So what can I do for you?" Cap said, punching the Save key on his computer with a flourish. "I'm on deadline, so I'm afraid we gotta make it quick."

"The Duarte Institute, Cap," Stephen said. "You were doing a story on it."

"Oh, them. Jesus." He took off his glasses and rubbed the bridge of his nose.

"What do you mean?" Stephen said.

"Tough story."

"In what way?"

"There's something going on up there, but I can't figure out quite what it is."

"Can you tell us what you know about it?" Stephen said.

"Let me ask you a question first. Why are you interested?"

"The pastor of Saint Xavier's wants me to donate my father's library to it," Beatrice said.

"Morton?"

"Yes."

"Figures. He's on the board. Well, they've got one hell of a spread up there."

"You can say that again. We were up there visiting yesterday," Beatrice said.

"You too?" Cap asked Stephen.

"Yeah; why?"

"I hope you didn't tell them what you used to do for a living. They're totally paranoid about reporters. Not that paranoia is bad. Paranoids are the only people who notice anything these days."

"I mentioned it."

"I'd like to have seen Morton's face." Cap laughed. "Seriously, you two: if I were you, I'd steer clear."

Beatrice crossed her legs and hunched over. She glanced at Stephen.

"Why, Cap?" Stephen said, fiddling with a pen on the desk. "What's the scoop?"

"Okay. Look, I've been working on this story off and on for about six months. It's a bitch. There's a lot of rumors flying around, but I can't pin anything down. They bill themselves as an educational and charitable society—an Institute for Philosophical Studies, quote, unquote. They're named after a guy called Inigo Duarte—I'll get to him later. That property they have up in Milbern is worth a fortune. Where are they getting the money? It sure ain't from weaving tapestries and making soap."

"They say they have big contributors who are interested in preserving books or some such bullshit," Stephen said.

"Father Morton told me people from all over the world go there to study," Beatrice added.

"Study *what* is the question. That's what I'm trying to find out," Cap replied. "And they're so goddamn secretive."

"Not so secretive. He invited me up there, after all," Beatrice said.

"Sure. You have something they want. That collection of your dad's is probably worth a fortune. They've got books up the wazoo. But I guarantee you, you didn't see anything they didn't want you to see. They pretend it's fucking Colonial Williamsburg, but if you ask me, it's closer to Salem."

"Why do you say that?" Beatrice asked, intrigued.

"A hunch—well, a little more than a hunch. I have a source who's been making some interesting observations. It's complicated and I just can't get into the whole thing right now, but it's scary. It's in the file."

"So who's Duarte?" Stephen asked.

"He's a fascinating character. He was from a very humble family in Spain. Born around 1900. He became a priest, then a kind of éminence grise, very close to Pius XII. Only a handful of people ever knew about him."

"He was a priest?" Beatrice said. "I thought they were supposed to be nondenominational."

"Inconsistency number nine hundred and eighty-four," Cap said. "These guys are something else."

"Remember how much my father loathed Pope Pius?" Beatrice said to Stephen. "He always said if that coward had threatened to excommunicate any Catholic who supported the Nazis, there wouldn't have been a war. I think that was when he turned off religion completely."

"Okay, so Duarte founded this very right-wing secret society within the Church in the late twenties—something called Defensores Fidei—"

"Shit!" Stephen cried, slamming his hand on the desk. "You're fucking kidding!"

Other occupants of the newsroom looked around briefly, then went back to their work.

"Stephen ... ," Beatrice said, startled by his reaction. "Calm down."

"That's why I mentioned them to you, Steve. Because you were going to South America."

"Defensores Fidei. Jesus!"

"I take it you found out what I was talking about," Cap said.

"I sure as hell did."

"Wait just a second, you two," Beatrice exclaimed. "In Father Morton's outer office, he's got a carved ivory Madonna with 'Defensores Fidei' written underneath it. I noticed it when I was waiting to see him. I was going to ask him what it meant, and I forgot. So what's Defensores Fidei?"

"It means Defenders of the Faith. And Father Morton, the old devil, is involved in it up to his eyeballs, if you want my opinion," Cap said. "What he is and what he says he is—two different things. I think the guy's a hard-nosed reactionary. To the right of Genghis Khan."

"Who are these people?" Beatrice asked.

"I'll explain later, Bea," Stephen said. "Cap, exactly what did you find out about them?"

"A whole bunch of stuff. We're talking tip of the iceberg here.

Unfortunately, I can't go into it right now: as I said, I'm on deadline. I would be damn wary of the Duarte Institute, though. I'm convinced it's a cover, but I can't prove it."

"When's the story coming out?"

"I don't think ever. I'm having trouble writing it, because I can't get the facts. Morton's got friends in high places."

"Cap, can I see your notes?"

"Sure. Let me see if I can dig them up. They're at home. Also, I'm going to send you a book that will interest you."

"What book?" Beatrice said.

"It's a lulu, believe me. It defies description. I'm not going to even attempt to tell you about it. I'll send it to you, you read it, and we'll discuss it afterward, okay?"

"It's not a grimoire, is it?" Beatrice asked.

"No; it's a historical document. They sell facsimiles of it up at the institute, because they have one of the original copies on display."

"The *Malleus Maleficarum!*" Beatrice said.

"That's it," Cap said.

"We saw it when we were up there. It's in a display case."

"Oh, and are they proud of it. But I've read it, and all I can say is fasten your seat belt," Cap assured them.

"God, I can't wait to see it," Beatrice said.

"I'm surprised they didn't try to foist a copy on you. Although it's probably smart of them, because after you read it, you ain't donating nothing to this place—not even comic books."

"Now you've really got me curious," Beatrice said. "What's in it?"

"It is literally indescribable," Cap said. "You'll see what I mean. Look, I'm going away tomorrow for a couple of weeks' vacation. I'll try to get everything to you before I go, Steve, but if not, we'll have a drink when I get back, and I'll give the stuff to you then."

"Try to get it to me now, Cap. This is urgent. Here're my address and my fax number." Stephen scrawled the numbers on a piece of paper.

"Listen, you guys, I gotta get back to work. Duty calls." Cap escorted them to the elevators. "If you find out anything I can use, will you let me know?"

"You bet," Stephen said.

· · ·

"So what's Defensores Fidei?" Beatrice said as she and Stephen walked along Forty-third Street.

"It's a very scary secret society. Want an ice?"

"Sure."

Stephen stopped at a little stand near the curb and ordered two raspberry ices. They watched as the vendor poured sticky red syrup over a ball of crushed ice in a paper cup.

"I remembered your favorite flavor, right?" Stephen said, handing Beatrice her treat.

"Right. So how do you know about them?" She licked the refreshing concoction as they strolled up Eighth Avenue.

"My drug-dealer book—the one I'm working on. One of my informants in Chile told me about a Jesuit mission they wiped out down there. Then they got the head of the national police to kill the investigation."

"Are you sure?"

"Oh, yeah. This guy's a real source. They're all tied in with the drug trade. That's how they get some of their money."

"So the big contributors to the Duarte Institute may be drug dealers?"

"It's possible."

"Why would they bother to wipe out a Jesuit mission?"

"Eliminating the competition. It's a real ecclesiastical power struggle down there. I like the Jesuits—some of them, anyway. They can be liberal thinkers—miles too liberal for Defensores Fidei."

"If everybody knows this . . ."

"No proof. And lots and lots of fear. These guys are fucking princes of darkness—about as close to the Inquisition as you can get in modern times."

"Stephen, you think the world is one big conspiracy, don't you?"

"It is." He gobbled down his ice in three swallows, crumpled the cup, and threw it into the gutter.

"Litterbug," she said, nudging him.

"They hate women, gays, minorities, activists—basically anyone who doesn't agree with the sovereignty of a Catholic, white, male-dominated world. They're 'Today the church, tomorrow the world' types. Lots of fun."

"So what do they want?"

"My informant says they want the world to go back to the fifteenth century. Since they operate a lot in South America, I suspect they want to control governments and possibly some drug trade through the Church. Anyway, that's part of what I'm working on. Small-world department."

"And what does the Church say about that?"

"Are you kidding? These guys aren't in the Church. I mean, they say they are, but they're fanatics. The Church is an excuse for their craziness. I wonder if the Pope even knows they exist. I doubt it. Like all secret societies, they usually operate under a cover."

"You mean like the Duarte Institute."

"Well, apparently so."

"Stephen, the United States isn't a third-world Catholic country. What do you think they're planning to do here?"

"As Cap said, no one really knows what they're up to."

"How'd you find out so much?"

"I didn't find out so much; that's just the point. But they must be getting bigger, and that's why we're beginning to hear more about them. This whole deal with the Duarte Institute is fascinating. One thing's for sure—it's a sticky web, and it's growing."

"Stephen? Look at this." Beatrice stopped in front of one of the seedy pornographic cinemas along the avenue. Laughing, she pointed to a big color poster of a movie entitled *The Witches of Dick's Wick*. Three buxom young women, dressed in black lingerie and witches' hats, were coiled around a virile, vacant-looking young man wearing only a jacket, shirt, and tie. He had an enormous erection, most of which was hidden by the thatch of an upside-down broom.

"You think John Updike knows about this?" she said.

Stephen guffawed. "Maybe we should go inside and do a review for him."

"You want to?" She eyed him.

"What? See a pornographic movie?"

"Yeah."

"Not particularly."

"Why not?"

"I don't know. They don't interest me that much."

"I'd like to."

"Come on, Bea, it's the middle of the day."

"So what? It looks amusing."

"No. Come on, let's go. Those places are too raunchy—not to mention unsanitary."

"That kind of sex really threatens you, doesn't it?"

"What? Group sex on a broom? That's not sex. That's sick."

"I'm talking about raw fantasy. That's all that is."

"Talk about demeaning to women . . ."

"I want to see this movie, Stephen. And I want to see it with you. Call it research."

Exasperated, Stephen shoved his hand in his pocket and pulled out a twenty-dollar bill.

"Two, please," he said to the cashier.

"Show's already started," the man said in a monotone.

"Good. I hope it's nearly over."

Stephen swiped up the two tickets, grabbed hold of Beatrice's hand, and marched inside. Several male patrons were scattered throughout the theater—no women, no couples. A rancid odor permeated the atmosphere, and many of the seats were broken and fraying at the seams.

"Notice they don't sell popcorn," Stephen said as they sat down.

The grainy-looking, amateurishly shot movie consisted mainly of women dressed as witches, wearing heavy, macabre makeup, going down on a hapless young man with an extraordinarily oversized penis. Intermittently, the women fondled one another—sucking each other's breasts and licking each other between the legs—all for his delectation. Though perpetually aroused, the young man seemed curiously bored by this display.

"Great plot line," Stephen said after a time, yawning conspicuously.

Beatrice sat mesmerized by the hard-core sex on the screen, feeling her wolf stirring inside her as she watched the passionless activity.

"Okay, I'm ready to go," she said before the movie was finished.

"I feel like I need a bath," Stephen announced, as they walked back out into the daylight.

"Take me to your apartment, Stephen. I need you to make love to me."

Stephen's studio apartment, on West Seventy-third Street, was just as Beatrice remembered it—bare-floored, sparsely furnished, cluttered with books, boxes of files, computer, laser printer, fax machine, and eccentric souvenirs he'd acquired on his travels. It was obviously the home of an itinerant writer. Stephen rinsed out a couple of glasses from the pile of dirty dishes in the sink and started to open a bottle of white wine.

Before he could finish, Beatrice came up behind him and started fondling his penis through his jeans. She unbuckled his belt and zipped down his fly. Stephen turned around and faced her, still holding the bottle of wine. Beatrice fell to her knees, yanked his pants down, and fished for his erect member, which she pulled out and began sucking hard, using her right hand to massage the shaft.

Stephen gazed down at her in utter astonishment. "Bea. What are you doing?"

She stopped and looked up at him. "What do you think? . . . Relax," she ordered, continuing to suck his cock.

"Oh God, baby . . ." He put down the bottle of wine and grabbed Beatrice's hair with both hands, forcing his penis deeper into her mouth. After a time, he pulled her to her feet. In taking off his jeans and Jockey shorts, he tripped slightly, which made Beatrice giggle like a schoolgirl. He abandoned the clothes in a heap on the floor, led her over to the bed, and threw her down, falling on top of her. They began to kiss with growing fury. Lust coiled around them, locking them together in a writhing dance. Then Beatrice suddenly stopped moving.

"What's the matter?"

"You mind if I take off my clothes?" she said playfully.

"I'll take them off."

Stephen undressed her. He unhooked her bra and slid her panties down her long, fleshy legs. She lay back on the bed as he flicked his tongue around her nipples, gently tugging at them with his fingers.

"You like that?" he said.

"Suck on them, baby . . . bite them." She groaned with pleasure.

Unable to hide his amazement, Stephen obeyed, tentatively at first.

"Harder," Beatrice commanded him.

After a time, Beatrice pulled away and stretched out like an odalisque, beckoning to him coquettishly with her index finger. He stared at her naked body.

"God, you're beautiful," he whispered.

"I'm a slut and a witch."

"Bea?" he said, disconcerted. "Is this you?"

"Use me. Just use me."

He slid on top of her and they began making love, moving together in a wild, joyous current that, for a brief moment, cut through the turbulent sea of their past to the exuberance of the shared moment. But the more Beatrice tried to break free of her troubled history with Stephen and tap into the well of deep feeling that existed between them, the more sorrow and frustration engulfed her. She found herself incapable of experiencing the ecstasy of pure lust she had felt with Luis Diaz. Despite all Stephen's efforts, she could not reach a climax. She pretended to, however, and pleased that he had been able to satisfy her, Stephen finally had an orgasm, after which he fell asleep, holding her in his arms.

Some time later, Stephen awoke. Beatrice was staring out the window, smoking a cigarette.

"What's the matter, honey?" he asked.

"Nothing."

"What? Come on."

"I want to love you, Stephen. I really do."

"Don't you love me?"

"I don't know."

"You just acted as if you did."

"Did I?" she said despondently.

"You came, didn't you?"

"Yeah, sure," she lied.

"Bea, I gotta tell you something. . . . You're much wilder than you ever were, you know."

"Yeah, I know," she said, dropping the cigarette into her wineglass.

"It's very exciting for me, Bea."

"Is it?"

"That was always one of the problems with our marriage, as far as I was concerned."

"What?"

"I never felt you really enjoyed sex."

"So you said. . . . Well, maybe I didn't. Maybe I was just like my mother."

"Your mother didn't enjoy sex?"

"I don't think so. I think she was threatened by it."

"You used to be. But not anymore."

"I'm not sure I know what sex is, actually."

"What do you mean?" Stephen asked, perplexed.

"I think I'm a little compartmentalized."

"What's that supposed to mean?"

"I'm not sure," she said. "I want to feel a certain way with you in bed, but because I know you and I like you, it's, uh, difficult." She got up and started wandering aimlessly around the room, searching for her underwear.

"How do you want to feel with me?"

"Carried away, transported," she said, putting on her underpants.

"And you don't?"

"Yeah, sort of," she said.

"So the earth did not move for you too, I guess," Stephen said petulantly.

"Don't get grumpy. I'm just trying to be honest with you so we can work things out. Be patient with me, okay?"

"Okay," he said, halfheartedly.

Beatrice put on her bra and sat down on the bed. They were silent.

"God, I'm just remembering my poor father," Beatrice said after a time. "He looked so old and frail and lonely, walking down that hall all alone after we had our fight. I wanted to call out to him and tell him I loved him, but something stopped me. Some horrible, perverse, self-righteous streak just stopped me dead. . . . It was the last time I ever saw him alive."

"It doesn't matter."

"But it does, Stephen, it *does*."

"No. He loved you, and you loved him. And he knew it."

"I miss him."

"Of course you do."

"I'm thinking about the baby too. Maybe I wouldn't have been such a great mother, though."

"It's not too late to find out," Stephen said.

"Sometimes I think I'm moving backward. I should have had the feelings I have now when I was a teenager. Now I should be more mature."

"What does that mean?"

"Oh, I don't know . . . better able to get those currents of desire and affection together. I wonder what would have happened if you hadn't met that girl. Would we have wound up like my parents, in an arid marriage, with a child? . . . Who knows?"

"Bea, I'd give anything to undo what I did to you. But I can't . . . I can't." Stephen's eyes grew moist.

"I'm sorry," Beatrice said, reaching out to comfort him. "I shouldn't bring it up all the time."

"No—you have a right."

"Stephen, I am so damn confused," she said, standing again. "I don't know—I have these tremendous feelings of loss, and then there are all these other feelings too."

"What other feelings?" he said, looking concerned.

"I don't know what they are or where they're coming from. But I guess I'm not the girl I once was."

"Yes, you are. You're just more interested in sex than you were."

"No, it's deeper than that. I think it has to do with being a woman. What it means. What it really means. I can't figure it out yet."

"I don't know what to say, Bea."

"Don't say anything. Just let me experience this thing, whatever it is. And be there for me."

"I am. I am."

Once more they lapsed into silence.

"So am I as good as he was?" Stephen said finally.

"Who?"

"Diaz."

Beatrice looked at him, amazed. "What makes you ask that?"

"I want to know," he said simply.

"It's always better when there's feeling, I suppose," she said noncommittally.

"You're not answering my question."

"It's different with you."

"Shit. So I'm not," he said, his pride wounded.

"It's different with you. And it's good, okay? Can we just leave it at that?"

"I guess we'll have to." He sighed. He paused for a long time. "Is my cock as big as his?"

"Stephen, I don't believe you're asking me that."

"Is it?"

"Is that what all men want to know? I mean, is that the bottom line?"

"No, it's just a matter of interest."

"Why is that so important? Because, in fact, it shouldn't be."

"Just answer the question."

"No."

"No, my cock is not as big as his, or no, you won't answer the question?"

"No, I won't answer the question, because size has nothing to do with anything."

"Oh, are you becoming the expert on this now? We've done a lot of research, have we?"

"It's none of your business," she said, laughing.

" 'Fess up, Bea. You were more attracted to this guy Diaz than you are to me, right?"

"You're so paranoid. It was different with him, that's all." She shrugged.

"Don't give me that. Hey—I know why you wanted to go to that sleazy movie today. You had to go so you could get turned on in order to sleep with me."

"That's not true."

"Listen, baby, you can't fool me. I've been there."

"Have you really?" she asked with interest.

"Damn right I have. I'll tell you something—we're both mongrels, Bea. But you seem to have caught up and passed me somewhere along the line."

"Does that make you mad?"

He considered. "I have to get used to it, I guess."

"God, it's almost dark outside," Beatrice said, anxious to change the subject. "What time is it?"

Stephen turned the digital clock radio on his night table around. "Nearly seven."

"Stephen, tell me something. Was I completely passive before?"

"Not completely. But you weren't anything like you are now. Sex didn't really interest you, I don't think."

"That's funny," she said dully. "Want some wine?"

"Sure."

Beatrice uncorked the bottle, poured the wine, and handed Stephen a glass. "I wonder what this bed would say if it could talk."

"That you're the hottest subject around," he said. "Cheers."

Beatrice propped up some pillows and lay down next to Stephen, nursing her drink. "I've been thinking about Lovelock," she said. "I wonder if he isn't mixed up in witchcraft in some way."

"Yeah. I was wondering that myself as we left."

"Do you think he might be a male witch?"

"Lovelock the warlock, you mean? He could be. Why not? He owns an occult bookstore. Who do you think buys that shit, after all? God knows he comes into contact with them."

"Do you think he really believes in black magic?"

"On some level, sure. If he didn't, he'd be sort of like a teetotaling wine merchant." Stephen chuckled.

"I like the idea of a former Jesuit being a witch, don't you? It has a nice symmetry to it. Are all witches bad, I wonder?"

"You are."

"Shut up," she said affectionately.

"He pissed me off, but he did say some interesting things. What the hell *was* Pope Pius XII doing with a grimoire?"

"And the fact that he thinks the Vatican has or had a collection of black magic."

"Bea . . . ? Do you realize how many years it's been since we made love?" he said, nuzzling up against her.

"Hmm," she replied, evidently uninterested.

"Okay!" Stephen said decisively. "Fuck romance. Time for action." He got up and put on a bathrobe. "We're going to treat this like a story. Come on over here."

Stephen sat down on the swivel chair in front of his desk, turned on his computer, and inserted a disk. A blue screen lit up. Beatrice walked over and stood behind him, watching as she sipped her wine.

"We're going to create a file and put all the information we have on it," Stephen said, turning toward her. "What do you want to call it?"

Beatrice thought. "What about 'Black Magic'?"

"Why not?" he said, pecking at the keyboard.

The words BLACK MAGIC appeared in white at the top of the screen.

"So right now, what we're going to do is put down a bunch of headings. Let's see—we have O'Connell, grimoire, Antonelli, Lovelock, Father Morton, the Duarte Institute."

Stephen typed in the names in capital letters on separate lines, leaving a large space under each one.

"You know the name of the guy who sent your father the grimoire?" he said.

"I have his letter in the grimoire," she said. "I'll get it."

"You're carrying it around with you?"

"I didn't want to leave it in the house."

Beatrice took the book out of her purse and extracted the letter.

"Schroeder," she said, reading the letterhead. "His address and telephone number are here too."

"Schroeder." Stephen added the name to the list.

"It's hard to believe people may have been killed for this little monster," she said, sitting down with Stephen in front of the computer. "I feel like it's going to fly out of my hand or something. What are we going to do with it?"

"Give it here. Hang on to the letter, though."

She handed the book to him, and he slipped it into the bottom tray of his printer, under the legal-size pages he never used.

"Will it be safe there?"

"Safe enough," he said.

"Now what?" Beatrice said.

"Now we do a kind of shorthand, stream-of-consciousness thing under each heading. For example. We take the heading 'Grimoire,' and under it we put: 'Legend in occult trade. Lovelock info: said to contain spell to raise dead and/or map for Knights Templar treasure. Belonged to Pius XII? Part of occult collection once belonging to Vatican? Lost during WWII. Sent Dr. O'Connell by Schroeder, former patient. Related to O'Connell's death? Interested parties: Antonelli— says he deals for private client. Who? Father Morton? Other? . . . ' "

Stephen continued typing. She drew up a chair and supplied him with relevant information about each subject.

"Under 'Father Morton' put 'Defensores Fidei,' 'Lavish offices,' and 'Wants to see grimoire,' " she said.

"Why 'Lavish offices'?"

"I don't know. You said this was stream-of-consciousness. Put 'Medieval gauntlet on desk.' "

"He has a medieval gauntlet on his desk?"

"Yes; it's quite striking."

"Sounds it," he said, adding her observations to the list.

They went through each category, bouncing ideas and impressions off each other. When they'd finished, Stephen saved the file and printed two copies. He handed one to Beatrice, who studied it carefully.

"You see," Stephen said, pointing out the paucity of information under the headings "Duarte Institute" and "Schroeder." "Now we know where we have to concentrate our efforts."

"Who's going to check them out?"

"We are. We're going to check out the Duarte Institute right now."

"How?" Beatrice said, perplexed.

"Watch me." Stephen reached up and picked out a directory from the shelf over the computer. "Foundations . . . Foundations," he murmured, as he searched through the thick paperback catalogue. "Ah, here it is."

"What?"

"This is a database of tax-exempt foundations. I'm a database junkie. I subscribe to several of these services." He punched in a telephone number.

The computer screen blinked as Stephen fed it his password, "K008QBB." After a few seconds, the words "What service do you require?" appeared on the monitor. Stephen typed in: "Tax exempt educational foundations." The screen registered the information by blinking again. He then typed in the words "Duarte Institute, Milbern, NY."

Another few seconds passed. Then white lines of text started scrolling across the blue field. Beatrice leaned closer to the screen.

"Oh my God!" she whispered, looking at the seven-man board of directors.

"Yup," Stephen said. "Your pals Father Morton *and* Giuseppe Antonelli, right at the top of the list. But look at those other names, will you? Pretty amazing, huh?"

"What do you mean?"

"Bart Winslow, the chairman of Fidelity Bank. Chuck Kraus, the congressman. George Cahill, the senior partner of Keegan and Goddard, the law firm. Phil Burgoyne, the right-wing talk-show host. And Desmond Crowley, the guy who donated the book. I'll tell you one thing, though," Stephen said, leaning back in his chair. "This is some heavy-duty board for such an obscure little institute. And what a strange collection of people to be drawn together. It's without doubt one of the—shall we say—most eclectic boards I've ever seen."

"What do you make of it?"

"I don't make anything of it yet. I'd like to know who this guy Desmond Crowley is."

"Well, you remember Father Morton said he's a scholar and a book collector. He donated the *Malleus Maleficarum* to the institute."

"Who he really is, I mean. What's he doing in such august company?"

"Can you find out?"

"I intend to. . . . Now, let's see." He continued to study the data. "It was incorporated in 1966 in Milbern. Here's a brief description of its purpose." Stephen read aloud: " 'An institution dedicated to all branches of philosophical studies—metaphyics, logic, epistemology, aesthetics—but particularly as applied to the branch of ethics." He paused. "Ethics, eh? Whose ethics, I wonder?" He went on. "Then it's all pretty standard stuff. . . . I better go out and see this guy Schroeder."

"Why you?"

"It might be dangerous. We don't really know anything about him."

"We know he was my father's patient."

"Yes, but we don't know anything else. And he sent your father a very strange book."

Beatrice thought for a moment. "I want to go."

"Okay. You can come along."

"No. I want to go alone."

"I won't let you."

"Look, Stephen, I'm very grateful that you're helping me, but I want to do this by myself. I have my reasons."

Stephen looked at her quizzically. "I don't think it's a good idea, Bea."

"I'm sorry, but I don't care what you think. You can direct me. I'll take your advice on certain things. But I want to remain independent as much as possible."

"Okay," Stephen conceded. "If that's the way you want it."

"That's the way I want it," she said firmly. "I could go out there tomorrow. I'm going to call him." She started to get up.

"Wait a minute." Stephen grabbed her.

"What?"

"I want to make love with you again."

"We just made love," she said. "I want to call Schroeder."

"You have time. It's one hour earlier in Oklahoma."

"What's that got to do with it?"

"I feel something coming between us, that's all," he said, directing her hand to his stiff cock.

Beatrice's eyes widened. "Stephen, you're amazing. One might think you were only nineteen."

"I'm not, but my cock is." He grinned. "That's the trouble with cocks. They stay forever young."

"You mean forever immature, don't you?"

He pulled her up and guided her over to the bed. "I'm going to make you forget this fucking guy Diaz," he said. "Then you can call Schroeder."

11

URING THE FLIGHT TO OKLAHOMA CITY, Beatrice thought about Stephen and Luis Diaz. She had no doubt that her familiarity with Stephen made her passion for him less intense. Like an addict, she now craved the pure drug of lust, untempered by tenderness or history—the kind of passion she had experienced with Diaz.

However, Beatrice was grateful to have Stephen spurring her on and directing her efforts. He was renowned for tenacity as well as his talent for ferreting out a good story, and his compulsion as a writer to dig deeper and harder had led him to rich soil beneath old, raked-over ground on many occasions. She admired his bird dog instinct for gathering intelligence and thought that even his slight paranoia, which slanted his view of the world toward cover-ups and conspiracies, could be useful to her now in the matter of her father's murder: this matter was becoming her preoccupation, her obsession; a malarial fever, raging, then abating, then raging again, a constant buzz in her system—like her craving for Diaz.

But there was something else brewing as well. With the excep-

tion of her marriage, where she had taken a great emotional risk and
lost, Beatrice had been content to stay in the background, not only
by her choice of a job but also by the sedate life she had led. Existence seemed less troublesome and less dangerous that way. Now
she felt a pearl of courage forming inside her, nurtured not only by
her fury over her father's murder but by her own sexual awakening.
She knew that pearl was the nucleus of real power.

After a brief stopover in Dallas, the plane landed in Oklahoma
City at twelve-thirty, slightly ahead of schedule. There were no taxis
at the airport, but Beatrice found a car service to take her to her destination. She made arrangements with the driver to deliver her to
Mr. Schroeder's house and pick her up there again at two-thirty, to
return to the airport in time for a connecting flight back to New
York.

It was a gray, sultry day. The black car made its way out of the
airport toward the city. Beatrice settled back on the warm vinyl up-
holstery and gazed aimlessly out the window.

"What parts are ya from?" the driver asked her after a time.

"New York."

"City?"

"Yes."

"Never been there. Wanta go, though. M'wife's scared to. She
thinks we'll get killed." He laughed. "I keep tellin' her don't believe everythin' you read. Whadda you think? Think we should go?"

"Yes, why not?" Beatrice replied absently, for she was hardly listening.

"Folks get killed 'round here often enough. But that doesn't
seem to bother her none. A minister shot his wife and kids over in
Enid just the other day. I guess the God business isn't goin' so well
these days." He snickered.

The driver rattled on. Beatrice paid him little attention. She
continued to stare out the car window, intrigued by the flat, jangly
landscape of neon signs, fast-food chains, gas stations, movie com-
plexes, furniture marts, and shopping malls. She wondered where all
the students of urban planning went after they got their degrees.
Clearly, it wasn't where they were most needed, she thought with
some amusement.

The car gradually worked its way through the long, dismal
blocks of commercial enterprise to a residential area. Here, at last,
were quiet, tree-lined streets and neat, patio-backed houses with

their all-weather barbecue grills, flower-bordered driveways, and tidy aprons of lawn. The driver slowed down for a group of children who were running and giggling as they took turns dousing one another with a garden hose. Here, Beatrice thought, was an innocent version of inner-city life, where kids played in front of the homeless on drug-infested streets, cooling themselves down with water from fire hydrants.

"This here's Eighteenth Street," the driver announced. "What address did you say?" He squinted at the sometimes obscured numbers on the houses.

Beatrice rechecked her piece of paper. "It's 3141."

"There's 3137. . . . Should be coming up."

Beatrice spotted *3141* in slanted gold numbers on the side of a black mailbox up ahead. Beneath it, just before one of the uniform driveways, a white sign was struck upright in the ground. The name SCHROEDER appeared in neat black capital letters surrounded by a small scene of flying ducks and a lone hunter aiming his gun at them.

"There it is," she called.

They pulled into the driveway, and Beatrice got out of the car. "Wait one second, please."

She climbed a small flight of slate steps, glancing at the American flag planted to the right of the front door. There was no doorbell. She was about to lift the brass eagle knocker, when the door opened. A man with white crew-cut hair and a ruddy complexion, built like a fireplug, stood very erect just inside the entrance, with a military bearing that made him look taller than he was. He wore cowboy boots, a navy-blue sports shirt buttoned to the top, and well-ironed khaki pants with razor creases dead center down each leg.

"Miss O'Connell—Hank Schroeder," he said in a crisp voice. "You're right on time." They shook hands. Schroeder's grip was firm and muscular.

"Mr. Schroeder . . . I appreciate your seeing me." She pointed to the car. "He'll be back to pick me up at two-thirty, if that's okay."

"Fine, fine. Come in."

Beatrice signaled to the driver. He nodded and backed out of the driveway.

"Had your lunch?" Schroeder said.

"No."

"Good. The wife is fixing some sandwiches. You look just like your dad, you know that?"

"Yes; people say so."

"Wonderful man, your dad. Wonderful man."

Beatrice didn't say anything. She followed Schroeder into the house, which was almost too cold from the central air-conditioning. It was a spacious, immaculate place, filled with reproduction Early American furniture and colorful braided rag rugs. The finial at the tip of the staircase banister was another brass eagle. Schroeder pointed out some things he was particularly proud of.

"I got these plates on a trip to Winterthur with my first wife," he said, pointing to a pair of decorative Chinese export saucers. "And this chair is an antique reproduction of one from Mount Vernon." Beatrice had always been amused by oxymorons like "antique reproduction," "fresh frozen," and "authentic copy."

Schroeder showed her into a pine-paneled den. Two sleek gray muskets hung above the stone fireplace. The furniture was all brown leather. On the floor was a navy shag rug. He led Beatrice over to a glass case in one corner of the room. Lined with pale-blue velvet, it displayed World War II souvenirs, including a Nazi helmet, a Walther PPK pistol, and an SS dagger. He lifted the top and reached inside.

"I took this little bugger off a dead officer outside Rome," he said, picking up an Iron Cross with an oak leaf cluster and holding it out to Beatrice. "One thing positive you can say about those bastard Krauts is that they had a damn fine sense of design."

Beatrice gave the medal a cursory look. Artifacts of that kind held little interest for her.

Schroeder replaced it carefully inside the vitrine. "The book I sent your father used to live right there," he said, pointing to a slightly depressed and darker patch of velvet on the right-hand side of the case.

Beatrice glanced around the rest of the room, which was very neat and orderly. The built-in bookcases were filled with volumes on oil and engineering.

"What do you do, Mr. Schroeder?"

"I'm a seismic engineer."

"What's that?"

"We use seismic surveying gear to find oil. I used to work for

Schlumberger. Know what this is?" He pointed to a strange-looking
metal object on one of the lower bookshelves.

Beatrice shook her head.

"It's a drill bit from the first well I ever spudded in. See here."
With his finger, he traced the words etched into the brass plate on
which it was mounted: DAISY MAE 23, 11/17/54.

"Why Daisy Mae?"

"You remember the character from *Li'l Abner?*"

"Sure," Beatrice said.

"That's what we called the well. You see, your first well's kinda
like your first girlfriend, if you get my drift." He smiled. "Oil's been
good to me. Now I'm retired, of course. Just relaxing and enjoying
life, thanks to your dad. How is he, by the way? I never heard from
him about the book. I guess he got it all right."

Beatrice looked him in the eye. "Mr. Schroeder, my father is
dead."

Schroeder's face darkened. "Oh Lord," he said with real sadness. "I'm damn sorry to hear that. He was a wonderful man. If I'm
not being too nosy, can I ask you how it happened?"

"That's what I need to talk to you about. May we sit down?"

"Sure, sure. Sit. Susie'll be in soon with the lunch."

Beatrice made herself comfortable on one of the two leather
couches flanking the fireplace. Schroeder sat down opposite her. He
offered her some peanuts from a small bowl on the coffee table between them. She declined. Schroeder munched on a few while he
listened attentively.

"About a month ago, my father was shot and killed in his library
by an intruder."

Schroeder winced. "Shot . . . Jesus," he said, under his breath.

"At first, nothing appeared to be stolen. But then I discovered
that the book you'd sent him was missing."

"No kidding."

"No kidding, Mr. Schroeder."

"I don't know what to say. I'm just real sorry about all this." He
squinted at her. "You think the book had something to do with it?"

"I don't know. I honestly don't know. That's what I'm trying to
find out. That's why I came out here to see you. I need to know everything you can tell me about that book—how you got it, where
you got it, everything you know about it. Everything."

"I see."

"You were fond of my father, weren't you?"

"Oh, I sure was," Schroeder said emphatically. "I'm convinced if it hadn't been for John O'Connell, I wouldn't be here today. Look, I wanna show you something."

Schroeder pulled his sport shirt up out of his pants and bared his chest. A long, ragged scar stretched across his rib cage.

"That's what your daddy did for me," he said proudly. "And I thank him and the good Lord I'm alive today to show it to you. So—anything I can do. Anything at all. It's a damn shame."

"Thank you," Beatrice said, touched at his evident deep feeling.

"Thing is, though," he continued, as he tucked his shirt back inside his trousers, "I don't know what all I can tell you about that book that's gonna help you."

"First of all, you said you got it during the war. How?"

"Well, now, that is kind of an interesting story."

"Do you mind if I take notes?"

"Be my guest."

Beatrice pulled out a small notebook and pen from her purse. "How, exactly, did you come across it?"

Schroeder leaned down and took a pipe from a round rack on the coffee table. Tamping in some tobacco from the tin nearby, he lit it and sat back reflectively.

"In August of '44, I was in Rome. We'd just gotten there. I was a captain in G-2. One of our patrols spotted a priest wandering around in a field at dusk, waving a flashlight at the sky—a pretty unpriestlike thing to be doing, especially when there was a plane circling overhead. So they picked him up, and sure enough, he was no priest but a German officer. They brought him back to corps HQ, and I was in charge of his interrogation. All he had on him were some forged identity papers and that book I sent your dad."

"Did he tell you anything about it?"

"The book? No. I mean, he said it was something he'd picked up as a souvenir. Of course, we thought it contained a code of some sort, so we went over it with a fine-tooth comb. Translated it, tested it for invisible ink—all the usual stuff. In the end, we couldn't find anything, so we just confiscated it."

"Did you know what it was? Did you know it was a grimoire?"

"A what?"

"A grimoire. That's a book of black magic."

174

"We knew it was a spooky little devil, all right. I didn't know there was a name for it. I got a kick outta some of the illustrations. But far as we could tell, it had no military implications."

"Didn't you wonder what he was doing with it?"

"Well, to tell you the honest truth, we thought he was up to other things."

"What things?"

"Well, we had to find out what he was doing there, number one."

"And did you find out?"

"Eventually. But we had a helluva time."

"In what way?"

"He was a tough bird. Didn't wanna talk at first. We interrogated him for a long time, and he gave us a song and dance about this and that. But after we kinda bent the rules of the Geneva Convention a little bit, he opened up."

"What do you mean, you bent the rules?"

Schroeder puffed on his pipe. "Little lady, you don't want to know, and I sure as hell ain't gonna tell you. However, I will say that our friend the fake priest never looked at a car battery in quite the same way again." He smiled grimly.

Just then, a squat, olive-skinned young woman with Indian features appeared at the doorway. Her jet-black hair was pulled back in a long ponytail, fastened with a silver barrette. She was wearing white jeans and an unbuttoned man's shirt, under which was a T-shirt and a string of turquoise beads. Not pretty but exotic looking, she had a dull expression on her face.

"Lunch is ready," she announced in a soft voice. "Shall I bring it in?"

Schroeder beckoned to her. "C'mon in for a second, Susie. I want you to meet Miss O'Connell, Dr. O'Connell's daughter."

Beatrice stood up.

"This is my wife, Susie. Susie, go on over and shake hands with Miss O'Connell. Go on," he urged her, as if she were a child.

The young woman walked across the room with lowered eyes, giving Beatrice a limp, perfunctory handshake and an embarrassed "Hi." Beatrice was taken aback by the apparent youth of the woman, who looked more like Schroeder's granddaughter than his wife.

"Hello," Beatrice said. "Very nice to meet you."

The young woman nodded without saying anything.

"What would you like to drink with your lunch?" Schroeder asked. "I take milk."

"Just some water, thanks," Beatrice replied.

"Okay, hon. You can bring in the lunch now."

The young woman quickly turned around and went out of the room.

"She's a registered nurse," Schroeder said. "I met her at the hospital after my first heart attack. Took care of me during my convalescence. She's a full-blooded Osage. Grew up on a reservation, oh, 'bout ninety miles from here. A man needs a pretty young girl around when he gets older, to take care of him. I was married before, of course. For thirty-eight years. Thirty-eight wonderful years. Four kids. My wife died, God bless her. Susie's younger than my second-youngest daughter, but they all seem to get along fine."

"How long have you been married?"

"Ten months. It was hard for some of my friends to understand it. But you see, we're both grateful to each other in a certain way. She takes good care of me, and I give her a nice home. She doesn't talk very much, which is fine with me. I just don't have the energy to start up a brand-new life with someone. I wanted someone quiet and capable, who doesn't complain. My first wife, Ginny, used to complain all the time, God rest her soul. I loved her, and I was used to it. But I don't think I could get used to it again."

Beatrice was fascinated by his candor. She wondered if that wasn't really what most men wanted in the end: a quiet, uncomplaining nurse to take care of them. And in exchange, a man gave a woman a home, financial security, and protection from a world that still, despite all the advances of feminism, looked askance at unattached women.

A few moments later, Susie appeared again, carrying a tray. Schroeder and Beatrice watched in silence as she laid the lunch out on the coffee table and handed them each a plate and some silverware. She offered them tuna-fish and peanut-butter-and-jelly sandwiches from a large platter and placed a bowl of potato chips in the center of the table, along with a creamy dip in a plastic container.

"Please help yourselves," she said softly.

Beatrice watched her closely as she waited on them, noting that her face was a mask of indifference. She avoided eye contact with both of them and behaved more like a servant than a wife. There was nothing about her to suggest she had anything more on her mind than the matter at hand.

After giving Schroeder his milk and Beatrice her glass of water, Susie left the room.

"Isn't she going to join us?"

"No. She's kinda shy around people. So," Schroeder said, biting into his peanut-butter-and-jelly sandwich. "Where were we?"

"The car battery," Beatrice said, picking at the insides of her tuna-fish sandwich with a fork.

"Oh, right. He loosened up after that."

"What did you find out?"

"His reason for being in Rome."

"Which was?"

"He gave up the six guys in an agent network he was servicing. He'd been flown in to pay them off and set up communications with them."

"And who were they?"

Schroeder chuckled. "You sure know how to ask questions. Let's see now. . . ." He leaned back and ticked off the list on his fingers. "Uh—two were in the *carabinieri*, one was with the railroad, another was with the phone company. There was a priest inside the Vatican. I forget who the other guy was."

"Inside the Vatican?" Beatrice said excitedly. "Do you remember the priest's name?"

"No; sorry."

"But he was definitely inside the Vatican? So it's possible your prisoner did see the Pope."

Schroeder looked at her quizzically. "The Pope?"

"Yes. You see, I think that book you sent my father was given to this man by the Pope."

Schroeder seemed interested but skeptical. "Uh huh . . . What makes you think that?"

"I've been told it by someone who's in a position to know."

Schroeder shrugged. "I somehow doubt it."

"Why?"

"Because this man was simply a courier. It was a pretty big deal, getting to see the Pope—even if you were a Nazi," he said with disdain.

"Yes, I'm sure. But you see, I think that was the real reason for his trip to Rome. Or, at least, an important one."

"What?"

"Seeing the Pope and getting that book."

Schroeder sipped his milk thoughtfully. "You do, huh? Lemme ask you something. Why would the Pope be giving this guy a book? Not to mention that particular book."

"I don't know. That's what I'm trying to find out."

"That book was strange—to say the least," Schroeder said, wiping a half-moon of milk from his upper lip with a paper napkin.

"But you never found out what he was doing with it?"

"At that point, it didn't matter."

"It didn't *matter?*" Beatrice said incredulously.

Schroeder looked at her sympathetically, as if she couldn't possibly get what war was about. "I told you. We had the book, and there was nothing in it. He told us it was a souvenir, and there was nothing to make us think it wasn't. And more important, we had him and we knew what he was doing. We got it out of him."

"I think he fooled you into thinking he was there for those other reasons, Mr. Schroeder. I think those reasons were a decoy."

"Oh, I doubt if he fooled us," Schroeder said with a sigh. "See, war's an impossible thing to imagine. You have to be in one to get the picture. It's like walking into a loony bin. That's the only way I can describe it. You may walk in there sane, but after a while you begin to lose it, pure and simple. You get something in your mind—an objective—and you go for that objective. You don't think much about anything else. I saw two of my best friends in the world buy it right in front of me. I still, to this day, don't know why it was them and not me. . . ." He stared away into space.

"I don't think you really understand," he continued. "My concentration was on who his contacts were in Rome. We'd just occupied the city, and we were in a precarious situation, as everyone is in wartime—to put it mildly. You got subversives all over, just waiting to blow you up or foul up your communications. You got to find out who they are, weed 'em out, and get rid of 'em. That was my main objective here. I wasn't interested in any old book."

"You didn't think the book was odd and that it might have been a code for something?"

"I told you we did," he said, growing mildly impatient. "But we checked it out thoroughly, and that did not appear to be the case. But even if it was, it didn't matter in the end. My job was to get names outta him that would lead to arrests. And he gave those

178

names to us, and we made the necessary arrests. Arrested everyone. All except the priest. We decided we couldn't touch him."

Beatrice nodded sympathetically. She thought for a moment. "May I ask you why you kept the book, Mr. Schroeder?"

"Same reason he did. As a souvenir. No one else wanted it. As you can see, I kept a lotta souvenirs." He gestured toward the case.

"Did he say where he got it?"

"Picked it up in a bookstore, I guess."

"Can you tell me anything else about him? Anything at all?"

"His name and the name of the town he came from, 'cause that's all he'd tell us for the first few hours of questioning."

"Yes?" Beatrice said anxiously.

"Erich von Nordhausen, from Hamburg."

Beatrice printed the name in large capitals in her notebook.

"Von—that means he was noble."

"There wasn't anything noble about that Nazi bastard."

"I meant he was from a noble family. Do you know what became of him?"

"Well, after we finished with him, we handed him over to the MPs, and I guess they would've taken him to a POW camp and held him till the end of the war."

"Do you think there's any way to find out what happened to him?"

Schroeder shook his head. "That'd be real hard. We took hundreds of thousands of prisoners, you know. Unless you've got a contact in Hamburg who could track him down. Who knows? He might still be around. He wasn't too much older than me, I don't think, and I'm still here ... well, barely." He gave a mordant little laugh. "You're not eating your sandwich."

"I guess I'm not very hungry."

"Chips?" He offered her the bowl.

"No, thank you."

"They're good with this dip," he said, helping himself. "Thousand Islands."

"Look, Mr. Schroeder, I don't mean to keep pressing you, but I don't think you got the whole truth out of this man."

"How do you mean?" he said through a crunchy mouthful of potato chips.

"It's true, I don't know anything about war and wartime. But I don't think he came to Rome just to contact agents. I think the real reason he came to Rome was to get that book."

Schroeder washed the chips down with the last of the milk and wiped his mouth. "So you have said." He sighed. "And I guess anything's possible in a war. But I'd say it's water under the bridge now, wouldn't you? What the hell difference does it make?"

"I suspect it made a great deal of difference to my father," Beatrice said with an air of defiance.

"Perhaps. I'm sorry about that," Schroeder replied softly.

Beatrice got up from the couch and began pacing around. "Are you sure there's nothing else you can tell me?"

" 'Fraid not."

"Mr. Schroeder, did anyone else know you had this book?"

"No. Well, my wife."

"And why did you send it to my father?"

"Well, as I explained in the letter, I knew your daddy was a book collector, and I thought he might like to have it. I figured your father, being a collector, would appreciate it."

"I knew. I knew it was evil," said a voice at the other end of the room.

Schroeder and Beatrice turned. Susie was standing at the door, her dark eyes glistening. The young woman, who had seemed so nondescript and flat to Beatrice at first, suddenly came into relief, gathering intensity as she spoke.

"I told him to get rid of it," Susie went on, her voice slightly twangy. "I told him it was bad luck."

"What made you think that?" Beatrice asked.

"I felt it. I felt it was a dangerous thing and that whoever had it would be in danger."

Schroeder waved his hand dismissively. "Susie's just superstitious."

"I'm not superstitious. I know when a thing is evil, that's all," she said. "I told him to burn it. Didn't I tell you to burn it?"

Schroeder nodded sheepishly. "She did. But I don't burn books. Nazis burn books."

"My people understand about magic," Susie said. "We're more interested in the things you can't see."

The comment struck Beatrice deeply, and she felt a sudden empathy with the young woman. She nodded at Susie, who nodded back knowingly, as if they were both members of a secret order.

"My father was like you, Mr. Schroeder," Beatrice said. "Pragmatic and principled. He was interested in the book from a collector's point of view. I don't think he attached much significance to it beyond that. But," she went on, "I'm afraid I agree with your wife. I sensed a palpable evil about that book the moment I saw it. It confused me, because I don't believe in black magic."

"Magic is magic," Susie said.

Schroeder shook his head. "I don't know. . . . All I know was that the guy was in Rome to contact German agents. And he gave those names up to us and we made the necessary arrests. I didn't think twice about the book—except as a souvenir of war," he said defensively.

"War," Susie said dully. "All men love war."

"Now look here," Schroeder protested. "We don't love it. But it's necessary sometimes. You have to fight for what you believe in."

"Or what other people believe in," Susie said.

"Yeah, well, you shouldn't be so smug. Wasn't it Leon Trotsky who said, 'You may not be interested in war, but war is interested in you'? And if women ran the planet, things wouldn't be any different."

"Maybe, maybe not." Susie shrugged.

"Look, Mr. Schroeder, I absolutely need to contact the courier." She glanced down at her notes. "This . . . Erich von Nordhausen."

Schroeder leaned back and sighed. "I think it's like looking for a needle in a haystack. But I s'pose you could try."

"How would I go about it?"

"If you know someone in Germany, you might try tracking him down through the army pension records. That's one way. Course, he was from Hamburg, so maybe you could just try looking up his name in the phone book. Who knows? You might get lucky."

Susie squinted. "If I was you, I'd leave it alone," she said.

"That's impossible." Beatrice glanced at her watch. "It's nearly two-thirty. I should be going. Thank you for all your help."

Schroeder and his wife saw Beatrice to the door. The car was waiting.

"Good luck to you," Schroeder said, waving good-bye.

"Thanks. I'll need it."

As the driver started the engine, Beatrice glanced back at the house. Schroeder had gone inside, but Susie was on the front steps, staring at her. The young woman extended her right arm, making a graceful sign with her hand, which Beatrice interpreted as an Indian blessing. She nodded in thanks. The two women locked eyes in a kind of understanding as the car pulled out of the driveway.

12

HE TRIP TO OKLAHOMA INVIGORATED BEATRICE. On the return flight, she thought about her life over the past few years and felt contempt for the routine that had become deadening and dry as dust. She was through with hunting up material for other people's stories, she thought, through with being a conduit, a literary and emotional pack animal—part of the hunt but never in on the kill. She was hunting for herself now, with her wolf as an ally. They were traveling together, her wolf and she—a pair of stalkers on a quest. "Magic is magic," Schroeder's wife had said, and Beatrice felt the power of her own magic for the first time in her life.

She called Luis Diaz from a phone at the airport.

"Luis?"

"Yeah," said a groggy voice at the other end of the line.

"I woke you up. I apologize."

"Who's this?"

"It's Beatrice O'Connell. Remember me?"

"Yeah, sure. The wolf woman," he said, laughing.

Beatrice hesitated. "I'd like to see you."

"What time is it?"

"About midnight."

"Where are you?"

"I'm at La Guardia."

There was a pause. "You want to come over?"

"Now?"

"Yeah. You got me up," he said suggestively.

"You're always up, Luis. That's what I like about you."

"So—do you want to come?"

"Oh, yes, Luis. I want to come. That's why I called."

"Airplanes do that to some people. I'll play with my toys until you get here."

"You have any condoms?"

"Sure."

"Then I'll see you in about a half hour."

"I'll meet you downstairs. It's dangerous around here at night."

"It's not so safe during the day, either," she said, hanging up.

Beatrice took a cab to Diaz's 103rd Street apartment. It was a hot night. When she arrived, he was sitting on the front stoop, wearing jeans and a T-shirt, smoking a cigarette. He was as beautiful as she remembered.

"Hey," he said, sauntering over to greet her as she got out of the taxi. "This is an unexpected pleasure. How've you been?"

He stood very close to her. The smell of his breath intoxicated her. She felt weak in the knees. "I don't want to talk, okay?" she said softly.

A mean smile crept over his face. "What do you wanna do?" Diaz drawled, running a single fingernail down the back of her dress.

Beatrice shivered with excitement.

"Huh, little researcher?' he whispered into her ear. "What do you wanna do?"

"Take me upstairs."

Diaz put his arm around her waist and pulled her close. As he fiddled with his keys at the downstairs door, Beatrice grabbed his hair, yanked his head toward her, and gave him a long, hungry kiss. Her lust for him sparkled throughout her body. They walked up the stairs of the dark building and entered his apartment.

· · ·

Beatrice left Diaz before sunrise the next morning and hailed a cab. At her house, she took a long, sensuous bath, coating her body in oil, running her hands over her slick thighs and breasts, recalling sensuous moments with Diaz. Why, she wondered, could she not feel this kind of attraction for Stephen, whom she loved? Why did her love for him somehow dilute her sexual pleasure? It was as if trust, familiarity, and tenderness were now unwelcome intruders in her newfound realm of the senses. Diaz was the serpent in the garden, offering her the forbidden fruit of pure desire. And at this time in her life, when her body was hovering on the cusp of middle age, there was nothing more tantalizing or delicious on the whole of God's earth.

The phone rang as she was drying herself. She hurried into the bedroom to pick it up, thinking it was Stephen.

"Beatrice, it's Father Morton. How are you today?"

She froze at the sound of his jovial voice. "Fine, thank you, Father, and you?" she said warily.

"Very well, thanks. Everything going all right? Are you keeping yourself busy?"

"Yes, indeed. Trying to get things in order."

"You mustn't work too hard. You must take some time off, relax, take a little trip somewhere to refresh the spirit."

Beatrice wondered if Father Morton knew of her trip to Oklahoma.

"I'm calling to see if you'd given any more thought to my little proposition regarding your father's library," he said.

"Oh, yes. I'm thinking about it all the time." She hoped he wouldn't catch the double edge in her tone. "I'll give you a call later in the week, if I may," she said.

"Of course, my dear. But don't forget us now, will you?"

"I won't."

"God bless you," Father Morton said. "I look forward to hearing from you soon."

After Beatrice hung up the phone, she couldn't shake the feeling that he had been spying on her.

Later that morning, she met Stephen at a coffee shop in the neighborhood, a bright little spot decorated in the style of a 1940s luncheonette. Two short-order cooks in white aprons were busy behind the long pink Formica counter. There was a pleasant aroma of frying bacon from an open griddle.

The café was crowded with customers glued to their morning papers. Stephen waved to her from a booth at the far corner. As Beatrice sat down opposite him, she noticed a thick manila envelope on the table.

"What's that?" she said.

"Cap's notes. How was your trip?"

"Fascinating," she said. "I found out the whole story of how Schroeder got the grimoire. And the name of the courier he got it from. Erich von Nordhausen."

"Great. I found out a few things myself." Stephen pointed to the envelope.

"Anything interesting?"

"Extremely. Let's order first. I'm hungry. How's your wolf?" he said, eyeing her over the top of a plastic-coated pink menu.

"Fine," Beatrice replied.

"Did he miss me?"

"Sure."

"You sound so cold."

"Sorry, honey. I wasn't aware I sounded cold."

He looked at her quizzically. "Why didn't you call me when you got in last night? I was worried about you."

"It was after midnight. I didn't want to wake you."

"I called you. You weren't there," he said.

"I guess I turned my phone off."

"Where were you, Bea?"

"I was home," she said. "I was exhausted. I went straight to bed."

He paused. "You may have gone straight to bed, but you weren't home, were you?"

"Stephen, don't. There's no point to this."

He stared at her. "Are you trying to get back at me? Is that it?"

"Don't be silly. Let's order."

"You were with Diaz, weren't you?"

"No. We've got so much to do. Let's order." She reached across the table and took his hand. He was shaking. "Stephen, let me go on my journey. You had to go on yours, after all."

"You *were* with Diaz, weren't you?"

"No," she insisted, not wishing to hurt him.

"What's all this crap about a journey, then?" he said, pulling his hand away.

"Don't ask me questions all the time, okay?"

"When I married you, you were so innocent. I was the one with the experience. Now . . . Shit, I can't get used to this. The tables have really turned, haven't they?"

"I wasn't *so* innocent when we got married."

"Comparatively. You were my little girl."

"And now you're my little boy," she said sweetly, signaling to the waitress.

Stephen sighed with exasperation and took up the menu. "I don't know what to make of you, Bea," he said, glancing at the breakfast specials.

"I don't know what to make of myself sometimes. . . . You know, I think Father Morton may be spying on me. I wonder if he knows I went to Oklahoma."

A tired-looking waitress with stringy blond hair and a pencil stuck behind her ear sauntered over to their table, pad in hand.

"What can I get you folks?" she said, removing the pencil and licking the point with her tongue.

Beatrice ordered tea and toast. Stephen ordered a double stack of pancakes, sausages, a large fresh orange juice, and coffee. Beatrice looked at him askance.

"Jealousy gives you an appetite, I see," she said. "Show me Cap's notes."

"Ladies first. What did Schroeder say?"

"I hate that expression 'ladies first.' We're not first in anything."

"Spare me the feminist rhetoric at this hour, if you don't mind. Tell me how the meeting with Schroeder went. What'd you find out?"

Beatrice decided not to argue. She took out her notes and filled Stephen in on all that the retired engineer had told her about the grimoire. He listened with a petulant expression, as if he was still preoccupied with the question of Diaz. After she'd finished, Stephen flipped through the pages of her steno pad.

"So, basically, Schroeder didn't think the book was at all important."

"I told you what he said. They examined it and found nothing. Nothing they thought was important, anyway."

"And he had no idea why Erich von What's-his-name had it or where it might have come from?"

"Von Nordhausen convinced him it was a souvenir—nothing more. But of course, I think he fooled them with all that bullshit about enemy agents. Don't forget, he was disguised as a priest when they picked him up, and he even admitted that one of the agents he'd been sent to contact was a real priest inside the Vatican. So there is a definite connection with the Pope."

"Lovelock's theory may be correct," he said.

"Stephen, assuming the Pope did have a book of black magic, why was he sending it by courier to Germany? Why did the Nazis want it? And why do people still want it?"

"We've definitely got to try and track down von Nordhausen."

"Schroeder says we could try the Hamburg phone book or the army pension records," Beatrice said. "But after all these years, it's a real long shot."

The waitress arrived with their orders. Stephen put Beatrice's notes aside. He poured a river of maple syrup on the large stack of pancakes and smeared on extra butter. Beatrice looked at him somewhat enviously as she dotted her dry toast with a stingy portion of marmalade.

"How do you manage to stay in shape?" she said, transfixed, as Stephen dug heartily into his meal.

"I'll go to the German consulate," he said, chewing vigorously. "They may be able to help us."

"I bet he's dead by now."

"Just tell me again—why did Schroeder send the book to your father?"

"I told you—his new wife wanted him to get rid of it. She thought it was evil and bad luck."

"So just like that, out of the blue, he sends it to your dad?"

"He was grateful to him for saving his life, and he knew Daddy was a book collector. You don't think there's more of a connection, do you?"

"No, I really don't. I think it's just damn bad luck."

"But you do think there's a connection between the book and Daddy's murder."

"Yeah," Stephen said, wiping his mouth. "And I think it has to do with the fact that your dad showed it to Antonelli. Antonelli's the key."

"What makes you say that?"

"A hunch. See, Antonelli's the link between your dad and Father Morton."

"And you definitely think Father Morton's a bad guy?"

"If he's mixed up with Defensores Fidei, he is. And since we're pretty sure that the Duarte Institute is a cover for them, and Father Morton is on the board—it just stands to reason."

Beatrice paused, staring into space. "I wish to God Schroeder had never sent it."

"You can't think about that. What's done is done."

Stephen dabbed at the syrup with his last forkful of pancakes. Beatrice pushed her plate of toast away.

"I really miss him," she said sadly.

"I know." He reached for her hand across the table and squeezed it tight. "Were you really with Diaz last night?"

"You know, Stephen, I'm beginning to think you're kind of turned on by the idea of me and Diaz together," Beatrice said in exasperation.

"That is below the belt, baby."

"Well, then, leave it alone, okay? It's not as if we don't have other things to think about."

"Okay," he said, taking a deep breath. "Something's definitely going on."

"What?"

He opened the manila envelope and extracted a handful of newspaper articles. "Here. Judge for yourself," he said, giving the clippings to Beatrice.

She sifted through them. "Some of these are fairly old: 1990, 1991 . . ." Beatrice scanned several of the articles with growing interest. "They're all about women who've disappeared from around this part of the country." She read some of the headlines aloud. " 'Utica Reporter Feared Dead' . . . 'Glenn Falls Mother of Three Disappears from Shopping Mall' . . . 'Helena Roberts Skips Town.' " Beatrice paused. "Helena Roberts. Where do I know that name from?"

"She was involved in that lesbian adoption case in Pennsylvania a couple of years ago. There are several articles there about it."

"Oh, right," Beatrice said, making the connection. She read aloud from one of the articles. " 'Ms. Roberts achieved notoriety when she and her live-in companion, Judith Osner, challenged state law by seeking to adopt a baby.' I remember now. And what happened?"

"Apparently, she vanished before the case could come to trial."

"No kidding?"

"It's all there in the clippings. Take a look at this one." Stephen thumbed through the pile.

" 'New York Assemblywoman Missing.' This happened last year," Beatrice said, noting the date.

"Read it."

Beatrice scanned the clipping and read the salient points aloud. " 'Police are seeking information on the whereabouts of Pat Slivka, a member of the State Assembly. . . . Ms. Slivka disappeared from her home in Albany sometime on Tuesday night and has not been seen since. Her husband reported her missing to the police the following morning,' et cetera, et cetera. 'During her campaign, Ms. Slivka described herself as a "humanist" as opposed to a "feminist." She was elected to the State Assembly by a narrow margin after a bitter fight where she infuriated conservative groups by her support of the Equal Rights Amendment and her pro-choice stance on abortion. She is currently backing legislation that would end restrictions on gay and lesbian marriages. . . . Police have yet to turn up any clues in her disappearance, and foul play has not been ruled out.' "

"The Utica reporter was someone called Tina Brand, who was a staunch advocate of women's rights," Stephen said. "That happened about six months ago. She's cute. Look at her picture."

Beatrice glanced at the grainy news photo of an attractive black woman in her mid forties.

"The latest one is Patricia Hall, the 'Glenn Falls Mother of Three.' She was abducted a couple of weeks ago from a shopping mall."

"And what's her story?"

"It's unclear from the article. But obviously there must be a connection, because here she is in Cap's clippings."

"It just says she vanished, but it doesn't say anything about her," Beatrice said, reading the small story. "Wait—'active in school politics,' it says."

"That's kind of amorphous, but it's the most recent episode, so we're going to take a little trip to Glenn Falls today and snoop around. I got the name of the reporter who wrote the piece. He's willing to talk to us."

"Great. Where's Glenn Falls?"

"Connecticut. Near New Haven."

Beatrice continued to peruse the articles. After a while, she looked up at Stephen. "Do you see a common thread here—other than the fact that they've all disappeared?"

"Yeah."

"They're all activists in some way."

"And here's a copy of the book Cap mentioned—the one they sell up at the institute. The one he said we'd have to read to believe."

He pulled out a large paperback book and handed it across the table to Beatrice.

" '*The Malleus Maleficarum* of Heinrich Krämer and Jakob Sprenger,' " she said, reading the cover aloud.

The book had a scarlet cover, with the title printed in black. A pair of medieval woodcuts flanked the names of the two authors. One was of a witch with hair of orange flames, riding backward on a ferocious beast, grasping the beast's huge, crooked tail like a phallus. The other was of a witch being burned at the stake, with a long green tongue protruding lasciviously from her mouth.

Beatrice paused for a second, searching back in her memory.

"What?" Stephen said. "What are you thinking?"

"It's interesting that Antonelli dismissed it, given that he's on the board of the institute where they sell it," she said thoughtfully.

"Cap's made some notes on the inside back cover. Have a look," he said.

Beatrice turned to the back and examined the black ink scrawls. "Doctors and reporters always have the most appalling handwriting," she observed. "What's this at the top?"

" 'DI,' " Stephen said.

"Duarte Institute?"

"Yeah. Here he lists the board of directors. See? 'BOD' and then the names: Phil Burgoyne, George Cahill, Chuck Kraus, Father Morton, Giuseppe Antonelli, Bart Winslow, and the elusive Desmond Crowley. Then underneath are the names of the women in the articles I showed you."

Beatrice raised her eyebrows. "He didn't say anything more about it?"

"I didn't get a chance to talk to him before he left. He just sent me this package, with a note saying he looked forward to seeing us when he got back from his vacation."

Beatrice examined the list. "What's this word after the names of the members of the board? 'Pre . . .' something?"

" 'Presenter.' See, it says: 'Phil Burgoyne—Presenter; George Cahill—Presenter; Chuck Kraus—Presenter,' et cetera. Father Morton and Signor Antonelli both seem to be presenters."

"What could that mean?"

"I have no idea. Must be some shorthand of Cap's."

"What do you suppose they're presenting?"

"Beats the hell out of me. I tried calling Cap, but he'd already left."

"Can't we get in touch with him?"

"He's fishing in the Canadian wilderness."

"Shit. What is it with men and the wilderness? Look here—there's something else after Crowley's name," Beatrice noted. "The initials 'GI,' What do you suppose 'GI' means?"

"Well, it usually means Government Issue or General Issue."

"So could it be an army thing?"

"I doubt it. It must stand for something else."

"Like what?"

Stephen shook his head. "No idea."

"The fucking Canadian wilderness! How come he couldn't go fishing somewhere where they have telephones, like normal people? . . . 'GI,' " Beatrice said, mulling the letters over in her mind. "Gift something? . . . If all the others are Presenters, then maybe the 'G' stands for 'Gift' or 'Giving.' Maybe it stands for 'Grimoire.' "

"That's a thought."

" 'Grimoire Iniquitous' . . . And all these women are somehow connected with the Duarte Institute?"

"Apparently."

"Well," Beatrice said, flipping through the pages. "I look forward to reading it." She put the book down. "So what now?"

"Now we drive to Glenn Falls."

Stephen took I-95 up into Connecticut.

"God, I've led a sheltered life," Beatrice said, as she read over the clippings more carefully in the car.

"True. But what makes you say it now?"

"Just reading these articles. Some women's lives are so bleak."

192

"Some *people's* lives are so bleak."

Beatrice turned her head toward the passenger window, staring out at the industrial landscape as they sped along.

"I can't explain it, but there's a certain sense of doom connected to being a woman," she said.

"How about just being a person?"

She shook her head. "You don't understand. I didn't feel it so much when I was young. Maybe that's because there were so many possibilities. But now that I'm getting older, and my options are beginning to narrow, I'm starting to feel it more and more: this doom— this doom of being a woman. And I'm someone who's had lots of advantages, comparatively. I haven't been the victim of a system that grinds women down. Except that maybe the whole system grinds women down," she said reflectively.

"I got news for you, baby—the system grinds us all down. That's what it's there for."

"Especially women. I felt it when I went out to see Schroeder. There he is, a widower, happily ensconced, starting life all over again with a young, healthy partner less than half his age. Now, I ask you, what are the odds of a widow, a woman in her seventies, say, like Schroeder, starting over again with a man—not to mention a man young enough to be her son? Schroeder's wife is going to take care of him until he dies, and when she gets old, chances are she won't have anyone to take care of her."

"Therefore you think men don't feel mortality as acutely as women? Lemme tell you—men are more obsessed with death than women."

"You think so?"

"I know I am. Shit, I wouldn't mind being shot in a war. I just don't want to get old."

"Maybe men feel the threat of death more acutely because they don't give birth and they don't menstruate, so there's no life cycle inside them. I think women probably are more spiritually connected in that sense. It's our one consolation. But, Stephen, men have got more options for a much longer period of time than women. Women's romantic lives are so damn finite, and romance is tied to a lot of options, let's face it. We have our childbearing years, and then—to put it bluntly—most of us are expendable."

"Everyone's expendable," Stephen said. "That's the lesson of history, of being alive. There's always someone else who can do what you do—better, longer, and more successfully."

"Yes, but women are far more interchangeable than men, Stephen. True, in civilized countries, we're gaining ground, struggling like mad to be accepted on our own terms in a man's world. But in most parts of the world, we're just broodmares. We have no status outside of whom we marry and the litters we drop. We have no real rights."

"Maybe ... but don't make it so simplistic."

"Just listen to this: 'Pat Slivka rose to prominence in her community defending a fourteen-year-old woman who was gang-raped, became pregnant, and then was denied an abortion by her parents, who are Catholic.' Jesus. What is it with the Catholic Church and women?"

"You ought to know. You're a Catholic."

"Was. Technically, I'm excommunicated because I divorced you. That's a man's church. They don't like women. They won't let us have abortions, won't let us use contraception, won't let us become priests. We're nearly in the twenty-first century, and as far as the Church is concerned, women might as well be parading around in coned headdresses and chastity belts. Vatican II notwithstanding, someone ought to write a history of women and the church and call it *Hold Back the Dawn.*"

Stephen laughed.

"It's not funny," Beatrice said. "It's deeply affecting."

"You'd make a lousy priest."

Beatrice shrugged. "We'll never know. I'd make a better one than you."

"In fact, I'd make a damn good priest," Stephen said. "I'd be swell in the confessional. Demonstrate a real reporter's gift for drawing people out."

"I think you've got the confessional confused with analysis, dear." She patted him affectionately on the knee.

"Want to move that hand up a little higher, please?"

"Concentrate on the road, you dog," Beatrice said.

Stephen glanced over at her. "You like us being together again?"

"I think so. But I don't really know." She closed her eyes. "I don't really know anything anymore, except that I feel for women in a way that I never have. I'm beginning to sense the strong undertow of anger and resentment against us. . . ."

"You know, Bea, it's not so easy being a guy, either."

"I know. But somehow you're not as vulnerable."

"You wanna make a bet?"

"Why have these women disappeared, Stephen? And why does your friend Cap think they're linked to the Duarte Institute?"

"Who knows? Hopefully, that's what we're on our way to find out," he said, looking for the exit.

13

EATRICE AND STEPHEN PULLED INTO GLENN
Falls just after noon. A little industrial town,
built up in the nineteenth century to make parts
for the gun factories of southern Connecticut,
Glenn Falls was gray and run-down now. Several
of the shops on the long, wide main street were
closed and boarded up. Others had signs in their
windows proclaiming sales and drastic price cuts on all merchandise.
There was a small amount of traffic on the street, with people shopping, taking their lunch hour, and generally going about their business. Yet a listless feeling pervaded the atmosphere. What little
activity there was centered around a pizza parlor called Luna's, in
front of whose unprepossessing facade a group of young men were
clustered.

Beatrice and Stephen cruised about the town, searching for the
bar where Stephen had arranged to meet his contact. Beatrice spotted a blinking red neon cocktail glass with the words JOE'S PLACE inside it. "There it is," she said, pointing it out.

Stephen cruised down to the end of the block and parked in

front of the seedy establishment. Beatrice got out and stretched her arms to the sky, feeling stiff from the long ride. Stephen tucked the manila envelope containing the clippings under his arm.

"Okay, Joe, let's have a look at your place," he said, holding the door open for Beatrice.

The bar, paneled in dark wood, was fairly dingy, despite the red-and-white-check tablecloths, red leather banquettes, and colorful electric signs advertising beer. A garish vintage jukebox was playing a Frank Sinatra tune. Some regulars looked up as Stephen approached the round-faced bartender, who was polishing glasses behind a long bar.

"What can I do you for?" the bartender said cheerlessly.

"You know a guy called Dick Ramsey?"

"Hey, Ramsey!" the bartender called to a balding middle-aged man in a brown suit who was sitting in a booth reading a newspaper and sipping beer. "You got company."

The man in the booth looked up over his bifocals and squinted, then waved Beatrice and Stephen over. He had a pasty face, and there were dark circles under his tired eyes. His jacket was open and the top button of his shirt was unbuttoned. His tie was slack around the collar, like a little noose.

"Mr. Ramsey? Steve Carson. Please don't get up," Stephen said, as Ramsey started to rise. "This is my friend Beatrice O'Connell."

The three of them shook hands. Ramsey had a flaccid grip.

"Have a seat," Ramsey said. "You folks want a beer or something?"

Stephen looked at Beatrice, who nodded.

"Joe! Two more beers!"

"I like that Joe's Place really has a Joe," Beatrice said as she edged her way into the cramped banquette.

Stephen and Beatrice sat facing Dick Ramsey, who removed his glasses and began shining them with a red paper napkin.

"You found your way up here all right, I guess," he said.

"Yeah," Stephen replied. "It's a nice, scenic drive."

"Oh, scenic's the word," Dick Ramsey said sarcastically, folding his glasses and sticking them into the breast pocket of his jacket. "So—what brings you folks up to scenic Glenn Falls? You mentioned something about the Patricia Hall case on the phone."

Stephen opened the manila envelope, pulled out the clipping

headlined "Glenn Falls Mother of Three Disappears from Shopping Mall," and handed it to Ramsey.

"You wrote this story for the *Glenn Falls Gazette,* right?"

Ramsey glanced at the article. "Yeah. That's the old byline."

"Has there been any follow-up on this? Did you ever find out what happened to her?"

"Nope. It's just like I say there. She was last seen over at Parsons Mall, about a quarter of a mile outside of town. It was around—oh—what'd I say in the article?" He referred to the clipping. "Eight-thirty in the evening, yeah. A clerk at the Kmart remembered waiting on her. And she never made it home. Her car was found in the mall, so the police figured she was abducted."

"Mr. Ramsey—"

"Call me Dick."

"Dick, did you know Patricia Hall?"

"Know her? No. Saw her around. Knew who she was. This is a small town, after all."

"Do you have any theories about what happened to her?"

Ramsey drew himself up and cleared his throat, as though he relished being asked his opinion. "Okay, there's been some speculation that she might have run off with someone. Supposedly, her marriage wasn't any too hot. But I don't buy it."

"Why not?" Beatrice asked.

"The kids. She has three kids. Women don't just run out on three kids, you know. And they're still youngsters. It's pretty unlikely she'd fly the coop with those chicks at home."

"So what do you think happened?" Stephen asked.

"It's hard to say. The Halls aren't rich, so kidnapping seems improbable. Anyway, there was never a ransom note."

"What does Mr. Hall do?"

"He owns a small lumberyard. It was some sort of a sex thing, most likely. Or just a straight murder, maybe. Something like that. I'm sure they'll find her body sometime."

Beatrice shuddered at the matter-of-fact way in which he proposed this. The bartender brought over a small tray of beers and handed them out. Stephen, who was thirsty, took a long draft.

"Do we know anything else about her? Your article mentioned she was active in school politics," Stephen said.

"To put it mildly," Ramsey went on, "old Patricia was kind of a free spirit, a flaming liberal."

Beatrice raised her eyebrows. "A flaming liberal?"

"You know the type. She was stirring the pot plenty."

"In what way?" Beatrice inquired.

"Just like I said. She was a liberal do-gooder. And she was try-ing to push through all sorts of stuff the folks up here just don't go for."

"Like what sort of stuff?"

"Oh, like, uh, you know—the kind of things they're into these days. She wanted to distribute condoms in the classrooms and make sex education mandatory for the kids. She was a big proponent of the 'alternative lifestyle' business that's going on up here now. I guess it's going on everywhere," he said in an aside. "And then there was the stopping-the-prayers-in-the-public-school bit. She also dem-onstrated against the closing of the abortion clinic. She was into all that."

Stephen and Beatrice exchanged glances.

"Would you say she was a feminist?" Beatrice asked.

Ramsey guffawed. "Yeah. She was a real little troublemaker."

"You think feminists are real little troublemakers, do you?" Beatrice said with an edge.

"I, personally, don't," Ramsey said, quickly backing off. "Lis-ten, I'm a just a lowly reporter—a 'just the facts, ma'am' kinda guy. Don't get me wrong. But what I'm saying is, she was poking her nose into places—particularly the school. But whenever there was an issue, she was on the liberal side of it. See what I'm saying?"

Ramsey paused to sip from his new glass of beer. He licked off a little mustache of white foam and cleared his throat.

"Please go on, Mr. Ramsey," Beatrice urged him.

"Dick. Call me Dick. . . . You have to understand—uh, Beatrice, is it?"

Beatrice nodded.

"A lotta folks around here are opposed to any kind of change, particularly where the youngsters are concerned," he continued. "And from what I understand, Patricia Hall was damn good at using her influence, which was considerable."

"And just why was her influence so considerable?" Stephen asked.

"Well, judging from the folks who knew her, she was a pretty charismatic gal—woman." He corrected himself quickly.

Beatrice produced a thin smile. Ramsey shifted uncomfortably on the banquette and looked squarely at Beatrice and Stephen, as if he was about to level with them.

"Okay," he said. "You want to know the rumor?"

Beatrice nodded.

"Well, supposedly Patricia was sleeping with the head of the school board. There was a big stink about it even before she disappeared."

"Is that true?" Stephen asked with interest. "*Was* she sleeping with him?"

Ramsey shook his head. "Who knows? That's the rumor. From what I understand, all the curriculum proposals were getting a little too racy for everybody's taste. And Midge Findlay, the wife of the head of the board, started saying Patricia Hall was some kind of witch." He laughed. "I think she got the first syllable wrong."

"What did Ms. Hall look like?" Beatrice asked.

"Oh, she was an attractive person, in an offbeat sort of way: kind of—what do they call it?—New Age. She had long, straight hair and wore one of those Egyptian things around her neck. She wasn't from here, originally. I think she was from up in Vermont somewhere. She made pottery and sold it out of her house. I guess she was kind of a hippie."

Just then the illuminated Budweiser Beer sign above the bar buzzed, sparked, and flickered out. The three of them turned to look at it.

"Goddamn thing," the bartender said, fiddling with it in exasperation.

"Go on," Stephen urged Ramsey.

"That's about it. That's about all I know."

There was a pause.

"Have you ever heard of something called the Duarte Institute?" Stephen asked.

Ramsey thought for a moment. "Nope. Can't say I have."

"How about a man named Desmond Crowley?"

Ramsey shook his head. "Why? Should I of?"

"No," Stephen said. "I was just wondering. And you've been a reporter here for how long?"

"Oh, Jesus—going on twenty years. The *Gazette*'s a good little paper. We're not going to win any Pulitzers, but we keep everybody informed."

"Well, listen, Dick, thanks for your time," Stephen said, starting to rise.

"You hardly touched your beer," Ramsey said to Beatrice.

"I'm not thirsty."

"May I?" Ramsey said.

"Be my guest."

Ramsey drained Beatrice's glass.

"Tell me, what's happened to all the things Ms. Hall proposed?" Beatrice asked, as they were leaving.

"Oh, you know—nothing," Ramsey said, wiping his mouth with the back of his hand. "People have more important things to think about right now—like getting jobs. This recession's killing all of us."

"Do you think the proposals might have gone through if she hadn't vanished?"

Ramsey considered. "Who knows? As I said, old Patricia was quite a lady. I can say that, right? Lady?"

"Yes." Beatrice smiled. "You can say that."

"The beers are on me," Stephen said, going over to pay the bartender.

"Thanks," Ramsey replied. "What's all this about? Why are you all so interested in this case?"

"Well, it's quite interesting when a woman just vanishes into thin air, isn't it?" Beatrice offered.

"Sure, but Glenn Falls is kinda out of the way for you folks, isn't it? How'd you happen to see the *Gazette?*"

"We have a friend who cut out the story," Stephen said.

"You're a reporter, right?"

"No; just an interested party."

"Come on—you gonna write it up for another paper, or what?"

"No," Stephen said evasively.

"Look," Ramsey said, "it's just a local story. And anyway, Hall's old news now. The police haven't come up with any leads that I know of. Level with me—you folks haven't heard anything, have you?"

"No," Stephen said. "We were just interested in the background of the case, that's all."

"We wanted to know a little bit about her—who she was, what she was up to," Beatrice added.

"Uh huh," Ramsey said. "Well, now you know."

· · ·

Before Stephen and Beatrice left Glenn Falls, they took a swing by Parsons Mall to view the scene of the crime. Beatrice was daunted by the sheer size of the place, with its three vast parking lots and the stores stretching for acres.

"Well, it certainly wouldn't be hard to be abducted from here," she observed. "At night, when it's dark, someone could just hit you over the head, drag you into a car, and no one would notice. Give me the good old unsafe streets of New York anytime."

"Let me tell you something," Stephen said, thinking aloud. "In my experience, there are two questions to which the answer is almost always yes: Did he or she steal the money? And, Are they having an affair?"

"So you think Patricia Hall was having an affair with the head of the school board?"

"Sure. Listen, she fits right in with the other women in the pattern—a feminist who's socially and sexually active in a threatening way."

"And what about the abortion clinic? He glossed over it, but that's certainly one of the big issues of our time. She fits the bill, and that's why she's in Cap's file of disappearing activists—female activists, to be specific."

"Old Cap's onto something big, and he knows it. I suspect we'll get the lowdown when he gets back from his vacation."

"I can't wait to take a look at that book—the *Malleus Maleficarum*. Maybe it'll give us a clue."

"Hope so," Stephen said, stepping on the accelerator. "In the meantime, I'm going to try to hunt up your courier, von Nordhausen. I think that's the next logical step."

Stephen and Beatrice spent the night together. They made love, but Beatrice, much to her chagrin, still felt none of the raw excitement she had felt with Luis Diaz. Stephen was more ardent than ever, and she couldn't tell if he was aware of her inner detachment. She seemed to be watching herself in the act, rather than participating, as she had with Diaz. The feeling troubled her, but she was powerless to change it.

The next day, they each pursued various aspects of what Stephen now dubbed "the story." He left after breakfast and went to the German consulate. Beatrice settled herself comfortably on the dilapidated sofa by the window, with a bottle of mineral water.

Opening the *Malleus Maleficarum*, she started reading the foreword, in which the book was praised not only as "one of the most effective and invigorating works in the vast canon of writings on witchcraft" but also as "a book for the present age, full of logic, clarity, and insight into the judicial system, even today. *The Witches' Hammer*," it concluded, "is a work for all eternity." It was signed "Desmond Crowley, 1955."

So Crowley wrote the foreword. She couldn't wait to tell Stephen. In the meantime, she settled into the text.

THE FIRST PART, TREATING OF THE THREE NECESSARY CON-COMITANTS OF WITCHCRAFT, WHICH ARE THE DEVIL, A WITCH, AND THE PERMISSION OF ALMIGHTY GOD

*

PART I

QUESTION 1

*Here beginneth auspiciously the first
part of this work. Question the First.*

Whether the belief that there are such beings as witches is so essential a part of the Catholic faith that obstinately to maintain the opposite opinion manifestly savours of heresy ...

Mildly intrigued at first, Beatrice soon became fascinated with the long tract. A feeling of horror crept over her as she read page after page of the most misogynistic rhetoric she had ever encountered in a serious work. Unable to believe what she was reading, she decided to make notes. She fetched some paper and a pen and started copying long passages from the text verbatim to show to Stephen.

Random Notes from the *Malleus Maleficarum*, by Heinrich Krämer and Jakob Sprenger:

Question VI: Why it is that Women are chiefly addicted to evil superstitions ... Therefore let us now chiefly consider women; and first, why this kind of perfidy is found more in so fragile a sex than in men. And our inquiry will first be general, as to the general conditions of women; secondly, particular, as to which sort of women are found to be given to superstition and witchcraft . . .

Now the wickedness of women is spoken of in Ecclesiasticus XXV: "I had rather dwell with a lion and a dragon than to keep house with a wicked woman" . . . All wickedness is but little to the wickedness of a woman. Wherefore S. John Chrysostom says on the text, It is not good to marry: What else is woman but a foe to friendship, an unescapable punishment, a necessary evil, a natural temptation, a desirable calamity, a domestic danger, a delectable detriment, an evil of nature, painted with fair colours!

When a woman thinks alone, she thinks evil.

Wherefore in many vituperations that we read against women, the word woman is used to mean the lust of the flesh.

As it is said: I have found a woman more bitter than death, and a good woman subject to carnal lust.

For as regards intellect, or the understanding of spiritual things, they seem to be of a different nature from men; a fact which is vouched for by the logic of the authorities, backed by various examples from the Scriptures.

And it should be noted that there was a defect in the formation of the first woman, since she was formed from a bent rib, that is, a rib of the breast, which is bent as it were in a contrary direction to man. And since through this defect she is an imperfect animal, she always deceives. For Cato says: "When a woman weeps, she labours to deceive a man."

Therefore a wicked woman is by her nature quicker to waver in her faith, and consequently quicker to abjure the faith, which is the root of witchcraft.

And as to her other mental quality, that is, her natural will; when she hates someone whom she formerly loved, then she seethes with anger and impatience in her whole soul, just as the tides of the sea are always heaving and boiling.

Can he be called a free man whose wife governs him, imposes laws on him, orders him, and forbids him to do what he wishes, so that he cannot and dare not deny her anything that she asks?

Let us consider another property of hers, the voice. For as she is a liar by nature, so in her speech she stings while she delights us.

Let us also consider her gait, posture, and habit, in which is vanity of vanities. There is no man in the world who studies so hard to please the good God as even an ordinary woman studies by her vanities to please men.

She is more bitter than death because bodily death is an open and terrible enemy, but woman is a wheedling and secret enemy.

All witchcraft comes from carnal lust, which is in women insatiable.

Three general vices appear to have special dominion over wicked women, namely, infidelity, ambition, and lust. . . . Since of these three vices the last chiefly predominates, women being insatiable, etc.

Question VIII: Whether Witches can hebetate the Powers of Generation or obstruct the Venereal Act . . . Is it a Catholic view to maintain that witches can infect the minds of men with an inordinate love of strange women, and so inflame their hearts that by no shame or punishment, by no words or actions, can they be forced to desist from such love; and that similarly they can stir up such hatred between married couples that they are unable in any way to perform the procreant functions of marriage; so that, indeed, in the untimely silence of night, they cover great distances in search of mistresses and irregular lovers?

Serpents are more subject to magic spells than other animals. . . . It is the same in the case of a woman, for the devil can so darken her understanding that she considers her husband so loathesome that not for all the world would she allow him to lie with her. Later he wishes to find the

reason why more men than women are bewitched in respect of that action; and he says that such obstruction generally occurs in the seminal duct, or in an inability in the
matter of erection, which can more easily happen to men;
and therefore more men than women are bewitched.

When the member is in no way stirred, and can never perform the act of coition, this is a sign of frigidity of nature;
but when it is stirred and becomes erect but yet cannot
perform, it is a sign of witchcraft.

And note, further, that the Canon speaks of loose lovers
who, to save their mistresses from shame, use contracep-
tives, such as potions, or herbs that contravene nature,
without any help from devils. And such penitents are to be
punished as homicides. But witches who do such things by
witchcraft are by law punishable by the extreme penalty.

Wherefore the Catholic Doctors make the following dis-
tinction, that impotence caused by witchcraft is either temporary or permanent. And if it is temporary, then it does
not annul the marriage. Moreover, it is presumed to be
temporary if they are able to be healed of the impediment
within three years from their cohabitation, having taken all
possible pains, either through the sacraments of the
Church, or through other remedies, to be cured. . . . Much
is noted there concerning impotence by Hostiensis, and
Godfrey, and the Doctors and Theologians.

Question IX: Whether Witches may work some Prestidigitatory Illusion so that the Male Organ appears to be entirely removed and separate from the Body.

There is no doubt that certain witches can do marvellous
things with regard to male organs, for this agrees with what
has been seen and heard by many, and with the general account of what has been known concerning that member
through the senses of sight and touch.

Peter's member has been taken off, and he does not know
whether it is by witchcraft or in some other way by the
devil's power, with the permission of God. Are there any
ways of determining or distinguishing between these?

First, that those to whom such things most commonly happen are adulterers or fornicators. For when they fail to respond to the demand of their mistress, or if they wish to desert them and attach themselves to other women, then their mistress, out of vengeance, causes such a thing to happen, or through some other power causes their members to be taken off.

When Beatrice finished, it was close to one o'clock. Her mind was racing, as the essence of the tract sank deeper into her psyche. She got up, lit a cigarette, and began pacing the room, rereading her notes. As she examined the vile nuggets that constituted the gist of the book, she grew more and more incredulous.

So this was the establishment view of women in the fifteenth century, she thought. And people say the world is worse off today. Like hell it is.

She then reread Desmond Crowley's foreword. When she saw that he deemed the book to be "an impartial and scrupulously reasoned account," she was more thoroughly stunned. How could he possibly think that, she wondered, given the volume's boisterously woman-hating tone? Albeit, Crowley had written the foreword in 1955, before the advent of modern feminism, it was nevertheless an astonishing accolade. Had the publishers printed it for its historical interest rather than as serious commentary? No, she thought. There was something far more sinister going on, and she was determined to find out what it was.

She knew that the one person who might be able to help her in that quest was Simon Lovelock. She immediately telephoned Lovelock in his shop and asked if she could come down and take him to a late lunch. He agreed, suggesting a restaurant on Spring Street, not far from his bookstore.

It was a little past two o'clock when Beatrice arrived at the place with the *Malleus* tucked under her arm in a paper bag. The café was light and airy, with white walls, a gray and white tile floor, and plants hanging from the ceiling in terra-cotta pots. Though it was still fairly crowded, Beatrice immediately spotted the black-garbed Lovelock sitting at a small round table in the corner, directly under a dripping fern. He stood up to greet her.

He looked different somehow, more polished and neat, as if he had made a special effort. A few of the plant's delicate tentacles whisked the top of his head, and for an awkward moment he appeared unsure whether to brush them aside or shake her hand, but finally he decided on the latter course. Though awkward and hesitant, he was obviously pleased to see her, and was very solicitous. He pulled out a chair and seated her, making sure she was comfortable. Then he sat down opposite her.

"This is my summer lunch spot," he said. "In winter, I prefer a rather cramped little restaurant right around the corner from me with no natural light. You see, in the winter I tend to gravitate toward dark places. I wonder why that is."

"Maybe you want to go into hibernation."

Lovelock thought for a moment. "No, I think it has to do with warmth. I always associate darkness with warmth. Don't ask me why."

"The womb, perhaps?" Beatrice said, intending to tweak him a bit.

"Oh, very possibly." He smiled, and Beatrice noticed that his teeth were cleaner.

"But enough of my proclivities," he said. "Are you hungry?"

"I could use a bite."

"Let me tell you what's good here," he said, handing her the small menu card. "This restaurant specializes in what I call hippie gourmet food. Most things come with brown rice, and if you're not careful, you'll order something with a flower on it. Nasturtiums make me ill. Do they you?"

"I don't think I've ever had one."

"I suggest the grilled vegetable sandwich, or any of their sandwiches, really, provided you like sandwiches, of course. I have the vegetable one every day. But without peppers. I loathe peppers."

"I'm in your hands, Mr. Lovelock."

He seemed quite pleased at her response.

"And what to drink?" he continued. "They have something called a 'jam fizz,' which is just crushed raspberries, sugar, and soda water. It's really quite refreshing. Anyway, I like it."

"Fine."

A waiter who obviously knew Lovelock came over to the table and took the order. "No peppers, right?" the young man said.

Lovelock nodded. "Well, now," he said, lighting one of his inevitable cigarettes. "I was delighted that you called. I felt our last meeting was extremely unsatisfactory."

"I've found out quite a lot since then, Mr. Lovelock—"

"Simon, please," he said eagerly.

"Simon . . . And you said I could come to you and ask you questions."

"I meant that very seriously. I want very much to help you, but as I told you, I'm in a difficult position."

"Yes, I understand." Beatrice slid the book out of the paper bag and handed it to him across the table. "Will you tell me everything you know about this book?"

"Ah," he said with a sigh. "So you've discovered the *Malleus*, have you?" He stared at the book in silence for a time. "Where, may I ask, did you get it?"

"From a friend of Stephen's, a reporter. He got it from the Duarte Institute." She saw him wince at the name. "They have an original edition up there and sell facsimiles of it. I saw it."

"You saw it?"

"We went up there."

"Where?"

"To the Duarte Institute."

Lovelock blanched. "I told you to stay away from there!" he said angrily.

"I wanted to see it."

"Who took you around?" Lovelock said.

"Father Morton."

"No one else?"

"No. Why?"

"You must promise me—*promise* me—that you will never go there again."

"Okay, okay. I promise. But why not? It's just sort of a scholarly Sturbridge Village."

"It's not, believe me. It's not."

"Tell me about it."

"No," he said, obviously agitated. "Let's get back to the *Malleus*. You don't pick easy subjects, do you, Beatrice? May I call you Beatrice?"

"Of course. More to the point, they don't pick me," she said.

He turned the book over in his hands. It seemed to weigh heavily upon him, as if it were stone.

"This is the most comprehensive edition," he said, thumbing through the pages. "It's got Innocent VIII's 1484 bull in it: here it is." Lovelock closed the paperback and put it down on the table. "You've changed your hair," he said. "May I say how pretty you look."

Beatrice was slightly taken aback. "Thank you."

"I probably shouldn't say that to you. I don't know whether you like to be complimented so directly."

"Oh, I do, I do."

"You've been in my thoughts a great deal, Beatrice. I wanted to telephone you, but I didn't think it was correct somehow."

"Why not?"

"You were with"—he seemed at a momentary loss for words—"a friend. I just assumed . . ."

"Stephen is my ex-husband. We're very close."

"Ah," he said, nodding. He stared at her for a long moment, as if he were memorizing the details of her face. Then he caught himself and, clearing his throat, got down to business.

"Well, literally translated, *Malleus Maleficarum* means 'The Witches' Hammer,' or, as some prefer, 'The Hammer of Witches.' It was written by two fanatics—Heinrich Krämer and Jakob Sprenger—and published around 1484: scholars generally accept that as the date. There were another fourteen editions between 1487 and 1520, and, oh, another sixteen or so between 1574 and 1669. These were printed by presses in France, Germany, and Italy. So you see, the work was very widespread, and its impact was incalculable . . . incalculable even today." He paused, seemingly lost in thought.

"Please go on," Beatrice urged him.

"Sorry," he said. "Forgive me. . . . Krämer was a German, born near Strassburg. A Dominican prior who became an Inquisitor for the Tyrol and the surrounding areas—Bohemia, Moravia, et cetera. Sprenger was born in Basel, and early on he was recognized as a genius and a mystic. He also became a Dominican and was an Inquisitor around Cologne, a very large district. By all accounts, he was saintly, and some chronicles of the day even refer to him as "Beatus." He's buried in Strassburg. Krämer and Sprenger both wrote a great deal on their own. But the *Malleus*, their masterwork, is a collaboration."

"Simon, I read part of the book this morning, and I'm kind of in shock. Can you tell me what it is, exactly, except a venomous diatribe against women?"

"Oh, it's a great deal more than that, Beatrice," he said somberly. "Though, granted, that's a significant part of it. How can I put it to you? No self-respecting magistrate or judge of that day was without a copy of the *Malleus*. It was the final and irrefutable authority on combating witchcraft and was accepted by both Catholics and Protestants as such. And not only did it tell them about witches and their nature and how to discover them; it outlined in detail how witches should be captured, brought before a court, tried, and punished."

"I understand. It was a lawbook, then?"

"No, no, that is an understatement. It was *the* lawbook on witchcraft for over two centuries."

"But it's so loathsome and dark and full of superstition."

"Yes, that's all true. But it wasn't superstition then. People really believed it. Do you understand what it is when people really believe something? They suspend logic, and emotion takes over."

"Well, religion, of course—"

"Exactly. Religion, love, hope, fear—the great opponents of logic."

"And hate."

"Yes, I know. I know all too well . . . ," he said thoughtfully. "You see, witchcraft was a tricky thing to prove. Plus, there were degrees of it. And then, you see, the witches themselves fell into different categories. So, for example, it addresses the problem of how to deal with a witch who has confessed to heresy but is penitent. Or a witch who has confessed to heresy but is *not* penitent. Or a witch who refuses to confess even though he or she has been convicted. Or a witch who has been accused of witchcraft by another witch. That last is a sticky one, to be sure. On and on like that, in the most minute detail. And then it outlines the various methods of punishment."

"Like burning at the stake," Beatrice said.

"Like burning at the stake. Precisely."

With that, their orders arrived.

Lovelock stubbed out his cigarette in the glass ashtray on the table and tucked his napkin up under his collar. He looked over the sandwich intently, then carefully removed the top slice of bread and placed it to one side of his plate. Next, he picked up his fork and began poking around the vegetables, careful to seek out only one variety at a time. He ate all of the carrots before he started on the zucchini, and all the zucchini before starting on the tomatoes, and on and on like that, down to the last bean sprout. Between bites of food, he took a tiny sip of the raspberry fizz concoction he had lauded, then he licked his lips, dotting them judiciously with his napkin. All this was accomplished with speed and precision.

Beatrice, who was mesmerized by Lovelock's eating habits, decided to wait until he had finished to ask him any more questions, especially since he seemed too engrossed in his food to be interrupted. Finally, he put down his fork and removed his napkin from his throat. With a little sigh of contentment, he leaned back in his chair and fumbled in his pocket for a smoke.

"That hit the spot," he said.

"Simon, may I ask you a question?"

"Certainly," he said, striking a large wooden match.

"Why do you order a sandwich when you only eat the vegetables? Why don't you just order the vegetable platter?"

"I always like to see bread on my plate," he replied, as if that made perfect sense. "Bread is the staff of life, as they say."

"You could order some rolls."

"I hadn't thought of that. Anyway, they might not come at the same time." As he exhaled, he waved the smoke away from Beatrice's direction with his hand. "I hope the smoke isn't bothering you."

"Not at all," she said, continuing to eat.

"By the way, do you taste the dill they use here in the vegetables?"

"I think so. Whatever it is, the flavor's delicious."

"An interesting herb, dill. In certain countries, it was believed to counteract the spells of witches."

"You believe in witches, then, do you, Simon?"

"You keep asking me that, Beatrice," he said, smiling. "Let's get back to our friend the *Malleus* for the moment."

"Tell me about this papal bull that was published with it."

"What do you know about papal bulls?"

"Not much. Even though I'm a Catholic."

"Let me tell you a little bit about them, in that case. The term 'bull' comes from the Latin word *bulla*—"

"Which means bullshit, right?" Beatrice interrupted.

Lovelock looked somewhat startled.

"Sorry, Simon. I'm a little irritated with the Church right now."

"Yes, it can be an irritating institution in the wrong hands. More than irritating," he said pensively. "Dangerous."

"But uplifting in the right ones," Beatrice said.

"Indeed."

"Please continue," Beatrice said, picking up her sandwich.

" 'Bull' comes from the Latin *bulla*, which means bubble. But in the vernacular, it came to mean a type of metal amulet. Gradually, it was associated with the lead seals used to authenticate papal documents. And by the end of the twelfth century, the word 'bull' was used to describe the document itself." Lovelock smiled with delight. "I love the way certain words drift around in a language, don't you?"

He raised his right hand, waving it gracefully back and forth through the air, as if he were conducting an orchestra. "They drift and drift and then—" His hand suddenly stopped. "Zap! They attach themselves like a barnacle to something seemingly unrelated to their original meaning."

"I never really thought about it," Beatrice said.

"To think that the word for a mere bubble came to mean one of the weightiest and most important of Church instruments. Don't you find that amusing?" He blew a perfect smoke ring.

"I do." She took a sip of her raspberry fizz. "Thanks for pointing it out."

"So—to go on," Lovelock said. "Of all the edicts issued from the Cancellaria, the bull was preeminent. A real papal bull was very different in both form and content from an encyclical or a decree, let's say, even though the latter are both sometimes described as bulls. Papal bulls were written in Latin, in an almost indecipherable Gothic script that was, interestingly, unpunctuated. They had seals on both sides—one depicting Saint Peter and Saint Paul, and the other either a likeness or else the name of the reigning pope.

"Now, the bull of Pope Innocent VIII, which accompanied the *Malleus* into the world, was written in the gravest possible language, giving the book enormous weight and prestige. Basically, it said that whoever defied the work would bring down the wrath of God and his Apostles on his own head."

"I see." Without finishing her sandwich, Beatrice pushed her plate aside. She squeezed her eyes shut and massaged her temples with her fingers.

"What's the matter, Beatrice?" Lovelock said with alarm. "Are you ill?"

She looked up and stared at him. Her face was tired and drawn. "I'm sorry, Simon. It's just that I sense that something extremely profound and dangerous is going on here."

"Do you?"

"You know there is, don't you?"

"Yes," he whispered, lowering his eyes.

She sat up straight and took a few deep breaths. "You know what I think this book is really about, Simon?"

"Tell me."

"Man's fear of impotency. And, by implication, his fear and loathing of all women. What do you think about that?"

"I think that's very astute," Lovelock said slowly. "But I also think it's rather a larger canvas than that."

Beatrice shook her head. "No. I don't think there *is* a larger canvas than that in the relations between men and women. That *is* the canvas, as far as I'm concerned. And everything else is just paint."

"Please elaborate," he said.

"Okay, hear me out now. In my opinion, *The Witches' Hammer* is a literal, as well as a literary, expression of man's primal fear of impotency. The authors use the generic term 'witch' to describe evil people. But you and I both know, Simon, as would any intelligent reader, that for them, 'witch' is really a euphemism for 'woman.' Do you agree with that?"

"Perhaps."

"Of *course* it is," Beatrice said emphatically. "The book states over and over that women are an inferior, lustful, and depraved sex. In those instances, the authors don't even bother to use the word 'witch.' According to them, all women are basically evil to begin with. And because of our weak minds and polluted bodies, we are more susceptible to becoming evil incarnate—that is, witches. Do you agree with *that?*"

"It seems to be the case they are making, yes."

"So you're with me so far. All right, then—what, according to this book, is the main power of witches?"

"What?"

"To render men sexually dysfunctional."

Lovelock nodded slightly. He appeared fascinated by her.

"Either by making them impotent," Beatrice continued, "or

else by making them so lustful that they have no control over their desires. Then they have to resort to whoring, which, in the authors' view, isn't their fault."

"Go on."

Beatrice, growing more and more animated, picked up the book and turned to a page she had marked.

She read aloud: " 'How Witches Impede and Prevent the Power of Procreation ... They can obstruct the procreant function in two ways. First when they directly prevent the erection of the member which is accommodated to fructification ... Secondly, when they prevent the flow of the vital essences to the members in which resides the motive force, closing up the seminal ducts so that it does not reach the generative vessels, or so that it cannot be ejaculated, or is fruitlessly spilled ... And the reason for this is that God allows them more power over this act, by which the first sin was disseminated, than over other human actions.' "

Beatrice looked up at Lovelock, who said nothing.

"And in the worst case, Simon," she continued, "witches have the power to steal men's members, to make them disappear entirely. Listen ..."

Again, she located lines she had marked in the text and read aloud: " 'Question IX: Whether Witches may work some Prestidigitatory Illusion so that the Male Organ appears to be entirely removed and separate from the Body ...' " Beatrice glanced up to see if Lovelock was digesting the enormity of what she was reading to him.

"Continue," he said, seemingly engrossed.

" 'And what, then, is to be thought of those witches who in this way sometimes collect male organs in great numbers, as many as twenty or thirty members together, and put them in a bird's nest, or shut them up in a box, *where they move themselves like living members, and eat oats and corn*, as has been seen by many and is a matter of common report?' Do you *believe* this?" she interjected.

" 'For a certain man tells that, when he had lost his member, he approached a known witch to ask her to restore it to him. She told the afflicted man to climb a certain tree, and that he might take which he liked out of a nest in which there were several members. And when he tried to take a big one, the witch said: You must not take that one; adding, *because it belonged to a parish priest.*' Whew!

How about that?" Beatrice shut the book and leaned forward, folding her hands on the table.

"And you say that this book was the law of the land in Christendom for over two hundred years, Simon?" she said, staring at him intently. "This is the sickest book I've ever read. It presents women as predators, abortionists, killers of fetuses. It speaks to the vilest aspects of the subconscious in no uncertain terms. It's an abomination!" She slammed her fist on the table.

"And," she added, "it's my belief that it is the virus which has infected not only the Catholic Church and its view of women but the whole of Western civilization up to the present time. This book is the root of the world's perception of women—even today, as we speak. . . . Let me read you a direct quote from the foreword."

She opened the book and read Crowley's words aloud: " 'A masterpiece . . . a scrupulously argued and convincing work, astonishing in its modernity . . . worthy of the attention of all mankind, even today.' "

They were silent for a long moment.

"There is a great deal in what you say," Lovelock said at last. "You've made an interesting connection."

"An interesting connection? Is that all?" she said, agitated. "Simon, listen to me. The word 'glamour' is used over and over. To 'cast a glamour' means to cast a spell. And who are glamorous, even today? Women! Tell me something—why have I never heard of this book before? Why is it a mere *footnote* in history?" She paused for effect.

"I'll tell you why, Simon." She leaned across the table and pointed a finger at Lovelock. "Because it has to do with women. And because of that, somehow it doesn't count!" She exhaled fiercely and wiped her brow with her napkin. Several patrons had turned around to look at her.

"Calm yourself, please, Beatrice."

"Simon," she said, shaking her head and lowering her voice. "Help me. Please. You implied on our last visit that there's a subculture of people operating in an extremely dangerous way: serious men who must be taken seriously. Your words, Simon, are they not?"

"Yes," Lovelock said softly.

"Then who are these men? And what the hell are they up to? This guy Desmond Crowley, who's written a foreword extolling this as one of the great books of all time? He's on the board of directors of the Duarte Institute, where they sell the damn thing. . . . And what about Phil Burgoyne, George Cahill, Chuck Kraus, Father Morton, Giuseppi Antonelli, and Bart Winslow? God knows Phil Burgoyne is a major reactionary. I can't even listen to his goddamn talk show. So are they involved in some terrible conspiracy against women? Can you answer me that?"

Lovelock paused. "I want to. I want to tell you so much." He was obviously moved.

"You said I had to find things out by myself and then ask you about them. Deep Throat, right? Well, okay—on the back page of the book, you'll see some notes. Here, look—"

She opened the *Malleus* and pointed out Cap Goldman's notes to Lovelock, who studied them closely.

"That's a list of the board of directors of the Duarte Institute," she said. "See, they're all the men I just asked you about—Burgoyne, Cahill, Kraus, Father Morton, et cetera. After each name, Goldman has scribbled the word 'Presenter,' as you can see. Except after this guy Desmond Crowley's name, where he's written simply the initials 'GI.' Now, question: Do you have any idea what these things mean? I mean, is there anything in the *Malleus* that would explain the initials 'GI' or tell us what a 'presenter' is?"

Lovelock shifted uncomfortably in his seat.

"I'm asking you, Simon. I'm begging you. Tell me what all this means."

"I wish I could. But I'm not free to."

"Why? Are you sworn to secrecy?"

"In a way."

"Well, I think these people are involved in kidnappings and God knows what else. So think—who are you protecting?"

He stared at her intently. "You," he said finally, with feeling.

"Me? What are you saying?"

"You're getting too close. I can only be of value to you if I remain neutral. Even though I'm not neutral. But I'm not holding back for the reasons that you think I am. It's not because I don't want to tell you things—I *do*. But I just can't. I'm caught. I'm caught. . . ." She saw tears welling in his eyes.

"You must believe me, Beatrice. I would do anything for you." Lovelock covered his eyes. "But I can't help you now," he said at last.

"You mean you *won't* help me."

"Have it your way, then."

"I don't want to have it my way, Simon. Look here," she pleaded with him, reaching out for his hand. "Is it because you're frightened of something? Because if that's the case, if we band together, we can combat this thing—whatever it is."

Lovelock caught her hand in both of his and held it gently, as if it were a precious object. He bowed his head.

"You're not the Enemy, are you, Simon?" Beatrice said sweetly.

"The Enemy?" He looked at her with horror. "Beatrice, I think I would die for you."

She was extremely moved, but perplexed. "Why? You hardly know me."

"I don't know. But the very first time I saw you, I knew. I'm like that, you see. I've only been in love once before in my life. And it was just like that."

"May I ask you a personal question, Simon?"

"Of course you may," he said gratefully.

"How old are you?"

"Fifty-one."

"Where were you born, Simon?"

"Why do you ask?"

"I'm just curious."

"Albany."

"Are you an only child?"

Lovelock hesitated. "Yes."

"Are your parents still alive?"

"My . . . my father is," he said with evident pain.

"Are you close to him?"

"I was very close to him at one time, yes."

"One more question," she said. "Why did you leave the Jesuits?"

Lovelock's eyes widened slightly. "How did you know I was a Jesuit?" he said.

"A bookseller told Stephen about you."

"Well, I suppose that wasn't too difficult to find out."

"I also know that you worked in the Vatican Library."

"I worked there, yes."

"So—I repeat: why did you leave the Jesuits?"

Lovelock sat motionless for what seemed to Beatrice an interminable time. She could see that he was making up his mind about something, and she remained silent, not daring to say anything. Finally, he spoke.

"I'm going to tell you something I've never told another human being. I don't quite know why I'm going to tell you, but I am."

Beatrice held her breath.

"I had an affair with a woman—someone I loved very deeply," he said at last. "She . . ." He paused, as if trying to fortify himself. "She took her own life."

Beatrice was stunned. "Oh God, Simon. I don't know what to say. I'm sorry. I'm so deeply sorry."

"Independent of the fact that I betrayed my order and went against my vow of celibacy," he said in a grave voice, "I could not, for many reasons and in all good conscience, find any consolation whatsoever in the Church. So I left."

"I understand," Beatrice said softly.

The clattering noises of the restaurant did not intrude upon their solemn moment of intimacy.

"You will forgive me now if I go back to my shop," he said, rising.

"Yes . . . Yes, of course. Let me take you to lunch. I'll get the check."

"Certainly not," he said. "It's been taken care of." Lovelock rose from his seat.

"Beatrice, know one thing, and know it always."

"What, Simon?"

"I'm on your side," he said. "And I will never let anything happen to you as long as I have a breath in me."

As he started to walk away, he appeared shaky. He held on briefly to the back of his chair. Having steadied himself, he took a few steps forward, then stopped.

"But you must stay away from Desmond Crowley at all costs. Promise me you will. Promise?"

Beatrice nodded solemnly.

"I promise," she said.

He turned around and walked out of the restaurant.

14

EATRICE SAT ON ALONE AT THE TABLE, THINKING about Simon Lovelock. At first, she had found him slightly offputting. His chain-smoking, his eating habits, his reticence, which seemed to mask a burning intensity of feeling under-neath—all contributed to the eccentricity of his personality. But Beatrice knew from experience that there was a difference between "personality" and "essence."

Beatrice judged the personality to be that which confronted her when she was face-to-face with someone—a person's appearance, manner, and conversation. Whereas the essence was intangible and independent of any concrete traits. An essence was the overall im-pression an individual left behind. Sometimes what lingered in Beatrice's mind about someone who was out of sight was, in fact, the very opposite of what she felt when she and that person were to-gether. Father Morton had a winning personality. He was outgoing, intelligent, and a good conversationalist. Though Beatrice found him rather likable, he left behind a rancid essence. The more she thought about him, the more she mistrusted and despised him.

Lovelock, on the other hand, had a strange personality. He was odd-looking, awkward, and shy. But to her surprise, Lovelock had a comforting essence. She liked him better and better as she reflected upon him, and she was oddly attracted to him, though in a very different way from either Stephen or Diaz.

Simon, she thought, was the courtly knight, who admired her from afar and protected her. Something about him reminded Beatrice of the delicate concept of *amour courtois* in the Middle Ages, first expressed by the lyric poetry of the troubadours and *trouvères* in the courts of southern France. She recalled the *lai* poems of Chrétien de Troyes, Henri d'Andeli, Jean Renart, Marie de France, and, of course, Guillaume de Lorris, who composed the first section of her beloved *Roman de la Rose*. These poets all described love as ennobling when directed toward a fine and virtuous woman. They chronicled lovers who won their ladies by feats of physical prowess, a strict code of worthy conduct, and, above all, patient hearts. In extolling the theme of chaste, contained passion as the highest form of love, they idealized woman and made her the catalyst for deeds of courage.

Lovelock's confession of constancy enchanted Beatrice, shimmering in front of her like a candle in the mist. Her imagination was as titillated by Lovelock's courtly love as it was by Diaz's crude lust. And in the middle was Stephen, who was, perhaps, her best hope for a complete relationship. She thought of the men in her life as she left the restaurant and started back to Stephen's apartment: her father, who gave her unconditional love; Stephen, who wanted her as a wife; Diaz, who took her purely as a sexual partner; and now Lovelock, who worshipped her from afar.

As she was walking up a side street in the Village, she saw an arresting vignette and crossed the street for a better look. There, in the window of a little shop with the enticing name Come Now, was a female mannequin presiding over a variety of vibrators, restraints, and other sex toys. Outfitted in a pointed witch's hat, a leather merry widow corset, black fishnet stockings, and black satin stiletto-heeled shoes, the dummy was holding a riding crop, like a skinny broom, sprouting a long black tuft of hair at the top. A sign underneath read: HALLOWEEN SPECIAL. The spectacle revived her wolf. Feeling it gnawing at her, she ventured inside.

A bell tinkled as she walked through the door. The small emporium was cheerful and cluttered. At the rear was an old-fashioned cash register on a counter that featured a display of condoms "in all flavors" and a row of dildos lined up like headless toy soldiers. One wall was devoted to pornographic magazines and videos. A second mannequin, in the center of the shop, was dressed in a red garter belt, a lacy bra with cutouts at the tips, and thigh-high red patent-leather boots. Hanging on a rack behind her was a variety of kinky outfits made of leather, spandex, and silk.

As Beatrice inspected this display, the proprietor, a beefy, baby-faced man dressed only in tight black leather trousers and a black leather vest, appeared from the back room. His greasy blond hair was pulled back in a long ponytail. He wore gold chains around his neck and a black leather bracelet studded with gold nails. His sleeveless vest revealed his thick arms and hairy chest. Popping the last bit of a sandwich into his mouth, he licked his fingers and wiped them on his trousers, polishing up his diamond pinkie ring in the process. He gave Beatrice a big grin.

"Howdy," he said. "What can I do for you today?"

"I'd like to buy that outfit in the window," Beatrice said, somewhat disgusted by his appearance.

"Oh, so you like Glenda, do you? That's what I call her. Remember Glenda, the Good Witch of the North, in *The Wizard of Oz?* Billie Burke, remember? I get a lot of comments on her."

Beatrice nodded. "Is the outfit for sale?"

"Everything in here's for sale—including me." He snickered.

"How much?"

"Me or the outfit?"

"Just Glenda's glad rags, thanks."

"Hat and everything?"

"What size are the shoes?"

"Seven or seven and a half, I think."

"The whole thing, then."

"Well, let's see now . . . The corset's one of a kind. And the fly whisk—that's the thing she's holding. They use it in horseback riding. I picked it up in a fancy riding store for the display. It's made of real horsehair and leather—"

"Just give me a total price, if you don't mind," Beatrice said, interrupting his sales pitch.

"Say, oh . . . four hundred bucks for the whole kit and caboodle.

It's worth more, but business has been in the toilet lately. Except for the small stuff, of course. I should've bought stock in flavored condoms."

"Okay," Beatrice said, opening her purse. "I'll take it."

"You'll take it?" He seemed surprised.

"Credit card okay?"

"Yeah, sure."

"Here." She handed him a MasterCard.

He looked Beatrice up and down, then shrugged, taking her card. "You live in the neighborhood?"

"No."

" 'Beatrice,' " he said, reading her name off the card. "I have an aunt named Beatrice. She hates it when people call her Bea. Do people call you Bea?"

"Sometimes. Excuse me, but I'm in a bit of a hurry."

"Okay, okay."

He ran her card through a little device by the register and made out a bill. Then he climbed into the window and began unfastening the hooks of the corset. Beatrice looked around the shop. She was fascinated by the sexual paraphernalia, which was presented in a disturbingly lighthearted way. She examined some of the packages: "Sindy's Cuffs—For Those Who Use Restraint"; "Inflatable Party Doll—Blow Her Up, Blow Your Mind. DD Cups"; "The Lone Ranger Mask"; "Silk Bondage Ropes—You'll 'Knot' Be Disappointed"; "Tit for Tat—The Clamps That Really Suck."

Having undressed the dummy, the proprietor climbed down from the window. "This is a great outfit," he said, as he wrapped the costume. "Hey, by the way. Have you noticed how weird people are getting these days? That's because the millennium is upon us. People go bats around the turn of the century. That's a fact."

Beatrice thought *him* one of the weirder specimens she'd seen in a while. He rolled the horsehair fly whisk in a sheet of newspaper and slid it into a plain brown shopping bag, along with the rest of the outfit.

"Happy Halloween," the proprietor said, handing her the package.

"It's a little early for Halloween, isn't it?"

"Are you kidding? Every day's Halloween around here."

"Yeah, I guess you're right," Beatrice said, going out the door.

"So—happy hunting!" he called after her.

"Jesus Christ—where the hell have you been?" Stephen said, as he opened the door. "I've been worried sick about you."

"I went down to the Village to have lunch with Lovelock. Then I did a little shopping."

"It's almost six," he said, hovering around her. "Why did you have lunch with Lovelock? Did he call you?"

"No; I called him." Beatrice put down the shopping bag. "Stephen, I think I've figured out something crucial."

"What?"

"I'll tell you after I freshen up. Stop fussing over me, will you?"

Stephen retreated to the couch and swigged down the last of a glass of Scotch. "What'd you buy?"

"I'll show you later." She went to wash her face and hands, feeling grubby from the day's activities. "What did you do today?" she called out from the bathroom.

"I've been with the Krauts all day. I feel like Poland must have felt in 1939," he complained. "You want some Scotch?"

"Sure."

"What a fucking day!" He sighed.

He poured two drinks and slumped down onto the couch, sliding off his moccasins. Beatrice returned from the bathroom and sat on the chair opposite him. She picked up her drink.

"Cheers," she said.

"Cheers," he responded wearily.

"Stephen, listen to me—"

"Bea, do me a favor, will you, before you start? Just let me just unwind for a while. I am really beat."

Beatrice stared at him hard. "Stephen," she began slowly, "you have no idea what we're up against."

"Listen, I've been dealing with so much red tape all day . . . But the good news is, it's paid off. I think I've located von Nordhausen."

Beatrice perked up. "Good going. Where is he?"

"Let me just get out my notes." He rolled over slightly and, with some effort, extracted a small notebook from the back pocket of his trousers. He thumbed through the pages. "Christ, I can hardly move. . . . Okay," he said, rallying a little. "Here's the deal. Ready?"

"In Germany, army pension records are restricted by a privacy act, so I couldn't find out anything about von Nordhausen through his war records. However . . ." Stephen raised a finger instructively. "Being ever organized, the Germans have something called the *Einwohnermeldeamt* . . . ," he said, reading from his notes.

"The what?"

"Don't ask me to repeat it, okay? It's a city organization enforced by the police—or the *Bundeskriminalamt*. Basically, it works like this. Every German citizen must register a change of address within ten days or else face severe criminal penalties. The small village registration office is called the *Gemeindeamt*. The big city registration office is called the *Einwohnermeldeamt*. So after I found all this out, I got this guy at the consulate to actually call the *Einwohnermeldeamt* in Hamburg, to see if he could track down von Nordhausen."

"Just like that?"

"Don't say 'just like that.' This has already taken two hours of waiting time and another hour of interminable bullshit before I could convince him to do it."

"At least he did it."

"Actually, he was a funny guy. He told me it's not a problem finding out who's registered where, 'ass long ass you don't vant to kill zem.' "

"How does anyone know what you want to do with them once you find them?"

"Good point. Luckily, he wasn't as scrupulous as you are. Although he did ask me four hundred million questions about why I wanted to locate von Nordhausen."

"And what did you tell him?"

"A lot of crap. I said I was doing a story on the new Germany and veterans of World War II. Some bullshit like that. You know me—I can wing it when I have to."

"So go on," Beatrice said. "I'm listening."

"Okay," he continued. "To make a long and incredibly tedious story short: Erich von Nordhausen moved to London in 1947. He lives in Highgate, and here's his address and telephone number."

Stephen ripped a piece of paper out of his notebook and handed it to Beatrice.

"Twelve Delphinium Street," she said, reading the page. "But 1947? Christ, that's over forty-five years ago. Do you think he's still alive?"

"I'm coming to that. So I call the number in London, and a

woman with one of those cheery English voices answers the phone.
And I say, 'May I speak to Mr. von Nordhausen, please?' And there's
a pause. So I say again, 'Is Mr. von Nordhausen there, please?' Another pause. Then click."

"Maybe you just had a wrong number."

"No. She wouldn't have hesitated after I asked for him the first
time. And she hesitated—she really hesitated."

Beatrice examined the paper again. "It's a long shot."

"Yeah, but I have a nose for these things. And there was something in her hesitation that told me she knew exactly who he was.
Otherwise why wouldn't she have said, 'I'm sorry, there's no Mr. von
Nordhausen here,' or 'He doesn't live here anymore,' or 'Piss off,
he's moved and we don't know where the hell he is'? Whatever." He
swallowed the rest of his Scotch. It burned his throat. "Ahh . . . ," he
said, taking in some air. "No. She knew damn well who he was, and
she didn't want me to talk to him, for some reason. Or more to the
point, she didn't want him to talk to me."

"Maybe," Beatrice said at last.

"I got news for you, kid. We're going to London."

"When?"

"As soon as possible. Tomorrow, how 'bout it? You game?"

"Sure."

"Remember that cute little hotel off Sloane Street we always
wanted to check out? We can stay there."

"Great."

"It'll be like a second honeymoon," he said, smiling at her.
"Now tell me why you went to see Lovelock. But first I need a kiss.
Come here."

"Just a second. I want to show you something."

Beatrice got up from the chair and retrieved the notes she had
made on the *Malleus* that morning.

"Take a look at these," she said, handing him the pages filled
with her neat, schoolgirl printing.

"I can't do anything until I have a kiss," he said.

Beatrice rolled her eyes heavenward and gave him a perfunctory
kiss on the mouth.

"Some kiss."

"Stephen, just sit up and pay attention, will you? Read."

She pulled him out of his slumped position and sat down beside him, reading over his shoulder. After looking over a couple of pages, he glanced at her.

"What the hell is all this about?" he said.

"Just keep reading."

Stephen continued until he had finished, then he put the notes down in his lap.

"Are these direct quotes from the *Malleus* whatever-it's-called?" he said.

"*Maleficarum.* They are verbatim quotes," she replied. "What do you think?"

"What do I think?" He scratched his head. "Is this stuff *real?*"

"It's real, all right. Don't you love the part about witches stealing penises and putting them in nests, where they feed on corn and oats?"

"It's amazing."

"That book was the law of the land for over two hundred years, Stephen. It was on the desk of every judge and magistrate in both Protestant and Catholic countries. Isn't it incredible? And no one's ever heard of it. It's like a footnote in history. And why? Because it deals with women."

"They certainly weren't overly fond of them in those days."

"So what's new?"

"Oh, come on, Bea. We're a little more enlightened today, don't you think? After all, I don't think of you as . . . what does it say here?" He read from the notes: " 'a foe to friendship, an unescapable punishment, a necessary evil, a natural temptation, a desirable calamity, a domestic danger, a delectable detriment, an evil of nature, painted with fair colours!' Although on second thought, you may well be 'a natural temptation.' " He reached out to stroke her hair.

She pushed his hand aside.

"Aw, come here, my 'delectable detriment.' Let's fool around," Stephen said.

"It's not funny!" Beatrice said. "I'm trying to tell you that nothing has changed. Look at my notes on the foreword—written in 1955, mind you, almost four hundred years after the fact. The author extols this little gem as one of the great works of literature. He calls it 'a book for the present age,' 'impartial,' full of 'scrupulous logic.' Read that," she said, pointing to the notes.

" 'The *Malleus Maleficarum* is one of the greatest books ever written, for it makes manifest the eternal conflict between good and evil and is, therefore, a tribute and an inspiration to all men who seek the truth beyond the finite realities of this world,'" Stephen read aloud. "The guy who wrote this sounds like a wacko, all right."

"Three guesses who that guy is, Stephen."

"Who?"

"Desmond Crowley."

Stephen raised his eyebrows. "Really?"

"If you ask me, they're doing more than selling it up there. I think they're teaching it."

"It's disturbing, I grant you."

"Disturbing? Yeah, you might say so. And all these feminists disappearing . . . ? Cap thinks there's a connection between that and the institute. Anyway, that's why I went to see Lovelock today."

"What'd he have to say?"

"Well, I think he knows what's going on, but he won't tell me. He thinks he's protecting me by not telling me—don't ask me why. However, he did say I was on the right track and that Desmond Crowley is an evil man. . . . Want to hear something amazing? He told me the reason he left the Jesuits was because he had an affair with a woman and she killed herself."

"I always said you should have been a reporter. You get the damnedest things out of people."

"Listen, Stephen—I want to go to London by myself."

"Oh, no, not this time, kiddo," he said emphatically. "We are now in deep water. Anyway, I don't want you sneaking off to see Diaz again."

"But you've got to stay here and find out more about Crowley and this damn Duarte Institute. You've got to, Stephen. I feel we're closing in on something."

"Seriously, Bea, it might be dangerous for you there alone."

"I can take care of myself."

"I'm sorry to hear that," he said, smiling ruefully. "You've really changed, Bea. You really have. There was a time when you were scared of your own shadow."

"Yeah, there was, wasn't there?" she reflected. "But no more, honey! I'm Athena with a sword now. I feel that women all over this country are in danger and somehow God has given me a mission to find out what the hell's going on. Anyway, I've made up my mind. I'm going alone."

"I guess I can't stop you," he said. "I just thought we'd have a really nice, romantic time there, that's all."

"I don't feel romantic. I feel like a warrior."

Beatrice picked up the phone and booked herself on a flight to London the next evening.

"Okay, that's done," she said. "By the way, Lovelock has a crush on me."

"Don't tell me I should be jealous."

"I'm not so sure you shouldn't be."

"What's that supposed to mean?" Stephen said irritably. "What are you turning into—the slut of the Western world? First Diaz, now Lovelock."

Beatrice slithered on top of Stephen and began kissing him, insinuating her tongue into his mouth.

"Jesus, Bea, what are you doing?"

"I want to fuck you. War gives me an appetite," she said. "Don't you want to fuck me?"

"Fuck? What happened to 'make love'?"

"I don't want to make love. I want to fuck."

"Right now?"

"Why not?"

"Sure, why not? Lovelock turned you on, did he?"

"Maybe."

"What's gotten into you, Bea? You're, like, sexually wired all the time."

"So? Don't you like it?"

"Yeah, I guess so," he said halfheartedly.

Beatrice undressed him. She massaged his penis until he had a big erection.

"Come on," he said, yanking her up off the couch. "Let's get into bed."

"Wait." She freed herself from his arms. "I want to show you something." Beatrice ran into the bathroom, grabbing her purse and the brown paper bag along the way. "Pull down the shades and light some candles," she called out to Stephen, as she was changing.

"What the hell for?"

"Just do it!"

"Okay, but hurry up. You've got me hornier than hell!"

Beatrice hooked up the merry widow and plumped up her breasts over the top of the cups. She drew on the fishnet stockings, fastening them with the black garters that hung down from the corset. She wore no underpants. Sliding her feet into the black satin stiletto-heeled shoes, she felt like a giant. Next, she teased her hair and rimmed the edges of her eyes in heavy black liner.

"I can only find one candle," Stephen called out.

"That's fine. Light it."

"It's lit. And so am I. What are you doing in there, for Christ's sake? My cock is about to explode!"

"I'm coming. Just hold your horses," she said, smearing on bright-red lipstick.

"I'm holding something else right now. Hurry up!"

Finally, Beatrice put on the witch's hat, setting it low on her brow so it shaded her face. When she turned to look at herself in the full-length mirror on the back of the door, her eyes widened. She saw another person reflected in the glass—the wild, lascivious creature of her subconscious. Baring her teeth, she snarled like a wolf, gripping the dark triangle of her pubic hair with her hands. She felt herself getting wet with excitement. Holding her mound, she opened the soft folds of her labia and massaged her clitoris with the tips of her fingers in slow circles. Then she ran her hands down her legs and plucked up the lace tops of the stockings, snapping them over the little bulges of flesh on her inner thighs. She stood still, her hands at her sides, looking at her Other Self with pleasure. She picked up the whip. She was ready.

The room was dark except for the aura of twilight creeping in around the shades. The candle was burning on the night table. Stephen was lying naked in bed, his penis standing up proudly. He was staring at the ceiling with a confident, lazy smile as Beatrice emerged from the bathroom. Rolling over on his side, he turned toward Beatrice, who walked to the center of the room and stood very still. Upon seeing her, he shot bolt upright, swinging his legs over the side of the bed. He gazed at her in disbelief.

"Jesus Christ!" he exclaimed. "What the hell ...?" He laughed self-consciously.

Beatrice took slow, undulating strides toward him, brandishing the whip.

"Bea ... For God's sake, what's going on?"

She stood directly in front of him, gently brushing the tail of the whip over his chest.

"Stop it," he said, reddening with embarrassment. "That tickles."

At that, she raised the whip high, stood back, and swatted him hard across his arm. He looked utterly stunned. She raised the whip again. Just as she was about to strike him once more, he sprang from the bed and grabbed her wrist in midair.

"Cut it out!" he cried. "What the hell do you think you're doing?"

She dropped the whip, yanked off her hat, and threw herself on top of him, knocking him back onto the bed. Sitting astride his pelvis, she gazed down at him with a lascivious expression.

"Fuck me, Stephen," she said. "Split me open with your big dick!"

Stephen grabbed her arms and pulled her down to his chest. She stretched out her legs and let him kiss her for a few moments. Then, suddenly, she responded, digging her tongue deep into his mouth, wiggling it around while she massaged his erect member with her hand. This is some cock, she thought. But then she felt the erection begin to wane and his blood-engorged flesh soften in her hand. He was losing his splendid hardness even as she tried to arouse him anew.

"I . . . I don't understand," he said after a time, letting her go. "I'm sorry."

Stephen lay on his back, his arms at his sides.

"That's okay, baby," she said. "I'll help you. Just relax."

She began to lick him all over, working her way down to his crotch. She flicked her tongue around the tip of his cock to wet it, then took it in her hand and massaged it while nibbling at his balls with her lips. Every once in a while she let her tongue slip down to the crevice of his ass. Stephen let out small cries of pleasure. When his cock began to get hard again, Beatrice slid her mouth over it, sucking it hard, her thick spittle coating his penis and running down into his groin. She moved her head up and down, up and down, forcing his member deeper into her throat until it became so erect, she gagged. Feeling the tip of his penis penetrating her gullet, he gasped with pleasure.

"Now," she said, climbing on top of him once more. "Fuck me, baby."

She straddled him, maneuvering his cock into the mouth of her vagina with her hand. She pushed down hard. But once again, his erection wilted. She started kissing him, but he pushed her away.

"Jesus, Bea, I don't know what the hell's wrong with me," he said apologetically.

"Don't worry, baby. Let's take a break." She cuddled up close to him.

"I think I've had too much to drink," he murmured, ashamed.

"You think that's it?"

"Yeah," he said in a tentative voice. "Why? What do you think it is?"

Beatrice paused.

"Maybe you don't want to fuck a witch."

"Oh. Are you a witch?"

"All women are witches underneath."

"Not all. Some. Not you."

"Yes, me, Stephen. But because you love me, you can't see me that way. And when you do see me that way, it frightens you."

"You think I'm frightened?"

"I think your cock is terrified."

Stephen diddled with his flaccid member. "Maybe," he said absently.

"Why do you think that is, Stephen?"

"What?"

"That you're terrified of this side of me."

"I don't know." He got up and padded over to the refrigerator. "You look ridiculous," he said.

"You think so?" Beatrice ran her hands over the cups of her bra. "I feel sexy in this outfit."

"I guess I'm not used to you looking like—"

"Like what?"

"A whore."

"What's wrong with that?"

"Nothing, if you are a whore. But you're not." He opened the icebox.

"Maybe I want to feel like one sometimes."

"Why?"

"Because it's part of my nature."

"What? Feeling like a whore?"

"Is a whore a witch, Stephen?" Beatrice said, raising her eyebrows.

"Yeah, sort of."

"Really? You really think so?"

"You know what I mean," he said, studying the contents of the refrigerator.

"You know what, Stephen?"

"What?"

"I think you're afraid that once your cock disappears into a witch, it will never come out again."

"Uh huh." He poured himself a beer. "You want something to drink?" he said flatly.

"No, thanks. I'll have some of yours."

Stephen returned to the bed and lay down, propping himself up on the pillows. He rested the glass of beer on his stomach. "So you wanna watch some TV, or what?"

Beatrice stroked his hair. "I'm sorry, baby. I didn't mean to frighten you."

"Tell me something—is this what you did with that asshole social worker of yours?"

"We didn't love each other, so I could be his witch."

"His whore, you mean?"

"Okay, have it your way. His whore. His witch-whore."

"In other words, he could get it up, and I can't."

"You can," she said, trying to reassure him. "Just not under these circumstances."

"Oh, and these circumstances are what? That you come out looking like Halloween, ready to whip me into submission? You call these circumstances?" he said hostilely. "I call this a fucking sado-masochistic costume party." He sipped his beer.

"You don't want to deal with my wolf," Beatrice said. "Not that I blame you. Wolves are dangerous."

"What do you want, Bea? You want to whip me? Or do you want me to whip you? Hit you? Slap you around a little? Does that make you hot? Is that what turns you on?"

"No, it's not that simple. I don't know if you can understand this, Stephen, but what turns me on is the power."

"What power? What do you mean?"

"The power of fantasy. The idea that I can take you into the kingdom of the senses and dominate you there. And that you can dominate me. I can bite off your cock, if I want. But I don't. I make

love to it instead. You can strangle me, if you want. But you don't.
You caress me instead."

"That's not love. That's just sick," Stephen said with revulsion.

"No . . . it's not love. But it's lust and it's anger. And it's the
doorway to the purest feeling of being alive that I've ever known."

"I'm sorry for you, Bea," he said, after a time.

"Why?"

"Because it doesn't connect you with the other person. It just
connects you with the sex."

"Well, that's how I feel now. I can't help it. And I want to feel
it with you, Stephen. I desperately want to feel it with you."

"Why me, when you've got fucking Diaz?"

"Because I *trust* you. I want to feel this way with someone I
trust."

"You didn't trust Diaz?"

"God, no," she said. "Don't you understand. I want to feel
whole. I'm so compartmentalized now, I need three different men to
bring me together."

"Three?" He looked at her askance. "Who's the third, for
Christ's sake?"

"Lovelock. He loves me from afar. He thinks I'm noble and
brave. I just can't get love and sex and nobility together, I guess."

"Bea, I want you to be the mother of my children. I don't want
a witch as the mother of my children. Are you doing this to get back
at me for running off during our marriage? Is that what this is
about?"

"It's not about you, Stephen. It's about me. I don't know if you
can understand that."

"So you don't feel sexy with me? Is that what you're saying?"

"I do, but not like I do with Diaz."

"You don't feel noble with me?"

"No. We've been through too much. You know me too well."

He turned away.

"Stephen, let me ask you a question. Why did you marry me?
Really?"

"I loved you."

"Why?"

"I don't know. Why do people love each other? They just do."

"I think it's because I wasn't a threat to you sexually. You didn't
want the mother of your children to be sexually challenging."

"That's not true," he said defensively.

"But you said yourself I didn't enjoy sex all that much. And then you ran off with—what's her name? I've blanked it."

"Margot," he said softly.

"That's right—Margot," Beatrice said, with contempt. "What did she have that I didn't?"

"I told you. That was about my own fear of commitment more than anything else. She was just a diversion."

"But she was sexy, right?"

"Yeah, she was sexy."

"Sexier than I was at the time."

"Okay, maybe she was."

"In other words, you married a good girl, but you needed to go elsewhere for your sexual gratification."

"I don't know."

"She turned you on. Admit it."

"Okay, she did."

"Why?"

"I don't know," he said, growing increasingly uncomfortable. "She liked sex."

"Then why didn't you marry someone who liked sex?"

"I don't know. Because I was in love with you, and you didn't like it."

"Maybe that's precisely *why* you were in love with me. Have you ever thought about that?"

"No," he said petulantly.

"I was no threat. And I was fairly innocent. Now I'm not so innocent. Now I am a threat. And it turns you off."

"But I'm still in love with you. Explain that."

"Are you? Or are you in love with the idea of me—your idea?"

"What's my idea of you?"

"You like to play rescuer. You rescued me from my family, and now you're rescuing me from the forces of darkness."

Stephen considered. "Okay . . . let me ask *you* a question. Why did *you* marry *me?*"

"Oh, that's easy," she said. "You led this exciting life. You were a writer, dangerous, non-Catholic, and my mother didn't approve of you. I married you to escape everything I'd been brought up to believe."

"But were you in love with me?"

"I don't know now . . . ," she said thoughtfully. "Sex is a big part of being in love. It's a kind of shock absorber to get people through fights and tough times. And as we both know, sex was not a major component of our relationship—even at the beginning. So, when we didn't have that shock absorber, the marriage ended."

Stephen rubbed his face with his hand. She loved his hands. They were muscular and strong.

"Look, Bea, I'm not into all this witch-costume shit, okay? Yeah, maybe your innocence appealed to me. But this stuff definitely doesn't. Is there no happy medium between not liking sex and this shit?" he said contemptuously.

"Too dark for you?"

He sipped some more beer and burped. "Yeah. It is too dark for me." He nodded.

"Well, this is part of me, Stephen. This is part of *me*. I am part witch. That is who I am."

15

T WAS DRIZZLING SLIGHTLY WHEN BEATRICE GOT off the plane at Heathrow. The sky was overcast with a dull gray haze. She changed some money and found a cab.

"Can you take me to Highgate?" she said, stepping into the large, beetle-black English taxi.

"Highgate. Right you are," the driver said in a bright Cockney accent. The meter clicked on.

"Nice flight?"

"Fine, thanks."

They drove for a while.

"So where're you from in the States?" he said.

"New York."

"Ah, New York. I been there. I'm very fond of you Yanks. You don't sound like you're from New York. You don't have a New York accent, do you?"

Beatrice responded with a tired smile. Ignoring her signal, he pressed on.

"Off to see the cemetery, are you?"

"What cemetery?"

"In Highgate, o' course," he said incredulously, glancing at her in the rearview mirror.

"Oh, right. Highgate Cemetery. I forgot about that. No, not exactly."

"You can't go to Highgate and not see the cemetery, unless you've already seen it. It's worth a trip, it is."

"I'm sure."

"You look like a literary type, if you don't mind my saying so. There's some literary types buried there, you know—George Eliot, the writer, you know? William Wordsworth, the poet. Then, o' course, there's Karl Marx. Everyone goes to see Karl Marx's grave 'cause of the big head. Looks like a big old lion, 'e does. Old Karl's prob'ly spinning in his grave now, what with all the problems in Russia. I wouldn't of thought I'd live to see the day those blokes gave in. World's turned topsy-turvy, though, hasn't it?" He gave out a little chuckle. "Course, my favorite grave is Frederick William Lillywhite," he said, pronouncing the name slowly, emphasizing each syllable. "Bet you don't know who 'e was."

"No," Beatrice said absently, wishing he would be quiet.

"A great bowler, 'e was. That's a cricketer, you know. Started round arm bowling?" She stared at the back of his head blankly. "But o' course you don't follow cricket, do you?"

"No, I'm afraid I don't."

"Nah." He shook his head. "Yanks don't follow cricket. . . . I follow American football sometimes. I like it better than our football, don't ask me why."

The driver nattered on and on as they sped along the M-1. Beatrice hardly listened. Feeling the effects of jet lag, she stared out the window at the monotonous road and finally nodded off. The driver didn't seem to notice, or if he did, he didn't seem to care.

"Now, whereabouts in Highgate?" he said, as they approached the main street.

"Twelve Delphinium Street," Beatrice said, snapping awake.

"Should be right around here. Don't you worry, now. We'll find it for you. We're like Scotland Yard, we are—always get our man."

Highgate looked to Beatrice like a fairly prosperous old suburb, preserved through the efforts of history-conscious home owners and civic groups. One side of the high street was interspersed with fake half-timbered buildings in the Elizabethan style. Little specialty shops lined the block—clothing boutiques, a chemist, butcher, bakery, greengrocer, and the like, along with several pubs and restaurants. There was a roundabout in the center of the wide road, where cars circled past a village green and a church. The people on the street, however, seemed less tinged with the smug, parochial bearing of a comfortable middle class in a comfortable setting. England was going through a depression, and more than in the surroundings, Beatrice could see it reflected in the somewhat grim faces of the inhabitants.

Veering off to the right into a narrow side street, the driver then took a sharp left turn down a cobbled alley.

"Delphinium Street," he announced, pointing up to a black-and-white sign nailed to a corner house.

Beatrice scanned the numbers on the doors as the taxi made its way slowly down the block. It pulled up in front of a small, three-story, pale-brick house. A sign hanging directly above the front door read, vertically, SNACKS & TEAS, in bold black lettering.

"Number twelve," the driver said, with evident satisfaction. "Told you we always get our man, didn't I?"

Beatrice gathered up her carry-on bag and her purse, got out of the taxi, and paid the fare.

"Oh, ta." The driver's grateful nod acknowledged her generous tip. "Have a nice visit. Don't forget the cemetery," he said, as he pulled away.

Beatrice stood in front of the building, then finally took a deep breath, threw back her shoulders, and pulled down the handle of the glass-paned door.

The tearoom was empty except for a ruddy-looking middle-aged man in blue jeans, sitting by himself at a table in the back, slumped over a book, reading. Stirring slightly as Beatrice entered, he called out at the top of his lungs:

"Katrine! Customer!"

Beatrice heard the muted squeals of children coming from a back room. The man returned to his book. Beatrice sat down near the front of the café, propping up her luggage on an empty chair. She looked around at the fairly seedy little parlor, with its fraying tieback curtains and peeling yellow walls. The rickety wooden tables, draped in faded pink cloths, were set with four thick cups, facedown in their saucers, and four folded napkins containing silverware. Bud vases at the center of each table sprouted withering little bouquets. A delicious aroma of baking bread filled the air.

Beatrice picked up the soiled printed menu card from the table. As she was reading over the selection of teas and cakes, a plump but rather pretty woman appeared from the kitchen, followed by two young children, a boy and a girl, who were giggling and dancing around her legs, much to her annoyance. She swatted the boy on the head with her order pad and cried, "Enough!" several times. Unheeded, she grabbed him by the ear.

"Ow, Mummy! That hurts!" he whined.

"You're both going upstairs if you don't behave! Now go and sit with your father. Mummy's got work to do."

"Come here, monsters," the man said, motioning to the unruly pair.

The children obeyed. The woman walked over to Beatrice's table.

"Please excuse the brood," she said with an exasperated smile. "You know what they're like."

She was wearing a loose-fitting sweater, a dirty apron over a pair of khaki trousers, and thick brown orthopedic shoes. A wilted white lace cap, tilting toward the back of her head, was haphazardly pinned to tufts of her short blond hair. Her round face was open and friendly.

"Just one, are we?"

"Yes."

"What'll it be, then?" she said, clearing the other places. "We have fresh scones and some nice lemon cake, baked yesterday."

"Just some tea, please."

"What kind?"

"I don't care."

"Lapsang souchong's nice. Goes nicely with everything."

"Sounds great."

"Any cakes? Scones? Toast?"

"No, thanks."

"Nothing else, then? You sure? You look like you just got in from a trip or you're going on a trip."

"I just got in. From New York."

"What brings you to Highgate, then? Wait, don't tell me." She held up her hand. "The cemetery. That's why most tourists come here."

"Uh, no. Actually, I'd like to speak with the proprietor here, if that's possible."

The woman cocked her head and looked more closely at Beatrice. "I'm the proprietor. Well, my husband and I are. What can we do for you?"

"I'm looking for a man named von Nordhausen."

As soon as Beatrice said the name, the woman's friendly expression evaporated. "I'm sorry. I can't help you."

Beatrice was sure she was lying. "Look, I don't know if I'm in the right place, okay? But we tracked him down to this address through a registration office in Hamburg. My, uh, boyfriend called here a couple of days ago and said that a woman answered the phone. When he asked for von Nordhausen, she hesitated. Are you that woman?" The woman stared at her coldly. "Please," Beatrice continued. "If you are, and if you know where von Nordhausen is, I beg you to help me."

"Aaron," the woman called out. "Come here, will you?"

Cautioning the children to stay seated, he got up and walked over to Beatrice's table. Slinging his arm around the woman's shoulder, he said, "What's up?"

"She says she's looking for a man named von Nordhausen."

He pulled her in closer. The couple eyed each other briefly.

"What do you want with him?" the man asked.

"I need to talk to him. Please. It's very urgent. Do you know where I can get in touch with him?"

"No. We've never heard of him, have we, Katrine?"

"No." The woman hung her head.

"If I told you that it's a matter of life and death? That I don't want anything from him except some information—"

"What information?" the man said.

"I can't tell you that. I have to speak with him directly."

He shrugged and looked at her dismissively. "Then I'm afraid we can't help you."

"Do you know him, at least?"

"What if we do?" the woman said.

Beatrice saw her husband squeeze her tighter to shut her up. But the woman pulled away slightly.

"What if we do?" she reiterated.

"Can you get him a message for me?"

"Maybe."

"No!" The man contradicted her emphatically.

"Maybe," the woman said again. "What's the message?"

"Tell him someone needs to speak to him about the grimoire. He'll understand."

The woman shuddered. The man stood as still as stone, glaring at Beatrice.

"Who are you?" he said at last.

"Won't you please sit down with me?" Beatrice said.

They looked at each other. The woman nodded slightly, and they sat down at the table.

"My name is Beatrice O'Connell," she began slowly. "My father was a surgeon and a book collector. A few months ago, a patient he'd operated on sent my father a book in gratitude for saving his life. That book was a grimoire. I gather from the look on both your faces that you know exactly what that is."

They both nodded.

"This patient wrote my father a letter, saying he'd picked up the book as a souvenir during the war. Shortly after my father received the book, he was—" Beatrice paused and swallowed hard, trying to gain control of her emotions. Her mouth was dry.

"He was murdered," she went on. "And the book was stolen. I tracked this patient down, and he told me the story of how he happened to come by the book. He said he'd gotten it in Rome from a German courier, disguised as a priest. The courier was trying to escape, when the Allies picked him up. They interrogated him, and he admitted he was a spy. He told them the grimoire was just a souvenir, and as they couldn't prove otherwise, they believed him. But I think he was lying. I'm convinced that the grimoire was his real reason for being in Rome. And I'm also convinced it's the reason my father was murdered. That courier's name was von Nordhausen, and I think you know exactly who he is and where I can find him. Now will you please help me?"

The three were silent. Then the woman looked at her husband. "Will you excuse us, please?" she said to Beatrice.

The couple walked over to a corner, where they talked in animated whispers. Beatrice watched them closely. They appeared to be arguing. Finally, the man shrugged and went back to his table, where the children were playing. The woman approached Beatrice.

"Come with me," the woman said. "Leave your things here. My

husband will look after them. By the way, my name is Katrine Silvers, and that's my husband, Aaron." She and Beatrice shook hands.

Katrine took a sweater from the coatrack near the front door and wrapped it around her shoulders. "Come," she beckoned.

Beatrice followed her out the door. They walked in silence through the town, up a steep hill to Highgate Cemetery. At the eastern entrance to the graveyard, Katrine paid the admission fee for both of them and led Beatrice along the main path. They passed Karl Marx's imposing monument. There, under a huge granite bust of the bearded philosopher, the words "Workers of All Lands Unite—Karl Marx" were chiseled in gold.

The cab driver was right, Beatrice thought. He does look like a great lion.

The ground was muddy and soft, and Beatrice's shoes kept sinking into the ground. Katrine, trudging on ahead, turned down a narrow path covered with tangled underbrush. Beatrice hurried to keep up with her. Finally, they reached a small clearing back in the woods. Katrine marched up to a relatively new-looking headstone. She knelt down and blessed herself. Beatrice came up behind her. Carved on the headstone was the simple inscription: ERIC NORTH, 1916-1988.

"You wanted to meet Erich von Nordhausen," Katrine said. "Here he is."

Beatrice stared at the simple white stone. "He changed his name."

"Yes."

"You knew him?"

Katrine paused. "He was my father," she said somberly.

"I had no idea," Beatrice said. "I'm so sorry."

The two women sat down on a small, moss-covered bench nearby.

"Do you smoke?" Katrine said, producing a pack of cigarettes from her trouser pocket.

"Thanks," Beatrice said, leaning in as Katrine gave her a light.

Katrine took a long drag of her cigarette and stared out into the mist. "I used to come here every day," she said. "Sometimes twice a day. My father was a tormented man, but I loved him very much. I haven't been here in months." Her eyes teared.

"How did he die?" Beatrice asked softly.

"Heart attack. That was the official verdict, anyway."

"What do you mean?"

"I mean he really died of the war. The scars of the war. He was dead a long time before his body gave out."

"Tell me about him," Beatrice said sympathetically.

"Oh, where to begin ..." She sighed. "My father was born in the town of Nordhausen. He came from a very old family. My grandfather was a baron and a monarchist. I have pictures of him. He looks exactly like Bismarck." She laughed slightly. "My father was a brilliant young man, a scholar and rather a mystic. In fact, he entertained the idea of going into the Church. But instead he became a philosopher—a devotee of Fichte. You know Johann Fichte?"

"No."

"He was a great German philosopher around the turn of the eighteenth century, much admired by Kant. But he eventually rejected Kant's theories. My father wrote a thesis on him, which brought him to the attention of Adolf Hitler." She spat out the name, as though it were poison in her mouth.

"Why?"

"You see, Fichte had a theory that the German people were the *Urvolk*, as he called them—the chosen people of nature. He believed that in the relationship between states, there is only one rule: the rule of strength. And that rule is in the control of a sovereign prince, who, simply because he is mighty, is above law and personal morals and even fate itself."

"No wonder Hitler liked him," Beatrice said.

"Yes. He used Fichte as a justification for his own pernicious goals. But all that is irrelevant, really," she went on. "Dad was a student at the university in Hamburg. He was having a brilliant career. And Hitler loved young aristocrats," she said, with bitterness. "That is to say, those with strong monarchist ties who were anxious to rebel against their parents and side with him.

"My father was young, impressionable, idealistic—perhaps too mired in academia to really understand at first what kind of monster Hitler was. Hitler was able to seduce my father with his passion for Fichte. My father told me he spent hours with Hitler, discussing the philosopher as an intellectual base for German nationalism. You see, Hitler knew how to prey on youthful vanity. Early on, my father swore a blood oath to Hitler and then became one of his favorite pets. This disgusted my grandfather so much that he never spoke to his son again."

Katrine flicked her cigarette butt away and immediately lit another. "Look at me, chain-smoking. All of this makes me so sad."

"Please go on," Beatrice said.

"I have no excuses for my father. And he had none for himself, believe me. Some of us take wrong turns in life and spend the rest of the time on a road we never bargained for. That was my father. . . . After the war, my father moved here and changed his name. He became a carpenter, of all things. It had been a hobby of his. He never studied philosophy or anything like that again. He married my mother, who was uneducated and not especially bright, but an extremely kind and understanding woman. I think he married her because he knew he could tell her the truth and she wouldn't be judgmental—which she wasn't. They had me. I'm his only child."

Just then a slight breeze ruffled Katrine's hair, dislodging her little lace cap. "God, have I still got this silly thing on?" She reached up and pulled the cap off. Stuffing it in her pocket, she continued her story.

"We lived a comfortable life, and I grew up happily oblivious of my father's past. But then, you know, when you get older, you begin to ask questions. My father was always very evasive about his past. He said he was born in Germany and moved here after the war. That was all I really knew.

"Then one day, in my twenties, I was in his shop, watching him make a table. And I asked him what he had done in the war. I'll never forget that moment. He put down his hammer and stood very still for a long time. And then he burst into tears. I had never seen my father cry. It was a shock," she said with profound emotion. "It was a real shock. He sat me down there in his shop and told me the whole story. We went upstairs to his bedroom, and he showed me pictures of his father and mother and a picture of himself with Hitler."

"What did you do?" Beatrice asked.

"I just listened. He told me that in 1942 he began to realize what Hitler was about. But he denied it to himself. He said there was a plan to deport all the Jews to Mozambique. He said Hitler kept toying with that idea. Meanwhile, the death camps were beginning to operate full force. And everyone knew about them, no matter what they say now. My father knew. But he'd sworn a blood oath to this maniac, and his code of honor was just—I don't know—twisted."

"My God. How did you feel about him after you found out?"

"I hated him," she said, clenching her teeth. "I hated him more than you can imagine. I didn't see or speak to him for over a year. I felt tainted and soiled and ashamed that I had his blood running in my veins." She shook her head. "I started to drink, take drugs, sleep with a hundred men. I think now that I was using my father's past as an excuse to destroy myself. It was a terrible time."

Beatrice put her hand on Katrine's shoulder to comfort her.

"Then one night I met Aaron at a friend's house. His parents were both concentration camp survivors. We were immediately drawn to one another. It was one of those mystical kinds of things. We spent the night together, talking about the war and our childhoods and forgiveness. Mainly forgiveness—and how it's necessary to forgive in this world, or you yourself become a victim, eaten alive by your own torment. I told him about my father."

"Was he shocked?"

"No. He was amused." Katrine forced a little smile.

"Amused?" Beatrice said incredulously.

"He started laughing. He said it was so ironic that we should have come together—me, the daughter of one of Hitler's favorites, and him, the son of concentration camp survivors. He said it was too crazy to be true. Anyway, we fell in love. I converted to Judaism. And eventually we got married. He was the one who pushed me into making up with my father."

"He sounds like a wonderful man."

"Yes, he is. Wonderful. I'm very lucky."

"So is he, Katrine."

"Thank you, Beatrice," Katrine said, with great feeling. "Come, let's go for a walk. I'm getting damp on this bench."

The two women got up and strolled through the cemetery, pausing every so often to take in an interesting headstone or mausoleum.

"I envy you in a way," Beatrice said, as they ambled along one of the paths.

"Why?" Katrine stopped short.

"Because your father knew he had your forgiveness before he died. Mine didn't."

"What do you mean?"

"It's too long a story. I can't go into it. But my father died thinking that I despised him for something he'd done. And it wasn't true. I was going to tell him I forgave him. Actually, I was going to tell him there was nothing to forgive. It was my own narrow-mindedness and stupidity that made me so judgmental about him. . . . But I never got the chance."

"I'm sure he knew you really loved him. My father said he always knew it, even when I wasn't speaking to him. They understand. They do."

"Katrine, whoever killed my father robbed me not only of the best friend I had in the world but also of the most important moment of my life—the moment when I was going to tell my father that I truly understood him, that I'm truly his daughter."

"I understand," Katrine said.

They continued walking, then stopped to pause at a grave marked William Alfred Westrupp Foyle.

"I wonder if he's the bookshop man," Beatrice said absently.

They walked on.

"Now I've told you the story of my life," Katrine said. "But I think what you really want to know about is the grimoire."

Beatrice felt her heart beat faster. "Yes, please," she said anxiously. "Anything you can tell me."

"Welcome back," Aaron said as the women entered the tearoom. "Did you get everything straightened out?"

The table he and the children were sitting at was now covered with crayons and coloring books.

"Not everything," Katrine said. "We're going upstairs. I have to show Beatrice something."

"Oh, that's fine and dandy," Aaron said. "And I suppose you want me to stay down here and wait on the customers?"

"There are no customers yet, my darling." Katrine walked over and patted him affectionately on the cheek.

"How am I supposed to get any work done?" he said, looking up at her with a petulant expression.

"You can work this afternoon. I promise. Noah . . . Rachel . . . I'd like you to meet a friend of Mummy and Daddy's."

Katrine introduced her children. Rachel, a blond, fresh-faced girl of nine, got up, curtsied, and shook Beatrice's hand in a forthright manner. Noah, an imp of seven, ducked under the table and stuck his tongue out.

"Noah, can't you ever behave?" Katrine sighed in exasperation.

"No!" squealed the little boy, who started playing a rambunctious game of hide-and-seek behind his father's chair.

"See you later," Katrine said.

She led Beatrice through the kitchen and up a flight of back stairs.

"What does your husband do, Katrine?"

"He's a poet."

"That's a hard life."

"He has a book coming out next year. Fortunately, my father left us a little money, but these days it doesn't go very far."

"How's your business?"

"What business?" Katrine shrugged. "We're off the main street, so very few people ever come here, as you may have noticed. But I love to bake, and I do a little catering to make ends meet. I sell cakes to the best teashop on the high street. I love pastries. It's the German in me, I guess."

Katrine showed Beatrice into a cheerful but sparsely furnished bedroom, with chintz curtains and a large brass bed. She went to the closet and took down a large, tattered dress box from the top shelf. Putting it on the bed, she removed the cover. Inside was a hodge-podge of loose snapshots, documents, military medals, cards, letters, and a couple of old photograph albums. Katrine sifted through the jumble and located a picture, which she handed to Beatrice.

"That's Baron von Nordhausen," she said. "My grandfather."

Beatrice examined the thick old black-and-white photo card. "You're right. He does look like Bismarck. I like his top hat."

"Dad told me Grandpapa always dressed formally for dinner, with his medals and everything. Here's one of my grandmother." Katrine handed Beatrice another photo.

"She was very elegant."

"A bit stout, no?"

"I suppose it was the fashion then."

"And here's my father," Katrine said, with a mixture of pride and sadness.

Beatrice turned the faded, sepia-colored photograph toward the light from the window. It showed a thin, pale, ascetic-looking young man dressed in a dueling society uniform, standing stiffly in the middle of a courtyard, clutching a small bundle of books in one hand

and holding a cigarette in the other. His expression was grim and distant.

"That was taken at the university," Katrine said. "He hated being photographed, as you can see."

"He was very good-looking."

"Do you see any resemblance between us?"

Beatrice held up the photograph, comparing it to Katrine's face. "Yes, a bit. Especially around the eyes."

"I take more after my mother, unfortunately. She was no beauty."

Beatrice returned the picture to Katrine, who sighed and put it down. She continued rummaging around in the box. "Ah . . . This is what I was looking for. Here he is with the devil," Katrine said, handing Beatrice another photograph.

Beatrice studied the picture closely. It was a snapshot of von Nordhausen, Hitler, and another young man, standing together in front of a low wall behind which a majestic view of sky and forest stretched to infinity. A German shepherd dog sat at attention at Hitler's side. Hitler was smiling at von Nordhausen as though the young man had just said something amusing. Von Nordhausen, who appeared far more relaxed in this photo, but less handsome, was smiling back at Hitler. Beatrice noted that von Nordhausen's teeth were slightly crooked and his ears stuck out a bit.

The other young man in the picture was standing off to one side with his hands sunk into his jacket pockets, his collar turned up, taking in the view. His face was shaded by a fedora, and a pipe dangled from the corner of his mouth.

"Who's that?" Beatrice pointed to him.

"Count Borzamo—the owner of the grimoire."

Beatrice took a closer look.

"I told you my father was a pet of Hitler's," Katrine continued. "Well, in 1944, my father denounced von Stauffenberg and the other aristocrats after the famous July twentieth attempt on Hitler's life. He was one of the few aristocrats to do so. Hitler then entrusted my father with a top-secret mission. My father spoke to me about this mission only once. He told me that Hitler ordered him to go to the Vatican to get a certain book from the Pope. That book was the grimoire belonging to Count Borzamo."

"And what the hell was the Pope doing with it?" Beatrice said, fascinated.

"I don't know. . . . But Borzamo would know. He and my father corresponded for a number of years."

"Is Borzamo still alive?"

"I don't know that, either. But I have his address in Italy. It was in my father's address book. I'll give it to you."

"Do you have any of the correspondence between them?"

"No. My father burned most of his papers before he died. All that's left is what you see here—pictures, a family album, diplomas, citations, a few letters from friends—nothing of any significance. Believe me, I've pored through all of it."

"Did your father tell you anything else about the grimoire?"

"No—except one thing."

"What was that?" Beatrice said, picking up the ominous tone in Katrine's voice.

"He said that if anyone should ever come here asking about it, I should tell them everything he told me," she said slowly. "And above all, I should make it clear that we didn't have it. He was adamant about that. 'Make certain they know you don't have it,' I remember him saying over and over."

"And has anyone else come?"

Katrine shook her head. "No; you're the first."

"So I'm right, then," Beatrice said, thinking aloud. "The real reason your father was in Rome was to get the grimoire."

"Yes; you are right. My father told me the preparations for the mission were extremely complicated. He had two cover stories prepared in case he was captured. The first was that he was a priest. He knew they would break that immediately, so it was the second he concentrated on."

"And what was that?"

"When they tortured him, he gave up the names of contacts in Rome in order to make them think he was an ordinary spy. That way he never had to reveal the true purpose of his mission. He was very proud of that fact."

Beatrice got up and began pacing around the room. "And he never said why Hitler wanted the grimoire?"

"No. I honestly don't think he knew. But Borzamo might know."

"And your father never found out what happened to it?"

"No. I'm quite sure of that. He just said they confiscated it and he never saw it again or knew what became of it. I think a number of people contacted him about it after the war. But he was always very secretive about that—just as he was about his past. Imagine if the good people of Highgate had known that they had a Nazi living in their midst," Katrine said, with a sardonic little laugh. "We all would have been stoned to death."

The two women looked at each other with mutual understanding.

"And you want to hear the final irony?" Katrine said. "The town of Nordhausen—my father's town—is where Hitler secretly manufactured the V-2 rocket in underground caves, using slave labor. The *Nibelungen*. Think of that—the death machines that decimated London," she said. "I wonder what my father thought of that."

"I guess everyone's a victim of some war, in one way or another," Beatrice said.

They were silent for a long moment.

"Will you give me Count Borzamo's address?"

Katrine copied down the address from her father's tattered address book. "Here it is," she said, handing it to Beatrice. "It's near Terni, in Umbria. Do be careful, though. My father warned me that Borzamo was a very, very strange man."

Invited for lunch, Beatrice, exhausted and jet-lagged, declined with regret. She hugged Katrine as she left the little teashop.

"Good luck," Katrine said.

Beatrice took a taxi back to the airport and checked into a hotel there. She immediately called Stephen, but there was no answer. She left a cryptic message on his machine, saying that she had arrived safely and had an "interesting meeting with our friends" and was on her way to Italy. "I'll be in touch," she added. "Don't worry. I'm all right, and I love you."

When she hung up, she calculated that it must have been close to 9:00 A.M. New York time, and she wondered where he was. No matter. She was exhausted. She got undressed and took a bath. After booking herself on a flight to Rome the next morning, she lay down on the bed and promptly fell fast asleep. She didn't wake until three the next morning. She tried Stephen again. The machine picked up. "Where the hell can you be, Stephen?" she said to herself. Unable to sleep, she read for a while. But her mind was racing with thoughts of the grimoire and von Nordhausen and Borzamo. She got up and took out the paper on which Katrine had written his address:

Count Giovanni di Borzamo
Villa Borzamo
Borzamo, Italy

She prayed he was still alive, for she felt, instinctively, that he was the key.

16

 N THE FLIGHT TO ROME, BEATRICE FELT LIKE A huntress, and the shadowy Borzamo was her game. Her plane landed at 1:00 P.M., and she disembarked from the aircraft, running into a curtain of sweltering heat. A helpful young man at the airport's car rental agency supplied her with a map, tracing the best route to Borzamo in thick red pencil.

"You are going to see the famous garden?" he said, in excellent English.

"What famous garden?"

"At Villa Borzamo, of course. The Garden of the Stone Monsters, as it is called."

"Well, yes. I guess I am."

She picked up a little white sedan and headed north toward Terni. As she sped along the autostrada, she noticed a change creeping over the countryside. The unsightly skein of factories and high-rise apartment buildings gradually unraveled into a lovely landscape of farms and patchwork groves of olive trees, sunflowers, mustard, and corn. Tall, stately cypresses stood at attention over sun-baked fields dotted with bales of hay. Sheep, seeking refuge from the heat, huddled together in tiny flocks spreading just to the edges of the sharply delineated shadows cast by the trees.

Every once in a while, a dark and cluttered little medieval town loomed in the distance, precariously perched on top of a steep precipice overlooking a valley. Isolated and forbidding, such towns looked as they had looked for centuries. Beatrice found herself thinking how full of magic and superstition they still must be.

Three hours later, she turned off the highway and headed east. Following the winding roads of the rustic countryside, she finally reached the village of Borzamo. She stopped at a café and had a cappuccino to revive herself. There, in halting Italian, she asked directions.

"*Dov' è la Villa Borzamo?*" Beatrice inquired of the friendly young waiter.

"*Villa Borzamo? Sì, sì, nei bosci, nei bosci,*" the young man said, proceeding to fire directions at her so rapidly she had no idea what he was saying.

Taking his cue from the bewildered expression on Beatrice's face, the waiter led her outside and explained the route, turn by turn, with hand signals. Beatrice got into her car and drove out of the sunny town, following the young man's instructions. Within a couple of miles, she came to a fork in the road. To the left was the beginning of a dense forest of pines. A small sign, barely visible through the foliage, read: VILLA BORZAMO, with an arrow underneath. Beatrice veered off the main route and headed toward the woods. About a quarter of a mile later, she came upon an identical sign, pointing toward a dirt road. She took the turn.

The car bounced along the bumpy path. The afternoon sun filtered down through the trees, creating a soft, smoky light. Presently, the road smoothed out to a fine carpet of pine needles, leading up to a heavy black wrought-iron gate flanked by stone walls. The name BORZAMO was worked in large iron lettering across the top of the gate. Underneath was an iron shield bearing the Borzamo family crest. A small sign hanging on the gate read: *Aperto.*

Beatrice pulled into an empty parking area to the right of the entrance. Her feet sank into the soft woodland ground as she walked through the gate onto the property. About a hundred yards in front of her, outside a tiny wooden shack, she spied an old man splayed out on a rickety canvas beach chair, his head resting against the back frame. He was asleep. His shirt was open at the bottom, and the flesh of his large belly bulged out over the tops of his trousers, heaving up and down to the rhythm of his snores.

"*Scusi, signore,*" she said, approaching him cautiously.

The old man snorted a couple of times and awoke suddenly. A pair of striking blue eyes shot out at her from his aged leather-skinned face. He was thick-featured, with a stubbly growth of beard. He rose from the chair with some effort and trudged into the shack. Seconds later, he returned with a white slip of paper.

"*Tremila lire,*" he said in a tired voice.

Beatrice hesitated. "Uh . . . *No, grazie. No biglietto,*" she said in awkward Italian. "*Voglio vedere il Conto Borzamo, per piacere.*"

He stared at her and licked his lips. "*Non è possibile, signorina.*"

"*Ma, è molto importante,*" Beatrice said. "*È possibile che Lei dice che*—" She struggled in vain with the language. "Shit," she said, opening her purse. She pulled out a hundred-thousand-lire note and handed it to him.

"*Per piacere,*" she pleaded. "*È molto importante.*"

The old man raised his eyebrows with pleasure and took the money from her, pocketing it. "Why do you wish to see Count Borzamo?" he said, quite unexpectedly.

"Oh, you speak English!" Beatrice cried with relief.

"A bit."

"Look, it's very important that I speak to Count Borzamo. Is he here?"

"Count Borzamo is in Rome. Are you one of his girlfriends?"

"No," she said, flushing with embarrassment. "How old is Count Borzamo?"

"Around forty years old."

"Oh." She felt deflated.

"You don't know him?"

"No." She shook her head. "And it's not him I need to speak to. It's his father. I suppose his father's dead," she said resignedly.

The old man studied her. "So it is the *old* Count Borzamo you wish to speak to."

"Yes," she said, sensing some hope. "Is he still alive?"

"Just barely," the gatekeeper said.

"Does he live here?" Beatrice said excitedly.

"Yes, he lives here. In the big house."

"Oh God, you've got to get me in to see him! Please. I'll give you anything you ask. I have over half a million lire in cash in my purse. You can have it all."

The flicker of a smile lit up the old man's expression. "I don't know. The count sees no one these days."

"Can you get a message to him?"

"It is possible."

"Then tell him that a woman has come all the way from America to see him. It's a matter of life and death."

"May I know what it is you wish to speak to him about?"

Beatrice shook her head. "No. I must speak with him personally. Can you arrange it?"

The old man looked Beatrice up and down in a way that made her feel slightly uncomfortable. "Yes, I think I can arrange it," he said at last. "Come with me. Ah . . ." He paused. "*Momento* . . . Wait, please."

He traipsed down to the entrance and turned over the sign, the back of which read: *Chiuso.* Beatrice watched him as he closed the gate and locked it with a large key he extracted from his pocket. He walked back, tucking his shirt into his baggy trousers, smoothing down his thick white hair.

"Come," he said, grinning at her. "I will take you to the count."

Beatrice followed the old man up a sloping path shaded by trees and lined with underbrush. Then they came upon a clearing, in the middle of which was a mammoth stone elephant saddled with a howdah. The sight was so arresting that Beatrice paused and blinked her eyes. The old man took no notice. He continued along the path. Soon there was another clearing and another gargantuan statue—this time of a tortoise, whose right front leg had sunk into the earth.

Beatrice ran to catch up with the old man. There were more clearings and more enormous statues—a horse, a lion, a dog, a hawk, a bear—all beautifully carved out of dark, pitted stone, covered with spots of moss, decaying amid the unkempt greenery of the garden.

"Wait!" Beatrice cried out.

The old man halted.

"What on earth is this place?" she said in awe when she had reached him.

"It is the garden of the Borzamo family. It was created in the sixteenth century by Luigi Borzamo, who had a passion for monsters." He smiled. "You like it?"

"It's marvelous," Beatrice said. "Very strange."

"People find it amusing," the old man said. "But I am used to it."

"Are there any more statues?"

"Yes, there are more. But they are not permitted to tourists."

"Oh, I'd love to see them," Beatrice said excitedly. "Won't you take me?"

"No," he said curtly, and walked on.

Presently, they came to another wrought-iron gate, identical to the first. Visible in the distance was a sprawling stone manor house set on a vast expanse of wild, untended lawn. The old man took out the large key from his pocket and unlocked the gate, pushing it open so Beatrice could pass through.

"Villa Borzamo," he muttered, closing and locking the gate behind them.

As Beatrice approached the house, she could see that it was extremely run-down. Chunks of the slate roof were missing. Thick cracks and chips scarred the weather-beaten stone facade. The flower gardens and low boxwood mazes in front of the villa had all gone to seed. A shabby old black Mercedes-Benz was parked in the cobblestone courtyard, alongside a battered pickup truck.

Beatrice and the old man walked up wide stone steps that led to an imposing front door, its wood reinforced with intricate iron hinges and large nails. Before he could knock or ring the bell, the door was opened by an ancient housekeeper in a cotton dress, a black kerchief around her head.

"*Buona sera*," she said, bowing slightly.

"*Buona sera*, Aldarana," the old man said.

They walked into a cool, dark, vaulted entrance hall decorated with tapestries and medieval armaments. A full suit of armor on a pedestal stood like a sentinel beneath a life-size oil painting of a young knight in full regalia, sitting astride a powerful stallion.

"Luigi di Borzamo—the creator of the garden," the old man said, pointing to the golden-bearded subject.

Beatrice stopped for a moment and studied the portrait. The young man had an arrogant expression and blue eyes that pinned the viewer. Beatrice followed the old man, her footsteps echoing on the stone floor. They walked through a series of grand rooms crammed with cumbersome Baroque furniture and huge, heavily varnished paintings in need of a good cleaning. Finally, they reached a paneled door.

"Stay here, please," the old man said.

Beatrice waited in the corridor while he slipped inside, closing the door behind him. She felt her heart racing in anticipation. A few moments passed. Then she heard a low voice call, "Enter."

Twisting the large black knob, she pushed open the door and stepped into the room. She found herself in a huge study. Two fraying red velvet couches flanked a cavernous fireplace. The mantelpiece was a grim stone eagle embracing the hearth with a pair of swooping wings. The walls were covered in tooled brown Moroccan leather, dry and peeling with age. A series of black-and-white etchings of snakes hung in ornate gold frames above a desk. Family photographs in silver frames were spread over the top of a grand piano. The quiet, insulated chamber smelled of old wood and sweet tobacco. Beatrice looked around. It appeared to be empty. She wondered where the gatekeeper had gone to.

As her eyes grew accustomed to the dim light, she spied a cloud of smoke rising in front of a high-backed wing chair facing a window in the far corner of the room.

"Count Borzamo?" she said tentatively.

"Yes," said a voice from the chair.

"I ...," she began. "My name is Beatrice O'Connell. Thank you for letting me come to see you."

"Beatrice ... *Beatrice*," the voice said, pronouncing her name in Italian. "Like Dante's chaste heroine."

Beatrice drew closer to the chair. "My father named me for her," she said, craning her neck, eager to get a look at the mysterious count.

"Ah ...," the voice sighed. "Your father was a literary man, then?"

"In a way. He was a doctor, but his hobby was book collecting."

"And it is my vocation," the voice said. "Isn't that a remarkable coincidence?"

With that, the man in the chair stood up and turned around to face her. He puffed on a pipe, grinning. She could hardly believe her eyes, for it was none other than the old gatekeeper. He had put on a wrinkled and worn-out red velvet smoking jacket.

"*You're* Count Borzamo?" she said, staring at him.

"At your service." He stepped out from behind the chair, removed the pipe from his mouth, and gave her a courtly little bow. "Please, do sit down," he said, ushering her toward the fireplace. "Let me offer you a special little liqueur."

Beatrice, still stunned, sank down into one of the worn velvet couches. She watched him closely as he walked over to a long sideboard and poured the drinks. Beatrice found herself searching for some resemblance between this unkempt, fat old count and the dapper young man in a fedora standing with Hitler and von Nordhausen in the photograph Katrine von Nordhausen had shown her. The pipe, she thought, with some disgust. The pipe is the only connection.

"This is called *limoncino*," he said, handing her a cordial glass filled with a filmy yellow liquid. "It is made from the lemons at my summer house near Ravello. Try it. Tell me how you like it."

Beatrice took a tiny sip of the syrupy liqueur. It tasted sweet and pungent and made her mouth pucker. "It's delicious. Very strong," she said.

"Drink too much and it has the effect of absinthe," the count said, taking a long swallow. "But a little clears the head." He sat down on the opposite couch and relit his pipe. "So," he said, leaning back and crossing his legs. "Tell me why you have come all the way from America to see me."

Beatrice put her drink down on the coffee table in front of her and stared at him. "Tell me something, Count Borzamo. Do you find it amusing to masquerade as the gatekeeper?" she said, irritated at his deception.

"But, my dear girl, I am not masquerading as the gatekeeper," he protested. "I *am* the gatekeeper. That is the job I have given myself."

"Why? Can't you afford to hire someone to hand out tickets for you? Or are you afraid they'll steal the entrance fees?"

Count Borzamo laughed heartily at this suggestion. "Steal the entrance fees! Oh, that is very good! Excellent! No," he said, calming down. "The truth is that I am an old man and I tire quite easily. It relaxes me to sit in the sun and look at the people who come to see my garden—especially the young women, like yourself." His eyes focused on her legs for a brief moment.

"My son lives in Rome," he went on. "My friends and enemies

are all dead, so there is no more amusement there. I find the newspapers a bore. The world is so repetitive, don't you think? Reading books is a chore, since it is difficult for me to see the print. So I guard my gate. It is really the only contact I have with the outside world these days. And in any case, there is not too much else I can do—so I do that."

Count Borzamo suddenly seemed an entirely different person to her. His voice, his manner, everything about him, exuded an air of jaded sophistication. She perceived his simple peasant shabbiness as a pose he cultivated to mask a complex man of no little experience and taste. Also, there was something about this seemingly affable old libertine that made her extremely uneasy. She suspected he had a dark side lying in wait, ready to pounce on her when she least expected it.

"*Allora,*" the count continued. "Answer my question. Why have you come to see me?"

Beatrice straightened up and folded her hands primly in her lap. "I need to know about a book you once owned."

"I have owned many, many books, my dear girl. Some of them I still own."

"This is a special book. It's a grimoire attributed to Pope Honorius III."

Beatrice studied the count closely, hoping for a reaction. He showed none. His facial expression didn't change in the slightest. He merely took a sip of the *limoncino.*

"Continue," he said flatly.

Beatrice proceeded to recount the entire story of the grimoire and her father's murder. She revealed to the count how she had managed to track him down through his old friend von Nordhausen's daughter. She mentioned all the principals in the drama—Antonelli, Father Morton, Schroeder, and Mr. Lovelock—offering thumbnail sketches of each one and how he was involved.

The count sat listening impassively, smoking his pipe and sipping his drink. Yet there was something about the way he looked at her that caused Beatrice to know she had completely captured his attention.

"So," she concluded after the long explanation, "Katrine von Nordhausen said that if anyone could help me, you could." She paused. "Will you help me, Count Borzamo? Will you please help me?"

The old man gazed at her, his blue eyes shining through the pipe smoke. "You would like my son," he said after a time. "He is extremely handsome. Do you like handsome men?"

Beatrice shifted in her seat, not knowing quite what to make of this question. "I suppose so," she said.

"He is—how do the English say it?—a fine, strapping young man. Forty years old. Well, maybe forty is not so young to you." He shrugged. "But it is very young when you are my age."

"Count Borzamo, I don't mean to be rude, but are you going to help me or not?"

He didn't answer. Instead, he got up and fetched the bottle of *limoncino*. Returning to the couch, he sat down again and filled his glass.

"You have hardly touched your drink," he said. "May I offer something else? Some wine, perhaps?"

"No, thank you."

"Tell me—are you married, *Beatrice?*" The count seemed to relish pronouncing her name the Italian way.

"Divorced."

"Divorced? You look quite young to be divorced. How old are you, my dear? I know it is a rude question, but I am old enough to ask rude questions."

"And I'm old enough not to answer them," she said.

"Ah, good. I admire a woman who will not reveal her age. Who was it who said, 'A woman who will tell her age will tell anything'?"

"It was probably a man. I'm thirty-five," Beatrice said playfully.

The count seemed delighted by her response.

"Thirty-five. *'Nel mezzo del camine de nostra vita,'*—in the middle of the road of life, as your biographer, Signor Dante, wrote." He paused. "My mother was a beautiful woman. She died many years ago, as did my father. So, like you, I am an orphan now. Orphans have a bond between them, don't you think?"

"I suppose so."

"I was married when I was very young. It was an arrangement. I did not care much for my wife, but she was elegant and rich and she suited the political ambitions of my family. After the birth of my son, we lived separate lives. She would have divorced me, but in Italy we do not divorce like you Americans. Tell me, do you have a boyfriend?"

"I didn't come here to discuss my private life, Count Borzamo."

"But that is the only life worth discussing," he said, tapping out the ashes of his pipe into an armorial dish on the coffee table.

Beatrice was growing impatient. "Count Borzamo, won't you tell me about the grimoire, please?"

He removed a small pouch of tobacco from his pocket and dug his pipe inside it. He tamped down the excess with his fingers and leaned back. "It is a very long story," he said. "Involving the entire history of my family."

"I need to know it."

"Why should I tell it to you?" He gave her a mischievous little smile as he lit the fresh pipe. "Give me one good reason."

Beatrice thought for a moment. She wanted to choose her words carefully.

"There is no one good reason. There is simply the fact that my father is dead and that I know his death is connected in some way with this book. And if I can find out more about the book, maybe I can find out who killed him. You seem like a kind man—"

"Do I?" he said incredulously. "I am certainly not a kind man. I am a selfish old bastard!" He roared with laughter.

His guffaws turned into a hacking cough. Beatrice watched as he sipped some more of the liqueur and gradually composed himself. She had no idea what to make of him.

"Well, if you're not going to tell me anything, I suppose I should go," she said, getting up from the couch.

"*No, no, per piacere, resta ancora.* Stay, please!" He raised his hand to stop her.

She sat down again, prepared to listen.

"I will tell you what you want to know, on two conditions."

"What are they?"

"The first is that you will stay and have dinner with me tonight."

"And the second?"

"I will tell you that after we have dined together."

Beatrice mulled over his offer.

"Yes, all right. I agree."

T WHAT HOTEL ARE YOU STAYING?" THE COUNT
said.

"Actually, I hadn't thought about that. I
came here directly from the airport. I should
make a reservation somewhere. You must know
of a place."

"I shall have Aldarana show you to a room."

"A room? Here?" She looked at him askance. "Now wait a minute. I said I'd have dinner with you—that's all."

"Yes, but you must prepare for dinner. It is almost time."

Beatrice glanced at her watch. She was surprised to see that it
was nearly seven. "I had no idea it was so late."

"Surely, you are not going to drive all the way to a hotel and
come back," the count said.

"No, I suppose not."

"Please—there are thirty-seven rooms in this house. All of them
empty. Aldarana will draw you a bath, and you may change. And
then, after dinner, you can go to a hotel, if you like."

"I'd better make a reservation right now."

"That might be a bit difficult for you," the count said. "This is the high tourist season, and most of the hotels are booked. But I am not unknown in this part of the world. If I telephone on your behalf, they will certainly find a room. Why not leave it to me?"

Beatrice felt as if she had no alternative, so she reluctantly agreed. The count rang for the housekeeper on an old-fashioned needlepoint bell pull. When she arrived, he gave her some instructions in Italian. While nodding obediently to the count, the old woman kept eyeing Beatrice dubiously.

"I have told Aldarana to bring your luggage up from the car. You will have my wife's old room. It has a rather nice view of the north garden. Do not worry," he added quickly. "It is in the opposite wing from mine."

"Thank you," Beatrice said.

As she was following the old housekeeper out of the study, the count called to her.

"*Beatrice,*" he said. "I should inform you that here in the Villa Borzamo we always dress for dinner."

She paused at the door. "Oh, dear," she said. "I'm afraid all I have with me is a fresh blouse and a ratty old pair of jeans."

"Do not worry," the count said. "We will provide something suitable for you."

"No, I really don't think that would—"

"Please do not protest," the count interrupted her. "As the saying goes, 'When in Rome . . . ' " He smiled. "Dinner will be served at nine o'clock."

Beatrice followed the old woman back through the house, up one flight of a grand staircase, and down a long corridor. They entered an enormous bedroom done up in pale-blue silk damask, with magnificent gilt furniture. Beatrice was struck by the affected piety of the room. There were crucifixes everywhere—carved into the furniture, perched atop the four posters of the bed, embroidered on the silk bedspread, and woven into the fabric of the chairs. A collection of icons was propped up on the bureau, and a saccharine portrait of the Madonna hung over the bed.

The room was musty. The old housekeeper immediately opened the doors leading to a balcony in order to let in some fresh air. Then she left. Beatrice poked around. She opened the closets:

they were filled with elegant but dated women's clothes. She peeked into the bathroom—a cavernous Art Deco room with marble floors, a sunken tub, and antiquated, oversized plumbing fixtures. Finally, she went out onto the balcony, which overlooked an intimate, well-tended flower garden. She stood there awhile, taking in deep breaths of the soft evening air, listening to the distant hum of cicadas. Gazing at the nearby forest, she thought about the great stone animals it contained and wondered what the other monster garden was like—the one Count Borzamo had refused to show her.

Just then, the housekeeper entered, carrying her suitcase. She set it on a carved storage chest at the foot of the bed. Beatrice walked back inside. *"Grazie,"* she said.

"Prego, signorina," the old woman answered. Then she asked something in Italian. Beatrice looked blank. The housekeeper motioned to the bathroom.

"Ah ..." Beatrice suddenly understood that the old woman wished to run her a bath. *"Sì, sì, grazie."*

As she bathed in the enormous sunken tub, Beatrice felt a sense of anticipation, for she expected that during the course of the evening, the mystery of the grimoire would surely be revealed to her by the old count, bringing her that much closer to solving her father's murder.

Returning to the bedroom, she was amazed to see on the bed, neatly laid out for her, two stylish evening dresses, one in black and one in white. Alongside them was a selection of lace undergarments, four evening bags, and four pairs of identical silk evening shoes in different sizes. An assortment of precious jewels glittered in a large black velvet tray.

At first, Beatrice was disconcerted by the idea of dressing up for the old count in clothes that he had provided. But as she held up each of the gowns to her body, admiring herself in the mirror, her distaste was overcome by feelings of titillation. The count's parting words to her in the study, "When in Rome ... ," echoed in her ears. She thought: This is an adventure. What the hell?

A clock chimed the hour of nine as Beatrice descended the staircase for dinner. Count Borzamo, in black tie and black velvet slippers embroidered with his crest, was waiting for her at the foot of the steps. Shaved, groomed, and formally dressed, the old count had managed to make himself quite presentable.

"Charming! Charming, my dear!" He extended his hand as Beatrice reached the bottom of the staircase. "I knew you would choose the white dress," he said with satisfaction.

"How did you know?"

"I was certain you would be true to your namesake in the *Divina Commedia*. Tell me, do you recall the scene in which *Beatrice* reproaches her beloved Dante for being unfaithful to her during her lifetime?"

"Yes, of course," said Beatrice. "And the virgins in the fields have to convince her of Dante's sincere repentance before she agrees to lead him into Paradise. . . ."

"Ah—I see you know the poem well," the count said, impressed.

He escorted her into a vast, candlelit dining room, where a liveried old servant was standing at attention at one end of the long rectangular dining table, set for two.

"I have always found the divine *Beatrice* a bit of a bore, if you do not mind my saying so," the count said, showing Beatrice to her place, to the right of his own.

"A bore—how do you mean?" she asked, as he seated her.

"Well, imagine poor Dante," the count said, pausing momentarily. "Here is a man who has *literally* been through Hell and Purgatory in order to find his beloved Beatrice—and all she can speak about when they finally see one another is what an unfaithful son of a bitch he was to her on earth! I cannot imagine anything less inspiring, can you?"

"That's certainly a novel interpretation of one of the greatest allegories ever written," Beatrice said, laughing.

The servant pulled back the count's chair, and Borzamo sat down. Shaking out an enormous white linen napkin, he tucked it into his collar and curtly instructed the man to pour the wine from a crystal decanter on the table. The count took a small sip and nodded his approval. The servant filled Beatrice's glass.

"I hope you like red wine," the count said, as Beatrice took a swallow.

She savored the velvety Burgundy.

"I have rather a good wine cellar. I used to own a vineyard, but the wine was inferior, so I sold it. I cannot tolerate inferior things."

"Well, this wine is magnificent," Beatrice said, drinking some more.

The count signaled to the servant to refill her glass to the top.

"What is absolutely true," the count said, continuing their discussion, "is that men and women do not think of sex in the same way."

"No. I agree with that. I'm interested in your opinion, Count Borzamo. How do you think they differ on the subject?"

The count, who seemed only too happy to answer the question, leaned back and made a little cathedral of his hands. "For women," he began, "sex is an altar at which they worship with more or less devotion at various times in their lives, depending on their lover. . . . For men, sex is simply a bath they need to take on a regular basis—and, unfortunately, not necessarily in the same tub."

Beatrice, highly amused, laughed appreciatively and toasted him. Another liveried old servant appeared, with dinner. He bowed slightly to Beatrice, handing her a pair of silver serving utensils. She helped herself to a small portion of chicken and some vegetables from the silver platter the man offered her. The servant then moved on to the count, who, in contrast to his guest, heaped his plate with food.

"I hope you like a simple dinner," he said.

"This is perfect," Beatrice replied.

The count used his hands to eat the chicken. His table manners left a lot to be desired; he seemed to approach his food and wine with a kind of lust.

"A woman makes a present of her body to a man," the count continued. "And most women must wrap that present up in emotion. Otherwise it feels rather cheap."

"To her or to the man?" Beatrice inquired somewhat mischievously.

"To her, of course. The man could not care less what the present is wrapped up in, as long as he receives it!" The count laughed and laughed, pointing a chicken leg at Beatrice.

"And in your opinion, are there women who don't feel that way? Women who, for example, use sex as a man uses sex—as a bath, to take your words?"

He considered. "In my experience, very few."

"But they do exist."

"They do." The count nodded. "And they are rather dangerous."

Their eyes met across the candle flame. Beatrice wondered

what the old count was thinking, but she didn't dare ask him, fearing he might tell her. He continued wolfing down his meal at a great rate, until he had cleaned his plate.

"So—" the count said, pushing his plate away and licking his fingers. "You wish to know about the grimoire."

"Yes, please," Beatrice said with surprise, for under the terms of their bargain, she hadn't expected him to bring up the subject until the meal was over.

She stopped eating and gazed at him in rapt attention. The count leaned in to finger a little mound of candle wax that had dripped onto the table. He concentrated on the wax as he spoke, glancing occasionally at Beatrice.

"To understand the grimoire, you must understand a bit about its background. The Borzamo family is extremely old. We go back many, many centuries, and we have always been great book collectors. Book collecting is more than an interest with us. It is a heritage, a birthright, a passion, which has been shared by the counts of Borzamo for hundreds of years. It is our destiny—or was until that stupid son of mine was born," he said bitterly.

"Your son isn't interested in book collecting?"

"My son collects women," the count said, disgusted. "He stopped reading books when he reached puberty."

"Where is your collection, Count Borzamo? I'd love to see it. It must be staggering after all these years."

"I am coming to that. You are an impatient young woman."

"Sorry," Beatrice said, looking down.

The count reached out and touched her hand. "No matter, my dear."

His hand was lingering on top of hers when the servant entered, and Beatrice quickly pulled away. The man removed Beatrice's plate, replacing it with a cut-glass finger bowl. He then took the count's plate. However, instead of bringing a finger bowl, the servant left the room and soon returned with a large silver basin filled with water. He knelt at the count's side and held the basin up to his master. The count turned sideways in his chair, washed his hands and face, and dried himself with a linen towel the servant provided. Beatrice was fascinated by this exhibition.

"Ah!" the count said, rubbing his hands together in a gesture of contentment. "Now I am refreshed. I hate the smell of grease."

He instructed the servant to bring in the next course. Then he resumed his story.

"Tell me, are you familiar with the history of the Vatican Library?"

Beatrice stiffened, for now she knew she was getting close to something, though she could not think what it might be. "Just a little," she replied. "I know that it was founded sometime in the middle of the fifteenth century—that's about all, I'm afraid."

"Not bad. It is more than most people know. The Vatican Library was really the work of two popes—Nicholas V and Sixtus IX. They must share the credit. The library was based on a collection of Latin and Greek codices—the *Bibliotheca latina* and the *Bibliotheca graeca*—as well as the *Bibliotheca secreta*."

"What's that?" Beatrice said, intrigued.

"The old papal library, whose contents were unrecorded for many, many years. But I shall come to that. . . . The Vatican Library really began to flourish in the seventeenth century. Maximilian of Bavaria donated the Palatine Library from Heidelberg in 1622. The great Latin manuscripts belonging to the dukes of Urbino and Queen Christina of Sweden were also acquired during that period. Then in the eighteenth century came the Capponiani collection, as well as the great Ottoboni library. The Borghese library, the Barberini library—so many great and famous collections came to the Vatican. . . ."

Just then the servant entered with fruit and cheese.

"Please go on," Beatrice said, for she was anxious to hear the rest of the story.

Once again, the count helped himself to gargantuan portions of everything. Beatrice chose a single peach.

"You do not like cheese?" the count said, shoving a large slice of Parmesan into his mouth.

"I'm not all that hungry, thank you. I guess I'm too riveted by your story."

He grinned at her. Bits of bread and cheese had lodged between his front teeth.

"To continue, then," he said, washing the food down with two large gulps of wine. "These are the collections that one has heard about: they are world famous. They form the nucleus of the Vatican Library. . . . But," he went on, spearing a wedge of apple with his fruit knife, "there is another collection in that library—one which is *not* famous and which nobody, outside of a tiny group of people, has ever heard of." He held up the knife with the apple slice on the tip, to punctuate his point. "Indeed, the Vatican denies all knowledge of it to this very day."

"What is that collection?" Beatrice said eagerly.

"That, my dear girl, is the Borzamo Collection!" the count cried, popping the slice of apple into his mouth.

"I don't understand. Why hasn't that collection been recognized and acknowledged along with the others?"

The count frowned slightly, as if he were searching for the correct words. "The Borzamo Collection is not—how shall I put it?— very traditional. . . . It consists of only two main areas of interest." The count sipped his wine.

"What are they?"

"Pornography and black magic," he said simply.

The count gulped down the rest of his wine and licked his lips. The servant, who had been waiting by the doorway, immediately refilled his glass. Beatrice peeled her peach and reflected on all the implications of this revelation. She remembered Lovelock's mentioning something of this at one of their first meetings, but decided not to say anything about that.

"So what you're saying is that the Vatican has a collection of pornography and black magic they don't admit to?" she said after a time.

"Well, they rather wink at the collection of pornography. Many people have seen it through the ages, so it really cannot be denied. Years ago, a friend of mine visited the library and asked the curator about it. 'Do you have a collection of pornography?' he said— knowing full well that they did—just to see what the poor curator would say. And the curator simply said, 'We are reputed to,' which I think is a rather good answer, as it is not, strictly speaking, a denial. However, when that same friend asked about the collection of black magic, the curator grew quite angry and said in a rather short temper, 'I think not', and he walked off very troubled—or so my friend said."

"And these collections were given to the Church by your family?"

"In a way. The collection of pornography, certainly. It was donated by my family in the eighteenth century for the amusement of some pope or another, who was most likely a bit of a rake. By the way, the eighteenth century was a marvelous time for pornographic works, in case you are interested. . . ." He studied her face for a moment. Beatrice remained expressionless. She remembered Lovelock had said the same thing.

"And then," he continued, "as is always the case with collections, they are added to by other sources. So I am sure the collection has enlarged quite a bit. But I am happy to say that the bulk of the pornographic collection was given to the Church by the Borzamo family," he said with mock pride.

"And what about the collection of black magic?" Beatrice asked.

"Ah—that is a slightly more complicated arrangement."

"I'm listening."

"Why don't we take our coffee in the salon, where we can be alone?" he said, glancing at the servant.

"That dress really suits you," the count said, as he and Beatrice sat in the living room, watching the old servant pour coffee into two demitasse cups from a small silver pot. "Let me give it to you as a present."

"I couldn't possibly accept it. But thanks, anyway."

"Americans are so puritanical," he said, shrugging. "Why not give an old man a bit of pleasure if he wishes it? Take it, please, with my compliments. After all, I cannot wear it, and there is no one else whom I wish to have it. . . . *Grazie*," he said, dismissing the servant with a wave of his hand.

The old man bowed and left the room.

"Count Borzamo, you were going to tell me about the collection of black magic," Beatrice said.

"So you will not accept the dress?"

"No. Please—I need to know about this collection."

The count finished his coffee in two swallows and put the cup and saucer down. He leaned back on the sofa and lit a pipe. "I have never liked this room. It is much too big. And all my ancestors stare at me from the walls."

Beatrice glanced around at the huge, grim-faced portraits in ornate gilt frames. "They're quite an imposing group."

"They have imposed on me a tradition which, whether I like it or not, is my birthright. You see, the Borzamos have always existed in a sort of symbiotic relationship with the Church. Ever since the

Vatican Library was founded, our family has been the source of works that are—shall we say—not sanctioned by the Church but are, nevertheless, of great interest to it."

"Books of black magic," Beatrice said.

"Exactly. In the past, the Church, as you know, always made a great show of confiscating such works and burning them—along with their practitioners and creators when they could find them. But the reality is slightly different."

"And what is the reality?"

"The reality is that God and the devil—like the Church and the Borzamos, if you will—also exist in a symbiotic relationship. After all, without evil, there can be no good—there is just boredom."

"I suppose you could put it that way," Beatrice said, amused.

"Do you recall that at dinner I mentioned to you the *Bibliotheca secreta*—the old papal library whose contents were unrecorded and which formed in part the nucleus of the Vatican Library?"

"Yes, I remember very well. Along with the *Bibliotheca latina* and the *Bibliotheca graeca.*"

"You are a good student," the count said. "Well, eventually, that secret papal library was catalogued—by an ancestor of mine, as it happened. And there were many classical manuscripts in it, of course—great works and fragments by Plato, Aristotle, Simplicius, Apollonius, Archimedes, Aristarchus of Samos, Euclid, Heroditus, Homer, Hipparchus, Ptolemy, Hippocrates, Seneca, Tacitus, Thucydides, Pliny, Plautus, et cetera." He reeled off the names with impressive speed.

"But there were other works, which were less acceptable. Grimoires, cabalas, magical papyri, Gnostic texts, and fragments pertaining to the Eleusinian, Orphic, Phrygian, and Mithraic mysteries. These works represented occult thought and knowledge from all over the world—Egypt, Persia, China, India, as well as ancient Greece and Rome. but it was not considered seemly for the True Church to harbor such a collection, as it would appear to detract from their mission on earth.

"Being extremely—what is that phrase Americans use?" He thought for a moment. "Image conscious. That is right, no?"

"Image conscious. Yes." Beatrice smiled.

"Being extremely image conscious, the Church was forced to hide such works. Nevertheless, they were available for study, and they formed the nucleus of a collection which grew rapidly throughout the Middle Ages and the Renaissance."

"In other words, a collection of black magic," Beatrice said.

"Let us call it a Collection of Opposing Thought," the count said, grinning. "After all, I don't want you to think of me as the devil."

"All right—a Collection of Opposing Thought, then."

"Because a Borzamo had catalogued the original collection and knew of its existence, my family was given the honor of continuing to seek out such works, in order that the Church could remain *au courant* with the forces which were against it. So for the next century, the Borzamo family business was to locate heretical works— particularly those of an occult or magical nature—and bring them to the Vatican. We were well rewarded for our efforts, as you can see. All this"—he gestured expansively—"we owe to the gratitude of the Church. It gave us protection from the Inquisition and from excommunication, which was very important in those days, since persons who were excommunicated had no civil rights."

"Let me get this straight," Beatrice said. "The Church paid you and protected you so that you could find books of black magic for them?"

"Basically, that is correct. But it sounds rather sordid when you put it that way." The count caressed the bowl of his pipe with his thumb and thought for a moment. "I like to think of it more as a sacred trust. The mission of my family on this earth has been to keep the Church informed about the nefarious workings of the Enemy."

"That Enemy being . . . ?"

"In a very small circle, the Borzamos are known as *Gli Agenti del Diavolo*—the Devil's Dealers."

Beatrice took a moment to digest this. "So these books are in the Vatican Library?"

"They were at one time."

"Where are they now?"

"During the first hundred years of the library, some of the popes were interested in reading them. Others were not. But with the fever of the Inquisition steadily rising in Europe, it was clear that the collection was in danger of being discovered. So in 1600, it was moved here, in the greatest secrecy."

"The books were kept *here?*" Beatrice said in amazement.

"That is the reason Luigi di Borzamo built the Monster Garden. The part that is not open to the public is where the collection was kept. People were very superstitious about that garden, and they would never dare to go near it."

"And"—Beatrice hardly dared ask the question—"is the collection still there?"

"No. When Napoleon came to power, it was moved back to the Vatican for safekeeping. Then, after the Second World War, Pope Pius feared that the Communists would take over Italy and such a collection would be in danger of annihilation. So it was moved yet again."

"Where is it now?"

"I believe it is somewhere in America, guarded by people who fear and loathe it but who recognize its power—like an important political prisoner."

The Duarte Institute, Beatrice thought.

"You don't have any idea where in America?" she said disingenuously.

"No." The count shrugged. She suspected he was lying. "As I say, I am retired from the family business."

"And the grimoire . . . ?"

"Was part of the collection."

"So von Nordhausen got the grimoire from the Vatican Library in 1944."

"Yes."

"And when it was taken, they wanted it back."

"Yes. But for other reasons."

"What other reasons?"

"Now we come to the real story of the grimoire," the count said with a sly smile.

Beatrice's mind was racing as she began to put things together. "So you must know Signor Antonelli?"

"Of course I know him."

Beatrice was stunned. "My God! Are *you* the private client who was interested in purchasing the grimoire from my father?"

"Let us simply say that I was an interested party."

"He called you, didn't he? To say that he'd found it."

"He did."

"Why? Why did he call you, if you didn't want to buy it?"

"He needed some information. And I am the only one who could give it to him."

"What information?"

"He needed to know for certain if it was the real grimoire."

Beatrice was flushed with excitement. "You mean because of the inscription from Saint Paul?"

The count looked at her with an amused expression on his face. "You are like a terrier with a bone," he said.

"Why? Why is this particular grimoire so important? What is its secret? You know, don't you?"

The count shrugged noncommittally. She knew he was toying with her.

"All right, then," she said. "Who's the private client who wants it so badly?"

He continued looking at her, saying nothing. When he finally spoke, there was something dark and menacing in his voice.

"We have a bargain," the count said slowly. "I said I would tell you what you wished to know, under two conditions. You have met the first. You have had dinner with me. Now you must meet the second."

Beatrice looked at him warily. "And what's that?"

"Come with me." The count rose from the couch. He walked over to her and offered her his hand. She put her hand in his and got up from her chair.

"Where are we going?" she asked.

"To the other part of the garden."

They walked out into the night.

18

HE COUNT PICKED UP A RUSTY HURRICANE LAMP
that lay on the terrace at the back of the house.
Lighting the wick inside, he held the lantern
straight out in front of him to illuminate the way
and beckoned to Beatrice. They walked down a
long flight of stone steps leading to a wide expanse of lawn. The dark forest, awash with the
silvery glow of the moon, loomed up ahead. It was hot and humid,
and Beatrice felt the satin dress clinging damply to her body as she
walked along the moist grass.

They reached the thicket. The count cautioned Beatrice to
watch her step as he led her along a rough little path winding
through the woods. The deeper they traveled into the forest, the
narrower and thornier the path became. Occasionally, the count bent
down to sweep aside twigs and branches in order to clear the route
for Beatrice. Despite his efforts, the pointy heels of her evening slippers kept getting caught up in the tangled underbrush, causing her
to stumble. She continued on for a quarter of a mile without com-
plaining. Then her patience wore thin.

"Where the hell are we going?" Beatrice called in an irritated voice.

"Have patience, *cara Beatrice*," the count replied, looking back at her. "It is Dante who is leading you."

Finally, they reached a clearing, in the middle of which were four dark structures of gargantuan proportions, grouped in a wide circle. At first, they seemed to Beatrice to be nothing more than big black boulders. Then, as her eyes became accustomed to the murky light of the grove, she could see that the dark shapes were more than just monster rocks. They were huge carved statues.

With theatrical flair, the count walked around to each sculpture in turn, as Beatrice watched.

"This is the Minotaur," he said, holding up his lantern to illuminate the strange entity.

The lamp cast a delicate light on the stone—enough for Beatrice to see that towering over the count was a terrifying version of the mythical beast with a bull's head and a man's body. Her eyes widened.

"And this is the Medusa," the count said, moving on.

Again, he held up his lantern, and Beatrice could make out the stone carving of the hideous Gorgon, its hair composed of snakes.

"And this is the Cyclops." He shone the light on a horrific monster with a recessed stone eye in the middle of its huge stone forehead.

The last piece of statuary, nearly twice the size of the others, appeared to be some sort of stone lizard, with great hollow eyes, a flaring snout, and gaping jaws big enough for at least three people to walk inside.

"What on God's earth is *that?*" Beatrice cried.

The old count stepped just inside the beast's mouth and turned to face her. His lantern glowed feebly against the immense black cavity around him. Seeing that he had her full attention, he recited some lines of poetry:

"All set with iron teeth in ranges twain,
That terrified his foes and armed him,
Appearing like the mouth of *Orcus*, grisely grim . . ."

"What does that mean?" Beatrice said.

"They are lines from *The Faerie Queene*, by Spenser. They refer to the mouth of a dragon. The great dragon is Satan. *Orcus* is the Latin name for Hades. And this, my dear girl, is the entrance to hell. . . . Follow me."

At these words, Beatrice was pierced by a sharp shiver of fear. But the moment quickly passed. She knew she could not afford to falter now that she was so close to her goal. Shimmering like a beacon in the forefront of her mind was the knowledge that the count possessed the secret of the grimoire. And besides, although she suspected him of incredible decadence, Beatrice still viewed the count as a harmless old man against whom she could easily defend herself if necessary. So she pressed on.

With his lantern swinging back and forth, the count led her into the dragon's mouth and down a long flight of stone steps. The farther they descended, the cooler and danker the atmosphere became, as if they were entering a crypt. At the bottom, abutting the last step, was a bronze door on which mystical symbols were modeled in low relief—pentacles, stars, crosses, numbers, snakes, astrological signs, and circles inscribed with strange writing. Beatrice recognized some of the designs from the grimoire.

The door was locked. The count, asking Beatrice to hold the lantern, removed two of the diamond-and-onyx studs from his dress shirt. He fished inside his shirt and soon produced a sizable iron key, which hung from a long gold chain around his neck. Unhooking the key, he bent down and inserted it into an ornate lock. He twisted the key this way and that until there was a resounding click. He put the key back on the chain, and as there was no knob, he shoved the door open, giving it a hefty push with his shoulder. Beatrice handed him the lantern and stood poised on the bottom stair as the count entered a black hole of a room. The darkness was so dense that it devoured the lamplight, leaving only a faint glow.

"Wait there," the count said.

Beatrice peered inside as he struck a match and lit two torches standing in tall iron receptacles on either side of the room.

"Come in," he called out when he had finished.

Beatrice stepped down and entered the large chamber. Deep, evenly spaced slots were cut into the jagged stone walls from floor to ceiling. Standing tall at the far end of the room was a plain black upside-down cross, in front of which was a long stone bench. The air smelled foul.

"Welcome to the old Borzamo library," the count said. The flickering torchlight made his face look ruddy and satanic.

"This is the family recreation room, I suppose," Beatrice said, looking around.

"It is extremely theatrical, don't you think?" The count grinned. "My ancestor Luigi had great dramatic flair, no?"

"You bet," Beatrice said.

"As you can see, the room was built for the purpose of housing the collection of black magic. Once, these shelves were filled with the devil's literature. It's quite amusing to think of it, don't you find?"

"Yes, it's fascinating. Now will you tell me about the grimoire?"

The count paused. "I have told you. There is one more condition."

Beatrice tensed. "And what is that?" she said with clenched teeth.

"It is a rather delicate matter."

The silence in the room was so marked, it seemed to crackle in the air.

"Go on. What is it? I'm ready," Beatrice said, trying to maintain a certain lightness of manner.

"You are a very beautiful woman," he said slowly.

"I am not," she said. "I'm interesting looking, but that's about it."

"You have a wonderful body."

Beatrice crossed her arms in front of her and assumed an aloof stance. "It's really not so wonderful. It's a bit saggy, in fact. I should do more exercise."

The count was staring at her. "I want you to take off your dress for me," he said at last.

Beatrice squinted at the old man. "Why?"

"Because I wish to see your sagging body," he said.

"Is that the condition?"

"It is the beginning of the condition."

"I'm not going to make love to you, Count Borzamo," she said firmly.

"I do not want you to make love to me."

"What do you want me to do?"

"Something else."

"Suck your cock, perhaps?" she said defiantly.

The count's loud laugh reverberated throughout the chamber. "Not that, either," he said. "Though I like the words in your mouth. You say them with such authority."

Beatrice sighed in exasperation. "Why don't you just cut the shit, Count, and tell me exactly what it is you expect me to do?"

The count eased himself down on the bench.

"I shall. But before you say no, consider what I am offering you in return."

"What do you mean?"

"I know the secret of the grimoire. I am the last hope you have of ever finding it out. I will tell you that I am certain your father was murdered for that book. I will also tell you that I am certain I know who murdered him. It seems to me that you are paying a very small price for something very valuable."

Beatrice hesitated for a long moment. "How can I be sure you're telling me the truth?"

"I am many things, but I am not a liar," he said. "And when you hear it, you will know it is the truth."

"If I do this *thing*"—she said the word with distaste—"that you want me to do, how can I be sure you'll live up to your part of the bargain?"

"Because I have given you my word."

"Why should I take your word? Why don't you take *my* word? I have an idea," she said brightly. "You tell me the secret first, and then I'll meet the second condition, whatever it is."

The count shook his head. "No."

"Why not?"

"Because what I am offering you is so much more valuable than what you are offering me. Forgive me, but it must be the way I say or no way at all."

Beatrice began pacing around the chamber. Finally, she faced him, put her hands on her hips, and sighed. "Is this some sort of kinky stuff?"

"Kinky. I love that word. I knew a call girl in Paris named Kinky."

Beatrice rolled her eyes. "Jesus! Are you going to hurt me?"

"No, no, my dear girl." He paused for a beat. "You are going to hurt me."

Beatrice glared at the count, inadvertently tossing back her head.

"Ah," the count said, leaning in. "That excites you?"

"No." Beatrice glared at him. "Not at all."

"I think it does. Look at you. You are defiant."

They stared at each other.

"I have your word?" Beatrice said after a time.

"You have my word."

Beatrice took a deep breath. Slowly and deliberately, she slid the right strap of her dress off her shoulder, then the left. She pulled down the zipper in the back of the dress. The gown fell to the floor with a soft wooshing noise and lay like a white satin puddle around her ankles. Stepping over it, she stood in front of the now mesmerized count, wearing the set of white lace undergarments he had so thoughtfully provided. She hoped that perhaps this glimpse of her would be enough. But the old count motioned her to continue.

Beatrice reached behind her and undid the strapless bra, letting it drop to the floor. She took off the shoes, then the stockings and garter belt, then the panties. Instinctively, she turned away and covered her private parts with her hands. The count cleared his throat and looked disapproving. He motioned to her to step forward so he could get a better view. Beatrice took another deep breath, dropped her hands to her sides, and moved to the center of the room. Standing up very straight, she faced the count squarely and let the old lecher run his eyes over her naked body.

"Put the shoes back on," he said in a hoarse whisper. "Just the shoes."

Beatrice nodded solemnly as she slithered her feet back into the high-heeled slippers. The count licked his lips and smiled in appreciation.

"Your body is beautiful, my dear. You have nothing to be ashamed of," he said at last.

"So now what?" Beatrice put her hand on her hip and rested her weight on one leg in a saucy posture, waiting for the count to reveal the rest of the condition.

He stood up, unzipped his fly, and lowered his trousers down around his knees. He was wearing baggy pale-blue undershorts, with a tiny crest embroidered on the right leg. Beatrice grimaced and stepped back slightly as he pulled them down. The dress shirt barely covered his limp penis. He turned his back to Beatrice and faced the stark inverted cross. Kneeling, he hunched over and placed his chest on the low stone bench. Then he rose up on both knees, arched his back, and lifted his rear end high into the air. Beatrice, repelled by the sight of the count's naked buttocks and dangling genitals, looked away.

"Now," he said in a whisper, turning his head to one side. "Spank me, my dear. Spank me as hard as you can."

Beatrice swallowed hard. She walked over to the kneeling count and timidly raised her hand. She smacked him once, lightly on the backside. Even this brief contact with his flesh made her cringe.

"Harder, my dear," he said.

She raised her hand again, took a deep breath, and struck him a second time.

"Harder!" he cried.

She slapped him once more. His loose old skin rippled under the sharp blow.

"Again!"

"How many times do you want me to do this?" she said with disgust.

"Until I tell you to stop. Again! Hard!"

Beatrice began to strike the count repeatedly. She shut her eyes and thought of Luis Diaz as she built up a pounding rhythm. The old man responded by emitting little cries of ecstasy after each whack. His drooping buttocks grew redder as she hit him over and over again, with increasing fury. She could see that the count had reached down to his penis, to massage it as she administered the blows.

Soon the airless chamber felt like an oven, and Beatrice began to perspire. Little drops of her sweat fell on the cold stone floor. Her hand was becoming sore. The count whimpered in pain. Squeezing her eyes shut, Beatrice prayed with all her might that he would beg her to stop. But the harder she hit him, the more excited he became and the more he seemed to relish it. She grew progressively angrier in the face of her humiliation.

Then an amazing thing happened. In the frenzy of the moment, though her right arm ached and her hand felt as if it were broken, Beatrice began to enjoy spanking the old count. She switched hands and walloped him with renewed vigor, until his flesh glowed. She was amazed and disconcerted at the power of the beating she was administering. However, the count's plaintive whines of pain titillated her, and she started crying out with him in unison. The beating hit a wild crescendo, as smacks and screams and moaning created a symphony of flagellation. Beatrice was just about to give up, when the old man stiffened all over and then went limp. She started to strike him again, but he yelled, *"Basta!* Enough! Enough!" He keeled over onto the bench, breathing hard.

Beatrice sank to the ground, exhausted and trembling. She put her hands over her face and began to weep. The old count rose to his feet slowly, without looking at her. He pulled up his underpants, then his trousers, buckled them up, and made himself presentable. Then he went over and picked up Beatrice's dress, which lay in a heap. He walked back and dropped it on the floor in front of her. He bent down slightly and started to stroke her hair. The touch of his hand made her recoil.

"Cara Beatrice," he said with tenderness. "You are a brave girl. You must have loved your father very much."

"Yes," she said, sniffing back her tears. "I did."

She put on the dress and stood up, facing the old man. She took a deep breath.

"Satisfied?" she said.

"Come," the count said, holding out his hand. "We both need a drink."

Beatrice and the count sat in the library, nursing tall Scotches. Beatrice lit a cigarette.

"Now, that was not so terrible, was it?" he said, puffing on his pipe.

"Yes, it was," she said sullenly.

"I am sorry. . . . Nevertheless, I am very grateful. It has been many years since—"

"Don't!" she said, interrupting him. "I don't want to hear it, okay? Just tell me about the grimoire."

"Yes, all right." The count sighed. "You have earned the privilege. The Honorius Grimoire is valuable for many reasons. First of all, it is said to contain the true spell for the raising of the dead. Second of all, it is supposed to be the key to the lost treasure of the Knights Templar. Historically, these are the two reasons for which it is famous."

"Yes; Mr. Lovelock explained all that. But it seems a little far-

fetched that anyone would be looking for a thirteenth-century treasure or seriously believing in a spell for raising the dead."

"Well, as to that," the count said, "Adolf Hitler himself was obsessed with necromancy and the occult. And the treasure of the
Knights Templar is thought by some to be as real as King Priam's
treasure in Troy—which was discovered within the last century."

"So is that it? My father was murdered for a goddamn spell and
a goofy treasure?" Beatrice said irritably.

The count smiled and shook his head. "No, my dear. These are
not the real reasons the grimoire is so important."

Beatrice leaned forward. "I'm ready. Spill it."

"I like the way you talk, *Beatrice,*" the count said.

Beatrice acknowledged the compliment with a weary little nod.
"Just get on with it, will you?"

"Hermann Göring was the Grand Acquisitor of the Third
Reich. His greed is legendary. He looted paintings and treasures
from every country the Reich took over. This is well known."

"And . . . ?"

"In the early days of the war, Göring wanted his own international intelligence network—independent of Reichsführer S.S.
Himmler's secret police and Admiral Canaris's military intelligence. . . .
I knew Göring quite well. He was a pig of a man but very sophisticated and, if you can believe it, quite funny and rather charming."

"I *can't* believe it," Beatrice said.

"No matter. I was working in the Vatican as a secretary to a corrupt old prelate named Cardinal Delorio, when Göring approached
me. He had a rather intriguing idea. The IOR, the Institute for Religious Works at the Vatican—actually a bank—was run by my supe-
rior, the dread cardinal. Delorio was a very austere man—forbidding
and judgmental. Like Robespierre, he preferred to dine on red wine
and bread. But more of him later.

"The three of us—Göring, Delorio, and myself—had a meeting
in the winter of 1941. Göring confided to us that he did not trust either Himmler or Canaris and that he wished to have his own agents
around the world. He told us that he needed the Vatican intelligence
network, which of course was vast." The count paused to relight his
pipe.

Beatrice sat on the edge of her chair, barely able to contain herself. "Please—go on."

The count waved away a large puff of smoke and continued.

"Göring agreed to pay Delorio with funds he was secretly looting from rich Jews and others in the Reich. It was his habit to confiscate property whenever he felt like it, and he was amassing an incredible fortune in this way. He wanted to put it into an account in Switzerland, and he asked Cardinal Delorio if he would set up such an account for him so that he would not come under suspicion by Himmler, Canaris, or even Hitler—though the chances of that were slim, as Hitler was obsessed by power and could not have cared less about money. Nevertheless, it was a precautionary measure to go through the Vatican."

The count cleared his throat and took a sip of Scotch. "As Delorio's secretary," he went on, "I was in charge of setting up Göring's secret account. We agreed that only the three of us would know the code names to access it. But what code names could we use? Anything well known was dangerous, and something too simple might be discovered. One evening, during the course of a rather long and drunken dinner, I had the idea of using the Vatican's copy of the Honorius Grimoire as a mnemonic device."

"A mnemonic device?"

"In order to get access to a secret Swiss bank account, you must present a name or a number. But one name would have been too easy to discover. So in order to get into Göring's account, we decided on a series of names. In the Honorius Grimoire, there is a page of names spoken by the devil—and I took this page as the key to the accounts. And as a precaution, I crossed one name out."

Beatrice was growing increasingly excited. "So whoever presented these names to the bank could tap into Göring's account?"

"Precisely. But the names had to be in sequence, exactly as they appeared in the grimoire, minus the one I deleted, of course—otherwise the sequence is of no value."

"It's so simple!" Beatrice exclaimed, hitting her forehead with her palm.

The count grinned. "And rather ingenious, no? We believe that the Vatican's copy of the Honorius Grimoire is the only one with the inscription from Saint Paul, so it is immediately identifiable. Delorio and I called the operation 'The Devil's Account.' "

" 'The Devil's Account.' Perfect!"

"It is a rather good joke, no? Who is the real devil? Göring? Satan? You see," he went on, "the book is quite unique. And with my little alteration, it seemed a safe key, as not many people will destroy an old book."

"No—just the Nazis."

The count smiled. "Yes, but they destroy only good books, and for show."

"So why did von Nordhausen have the grimoire?" Beatrice said.

"Because I was sending it to Göring. Göring had convinced Hitler that it was something magical. Something to make him immortal. Göring told Hitler about the spell for raising the dead that it was said to contain. Hitler was quite mad at that point. He knew his life was in danger, so of course he was willing to try anything, especially to do with the occult. But Göring's real objective in getting the book was of course to secure the names for himself."

"And he never got the book, so he never collected his money! How much would you say this account is worth today?"

"With the interest? . . . I should say Göring's fortune is worth well over a billion dollars. Perhaps more."

Beatrice exhaled fiercely. She thought for a moment. "Count Borzamo, why didn't you and Delorio just keep the money yourselves? You had the key, after all."

"Because, quite simply, they would have killed us. A man like Delorio had no use for any more money than Göring had agreed to pay him for his services. And I am a terrible coward, as everybody knows. No, no, my dear girl—I did not wish to wake up one dark night with a Gestapo pistol at my head. . . . I did, however, think to myself that after the war I would try to locate the grimoire. But then, as you know only too well, it vanished. Until your father received it."

Beatrice got up and walked around the room, thinking. Then she returned to her chair and sat down. "There's one thing I don't understand, Count. If only you and Göring and Cardinal Delorio knew about it—how did all these people find out? And who are they?"

The count nodded. "A good question, my dear. Before he died in 1948, Delorio spoke of the scheme to another member of the clergy—a man who, like himself, was a member of a secret order: an order that guards the Borzamo Collection; an order that believes in the books of black magic as if they were science manuals; an order that is convinced the world should go back to the fifteenth century and that the Inquisition is the true law on earth."

"What order is that?"

"It is called Defensores Fidei—Defenders of the Faith."

"Defensores Fidei?" she whispered.

"Do you know of it?"

"Was this man whom Delorio told named Inigo Duarte?" Beatrice said anxiously.

The count toasted her with his Scotch. "Exactly," he said. "So you know of the elusive Duarte, do you?"

"He was the founder of Defensores Fidei."

"Indeed he was. I knew him slightly when I worked at the Vatican. He was a very strange man. He looked like a corpse."

"And have you ever heard of the Duarte Institute?"

The count shook his head. "No. What is that?"

"It's in upstate New York. They call it an institute for philosophical studies."

"Philosophical studies. How interesting." The count mused.

"What?"

"This institute . . . Have you ever been there?"

"Yes. They want my father's book collection."

"They do, do they? That is most intriguing. So they are interested in books. Well, I wonder if the Borzamo Collection could be there."

"I'm sure it is. You said it was moved to America after the war."

"Yes, that is what I heard. I do not keep up on these things anymore." She felt he was lying.

Beatrice clasped her hands together. "It's there, Count Borzamo. You know it is." She pinned him with her eyes.

"Well, it would make sense after all," he said noncommittally. "You have no idea how pernicious the Defensores Fidei are, for they carry what they consider to be a moral banner. And people who are so concerned with the morality of others are far more dangerous than those of us who simply exist and accept the world as it is and has always been."

"Signor Antonelli is *their* dealer, then," she said, now making the connection. "*They're* the ones who are interested in 'such oddities.' "

"Yes, indeed. Defensores Fidei is extremely interested in black magic. They entertain a truly childlike belief in heaven and hell, and not just as abstractions but as a complete reality—angels and devils, halos and pitchforks, clouds and fires—all that sort of nonsense. It would be amusing if they were not so dangerous."

"Tell me something, Count Borzamo. What do you know about a book called the *Malleus Maleficarum?*"

"Ah!" the old count said, lighting up. "The *Malleus!* You know of it as well?"

"I've read it."

"A fascinating book, eh? The result of a fever in human thought."

"More like a virus. It's abominable—a misogynistic diatribe. It's nothing more than a manual for finding witches, trying them, and killing them. And witches are a euphemism for women."

"And rather detailed, no? It states very clearly who the enemy is and how she must be destroyed. It was the law of Christendom for two hundred years."

"I know. And I think it's connected in some way to Defensores Fidei."

"Connected?" He laughed. "My dear, the *Malleus Maleficarum* is the bible of Defensores Fidei!"

"What do you mean?"

"It is the code by which they live. The reason they are so interested in books of black magic is that they believe evil truly exists and must be eradicated. The *Malleus* is the hammer—literally, *'the hammer of witches.'*"

Beatrice shook her head in despair. "And do you think it's Defensores Fidei who killed my father?"

"Oh, undoubtedly they are involved," the count said. "You see, the *Malleus Maleficarum* is their bible, but the grimoire is their gold. They will stop at nothing to get the grimoire, for with it, they will have the power to make their wretched bible sacred on earth and its word law. They will have the funds to carry on a war against modern life, which they detest and which they believe is the work of the devil. And make no mistake, they believe it is the devil himself against whom they are fighting. Anyone who knows the *Malleus* should be convinced of that. . . ."

"Have you ever heard of a man named Desmond Crowley?"

The count shook his head. "No. Who is he?" Again, she could not be sure if he was lying.

"He wrote a foreword to the *Malleus,* calling it one of the great works of literature."

"In this century?"

"Yes. In 1955."

"Then I should say without reservation that he is a man of whom you should be extremely careful. And perhaps . . ."

"What, Count Borzamo? What were you going to say?"

He looked at her. "I think, *Beatrice*, that you took slightly more pleasure in our little adventure than you care to admit. And in that case, you must be very careful of yourself as well."

"Yes . . . I know," she said softly.

The count took a final sip of Scotch. "So my advice to you is this, my dear: find out who is the head of Defensores Fidei—and I suspect he is connected in some way to this Duarte Institute you have spoken of," he said. "Find that man, and you will have your father's murderer."

19

TEPHEN! I'M BACK!" BEATRICE POUNDED ON THE door of the little apartment. "Let me in!"

Beatrice stood in the hallway, anxiously tapping her foot.

"Stephen?" She pressed her ear against the door. "Are you in there? Open up!"

She heard scuffling inside.

"Stephen . . . ? I know you're in there. Have I got news for you!"

Presently, the door cracked open. Stephen, wearing only his Jockey shorts, poked his head out. His hair was disheveled, and he seemed half asleep.

"Hello, Bea," he said somberly. "I wasn't expecting you."

"I tried to call you a hundred times, but there was never any—"

Before she could finish, Beatrice saw that he was not alone. A voluptuous young blond woman, wearing Stephen's bathrobe, was standing in front of the unmade bed, looking sheepish.

"Uh—Sally, this is Beatrice. Beatrice, this—uh—is Sally." He winced ruefully.

"Hi," the young woman said, waving weakly.

Beatrice stood still, not knowing where to look.

"I—I—I'm sorry," she stammered. "I—I should have— Oh, shit!" she cried at last. "You asshole. Why'd you let me in?"

"Bea—uh—"

"I was just going," the young woman said perkily, gathering up her clothes and heading for the bathroom. "I won't be a minute."

Beatrice stood in the middle of the room, shaking her head. Stephen attempted to put his arms around her.

"Don't touch me," she said, backing away.

She took deep breaths and tried to compose herself while Stephen swiped up his crumpled shirt from the floor and started getting dressed. Soon the bathroom door opened and the young woman came out, wearing a tight-fitting halter dress, a large leather bag thrown over one shoulder.

"Well, I guess I'll be going," she said apologetically. "Sorry about all this," she muttered, as she closed the front door behind her.

Stephen and Beatrice stood looking at each other.

"Bea," Stephen began, "I don't know what to say."

"Just leave me alone for a second, okay?"

Beatrice sank down onto the couch and took a cigarette from the pack on the coffee table. Stephen sat next to her.

"Got any matches?" Beatrice asked.

Stephen gave Beatrice a light and took a cigarette for himself. The two of them sat in silence for a long time, smoking.

"She's nothing to me, Bea. I want you to know that."

"It doesn't matter," Beatrice said.

"Yeah, it does. I feel really lousy about it." He clenched his teeth.

"Just out of curiosity, who is she?"

"She's just a nice girl. I don't know. She does PR for a software company."

"How'd you meet her?"

"I've known her for a while. I met her at a party a few months ago. Then I ran into her again on the street yesterday and . . ." His voice trailed off.

Beatrice crushed out her cigarette, got up from the couch, and walked over to Stephen's printer. She slid open the bottom tray.

"What are you doing?" he said.

"Getting the grimoire."

"Why? It's safe here."

"I just want it, that's all. I need to look at it."

She pulled out the book and stuffed it into her pocketbook. Then she picked up her overnight bag and headed for the door.

"Where are you going?" he said, alarmed.

"Look, Stephen, I just got off a plane. I'm tired. I've had an amazing trip. I'm going to go home and take a bath and think about things, okay?"

"Bea, please stay with me . . . please?"

"No. It's too emotional right now. Um—call me later."

"Can we have dinner? I want to know about your trip."

"Maybe."

Stephen grabbed her arm just as she was about to go. "Listen, Bea, I'm sorry," he said, looking desperate. "I'm so sorry, baby."

"I know," she said wearily, pulling her arm away. "So am I."

Leaving the apartment, Beatrice thought what a child Stephen was. To her surprise, she wasn't particularly angry—just resigned. He would always retaliate sexually for his insecurity; it was his nature. She knew she had outgrown him and the pathology of needing to be disappointed by men. But as she unlocked the front door of her house, she was hit by a sharp pang of sorrow—for her father, for Stephen, for all the losses in her life. God, being a woman is complicated, she thought with vague annoyance. She resolved not to dwell on these things, for that was simply another way of punishing herself. She had work to do.

Thumbing through the stack of mail on the hall table, she was stopped by a postcard with a striking painting of a grim-looking man wearing round black spectacles, seated tensely in a chair, dressed in the magisterial red regalia of a cardinal. She turned it over and read the message:

"The *Roman de la Rose* is ready to be picked up at your earliest convenience. As ever, Simon Lovelock."

The small black print on the upper-left-hand corner identified the picture as "Cardinal Don Fernando de Niño de Guevera, by El Greco. Metropolitan Museum of Art, New York."

Beatrice absently flicked the card against her cheek. It was an odd choice, she thought. She felt that Lovelock was trying to tell her something—but what? She tucked the card into her pocket, gathered up the rest of the mail in a little bundle, and went upstairs to the library.

Sitting at the desk, she played back the answering machine tape. There were messages from Father Morton, once again entreating her to make a decision about her father's library; from Detective Monahan, who said he had "nothing new to report"; and from Signor Antonelli in Rome, who said he was calling "merely to say hello." A couple of friends had checked in, wondering how she was, and there were a number of calls from real estate brokers, who wanted to see the house.

Beatrice sorted through the rest of the mail—bills, a bank statement, catalogues, and condolence letters, which she opened, read, then tossed into a shoe box on the desk. The box was filled nearly to capacity with sympathetic cards and letters about John O'Connell's death. She intended to answer them all by hand, but now was not the time.

Then Beatrice opened a letter from one of the tonier real estate firms in the city. It read:

> *Dear Miss O'Connell:*
> *I have a client who wishes to purchase your town house for the asking price of $2,500,000. I have tried to telephone you several times at your home without success. Would you be so kind as to call me at your earliest possible convenience so we may discuss the matter?*
> *Yours sincerely,*
>
> *Edwin Moore, President,*
> *Edwin Moore Associates*

Beatrice picked up the phone. After identifying herself to the smooth female voice at the other end of the line, she was connected to Edwin Moore and exchanged preliminaries. To Beatrice's inquiry regarding this client, Moore replied:

"Well, he prefers to remain anonymous for the moment. He would very much like to see the house first. I can tell you that he's a very well-to-do old gentleman. And he has a book collection."

"Does he indeed?" Beatrice said.

"Yes, he needs a house with a large library. It just happens to be one of those perfect fits. He knew of your father, actually. . . . By the way, my sincere condolences."

"Thank you."

"He seems very serious. And as I indicated in my letter, he's not going to quibble about money. He's bid the asking price."

"But he hasn't even seen it."

"I described it to him in detail, and he tells me it's exactly what he's looking for. I said I was sure it had been kept up well, given the owner's reputation. I know he would very much like to see it and to meet you."

"To meet me?"

"Well, as I mentioned, he said he knew of your father. I wonder, is there any chance I could bring him by sometime in the next week or so?"

"Mr. Moore, I'm going to have to get back to you on this, if you don't mind."

"No, of course not. In the meantime, we have put in our bid, so please don't take any other offers."

After a final exchange of pleasantries, Beatrice hung up and immediately dialed Stephen's number.

"Yeah?" he answered.

"Stephen, it's me."

"You forgive me?" he said hopefully.

"Stephen, put that aside for the moment. I just had an interesting telephone conversation. Someone wants to buy the house, and he's bid the asking price, sight unseen."

"Who is it?"

"I don't know. The broker won't tell me his name. I smell the aroma of fish, don't you?"

"Why?"

"What if whoever it is suspects Dad hid the grimoire here and he's willing to pay two and a half million dollars to find out. What do you think?"

"Two and a half million dollars is a lotta money for a book."

"Not this one, believe me," Beatrice said. "So did you find out anything more about Crowley while I was gone, or were you otherwise engaged?"

"Don't rub it in. . . . He lives up in Milbern. He's a retired professor with two Ph.D.'s—one in philosophy, one in religious studies. He's written a number of books—hagiographies, mostly. He's a wid-

ower. He's a respected member of the community and heavily involved with the Duarte Institute. I couldn't find out anything else."

"You better get over here tonight."

She hung up and took the grimoire out of her purse. "Okay, you
little billion-dollar baby," she murmured aloud. "Let's see if we can
find this famous list of names."

She thumbed through the book, page by page, pausing to look
at the woodcuts in the center. Then on page eighty-one, she came
to what she was certain she was looking for. The type changed to
Gothic script, and she read the following:

*Je suis Lucifer! J'ai beaucoup de noms: Alpha et Omega, Acorib,
Agla, Amaymon, Bamulahe, Bayemon, Beelzebut, Egym, Enga,
Englabis, Imagnon, Ingodum, Ipreto, Madael, Magoa, Meraye,
Obu, Ogia, Oriston, Penaton, Perchiram, Phaton, Ramath,
Rissasoris, Rubiphaton, Satan, Satiel, Septentrion, Tetragram-
maton, Tiros, Tremendum!*

It was the only such list in the book. A fine black ink line had
been drawn through the name Tiros. She knew that was Count
Borzamo's deletion. A shiver of excitement went through her. Here
it was—the access code to Göring's fortune. She stared at the names
intently, committing them to her photographic memory. Then she
repeated them aloud. She found they had an incantatory power, reinforced by the alphabetical order. Book in hand, she climbed the
stairs to her bedroom, reciting the names in rhythm as she walked.

Suddenly, a figure darted out at the top of the stairs. Startled,
Beatrice looked up and nearly dropped the book.

"Nellie!" she cried with relief. "I had no idea you were here."

"Jesus, Mary, and Joseph, Miss Beatrice!" the old housekeeper
said. "You nearly scared the living daylights out of me! ... And do
I have to be asking where you've been for the past few days?"

"With Stephen," Beatrice said evasively. Seeing Nellie's eyes
riveted to the grimoire, she quickly closed the book and tucked it
under her arm.

"What are you doing here, Nellie?" Beatrice said suspiciously,
reaching the top of the landing.

"My job, if you please," Nellie retorted. "I'm after cleaning up
your room and your father's room just now. You could have let me
know what you were up to, you wicked girl. I've been worried sick

about you. The real estate agents have been calling and calling. Will you be wanting any dinner?"

"No, thanks, Nellie."

"Well, then, I'll be going home now, Miss Beatrice, if it's all the same to you."

"Just a minute, Nellie. You never let anyone in this house without my permission, did you?"

The old housekeeper lowered her eyes. "Why, no, Miss Beatrice."

"Are you telling me the truth?"

"Sure I am."

"You swear?"

Nellie hesitated. "I don't like to swear to things."

"Why? Are you afraid you'll go straight to hell?" Beatrice said, half joking.

Nellie glared at her. "I wish you wouldn't make light of things like that, Miss Beatrice."

"Nellie, do you really believe there's such a thing as hell?"

"I do," she said emphatically. "I fear the fires of damnation more than anything. And you should too."

"Well, you're safe, Nell. I may not be, but you are."

"No one is safe from Satan," Nellie said, glancing at the grimoire.

The fear in the old woman's eyes made Beatrice uneasy.

"All right, Nellie." Beatrice sighed. "I'll see you tomorrow."

Beatrice slid the grimoire under the mattress. She took a hot bath and washed her hair. Then she lay down on the bed and, exhausted from her journey, fell asleep. At seven o'clock, she was awakened by the ringing doorbell. She looked down from her window and saw Stephen standing on the steps, peering upward at her. Putting on a pair of jeans and a T-shirt, she went downstairs.

"Hi," he said when she opened the door.

"Come on in," Beatrice said.

"I brought us some stuff for dinner," he said, holding up a large shopping bag.

"Thanks, but I'm not very hungry."

"You have to eat something." He headed for the kitchen.

Beatrice got out plates and silverware. Stephen took plastic containers from the shopping bag. They hardly spoke as they set cold cuts and salad on a tray and brought it into the dining room. Beatrice lit the candles on the dining table, near the window, and Stephen opened a bottle of red wine.

"I'm glad you're back," Stephen said, toasting her with his glass of wine.

"Gee, thanks," Beatrice said. "That was one hell of a welcoming committee."

"Look, Bea," he said, reaching out for her hand. "I've been doing a lot of thinking. . . . Why don't we get married again?"

Beatrice raised her eyebrows. "You're kidding, of course."

"No. I'm serious. I think we ought to just cut all the shit and do it."

Beatrice regarded him for a long time. "You're just feeling guilty."

"No," he protested. "Well, maybe. But I love you. I do."

"Listen, she was cute. I don't blame you."

He looked at her askance. "Yeah, you do. Come off it."

"No, I really don't." Beatrice stared at the black garden outside the window. "People's sexuality is so damn complex. If I were a man, I'd probably have done exactly what you did."

"Are you kidding?"

"No," she said, taking a sip of wine. "I understand. I really do."

He stared at her in disbelief. "You've really done a one-eighty on this, Bea. I thought you'd be furious. I thought you'd never want to speak to me again."

Beatrice shrugged. "What would be the point of that? I'd lose my best friend."

"Yeah, but . . ." He toyed with his food. "I betrayed you again." He looked up at her like a little boy.

"You slept with someone else who didn't mean anything to you. I'm not sure anymore that constitutes betrayal."

Stephen furrowed his brow, looking perplexed.

"I've really changed, Stephen. I see men and women in a whole different way now."

"What way is that?"

"Our sexuality is just different, that's all. There's no use fighting it." She shook her head. "Sexually, we're just two entirely different machines. The notion of love and fidelity being one and the same thing may be erroneous. And when people are together for a long period of time, it may be impossible."

"What do you mean?" he said, riveted.

She sighed and leaned back in her chair, holding her glass up to the candlelight, intrigued by the shimmering ruby wine. "I think you love me," she said at last. "I don't think you can be faithful to me."

"But you think you can be faithful to me?"

Beatrice pondered. "Who knows?" She shrugged, putting the glass down. "The fact is that there's something about rogue-male sexuality that turns me on." She stared at him over the candle flame, thinking of Count Borzamo.

"Turns you on? How do you mean?"

"When I was in Italy, I met a jaded old roué who told me that sex, for men, was like a bath they had to take periodically, and not necessarily in the same tub. And that women have to wrap up their sexuality in emotion and commitment so they don't feel used. I think that's true. Otherwise we'd just think of ourselves as receptacles, right? Whereas men can think of themselves as warriors. . . ."

"Who was this guy?" Stephen said, narrowing his eyes.

"Just let me finish, okay?"

Stephen shifted uneasily in his chair.

"I'd like it not to be that way," Beatrice continued dispassionately, lighting a cigarette. "I'd like to believe there's such a thing as home and hearth and fidelity forever. But I think men and women are too threatened by one another. The truth is, Stephen, that men and women envy each other profoundly."

"How is that?"

"You envy us our ability to feel so deeply about sex and to be able to commit to one person. And we envy you your ability not to feel so deeply about it, to take it simply as it comes—pardon the double entendre," she said, smiling. "Look, I know I threatened you with the dark side of my sexuality, Stephen—the lusty, impersonal side of me. The male side, if you will. So I don't blame you for trying to get some of your potency back with someone who meant nothing to you."

"I don't think Sally's going to get hung up on me. She knew what the deal was before she slept with me. . . . I told her about you," he said, reminding her of a little boy anxious to get back in his mother's good graces.

"Take it from me—she knew and she didn't know. Women always live in the hope that they'll be able to change a man. That they'll be the one who'll awaken him to the joys of fidelity and commitment. We strap on our toeshoes for you—do a lot of pretty dances. It's sort of a challenge being at concert pitch all the time, trying to win you. And men always live in the hope that their real desires won't be found out by the women they truly love—or think they love."

"Do you really believe that?"

"I really believe that."

"Shit. Maybe you're right. I don't know. All I know is that I have this profound desire to protect you from the world."

"But that's just the point, Stephen. Maybe I don't want to be protected. Because if you protect me from the world, you protect the world from me."

"And are you so dangerous?"

"According to the *Malleus Maleficarum* I am. All women are dangerous because we can zap men's powers. We can make you impotent just by being near you."

"Come on, for Christ's sake. That thing's five centuries old. No one takes it seriously. No one even knows about it."

"Don't kid yourself," Beatrice said, shaking her head. "It's infected Western civilization like a hidden plague, because there's a fundamental truth in it. In that respect it's as modern as a modem. The truth is that men don't know who women are and women don't know who men are. We've existed side by side, like two different species, for thousands of years. And now we're just beginning to scratch each other's surfaces. Don't you feel it? Don't you feel the emotional climate changing? We're not just in a technological renaissance; we're in an emotional renaissance as well. There are no rules anymore. It's all a search. That's what all these so-called alternative lifestyles are about.

"And," she went on, taking a deep breath, "to some of us, it's liberating. It's exhilarating. It's freedom at last. But to others, it's bewildering, ominous, and threatening beyond belief. Those are the people who fear the renaissance, Stephen. They're the ones who want to stay firmly in the Middle Ages, where life was more restricted and therefore more easily defined."

"And who are these people?"

"I think some of them are up at the Duarte Institute."

She threw her cigarette into her wineglass. It made a hissing sound and went out, floating on top of the red liquid. Stephen put his head in his hands.

"What's the matter?" Beatrice said.

"Nothing," he said gloomily. "I was just thinking what a jerk I am."

She tousled his hair. "Oh, buck up. You're just . . . a man."

"So there's no hope for any of us, right? Is that what you're saying?"

"It's not a question of hope. It's a question of acceptance. That's the way it is."

"What time is it?"

"Around eight-fifteen."

"I have to give Cap Goldman a call," he said, getting up. "He's been trying to reach me."

"Is he back?"

"No, he's still up in Canada. But he's back at the lodge."

"You finished? I'll clear up."

Stephen paused at the door of the dining room. "I'm going to get you to change your mind, sweetheart. You've got to tell me there's some hope, though, okay?"

"Okay."

Laughing, Beatrice started to clear the table.

Just as she was about to go into the kitchen, Stephen appeared at the door, ashen-faced. "Bea," he said softly.

"What's the matter? You look like you've seen a ghost."

"Cap Goldman is dead."

"What!" Beatrice gasped, putting the tray down.

"He's dead." Stephen walked over and sank down on one of the dining chairs.

She pulled up a chair close to him. "What happened?"

"A car accident. His neck was broken."

"Jesus." She looked at him. "You think it was really an accident?"

"I don't know."

"What does your gut tell you?"

"They said it was an accident."

"Who said it was an accident?"

"The woman at the lodge. His car went out of control, into a ravine."

"When did it happen?"

"This afternoon."

"And when did he call you?"

"This morning sometime. He left his number on the machine. I told you."

"Is that all?"

"No. He said he had some interesting information for me."

"But he didn't say what it was?"

"No. He just said to give him a call tonight."

"Stephen, they found out he was talking to us."

"Who found out?"

"Oh, Stephen, I've got so much to tell you."

They went upstairs to her father's library and stayed awake half the night, talking. Stephen listened with growing amazement as Beatrice took him through her recent odyssey step by step, omitting only her bizarre sexual encounter with Count Borzamo.

"So what do you think?" she said, when she had finished her story.

Stephen took a deep breath and shook his head. "I think you're the bravest girl I've ever known," he said, looking at her with admiration.

"No, seriously, Stephen."

"Seriously? It sounds too crazy not to be true. So Borzamo thinks the Duarte Institute is a front for Defensores Fidei too."

"Yes. I suspect he knew a lot more than he told me."

"And they might have the Vatican's collection of black magic."

"The Borzamo Collection, as he so proudly calls it. A 'Collection of Opposing Thought.' I know it's up there, Stephen," Beatrice said. "Remember that room marked 'Danger—No Admittance' in the basement? What do you bet it's in there?"

"Maybe that's what Cap wanted to tell us. Poor old Cap."

"Yeah, Jesus . . . It all fits perfectly. The *Malleus* is their bible, and the grimoire is their gold—Borzamo's words. They want that grimoire so they can access Göring's secret account in Switzerland and fund their little war on witches."

"And the so-called witches are activists and feminists—the ones from Cap's clippings. But what's the point? There must be a grander scheme. Why would they bother with a bunch of innocent women?"

"Witches have always been innocent women," Beatrice said bitterly.

"I know, but nobody's ever heard of these women."

"Can you name me one of the witches who was burned at Salem? It's the principle of the thing, don't you see? Defensores Fidei are fanatics. This is their vision. The Virgin Mary is their symbol because she's chaste. Unviolated by lust. Lust is evil, and they really believe in evil. We can't conceive of that."

"I can. I've seen their handiwork. Old Count Borzamo's sure right about one thing," Stephen said.

"What?"

"Göring's secret account. I've heard about that for years. It's one of the great unsolved mysteries of World War II—like King Priam's treasure from Troy, which was stolen from the Reich at the end of the war and only recently turned up in Russia."

"Look, Stephen, I'm sure Borzamo was telling the truth about everything. You should have seen that monster garden where they used to keep the collection. It's the most frightening place I've ever been in." Beatrice stared at nothing in particular, shuddering as she relived the horrifying climax of that night.

She got up from the couch and stood in front of the window, nervously flicking her cigarette lighter on and off. "Cap Goldman was murdered, Stephen. I'm sure of it. I wonder what it was he wanted to tell you. . . . It had to be about the Duarte Institute. I know they're responsible for all those women disappearing."

"You think they've been killed?"

Beatrice considered. "Maybe it's not that simple. Maybe they wanted to make examples of them."

"What do you mean?"

"Well, if the people in Defensores Fidei literally believe in the Inquisition, they might believe that these women are modern-day witches. After all, feminists and activists are usually for gay rights and abortion and women in the priesthood. All those things used to be considered heresy. If you believed in them or practiced them, you were a witch."

Stephen mulled this over. "Feminists as modern-day witches. Yeah, why the hell not?"

"And think what the Inquisition did with witches. . . ."

Beatrice turned, locking eyes with Stephen across the room. The silence of the night closed in on them. She flicked on the lighter one last time and held it in front of her face.

"They burned them, Stephen," she said slowly, staring hard at the tiny flame. "Burned them at the stake."

20

EATRICE WAS AWAKENED NEXT MORNING BY THE sharp ring of the telephone. She fumbled for the receiver.

"Hello?" she said groggily.

"Beatrice? It's Simon."

"Simon," she said, barely registering his voice. "What's up?"

"Meet me at the Metropolitan Museum at ten o'clock. Meet me in front of the portrait."

"What portrait?"

"You got my postcard?"

"Oh, yes—the El Greco."

"Meet me there. Don't fail me."

"Simon . . . ?"

He'd hung up.

Alarmed by his urgency, Beatrice got up immediately. She took the grimoire out from under the mattress, wrapped it in a small, odd-size book jacket, and inserted it in her bookcase. The fit was not exact, but she was confident it would not be noticed in among the other books. At ten o'clock, she was standing in front of El Greco's portrait of Cardinal Don Fernando de Niño de Guevera at the Met. She was alone in the gallery.

"Beatrice . . ."

She turned around. Lovelock was out of breath and disheveled.

"Simon . . . What's the matter?"

"I ran all the way from the subway. It's so good to see you." He gazed at her lovingly, trying to calm down. "Let me look at you."

"Simon, please, what is going on?"

"Forgive me . . . I'm out of breath." He turned to the painting. "So what do you think of our friend the cardinal?"

"Well, I didn't know that he was called 'The Grand Inquisitor.'" She indicated the plaque on the gilt frame.

"His face is an interesting study, is it not?" Lovelock said. "His expression is stern, somber, and righteous. Yet his eyes are evasive. He looks down and off to the side, not addressing the viewer at all. He doesn't care about his audience, you see. As an inquisitor, he's a universe and a law unto himself. . . . And note how the right hand dangles loosely over the wooden arm of the chair, while the left hand grips the armrest like a claw."

"He looks as if he's very wary of something."

"He is," Lovelock said. "The devil. To his twisted mind, the devil is all around us, and we must be ever vigilant."

The two of them stood transfixed by the painting.

"Simon, why did you get me here at this hour? What's all this about?"

"Wait. First, look." Lovelock handed her the *Roman de la Rose*, neatly wrapped in tissue paper. "She's all healed."

"Thank you. . . . Are you going to tell me what's so urgent?" She stared hard at him.

He looked away. "Yes, of course. Just let me compose myself for a moment."

They strolled into the adjoining gallery, where the work of the seventeenth-century Spanish Baroque artist José Ribera was on view.

"How deeply violent religion is," Lovelock said, looking around at Ribera's darkly dramatic paintings of martyred saints.

"The 'GI' in Cap Goldman's notes stands for Grand Inquisitor, doesn't it?"

"Yes," Lovelock said.

"And the 'Presenters'—they present the witches, don't they?"

"Yes."

"So we are dealing with an inquisition?"

"Ribera was very influenced by my favorite painter, Caravaggio," Lovelock went on, ignoring her question. "Caravaggio was a thief and a murderer. But he was touched by the sublime fire of creative genius. Ironic, is it not, that a man of his low and bestial character should have created some of the greatest religious works ever painted."

"Desmond Crowley is the Grand Inquisitor, isn't he?"

Lovelock looked at her, his bright black eyes full of concern. "Oh, Beatrice, I fear you're in great danger."

"I know all about the grimoire, Simon. I visited Count Borzamo in Italy."

Lovelock's expression flickered. "Yes . . . I know."

"You *know!*" Beatrice cried.

Her exclamation echoed throughout the empty gallery, and she clapped her hand over her mouth.

"How do you know?" she whispered.

"You are being closely watched. That's what I've come to tell you."

"By whom?"

"I'll get to that. What did Count Borzamo tell you?" Lovelock said, continuing to walk around the exhibition.

"He told me about the Borzamo Collection of books of black magic. He told me about Defensores Fidei, and he said that if I found out who the head of it was, I would have my father's murderer. And," she added, "he told me the secret of the grimoire."

Lovelock stopped and looked at her. "How badly did he abase you in exchange for this information?"

Beatrice flushed. "What do you mean?"

"He's a vile man, a man of no morality whatsoever—the product of centuries of corruption and inbreeding. I knew him when I worked in the Vatican Library. Borzamo is like a disease that infects everyone with which it comes into contact. That's his nature. He does nothing for free. There's always a price."

"Yes," Beatrice said, lowering her eyes. "It's true."

"What did he do to you?"

"I can't tell you. Please don't make me."

"Of course not, my love. You mustn't distress yourself."

His tenderness and concern toward her made her want to confess.

"He made me do something to him," Beatrice said at last. "He took me to the underground chamber where the books were once kept.... And then . . ." Beatrice looked around to make sure no one was nearby. "He made me undress for him," she said softly. "And made me spank him until he reached a climax."

Lovelock shook his head sadly. "You have great courage." He enveloped her hand in his and squeezed it tight.

Beatrice, feeling him trembling, saw his eyes glittering with tears. She wiped a tear from his cheek. They regarded each other fondly.

"Thank you for understanding, my knight," she said.

Hand in hand, they walked around the gallery in silence, marveling at the gruesome majesty of Ribera's tortured saints. At length, Lovelock led Beatrice back to the first gallery and the portrait of the Grand Inquisitor.

"Dear Simon," Beatrice said, as they stood before the painting once more. "Why did you bring me here?"

Simon avoided her gaze as he began to speak slowly, in a measured voice. "I want to tell you a story—the story of a little boy. When this little boy was four years old, his mother abandoned him and his father. She was pregnant at the time. Rather than have the child of her husband, whom she didn't love, she had an abortion and ran off with her lover. For a long time, the father of this little boy tried everything he could to get his wife back, even though she'd hurt him so badly. He was obsessed by her. But she wouldn't have anything to do with him. She moved away, cutting her husband and her little boy out of her life completely." Simon's voice, choked with emotion, trailed off.

"Go on," Beatrice gently urged him.

"As the years went by, the little boy saw his father turn against all women, but particularly the ones who questioned or flouted the conventions of motherhood and traditional family life. He blamed these women for his wife's infidelity, for her abortion, for her leaving him, for the failure of his marriage. This blame flowered into a deep rage, and he searched for a weapon he could use against them.... He found the *Malleus Maleficarum*, which confirmed his view that all women are essentially evil, or conduits for evil. The *Malleus* became his bible, his justification, and, ultimately, his blueprint for their destruction. Because the father was rich and brilliant, he was able to find followers who adhered to his warped vision. He had a truly satanic gift for oratory, and he united these sick people in search of a leader."

"And the little boy?" Beatrice said, holding her breath.

"He still loved his father," Simon replied almost inaudibly. "And he either refused to see or could not fathom the extent of his father's madness. But he understood that he had to get away. So when he was of legal age, he assumed his mother's maiden name and became a Jesuit."

"Oh, Simon . . . ," Beatrice said with compassion, for she knew he was talking about himself.

He looked at her pleadingly. "He wanted desperately to do good in the world in order to make up for his father's fanatical hatred. Then suddenly, unexpectedly, and even against his will, he fell in love. But that love ended tragically. . . . And the little boy—now a disillusioned young man—lost his faith in the Church completely. Leaving his order, he turned to books, which were the only true friends he had ever known. He had only slight contact with his father. Then one day, he met a beautiful woman and fell in love again. He knew that she was the love of his life. And when she unwittingly became involved in his father's nightmarish world, he could no longer close his eyes. He understood once and for all what a sick and depraved old man his father had become."

Beatrice stared at Simon. "You're Desmond Crowley's son, aren't you? You're the son of the Grand Inquisitor." Simon nodded. "Oh, my dear friend, I'm so sorry for you," she said at last.

"They know everything," he said slowly, pulling her close.

"Who are they?"

"Defensores Fidei. They know you have the grimoire."

"*How?*" she said, astonished. "Did you tell them?"

"No, of course not."

"Who, then? Only you and I and Stephen know I have it."

"And one other person."

"Who?" Beatrice was utterly perplexed.

"Your housekeeper."

"*Nellie!*" Beatrice gasped. "Oh my God! That's right. She saw me with it yesterday. I wondered what she was doing upstairs. She must have been searching for it all along."

Lovelock nodded.

"But surely Nellie's not in with them?" Beatrice said.

"Who do you think let them in to see your father that day?"

Beatrice felt light-headed with horror. "That's why she was so upset. That's why she kept begging my forgiveness. It wasn't about finding him dead. It was about letting them in. . . ." Beatrice reflected. "But she loved my father. She loves me. She's like a member of our family. She wouldn't have collaborated in his murder . . . would she?" She regarded Lovelock in bewilderment.

He looked at her compassionately. "Beatrice, Beatrice my darling, you *still* don't understand the hold they have. Your housekeeper, Detective Monahan, Father Morton—they're all in on it."

"Monahan!"

"Certainly. Why do you think the investigation came to a halt?"

"Oh God . . ."

"I could protect you up to a point. As long as they thought you didn't have the grimoire, you were safe. But now that they know you have it, and they suspect Borzamo told you of its value, they're going to try to get it."

"I'll destroy it first," Beatrice said angrily.

"Oh, no! You mustn't do that."

"But I'll never give it to them, never! You think I'd willingly give them the key to all those millions? They murdered my father. . . . I'll tell the police or the newspapers. There'll be an investigation. I'll go up to the institute and find out what's going on there. I'll get them. I will!"

"What if you tell the wrong person? Look at Monahan. Would you have suspected him?" Beatrice shook her head. "Don't you see, they have tentacles in too many places. You can't know whom to trust. And there's no way to prove anything. They cover their tracks."

"I'll find a way, Simon. You can help me. We can help each other. If what Borzamo says is true, if it really is the key to Göring's fortune, they'd be so powerful with it—" Beatrice interrupted herself. "But, then, so would I," she added slyly.

"You are powerless against them, don't you understand? How can I make you understand that?" he said, agitated. "They believe they're fighting the ultimate war on earth. Remember I once told you that the doctors are sometimes more dangerous than the disease? They believe that anyone who opposes them—anyone who gets in their way—is the Enemy and on the side of Satan. They be-

lieve in the reality of hell more strongly than you and I believe in
the reality of anything on this earth! If you cross them and try to get
the money yourself, they'll destroy you!"

"Maybe. But maybe I'll destroy them. A billion dollars buys a
lot of power, and power is protection. . . . Simon, listen to me," she
said with new resolve. "It's simple. I've got to go to Zurich and get
the money myself. It's our only chance."

Simon thought for a moment. "Yes, all right. That might just be
possible. But you must be very careful. There's still time. Go back
to your house, get the grimoire, and pack a suitcase."

He took hold of her shoulders and faced her squarely. Gone was
the ineffectual Lovelock she had known. He was full of strength and
conviction.

"Beatrice," he said, "you're very precious to me. I won't let any
harm come to you. But you must do as I say. . . . Do you trust me?"

"Yes," she whispered.

"Then go home. Do as I've told you and wait for my call. Do
you understand?"

"Yes."

"I must hurry back to my shop now and make arrangements."

"Just a second." She grabbed his sleeve and looked at him
pleadingly. "Simon, you've got to tell me who killed my father."
Shaking with emotion, she pinned him with her eyes. "Was it Father
Morton?"

"No."

"Monahan?"

"No."

"Surely, it wasn't Nellie?"

Lovelock shook his head.

"*Who* then?" Beatrice implored him.

Simon hung his head. Beatrice could see the torment in his
face.

"Pity me, Beatrice," he said at last. "I am a soul divided."

"Simon, please, I beg of you—whoever you're protecting is a
murderer. He must be brought to justice. Don't you see that?"

He started to walk away, his footsteps echoing on the wooden
floor of the gallery. When he was halfway across the room, Beatrice
called out to him.

"Is it your father—Desmond Crowley?" she cried.

Lovelock stopped for an instant, glanced over his shoulder at her, then turned and kept walking through the succession of rooms. Beatrice watched him until he was out of sight. She stared at El Greco's painting of the Grand Inquisitor one last time.

Beatrice called Stephen from the museum. His answering machine picked up.

"Stephen—where the hell are you?" she said frantically. "I've just had the most amazing meeting with Lovelock. They know I have the grimoire. He says I'm in danger. I'm at the Met, but I'm going home to wait for his call. I know who killed my father, and you won't believe it when I tell you who it is. Get in touch with me as soon as possible."

Back home, Beatrice rushed upstairs to her bedroom and retrieved the grimoire from the bookshelf. She pored over the list of names once more, to make sure she had memorized them correctly. The book really was a little repository of evil, she thought. Purposefully and decisively, she decided to ignore Lovelock's warning and destroy it.

"Your destructive power in the world is no more!" she declared aloud.

Ceremoniously, she slid the metal wastebasket out from underneath her desk. She got a pack of matches from the bureau.

"I commit you to the fires of hell whence you came," she announced, striking a match.

At first, the flames drifted slowly over the grimoire's old pages, crinkling them, turning them brown. Then, suddenly, the book ignited with a furious hiss—an evil spirit burning into nothingness. The fire singed Beatrice's fingertips, and she quickly dropped the grimoire into the wastebasket, watching it disintegrate.

As Beatrice stared at the smoking remains, she heard voices. She ran out of the bedroom and stood poised on the landing, listening. The voices grew louder. She peered down the staircase. Though she couldn't yet see the figures climbing the stairs, she judged that they were headed toward the library.

Clutching the banister, she crept downstairs, reaching the second-floor landing just as Nellie ushered two men inside the library. Beatrice felt a profound sense of revulsion at the sight of the woman who had betrayed her.

"Nellie, who's in there?" she said coldly.

"Oh, Miss Beatrice!" Nellie exclaimed. "I thought you'd gone out."

"I'm back. Who's in there?" she repeated.

A meticulously groomed, rather boyish-looking man in a three-piece suit appeared at the library door. Nellie lowered her eyes and slunk back against the wall.

Stepping forward, Beatrice looked at the stranger suspiciously. "I'm Beatrice O'Connell," she said.

The man's face lit up with a sycophant's smile that looked more like a frown. "Miss O'Connell, I'm Edwin Moore. So very nice to meet you." He walked over to shake her hand. "I spoke with you on the telephone yesterday."

"Oh, Mr. Moore," she said, with some relief. "I wasn't expecting you."

"I know. Please forgive me. I do hope you don't mind my showing up unannounced like this, Miss O'Connell. I did phone you this morning, but your kind housekeeper here said you were out." He wrung his hands. "I'm afraid I pestered her until she agreed to allow us to come over and take a look at the house without you. My client just happened to be in town today and . . ." He lowered his voice, adopting a confidential air. "He's an older man, you know, and he must get back to his house in the country this afternoon. He'd very much like to meet you. I wonder, could you spare us a moment of your time?"

"I was just about to go out."

"Oh, please, do come and say a quick hello," Edwin Moore implored her. Beatrice reluctantly gave in. "What a magnificent house," Moore said, accompanying Beatrice down the hall toward the library. "I saw it at the viewing, of course, but it seems even better now, with all the books back in place."

The man seemed harmless enough, though his smothering affability got on Beatrice's nerves.

"He's so anxious to meet you," Moore said as they entered the room.

At the far end of the library was a tall, imposing figure, standing sideways in a streak of sunlight with his head bowed, examining a book he had pulled from the shelf. Seeing Beatrice, he looked up, peered over his bifocals, and beamed at her. He had a round, impish face, which presented a striking contrast to his great size. His head was completely bald, and the bumpy configuration of his skull was well articulated beneath the shiny pate. His neck muscles seemed to be straining against the restriction of a too-tight bow tie. His tweed suit was baggy, and he had a dithering, professorial manner, which was betrayed only by keen black eyes that stood out against the pallor of his skin.

"Miss O'Connell, may I present Mr. Desmond Crowley," Moore said.

Though Beatrice had already guessed who he was, she felt cold fear at the sound of his name. She was trapped, and she knew it.

"Do forgive us," Crowley said, shambling across the room, holding up the large volume. "This is a marvelous, simply marvelous, fascinating book. One wonders where on earth your father found it." He spoke with a curiously unplaceable but vaguely mid-Atlantic accent.

"Which one is it?" Beatrice said lightly, trying to appear relaxed, though she was leaden with dread.

"*Anatomia del corpo humano*, by Juan Valverde de Amusco—a simply glorious, glorious book on anatomy. It's the Italian translation published in Rome in 1560. A great part of the text and the illustrations, of course, were plagiarized—and I do mean stolen with a vengeance—from poor old Vesalius, who loathed Amusco and accused him of being a thief." He snickered. "There's a copy in the Vatican Library, I believe. One hasn't seen it, though."

Carried away by enthusiasm, Crowley opened the tome and showed Beatrice a gruesome illustration of a skinless man with his raw musculature exposed, holding up the dripping hide of his own flesh in one hand and, in the other, the knife he had used to flay it. Beatrice, who was familiar with her father's small collection of rare anatomical works, nodded in recognition.

"You see here?" Crowley turned to the front pages. "Amusco dedicated it to his patron and patient, Cardinal Juan Alvarez de Toledo." He paused. "He was a Grand Inquisitor," he said with reverence.

Crowley made an awkward move to shake hands, but the large volume got in the way.

"One doesn't know quite what to do with this book," he said apologetically, finally handing it over to Edwin Moore. "There," he said. "Now . . . Howdoyoudo?"

Crowley hunched over slightly and shook hands with Beatrice, who was struck by the strength of the old man's grip.

"I've just been looking at the portrait of another Grand Inquisitor," she said nervously.

"Oh? Have you indeed?" Crowley said with interest.

"Yes. El Greco's portrait of Don Fernando de Niño de Guevara, in the Met. Do you know it?"

"One most certainly does. A very distinguished picture—the sinister cardinal in his scarlet robes, with his elongated hands and his comical round black glasses."

"I see you know it well, Mr. Crowley."

"It's a period that interests me," Crowley replied with a sigh.

"Yes, well, it's an interesting period," Beatrice said. "It seems the world was just chock-full of Grand Inquisitors in the good old days." She flashed him a perfunctory smile.

"The world was young then. Young and innocent and fresh, like the spring," Crowley said.

"Uh—Mr. Crowley, Miss O'Connell wasn't really expecting us, so perhaps . . ." Moore turned to Crowley with a hopeful expression.

"Oh, yes, certainly. You must forgive one. One has come to see your house, and here one is just chattering on and on like a mynah bird," Crowley said.

There was a marked tension in the air as Beatrice and Desmond Crowley seemed to size each other up.

"Well, of course, one hasn't seen the whole house, but the library's perfect, perfect. As a book collector, it is just what one needs."

Her heart pounding, Beatrice nodded reflexively.

"Yes, yes," Crowley went on. "One has a modest collection—the fruit of many years of hard labor. But it doesn't match up to this brilliant, brilliant assemblage here. Your father is a legend, of course. A legend in the trade . . ."

As Crowley spoke, Beatrice studied him closely. The situation struck her as slightly absurd: here she was, she thought, engaged in a polite, civilized conversation about her father with the man who had murdered him—and in the very room in which the murder had occurred! This, coupled with the fact that Crowley's own son—hints of whose expressions she could see in the old man's face—was out to save her from him, gave the drama a further sense of unreality.

"One is struck," Crowley went on breathlessly, flaring out the fingers of both hands for emphasis, "by the magnitude, the breadth, the scope—the eclecticism, if you will—of the contents. Because, you see, there seems to be no one unifying theme to the collection, and that's rare, rare."

"My father just bought whatever appealed to him."

"And more power to him, more power to him. Knew what he liked, eh? Can't fault that in a man," Crowley said, with slight disdain.

"Where is your collection?"

"My collection lives in Milbern, where I live. We all live together. Quite happily sometimes and not so happily at others. But that's life, isn't it, isn't it?" His laugh was more like a cackle.

"But Mr. Crowley wants to move to New York," Edwin Moore interjected. "Isn't that right, Mr. Crowley?"

"Oh, yes, I do, indeed I do. The winters upstate are very severe. And I'm getting on. I'm going to be seventy-four in October."

"You certainly don't look it," Beatrice said, astonished.

"Thank you, my dear, thank you. But one feels it nonetheless, you know. One feels the cold of the grave creeping into one's bones year after year, and that makes the winter months so much less tolerable. One longs for the sun and the warmth of youth."

"I don't think there's much sun and warmth of youth in a New York winter, Mr. Crowley."

"No, but it's not quite as dismal as the bleak of the countryside. Nothing is quite as dismal as that."

"Why don't you take a little tour of the upstairs?" Moore said, seeming anxious to interject a note of purpose into the darkening conversation.

Beatrice froze, for she knew that they would see the burned grimoire.

"No, no, not just yet," Crowley said, waving at Moore blithely. "One can just picture oneself on a chilly February afternoon, seated at the desk, a log fire blazing, composing bits of this and that for posterity."

"You're a writer, Mr. Crowley?" Beatrice asked, playing for time until Simon called.

"Oh, well, you know, a dabbler, a dabbler."

"Mr. Crowley is a renowned scholar," Moore proclaimed.

"What's your field?" Beatrice asked.

"Oh, just philosophy and boring religious studies," Crowley said evasively. "Nothing to write home about; stodgy stuff."

"What have you written?"

"Terrible, tedious old things. Nothing that young people are interested in nowadays."

"I'm interested," Beatrice said.

"Oh, well, hagiography mostly. Lives of the saints, you know. One has written monographs on Saint Augustine, Saint Alban, Saint Francis of Assisi, Saint Catherine, Saint Teresa of Ávila, Saint Mark, Saint Paul—and the Virgin Mary, of course, who is the chief saint. That sort of thing."

"What about your book on the Spanish Inquisition, which I found so fascinating?" Moore inquired.

"You wrote a book on the Inquisition?" Beatrice asked.

"The Spanish Inquisition, as distinct from the medieval Inquisition," Crowley said. "The Spaniards were much more thorough, much more bloody. And much less forgiving."

"Forgiving?"

"Well, the usual penance, fine, and imprisonment wasn't generally enough for the Spaniards. They burned and flayed people left, right, and center. . . . Left, right, and center—that's rather a good political joke!" Crowley guffawed.

"Well, Mr. Crowley," Moore said, "what's the verdict?"

"One is very impressed, very impressed. It's a fine house. And very well maintained. My offer still stands."

"There we have it, Miss O'Connell. If I may take a shortcut here, Mr. Crowley is offering two and a half million dollars—an extremely generous sum."

Beatrice said nothing.

Desmond Crowley leaned forward. "One wonders, Miss O'Connell, if one might prevail upon you to have a little talk with me—alone," he said pointedly, glancing at Edwin Moore.

"Oh, yes, of course," Moore said. "I'll be downstairs." He walked out of the library, closing the large double doors behind him.

"Well, Miss O'Connell," Crowley said, "we both know why one has come here, don't we?"

Beatrice was suddenly conscious of how physically small she was in comparison to Desmond Crowley, who seemed to tower over her like a great shadow.

"No," she said, looking up at him ingenuously. "*We* don't."

"Come, come now. Coyness is attractive only in small doses." Crowley sat down and spread himself out on the sofa, patting the cushions on either side with his hands. "One has made an offer on your house for two and a half million dollars," he continued. "Two and a half million dollars is a great deal of money."

"Yes, it is. It's a very generous offer. But I've changed my mind. I don't want to sell it."

"Nevertheless," Crowley pressed on. "Would you like two and a half million dollars? In cash? This afternoon?"

"If I change my mind, you'll certainly be the first to know."

"Miss O'Connell, one is trying to conduct matters in a civilized manner. One is prepared to give you two and a half million dollars in cash this afternoon. No one need know about it, not even the government."

Beatrice could feel her heart beating wildly as she stared at the old man in silence.

"All right, all right. Let us not beat about the bush any further, Miss O'Connell. One wants the grimoire," Crowley said.

Beatrice swallowed hard, trying her best not to betray any emotion. "I don't know what you're talking about."

"One had hoped to spare you any unnecessary . . . shall we say inconvenience?" Crowley said.

"I can't help you," Beatrice said flatly.

"You realize that by keeping it from us, you become an agent of the devil?"

Beatrice let out a little laugh. "If there's an agent of the devil here, it's not I."

"As one has just pointed out, coyness is attractive only in small doses. You have the grimoire, and it belongs to us, Miss O'Connell. Look at it this way: you would only be giving back stolen property."

"I don't have it."

"One must impress upon you that this is a crusade. We are fighting the forces of evil. You have only to look at modern life to know that the world has slipped into the devil's hands, Miss O'Connell. And Satan must be stopped before it's too late."

"I think *you* must be stopped before it's too late," Beatrice said, starting for the door.

Crowley reached out and grabbed her wrist. "One has been very patient," Crowley said in a monotone, strengthening his grip. "One is now running out of patience."

"Let me go!"

"The grimoire, Miss O'Connell. Where is it?" His eyes glinted with anger.

Beatrice yanked her wrist free and backed away.

"It's no use. Your precious grimoire no longer exists."

"What have you done with it?" he said.

As if on cue, the library doors burst open. Edwin Moore was standing at the entrance, holding the wastebasket. Nellie was behind him, wringing her hands.

"She's burned it!" Moore cried.

Desmond Crowley sniffed the air. Slowly and deliberately, he walked over to Moore. Beatrice held her breath as Crowley reached down inside the basket and lifted out the burned remains of several pages, to examine them more closely.

"Shut up, woman!" Crowley barked at Nellie, who was sobbing softly. Nellie fell silent immediately.

Crowley slapped his hands together, dusting the cinders off his palms. He turned around to Beatrice, his eyes bulging with a maniacal rage. Then he opened his mouth and tried to speak but, choking on his anger, was mute. Finally, a dreadful sound churned up from his bowels, and he produced a horrific roar.

"You witch!" he thundered. "You shall pay for this!"

Pinning her with his black eyes, glistening with rage, he crossed the room in mighty strides. Beatrice shrank back, mesmerized by the size of him and by the force of his fury. She stopped behind a chair and prepared to defend herself.

"Get away from me, you bastard! You murderer!"

With that, Crowley raised up his enormous right hand. As Beatrice attempted to duck, he struck her with the full force of his being, delivering a stunning blow to the side of her skull. A bolt of red lightning flashed before her eyes. Staggering, she fell to the floor.

21

ONSCIOUSNESS SEEPED BACK SLOWLY INTO BEA-
trice. She was lying flat on her back. The sur-
face underneath her body was cold and hard,
like a slab. Her head was pounding. She wanted
to touch it, to relieve the pain. She raised her
arms but got only so far, when something
stopped them and they dropped down, making a
clanking noise. She could hear water dripping. Her mouth was dry.
She licked her lips and opened her eyes.

At first, there was only darkness. Gradually, however, as she
became accustomed to the gloom, she perceived that she was in
an enormous space. Up ahead, to her left, she could just make out
a black grille, with steps behind it. That must be the entrance,
she thought, for the steps led up to what looked like the faint
glimmer of daylight. She turned her head from one side to the
other. Her wrists were held fast by manacles, which were attached
to chains linked to two iron rings embedded in the stone floor.
Her legs were free. With great effort, she managed to haul herself
onto her elbows and prop herself up against the rough stone wall

behind her. The exertion was more than she could endure, and she sank back into oblivion.

When she awoke the second time, she was more alert. The pounding in her head had been replaced by a dull ache. Struggling to sit up, she remained motionless for a long time as recent events began coming back to her: Edwin Moore, Desmond Crowley, Nellie, the grimoire . . . Where am I? she wondered. She tried yanking her wrists free of the shackles, but it was no use. As she came to the realization that she was chained up in a kind of tomb, a fire-ant panic swarmed through her body.

"Help! Help me!" she began to scream, her voice bouncing off the walls of the vast, cold chamber.

"It won't do any good." A small female voice came from somewhere in the room.

"Who is it? Who's there?" Beatrice called, alarmed but oddly comforted by the human sound.

"Over here," the weak voice said.

Beatrice squinted through the gloom. She could just make out the figure of a woman with long blond hair, slumped back against the opposite wall, her wrists, too, in chains.

"What is this place?" Beatrice cried.

"A root cellar," the woman said.

"How long have I been here?"

"They brought you in last night."

"Who are you?"

The woman hesitated. "I'm Trisha . . . I think. Who are you?"

"Beatrice."

"Hey, Beatrice. Pleased to meet you. I would shake hands, but I'm all tied up." The woman laughed somewhat hysterically.

Beatrice was not ready for jokes. "Oh God, what are we doing here?"

"We're in prison, awaiting trial."

"What are you talking about?"

"We've committed crimes. . . . At least that's what they say. They're going to try us."

"Who?"

"The Inquisition," the woman said.

Beatrice squeezed her eyes shut. "This isn't happening," she said. "This isn't happening."

"Oh, it's happening, all right. . . . They're going to try me. It will be a fair trial, and they'll find me guilty," the woman said. "They have to, you see, because I am. And after they find me guilty, they're going to burn me. And you're going to watch. I've watched the others. They make you watch, you see. It's part of the punishment—knowing how much you'll suffer when your time comes. There's no escape."

The woman emitted a maniacal laugh. When she calmed down, Beatrice tried to question her again.

"How did you get here, Trisha?"

"Oh, I had a choice between coming here and going to the Ritz in Paris!" Again the terrible laugh.

"Trisha . . . Patricia." Beatrice suddenly remembered. "Your name is Patricia Hall, isn't it?"

"Ohhh," the woman said, releasing a pathetic cry. "You know my name! How do you know my name?"

"You were kidnapped from a shopping mall in Glenn Falls."

"Yes! Yes! How did you know?"

"I went up there to try and find out what had happened to you."

"You did?" Her voice was that of a little girl. "That was so nice of you. Thank you."

"Trisha, you've been here for months!"

"Have I? . . . I don't know." She began to moan. "Ohhh, I want my mommy . . . I want my daddy . . . I want my babies . . . My babies, ohhh!"

Beatrice felt a sharp pang of sorrow for this deranged woman.

"Have you ever seen anyone burned at the stake?" Trisha said suddenly.

"No."

"Oh, it's terrible. The smell is so terrible. And they don't give you anything—any drugs or anything to dull the pain. So you scream and scream. . . . We had to watch, you see. We all had to watch. And then, one by one, they took us. . . . I'm next. Ohhh, I'm next!" She started to howl.

Beatrice, utterly powerless, sank down and listened to the poor creature wail. "Trisha," she said. "Trisha, listen to me. How many were there?"

"What?"

"How many women have they burned?"

"Oh, I don't know. I've seen five. The flesh melts. Ohhh, it's so terrible! I asked them if they could just behead us. That's quick, at least. But they said no. We have to die in the fires of hell, because hell is where we come from."

"Do you understand why you have to die?" Beatrice said.

"Yes . . . I'm an instrument of the devil. I'm a fornicator and an adulteress. I've led men down the paths of wickedness. I used to believe in abortion. I used to believe that people should be allowed to do as they wish, to love who they want. . . . But that's wrong, you see. I didn't know it then, but now I do. You see, I was a witch and I didn't know it. But now I know it. And I repent. I repent! I do!"

"What do you mean, you were a witch?"

"Oh, yes. I was—I *am* a witch. I know that now. But they said there was hope for me because I've repented. I repent! I repent!" she cried.

"You're not a witch, Trisha. You've done nothing wrong. They're the witches, don't you see?"

"Don't tell me that! They've sent you here to trick me. I am a witch, and I deserve to burn. I can see that now. But maybe I won't burn because I repent," she said hopefully. "Maybe they won't burn me. Will they?"

Trisha Hall started rocking back and forth, humming a child's aimless ditty. Shafts of sunlight began to pierce the grille, creating a dusty light in the cellar. Beatrice took note of the stacks of kindling and cords of firewood piled neatly against one wall. She could also see Trisha Hall more clearly. Dressed in rags, the woman looked emaciated. Her pretty face was swollen and bruised. There were welts all over her body. Her bare feet were black with filth. Every once in a while, she shuddered ferociously and cried out like a madwoman, as if she were reliving the ghastly events she had witnessed.

Beatrice had to relieve herself two or three times during the course of the day. She tried to stand up and pull down her underpants, but the chains restricted her movements. Squatting, she peed through her underpants and watched her urine trickle across the stone floor. She remembered ironically her comment to Father Morton during their first meeting: "If women could have peed from the saddle of a horse, the history of the world would have been different."

The light began to fade. The temperature dropped. Beatrice felt a chill. Without the full use of her arms, there was no way to get warm. She began to shiver. Her damp underpants clung to her crotch, chafing the skin. Presently, she heard shuffling overhead, then the sound of feet scraping the stone steps. She looked up.

Trisha Hall began to tremble and cry. "It's them. . . . They're here. . . . Oh, please . . . please . . . I repent. . . . Please, God . . . I repent. . . ." The woman prayed softly, her teeth chattering in fear.

Beatrice felt her own terror and froze. As the footsteps neared, the chamber became awash with flickering light and shadows. A dark figure entered, carrying a torch. He wore a long black soutane, the front of which was emblazoned with a large white cross. The torchlight illuminated his face. Beatrice recognized him as the young man behind the reception desk at The Bungalow of the Duarte Institute, at whom she had smiled without success. He was followed by two men in similar garb. The three of them worked together efficiently. The torchbearer stood perfectly still, staring straight ahead, while his confederates set about unlocking the wrist manacles restraining Beatrice.

One of the men pulled Beatrice to her feet. Weak from hunger, fatigue, and fear, she fell back against the wall. He yanked her up again and set her in front of him, face forward, tying her hands behind her back with a rope. Having finished, he struck her lower back with his fist to get her to straighten up and walk. She cried out but he paid no attention. They ascended the stone steps to the outside, leaving Trisha Hall behind.

The night was cool and clear. Soft country sounds of crickets and birds resonated through the woods. Beatrice took a deep breath, filling her lungs with the fresh air. The leader extinguished his torch in a vat of water outside the cellar. It made a bright, hissing sound. He strode toward a sleek black golf cart parked nearby and got in. Though it was twilight, Beatrice was able to make out some familiar stonework in the distance—a small bridge and two statues. It was then that she knew for certain she was somewhere within the verdant grounds of the Duarte Institute.

The young man pulled the golf cart up in front of Beatrice and slammed on the brakes.

"Get in!" he barked.

Feebly, she managed to climb into the back of the small vehicle. One of the attendants jumped onto the seat next to her, shoving her aside. The other man got in beside the driver.

As they drove down the road, Beatrice could not help but think what a comical sight they presented: three men in medieval garb and a woman with her hands tied, careening down the road in a golf cart.

Beatrice saw the library ahead, standing out like a black fortress against the night sky. They pulled up to the front entrance. The driver hopped out of the cart and motioned the attendants to follow suit. One of them grabbed Beatrice's arms and led her inside, marching her downstairs to the basement.

Passing the humming Cray computer and the large boiler, Beatrice and her guard stopped in front of the black metal door marked DANGER—NO ADMITTANCE. There was a small bowl filled with water to the left of the door. The young man dipped his hand in the water and blessed himself. Then he hiked up his soutane and took out a circle of keys from the pocket of his trousers.

After turning three keys in three separate locks, he untied Beatrice's hands, swung the door open, and pushed her inside. Remaining behind, he slammed the door closed.

Beatrice found herself in a vast, cool room with a rough floor and no windows. Harsh fluorescent light illuminated gray slate floor-to-ceiling shelves filled with books and manuscripts. On the right wall, some shelves had been removed to make room for an enormous television screen and an accompanying VCR. Above the screen were rows of videotapes in black boxes. On the floor to the left of the television was a large copying machine.

Beatrice approached one wall of shelves and began to examine the books, most of which looked fragile and ancient. The more cumbersome tomes lay stacked on their sides. The smaller volumes were lined up neatly in long rows. On the bottom were mammoth black folders bursting with loose papers that peeked out over the edges.

At random, Beatrice pulled out a large brown book with a pentacle emblazoned in gold on the front and placed it on top of the copier. The old binding crackled as she opened the cover. She leafed through page after page of moons, stars, inverted crosses, and circles containing occult symbols and writing. These were interspersed with Latin, Greek, and Hebrew words, as well as pyramids of upside-down numbers and intricate drawings of planets with intersecting lines.

Replacing it in its niche on the shelf, she extracted another book that caught her fancy. It was handwritten on parchment in minuscule Arabic calligraphy. She pulled out a variety of books and examined them. One consisted solely of hieroglyphics. Another was written in Hebrew; still another, in Greek. And several were printed in languages she could not identify. Most of them contained mystical signs artfully sprinkled throughout the lines of text.

Surely this was the long-lost Borzamo Collection of black magic!

Presently, the door creaked open and Desmond Crowley entered the room. He was wearing a black soutane. A great gold cross was suspended from a thick gold chain on his chest. Illuminated by the fluorescent light, the pale skin of his face and skull took on a greenish, putrid cast.

"Good evening," he said, smiling.

Feelings of revulsion welled up inside Beatrice. She felt light-headed with dread, but she stood her ground, neither moving nor speaking.

"So, Miss O'Connell, we are sorry your stay with us is not as pleasant as it might have been."

Crowley walked toward her, absently running his fingers over the spines of the books. Beatrice cringed slightly as he neared.

"What do you think of our collection?" he inquired, stopping in admiration. "Quite impressive, no? Are you not excited by its power? Hmm? You won't speak? No matter," he said, flicking his huge hand in the air.

"The contents of this room represent centuries of heresy, sorcery, and demonology. . . . All Satan's tricks written down—some of them indecipherable as yet. But we are working on that. It is our mission . . . God's work. Tell me, can you feel the evil in this room? One must bless oneself before one comes in here, lest it should infect one."

Beatrice remembered the font of water outside.

"One feels its dread power vibrating all around one, even now. . . ." He glared at her. "But you feel nothing, do you, Beatrice? This is home to you," he said.

"You bastard," she whispered. "You killed my father, didn't you?"

"Ah! The cat has a tongue! I can see you're not a woman who enjoys small talk. As for your father, he was a brave man. But unfortunately for him, a remarkably foolish one. One didn't like doing away with a fellow collector, but he refused to see reason."

"What reason are you talking about except the reason of your own madness?" Beatrice said angrily.

"Our madness, you say? Would that it were mine alone, for then it would present no threat. No—it is Satan's madness. And now it has become the world's madness. We are in a holy war, my dear. Surely you understand that by now."

"I understand that you're the devil, Desmond Crowley—you and no one else."

"If only one had the devil's power, one could rid the earth of him once and for all. Tell me, do you not watch television and read the newspapers? Do you not see what is going on all around you? The murder of innocent fetuses. Men proud of becoming women. Women proud of becoming men. Genetic engineering, which threatens God's work. Blasphemy, heresy, and pornographic filth all around us, sanctioned, protected, and venerated by the laws of the land! Everything is topsy-turvy. 'The first shall be the last; and the last shall be the first.' That is what the Bible says. We are living among the whited sepulchres of sin, 'which indeed appear beautiful outward, but are within full of dead men's bones! . . . O Jerusalem, Jerusalem, thou that killest the prophets, and stonest them which are sent unto thee, how often would I have gathered thy children together, even as a hen gathereth her chickens under her wings, and ye would not!' "

Crowley's eyes seemed to spin madly in their sockets as he shook with rage. Steadying himself against the wall, he took deep breaths in an effort to regain his composure.

"We are on the brink of Armageddon, and there is no hiding place," he continued in a low voice. "This is all the work of Satan and his minions. And those of us who see it clearly have no choice but to fight back."

"You think killing innocent people is God's work, do you?"

"Innocent people, you say? Witches are not innocent, just as Eve was not innocent. Witches are vile, corrupt beings, easily tempted by the devil, just as Eve was. Is Satan so firmly in control of your soul that you cannot even hear the word of God?"

Beatrice shook her head and sighed. "Mr. Crowley, what's the point? What do you hope to accomplish by killing these poor women? It's not as if they're famous or have any real influence in the world. They're just poor, unfortunate women who happen to believe differently from you about certain issues. What purpose does it serve?"

Crowley drew himself up to make a pronouncement. "Just as a

single microbe can infect an entire body, causing that body to degenerate physically, so a single witch can infect an entire population, causing that population to degenerate in spirit," he said, pointing the long index finger of his right hand at Beatrice.

"The Inquisition never underestimated Satan's power in that regard," he continued. "They understood what a wily one Satan is. Inquisitors traveled to little towns all over Europe, rooting out the infection at its source."

"The Inquisition was disbanded centuries ago."

"Yes! And look what has happened to the world in the interim. Satan made great inroads during that dangerous period of inactivity on the part of the Church. Now we are eating the fruits of his evil anarchy. But we are fighting back."

"You don't speak for the Catholic Church, Desmond Crowley!" Beatrice proclaimed indignantly. "If the Pope ever got wind of what you and your depraved band of misogynists were doing up here at the Duarte Institute, he would excommunicate you all on the spot and have no pity on your souls!"

Crowley paused, fingering the outer edges of the gold cross around his neck. He seemed lost in thought. Then he sighed. "You're right. But the Church doesn't know about us, and they're not going to.... Unfortunately, most modern-day popes have been far too moderate in their approach to the war between God and Satan. This is most lamentable, as it is the only war of lasting consequence on earth. Well-intentioned as they may be, these popes have all lost sight of the enemy with whom they are dealing. And when that happens in any war, the enemy cannot fail to prosper. We think you will agree that a weak, beclouded commander in chief can be worse than no commander in chief at all...."

"Is that how you think of the spiritual leader of Catholics on earth—as a 'beclouded commander in chief'?" Beatrice found it ironic that she should now be defending the church she had abandoned.

"The Catholic Church is, at the present time, misguided. Vatican II, that disgraceful conference of libertines, was simply a harbinger of more changes to come. Dangerous changes, in our view. They are far too lenient. And so," he continued, "reluctantly, very reluctantly, we have found it necessary to take matters into our own hands. We are all fighting for the same cause, after all, but in a different way. Let us simply say that we here at the Duarte Institute are devotees of the older methods. Which simply means we are more zealous in our approach to eradicating evil."

"And why women? Why do you take it out on women?"

"Because women, as one has explained and as is pointed out so many times in the scripture and in the writings of other eminent ecclesiastical authorities, are universally recognized to be conduits of the devil. Their lascivious natures and unclean bodies are fertile ground for the seeds of evil. Evil flourishes in them as a crop flourishes in rich soil. The *Malleus Maleficarum* makes that quite clear."

"You're insane, Desmond Crowley," Beatrice pronounced with disgust.

"On the contrary," he replied. "One is directed by God in this matter. It is God Himself who directs one in all matters. It is the Almighty Himself who has given one the strength and vision to vigorously pursue His Enemy on earth."

"God is as far removed from what you're doing as good is from evil."

"Dear, dear Beatrice . . . would that one could bring you out of the darkness and into the light. One has at least spared you for the moment, because one feels that you are hiding something and one is hoping that you, Beatrice, will not prove as stubborn as other members of your family. . . ."

Beatrice glared at him.

"You see that your hand is resting on a copying machine," he said.

Beatrice immediately pulled back her hand and crossed her arms in front of her.

"We make copies of all our books. They are distributed among our scholars so that we may learn more about Satan and his ways. If it were not for the foresight and vision of our founder, Inigo Duarte, the Borzamo Collection might have perished, and we would never know the strategies and wiles of our enemy. But now, with diligence and patience, those strategies and wiles are being made known to us. Our scholars come here to help us decipher his nefarious works. . . . And upon reflection, it is one's conviction that you, Miss O'Connell, being the daughter of a collector, would not have destroyed the grimoire without having first made a copy yourself."

"I assure you I didn't make a copy of the grimoire, Mr. Crowley. I intentionally destroyed it to keep the likes of you from getting your hands on it."

"Come, come now," Crowley coaxed. "You knew of its secret. One cannot believe, in all good conscience, that you would have burned so valuable a book without some recourse to its treasure."

"Believe what you like."

"No? Truly? You made no copy? No notations hidden away somewhere? One is convinced to one's fingertips that you are holding it back from us."

"Then you can't kill me, can you?"

"Kill you? No, perhaps not . . . But one has other means at one's disposal for getting the truth from witches."

"You're going to make me watch a burning and try to frighten me, like you did that poor woman Trisha Hall?"

Crowley shook his head. "Patricia Hall is an adulteress and a fornicator. She has espoused many harmful causes. She is a witch. She knows that eventually she must perish in the fires of hell whence she came. But enough of her. Here—one has something to show you."

Crowley walked over to the shelf above the television. Pulling out one of the black boxes and opening it, he extracted a videotape. He slid it into the black slot of the VCR, picked up a small remote-control device, and pressed a button.

While he worked, Beatrice assessed her options. Crowley was very large, but he was old, and she had noticed a hint of frailty in his step. She wondered if, in some way, she might be able to find a way to strike at him.

The large black screen flickered for a few seconds, before the picture suddenly snapped on. A woman tied to a stake that rose from a pile of logs and kindling was screaming hysterically. Beatrice recognized her immediately as one of the women in Cap Goldman's clippings. She was Tina Brand, the attractive black activist reporter whose picture Stephen had pointed out to her in the luncheonette.

"Do you mind if one turns off the sound?" Crowley said. "Screams are always so grating on one's ears." He pressed the Mute button on the remote control, and the sound went dead.

Beatrice and Crowley continued to watch the silent picture. A man in a black soutane, carrying a torch, lit the pile of wood in front of the stake. The flames smoldered at first and then ignited all at once. The woman tried to squirm away as the flames licked at her bare legs. Her ragged clothes soon caught fire, and she writhed in pain, turning her head from side to side, her face contorted as the fire charred her flesh. Her skin seared and blackened. Then her hair lit up in bright flames. Her torment was so grotesque, it seemed unreal—a special-effects concoction for some horror film. Long before the wretched soul lost consciousness, Beatrice had turned away.

"For God's sake, turn it off," she whispered.

Crowley didn't move. Beatrice studied his profile as he stared sullenly at the screen.

"But see here," Crowley said matter-of-factly. "Burnings are not so unusual here. And we have other ways as well to deal with the stubborn."

When Beatrice turned to look at the screen again, she saw another woman, stretched out on a rack. The flesh of her armpits was beginning to tear as a hooded torturer tightened the screws of the medieval machine. The woman's eyes were bulging, her face convulsed in a harrowing display of pain.

Beatrice avoided watching the screen and stared, instead, at Crowley. The cold concentration in the old man's eyes as he witnessed this excruciating sight was the purest distillation of evil that Beatrice could ever have imagined. She thought briefly of Simon. Could he possibly know the extent of his father's depravity?

Crowley was so engrossed that Beatrice saw her chance. Picking up the heavy book on top of the copier, she leveled it at him, slamming it into the back of his neck. The unexpected whack caused the old man to keel over and fall to his knees. Beatrice continued to hammer away at him with the book, but it was no use. The book was an imperfect weapon, and she wasn't strong enough to deliver an incapacitating blow. Crowley stumbled to his feet and scuttled to the other side of the room, where he stood up tall and glared at her, rubbing his neck with his hand.

"One can see that our negotiations have failed. One's patience has run out. You are the devil's mistress!" he cried, pointing an accusatory finger at her. "And now you shall be punished!"

With that, he opened the door.

"Guards!" he called out.

Two attendants rushed inside the chamber and grabbed hold of Beatrice, who struggled against them to no avail. Dragging her into the night, they threw her back down into her underground prison.

22

OU'RE BACK," TRISHA HALL SAID, AWAKENING. "I was so afraid . . ." Her voice trailed off. "Where did they take you?"

"Never mind," Beatrice replied, for she knew poor Trisha could no longer process reality. "Go back to sleep."

Beatrice closed her eyes, hoping she could sleep herself. It was no use; her mind was racing. The dust from the firewood and the dank of the cellar made her head ache. In order to steady her nerves, she recited the list from the grimoire over and over in her mind. She knew this knowledge was her power over the forces of evil. She had something they wanted. She would figure out a way to use that, she thought as the demonic names rolled through her brain.

Then she heard soft footsteps. Peering into the darkness, she saw a black figure descending the steps. She stiffened.

"Beatrice?" whispered a voice.

"Yes?" she replied warily.

"Where are you?"

She remained silent. A narrow beam of a light pierced the gloom of the cellar and shone in her face, blinding her.

"Who's there?" she said.

The beam zigzagged through the darkness as the figure made its way across the cellar and slid down on the floor next to her, turning off the flashlight.

"Simon!" Beatrice cried.

"Shhh! Keep your voice down," he warned her.

"Who is it?" Trisha Hall asked groggily.

"Go back to sleep, Trisha," Beatrice whispered.

"We don't have much time," Simon said, extracting a ring of large, old-fashioned keys from his pocket. "Are you hurt, my love?"

"No, I'm all right. They've chained us up."

"I thought they might. I stole these keys from my father's room. He likes to keep control of everything. One of them should fit."

"What if it doesn't?" Beatrice whispered, feeling oddly more panicked now that freedom was at hand.

"I have a file. But that will take longer. Here, hold this." He handed her the flashlight.

Beatrice directed the light onto the manacle shackling her left wrist. Simon raised her arm gently and kissed the back of her hand. Feelings of relief and tenderness swept over her as she felt his lips on her flesh. Their eyes met briefly. Simon began trying the keys in the lock of the heavy iron cuff.

"Simon, thank God you found me," Beatrice said. "How did you get in?"

"We don't have a second to lose. Trust me, I know my way around here."

There was a click. The manacle sprung open. "There's one," he said in triumph. "Give me the other."

Beatrice switched the flashlight to her left hand and shone the beam onto her bound right wrist so Simon could see where to insert the key. There were red marks on her wrists where the irons had cut into her flesh.

"Simon, do you have any idea what's going on up here? It's the worst thing you can imagine. Your father is truly insane." The second lock clicked open. She was free! As Simon helped her up off the ground, she detected a glint of metal in the right pocket of his familiar black suit jacket. Looking more closely, she saw the butt of a heavy automatic pistol.

"You really think that gun will do any good?" she asked.

"I don't know. I pray we don't find out. Come on. We've got to run for it."

"What about her?" Beatrice nodded at Trisha Hall.

Simon glanced at the dazed, emaciated woman.

"She's too weak. Let's go." He grabbed Beatrice's arm, pulling her toward the steps.

Beatrice stood her ground. "No," she said firmly. "I won't go without her."

"You will. You *must*," he urged her. "Come on!"

"No." She shrugged him off. "You've got to free her too."

"I can't get the two of you out," he said in exasperation. "She's too weak to run for it, can't you see that? The only chance she's got is if we get away and get help."

"I won't go without her. We either try it all together or not at all."

Simon nodded curtly with combined admiration and annoyance.

"All right. We'll do it your way. Hold this," he said, handing her the flashlight.

Simon bent down and picked up Trisha Hall's limp right wrist. Beatrice focused the beam of light on the manacle, as he began fiddling with the lock.

"What's happening?" Trisha said, in a sleepy voice.

"Be quiet, Trisha," Beatrice admonished her. "It's all right."

"This lock is different," Simon said, aggravated that the first key refused to turn. As he tried several others, Beatrice gazed at him intently.

"Do you know about the burnings?"

Simon looked up at her. The flashlight beam bounced an eerie glow over his long, pale face. "I do now," he said. "I've just seen the scaffold and the stake. I knew you were in danger, but I had no idea ..."

He stared at her briefly, then went back to work, trying a succession of keys in the stubborn lock.

"Did you call the police?"

"No."

"Why not?" Beatrice cried.

"There was no time. Anyway, I'm not sure we can trust the police up here. My father may have paid them off."

"How is that possible?"

"How is any of this possible?" he replied, sadly shaking his head.

"Do they know you're here?"

"No, of course not. They would never have let me in tonight."

"Your father's a truly evil man, Simon."

"I know. I know that now."

His hands trembling, Simon unlocked one of the manacles and went to work on the other. Beatrice and Simon froze as they heard voices in the distance.

"Oh my God, Simon! They're coming back!"

Simon worked furiously as the voices grew nearer.

"Hurry! They're almost here."

A faint glow illuminated the steps.

"I can't. It's no use," Simon said, giving up. "Come with me *now!*" he implored, grabbing Beatrice's hand.

"No!" She pulled away. "Listen to me, Simon. Lock us up the way you found us. Hide over there against the wall behind the wood. They won't see you."

"Beatrice, if they take you out of here, it will be the end, don't you understand?" Simon implored.

"Quickly, Simon! Do as I say! There's no time!"

Reluctantly, Simon obeyed. Then he hurriedly burrowed behind one of the large stacks of firewood abutting the wall. Carefully wedging himself down, he lay stretched out sideways on the cold floor and waited.

Beatrice held her breath. Bright torchlight flickered on the walls and steps of the entrance. The men in black soutanes descended once more. Trisha Hall wept in fear as they released her from her shackles and tied her hands behind her back. They worked in silence, their faces masks of indifference even as Trisha cowered and screamed, sobbing that she had repented. Beatrice was praying they would not see Simon in the corner. They paid attention to nothing except the task at hand. Having bound Beatrice's hands, the men led the hapless women up the stone steps to the outside. In the open air, Beatrice sighed with relief that Simon had gone unnoticed.

The woods were black, deep, and still. A crescent moon hung in the sky, partially obscured by lead-colored clouds. Trisha marched deliberately, as if she knew the way. After what seemed like half a mile or so, Beatrice perceived a faint glow, which grew more intense as they approached it. Emerging from the forest, they reached a clearing, in the middle of which a mighty bonfire blazed toward the night sky. Twelve men in black soutanes with white crosses sewn on the breast sat side by side on a bench. Behind them were five rows of benches occupied by men in plain black soutanes. Facing the company was a wooden scaffold, lit by oil lamps blazing atop tall iron stands at each of the four corners. A pair of solid wooden chairs were bolted to the platform.

The scaffold was flanked by a giant stake embedded in a hive-shaped pile of logs and kindling and, on the other side, by an enormous rack, like the one Beatrice had seen in the video. Two guards, wearing black warm-up suits and ski masks, patrolled the grounds with shotguns. Their modern terrorist-like garb presented a striking contrast to the macabre medieval atmosphere of the setting.

At the sight of the pyre, Trisha Hall stumbled and fell to her knees. Her attendant yanked her up by the hair and shoved her onward.

"Enter the accused!" the torchbearer cried out, over the crackle of burning wood.

The assembled company turned their heads to the right in unison, their faces now fully revealed by the soaring flames. Cold-eyed and tight-lipped, the seated men stared as Beatrice alone was led up to the scaffold. Trisha Hall remained below, accompanied by a guard.

As she was prodded up the rickety wooden steps, Beatrice recognized the men in the first row. Father Morton was there, and Detective Monahan, Phil Burgoyne—the talk-show host, whom she had seen on television—Edwin Moore, and seated at the far end of the grim line, Signor Antonelli, who watched her impassively, his hands resting on the hawk's-head cane.

Then Desmond Crowley strode out of the darkness, his huge bald head gleaming like a white orb. The large gold cross around his neck swayed from side to side across his black soutane as he walked. He was clutching a book.

"Hail to the Grand Inquisitor!" the minion announced.

The men stood up and cried: "Hail to the Grand Inquisitor!"

They sat down as Crowley mounted the scaffold, where Beatrice was standing alone. Crowley placed the book upon a small lectern.

"All rise!" he commanded.

Once again, the men rose from their seats and stood solemnly at attention.

"Do you, Learned Judges, swear by virtue of your oath and in the name of the Lord God Almighty to keep secret all that is about to transpire here in this court?"

"We swear!" the men replied.

"Be seated."

Crowley put on a pair of bifocals. Opening the book with marked reverence, Crowley crossed himself and spoke in a sonorous voice.

"In the words of the right and true *Malleus Maleficarum*, otherwise known as *The Witches' Hammer*, an accurate and fair translation of which is here before us, we now address this august body: 'Whereas we the Grand Inquisitor, do endeavour with all our might and strive with our whole heart to preserve the Christian people entrusted to us in unity and the happiness of the Catholic faith and to keep them far removed from every plague of abominable heresy; Therefore we the aforesaid Judge to whose office it belongs, to the glory and honour of the worshipful name of Jesus Christ and for the exaltation of the Holy Orthodox Faith and for the putting down of the abomination of heresy, especially in all witches in general and each one severally of whatever condition or estate . . . ,' do begin this trial. Presenter, make yourself known to this company."

Giuseppe Antonelli stood up from the ranks of the audience. Leaning on his cane to steady himself, he mounted the scaffold with effort and stood directly behind Beatrice.

"Make your presentation," Crowley said.

Antonelli placed his hand on Beatrice's head. She withered at his touch.

"Stand still!" Crowley ordered her.

Beatrice straightened up, rigid with disgust, and gritted her teeth as the old man's shaky hand rested on her scalp.

"Your Honor, Learned Men," Antonelli said in a low but clear voice. "I present Beatrice O'Connell to this court."

"In what capacity is she presented?"

"As a defendant, Your Honor."

"Of what crimes is she accused by you?"

"The crimes of heresy and witchcraft."

"Do you yourself accuse her?"

"I myself accuse her."

"You may step down."

Antonelli descended the steps of the scaffold and returned to his seat. Crowley addressed Beatrice.

" 'I conjure you by the bitter tears shed on the Cross by our Saviour the Lord Jesus Christ for the salvation of the world, and by the most glorious Virgin Mary, His Mother, and by all the tears which have been shed here in this world by the Saints and Elect of God, from whose eyes He has now wiped away all tears, that if you be innocent you do now shed tears, but if you be guilty that you shall by no means do so. In the name of the Father, and of the Son, and of the Holy Ghost, Amen.' "

Beatrice did not flinch. Crowley narrowed his eyes.

"Bring the Holy Gospel," he ordered.

One of the minions scurried up to the scaffold, carrying a Bible. He handed it to Crowley.

"Untie her hands," Crowley said.

The young man obeyed. Beatrice rubbed her wrists where the rope had cut into her skin. Crowley held the Bible in front of her face.

"Beatrice O'Connell," he said in a sonorous voice. "We put to you the Question: are you guilty of the following sins: the sin of stealing property from the Right and True Church and of willfully destroying that property though you knew it to be of value to the true Defenders of the Faith?"

Beatrice stared at him coldly.

"Answer me, Witch."

Beatrice remained silent.

"Are you guilty of being a fornicator and an adulteress?"

She continued to stare at him without speaking.

"The sin of using contraception?"

Despite herself, Beatrice smirked.

"The sin of casting a glamour on unsuspecting men and stealing their manhood by cohabiting with them outside the bonds of matrimony?" he went on.

She still refused to answer.

"And finally, are you guilty of the sin of sodomy and of performing other unnatural sexual acts?"

Beatrice could no longer control herself. She let out a peal of laughter.

"Shut your foul mouth, Witch!" Crowley warned her. "Put your right hand upon the Book of the Holy Gospel."

Clasping her hands behind her back, she planted her legs firmly apart and stood her ground.

"We, Desmond Crowley, Grand Inquisitor, have, by public report and the information of credible persons, before us one accused of the sin of heresy. What is your name, accused?"

"Rumpelstiltskin," Beatrice said boldly. She heard herself and knew she was out of control. Secretly, it pleased her.

Crowley ignored her.

"We command you to put your right hand upon the Book of the Holy Gospel, Witch, and swear that you have committed these sins!"

Beatrice looked down at the book, then back up at Desmond Crowley. She held her breath, watching the firelight dance on the stern faces of the judges. The short silence was punctuated by a popping sound in the bonfire and a flurry of shooting sparks. Then Beatrice suddenly raised her head high and spit in his face.

The company gasped in unison.

"Burn her now!" one of the men called out.

Using the back of his sleeve, Crowley slowly wiped the spittle from his cheek. An even greater seriousness crept over his face.

Isolated cries of "Burn her! Burn her!" swelled into a chanting chorus. Crowley raised his right hand abruptly to silence the assembly.

"Stop!" he cried.

The men immediately fell silent.

"This august and learned body shall do nothing but proceed according to law," he said with civility. "Your name is Beatrice O'Connell, and since you have for many years been infected with heresy, to the great damage of your soul; and because this accusation against you has keenly wounded our hearts: we whose duty it is by reason of the office which we have received to plant the True Faith in the hearts of men and to keep away all heresy from their minds, wishing to be more certainly informed whether there is any truth in the report which has come to our ears, in order that, if it is true, we might provide a healthy and fitting remedy, will now proceed in the best way open to us to question and examine witnesses and to interrogate you on oath concerning that of which you are accused. . . ."

He opened the *Malleus* and read: " 'Note that persons under a sentence of excommunication, associates and accomplices in the crime, notorious evildoers and criminals, or servants giving evidence against their masters, are admitted as witnesses in a case concerning the Faith. . . . For it says: So great is the plague of heresy that, in an action involving this crime, even servants are admitted as witnesses against their masters, and any criminal evildoer may give evidence against any person whatsoever. . . . And if any through damnable obstinacy stubbornly refuse to take the oath, they shall on that account be considered as heretics.' " He closed the book and removed his glasses.

"Bring forth the witnesses!" he bellowed.

Three figures wearing black hoods over their faces, only their eyes visible, appeared in the distance. Beatrice saw that one of them was a woman, wearing a blue flowered dress. Their hands tied behind their backs, they marched toward the scaffold, accompanied by a guard. Standing in the shadows, they awaited Crowley's orders.

"Bring up the first witness," he said.

The guard escorted the woman up to the scaffold. She was placed next to Crowley, facing Beatrice. The guard removed her hood and Beatrice gazed at Nellie. Crowley addressed the old woman, who, though trembling, appeared purposeful.

"Put your left hand on the Gospel and raise your right hand."

"Yes, Your Honor," she said with reverence.

Crowley held the Bible in front of her. Nellie put her left hand on the book and timidly lifted her right hand.

"Do you swear to tell the truth, the whole truth, and nothing but the truth, so help you God?"

"I swear."

"What is your name?"

"Nellie Riley." The old woman was barely audible.

"Speak up, please," he commanded.

"Nellie Riley," she said, louder.

"Are you a member of Defensores Fidei?"

"Yes."

"Do you believe in the authority of the Grand Inquisitor?"

"Yes! I affirm your authority, Your Honor!" she cried fervently.

"Good, my child." Crowley smiled. "Are you employed as a housekeeper by the accused?"

She paused. "Yes," she said, her voice cracking.

"And on the fifth day of this month, did you yourself see the accused in possession of a book which you knew to be the rightful property of Defensores Fidei and the True Church?"

"Yes," Nellie replied, avoiding Beatrice's scornful gaze.

"And did the accused subsequently burn that book in defiance of its rightful owners?"

"Yes," Nellie repeated.

"How do you know that?"

"I went up to her bedroom with Mr. Moore, and we discovered the ashes of the evil book in the wastebasket. She was the only one in the house who could have done it."

"And how did you know it was the book in question?"

"Mr. Moore looked at some of the part that wasn't burned through, and he told me it was the one they were looking for."

"Nellie Riley, do you pity the accused?"

"Yes." She lowered her eyes.

"Nellie, *I* pity *you!*" Beatrice cried. "They're just using you! You're the one who's been bewitched—by *them!*"

"Silence, Witch!" Crowley turned back to Nellie. "Tell us why you pity the accused."

Nellie looked at Beatrice blankly. "Because she has abetted Satan in his war with God on earth and she is, therefore, a heretic and a witch." Nellie's flat patter sounded rehearsed.

Despite the anger she felt toward Nellie for the part she had played in the murder of her father, Beatrice realized the old woman had been brainwashed by the evil Crowley and his hateful interpretation of what he called the True Church.

"You may step down," Crowley said to Nellie, obviously pleased.

Nellie descended the rickety steps and took a seat among the company of men, avoiding Beatrice's gaze.

"Next witness!" Crowley bellowed.

The first hooded man was prodded up the scaffold. He stood where Nellie had stood, facing Beatrice. When the guard removed the black cloth covering his head, Beatrice gasped. It was Luis Diaz, his beautiful face swollen and bruised. His upper lip was split, and two of his front teeth were missing. His eyes were glazed. The attendant untied his hands, and Crowley swore him in, then began his interrogation.

"What is your name?" Crowley said.

"Luis Diaz," he answered in a low monotone.

"Do you know the accused, Beatrice O'Connell?" Crowley said, pointing to Beatrice.

Diaz nodded.

"Speak up."

"Yes," Diaz replied.

"Have you had carnal knowledge of the accused?"

"Yes."

"Did the accused insist that you shield yourself with a contraceptive device?"

"Yes."

"Did the accused seduce you with the aid of the devil rites known as Santeria?"

"Yes."

"Did the accused perform unnatural sexual acts upon you?"

"Yes."

"Did you perform sodomy upon the accused?"

He paused for a moment. "I did," he said at last.

Beatrice felt sympathy for Diaz, who stood perfectly still, answering Crowley's questions like an automaton. She thought back to that fateful afternoon in Diaz's dim apartment when he had penetrated her virgin anus and she had let out a wild cry. She knew she could never renounce that moment.

"Luis Diaz, do you pity the accused?"

"Yes."

"Tell us why."

"Because she has abetted Satan in his war with God on earth and she is, therefore, a heretic and a witch"—Nellie's exact words, delivered in the same rehearsed manner.

"You may step down."

The attendant retied Diaz's hands behind his back and escorted him down the steps and into the darkness.

"Next witness!" Crowley cried.

Beatrice's heart was pounding. She knew immediately who was mounting the steps.

"Stephen!" she exclaimed, when the attendant removed his hood. She reached out to him.

The attendant blocked her way.

"Hands at your sides, Witch!" Crowley commanded her.

Beatrice retreated, though she tried desperately to catch Stephen's eye as the flickering torchlight illuminated his face. He stared straight ahead as the attendant untied his hands.

Crowley swore him in and began his questions. "Do you know the accused, Beatrice O'Connell?"

"Yes."

"Are you married to the accused?"

"We're divorced." His voice was weak and hollow.

"The question of divorce shall be addressed later," Crowley said. "In the meantime, what was the reason for your alleged divorce from the accused?"

"I . . ." Stephen began slowly, "I was unfaithful to her. And she left me."

"And what was the reason for your infidelity?"

"I was frightened of marriage."

"And yet you saw no connection between this fear and the accused? Did it never occur to you that she had cast a glamour upon you and caused you to be unfaithful?"

Stephen squeezed his eyes shut. He appeared to be in pain. "What are you talking about?" he said finally.

"Let me read to you from the *Malleus*," Crowley said, once again referring to the book. " 'Witches can infect the minds of men with an inordinate love of strange women, and so inflame their hearts that by no shame or punishment, by no words or actions, can they be forced to desist from such love. . . .' "

As Crowley read, Beatrice studied Stephen's tortured face. It was clear that he was under the influence of a powerful opiate. At times, his head drooped forward and his eyes rolled aimlessly in their sockets. He appeared to nod off, then suddenly revive, smacking his lips together and blinking violently, as if trying to awaken from a terrible dream. Beatrice tried to engage him visually, staring at him hard, shaking her head from side to side in a signal that he must not answer the questions Crowley put to him. But Stephen appeared uncomprehending. He looked back at her with a distant, perplexed expression on his face, as though he vaguely recognized her but did not think her real.

" 'It is to be noted,' " Crowley continued reading, " 'that impotence of the member to perform the act is not the only bewitchment; but sometimes the woman is caused to be unable to conceive, or else she miscarries. . . .' " Crowley looked up and peered over the tops of his bifocals. "Stephen Carson, did the accused suffer a miscarriage?"

Beatrice quivered at the terrible memory these words evoked.

"Yes," Stephen said softly.

Crowley adjusted his bifocals and again read impassively: " 'According to what is laid down by the Canons, whoever through desire of vengeance or for hatred does anything to a man to prevent him from begetting or conceiving must be considered a homicide ... and that witches who do such things by witchcraft are by law punishable by the extreme penalty.' *Res ipsa loquitur,*" he concluded, raising his index finger heavenward as a coda to the pronouncement.

"Are you saying I caused myself to miscarry!" Beatrice screamed at him, her face as taut as a fist.

"Silence, Witch!"

"You bastard! You bastard!"

"One more utterance that interrupts the proceedings of this court, and you shall be bound and gagged," Crowley said coldly.

Beatrice gazed at him, feeling nothing but pure hatred. In all her life, she had never known such a powerfully distilled emotion.

Crowley cleared his throat and read from the book: " 'Question Nine of the great *Malleus* asks whether witches can with the help of devils really and actually remove the Male Organ, or whether they only do so apparently by some glamour or illusion.... Answer: There is no doubt that certain witches can do marvellous things with regard to male organs ... through some prestige or glamour. But when it is performed by a witch, it is only a matter of glamour; although it is no illusion in the opinion of the sufferer. For his imagination can really and actually believe that something is not present since by none of his exterior sense, such as sight or touch, can he perceive that it is present.' "

Crowley addressed Stephen. "Did the accused cause you to be impotent on one or more occasions by declaring herself a witch and dressing in the vile habit of such creatures?"

"I ... I don't remember," Stephen said groggily.

"Bring the evidence," Crowley ordered.

One of the attendants marched up onto the scaffold, carrying the witch costume that Beatrice had purchased in the Village. She stared in stunned disbelief.

"These clothes were confiscated from the apartment of the witness," Crowley said, as the attendant held up the pieces one at a time: the black merry widow, the garter belt, the pointed hat, the stockings, the shoes, the fly whisk. The appearance of each article caused murmurs of disgust through the audience.

"The witness has acknowledged that they belong to the accused and that, by means of a glamour, she did render his member powerless and thus declare herself outright to be a witch!"

Beatrice didn't know whether to laugh or to scream in horror. The sexy costume, which was a harmless physical expression of her darker side, was being used by an insane court to condemn her of *actual* witchcraft! The madness of it was inconceivable. And yet it was real. It was happening. These people—these Defenders of the Faith, as they called themselves—actually believed she was a witch, in league with the devil! In that moment, she knew they intended to destroy her, no matter what.

She felt she had stepped into a world of total insanity. The organization, the ceremony, and the abominable *Malleus Maleficarum*, which appeared to give weight and purpose to the court but only made the proceedings all the more obscene, could not mask their true nature—unutterable fear and abhorrence of females. Now Beatrice knew that she was not on trial for being a witch. She was on trial *for being a woman—a sexual woman!*

So powerful was this illumination that Beatrice barely listened as Crowley continued his interrogation of Stephen.

"Is the accused a Catholic?"

"Yes."

"Has your marriage been annulled by His Eminence the Pope?"

"No."

"Then you are still married to the accused in the sight of God."

"Wait a minute! He's not a Catholic. And anyway, I thought a husband couldn't testify against his wife," Beatrice interjected.

"The witch's objection is noted," Crowley said, thumbing through the copy of the *Malleus Maleficarum* on the lectern.

He turned and addressed the seated men, reading from the text. "According to the good and great *Malleus*, 'Just as a heretic may give evidence against a heretic, so may a witch against a witch; but this only in default of other proofs, and such evidence can only be admitted for the prosecution and not for the defence: this is true also of the evidence of the prisoner's husband, sons, and kindred; for the evidence of such has more weight in proving a charge than in disproving it.' "

There were murmurs of approbation from the assembly.

"It is the judgment of this court that the witch, being still married in the eyes of God, may now be accused of the sin of adultery with the aforeseen witness Luis Diaz. How say you all?"

"Yea!" the men cried out together.

Stephen's hands were retied behind his back and he was led down the scaffold. Beatrice and Desmond Crowley faced each other.

"Beatrice O'Connell, do you repent?"

"For what?" she cried. "Go to hell!"

Curiously, she felt more in control of herself as she put herself at greater risk.

The company hissed.

Crowley spoke after a moment. "The right and true *Malleus Maleficarum* has made provisions for the unrepentant. On your knees, witch whore."

Beatrice took a deep breath, threw back her shoulders, and stood up straighter. Crowley, in a fury, bent over to the side and slammed the Bible against the backs of her knees, causing her legs to buckle. She fell to the floor. He put his hand on her head and held her down.

"Do you repent?"

"Fuck you!" Beatrice said, still gaining strength.

Crowley snorted in anger. " 'Wherefore since the Church of God can do nothing more for you, having done all that was possible to convert you, We the Grand Inquisitor and Learned Men, sitting in tribunal as Judges judging, having before us the Holy Gospel that our judgement may proceed as from the countenance of God and our eyes see with equity, and having before our eyes only God and the honour of the True Faith, on this day at this hour and place, we pronounce judgement upon you, Beatrice O'Connell, here present before us, and condemn and sentence you as a truly impenitent heretic, and as such to be delivered or abandoned to secular justice.' Learned Men," he called out. "All rise."

The men rose in unison.

"Learned Men, you see before you the accused, who is unrepentant. Judge her now. Is she a witch? How say you: yea or nay?"

"Yea!" they shouted without hesitation.

"Beatrice O'Connell," he resumed. " 'Because we cannot and must not in any way tolerate that which you have done, but are in justice compelled to abominate it, and that your crimes may not remain unpunished, and that others may not be encouraged to fall into the like sins, and that the injuries to the Creator may not easily be passed over: Therefore against you, Beatrice O'Connell, unrepentant witch, We the aforesaid Grand Inquisitor and Learned Men, sitting in tribunal as Judges judging, having before us the Holy Gospel that our judgement may proceed as from the countenance of God and our eyes see with equity, pronounce sentence in the following manner:' That you shall be put on the rack and stretched until you tell us that which we wish to know concerning the grimoire. And if you do not tell us that which we wish to know, we shall then tie you to a stake this very night and you shall burn, burn, burn!" He said this with relish.

The two attendants mounted the scaffold. As they took hold of Beatrice's arms to escort her down, she screamed:

"Fuck you, you hypocrites! What about your wives, your sisters, your daughters, your mothers! Who gave you life? Women! If we're evil, so are you! You come from inside us! Hypocrites! Hypocrites!" she screamed.

One of the attendants clapped his hand over Beatrice's mouth as the two men grabbed her tight and marched her down the steps. They dragged her over to the rack and lifted her onto it, faceup. Jamming her down against the thick wooden slab, they locked her wrists and ankles into manacles. One of the men put a black hood over his face, his eyes visible through two small slits. He stood in front of a pulley around which wound chains that connected to the manacles.

When they finished binding her, and she was firmly in place on the instrument of torture, Beatrice looked over at Trisha Hall, who was being led up to the scaffold.

Simon, Simon, where can you be? she thought frantically. Time is running out.

Crowley turned to Beatrice. "We shall deal with you later, Witch . . . Patricia Hall," he said. "I put to you the Question: Are you guilty of being a fornicator and an adulteress?"

"Yes," the woman said weakly.

"Have you had an abortion and advocated the right of such in others of your sex?"

"Yes."

"Have you maintained the right of persons of the same sex to cohabitate and fornicate as lovers and sodomites together?"

"Yes."

"Do you recognize these crimes as heresy?"

"Yes."

"Are you guilty of witchcraft?"

"Yes."

"Do you now repent?"

"Yes, yes! I repent!"

"Put your right hand upon the Book of the Holy Gospel."

Trisha Hall put her hand on the Bible and looked at Desmond Crowley.

"Do you, Patricia Hall, of Glenn Falls, Connecticut, standing your trial in person before these Lords and before the Grand Inquisitor, having touched with your hands the Holy Gospel placed before you, swear that you believe in your heart and profess with your lips that Holy and Apostolic Faith which the Roman Catholic believes, professes, preaches, and observes?"

"I do."

"And consequently do you abjure, detest, renounce, and revoke every heresy which rears itself up against the Holy and Apostolic Church, of whatever sect or error it be?"

"I do," said the terrified woman, her hand trembling on the book.

"And do you also swear and promise that you will never hereafter do or say or cause to be done such crimes as you have already committed for which you are justly defamed as having committed them and of which you are held suspected?"

"I swear."

"And do you also swear that you will perform to the best of your strength whatever penance the august body imposes upon you, nor omit any part of it, so help you God and this Holy Gospel?"

"I swear."

"On your knees," Desmond Crowley said.

Trisha Hall sank to her knees, cowering before the old man.

"We, Desmond Crowley, Grand Inquisitor, have, by public report and the information of credible persons, before us one accused of the sin of heresy. What is your name, accused?"

"Trisha . . . I mean, Patricia Hall," she said, her head bent.

"Patricia Hall, since you had for many years been infected with that heresy to the great damage of your soul, and since we wish to bring your case to a suitable conclusion and to have a clear understanding of your past state of mind, whether you were walking in the darkness or in the light, and whether or not you had fallen into the sin of heresy: having conducted the whole process, we summoned together in council before us learned men of the theological faculty and men skilled in both the Canon and the Civil Law, knowing that, according to canonical institution, the judgment is sound which is confirmed by the opinion of many; and having on all details consulted the opinion of said learned men, and having diligently and carefully examined all the circumstances of the process: we find that you are by your own confession, made on oath before us in the court, convicted of many of the sins of witches."

Desmond Crowley now addressed the seated men.

"All rise."

The congregation rose in unison.

"Learned Men, you see before you the accused, Patricia Hall. You see that she weeps and abjures her sins. Now you must decide, does she shed false tears, a common ruse of the incorrigible witch? And, by the shedding of false tears, does she remain unrepentant in her soul despite her appearance to the contrary? Is she a witch? How say you, Learned Men—yea or nay?"

Beatrice held her breath, watching the firelight flicker on the stern faces of the judges.

Then the men rumbled in unison: "Yea!"

Trisha Hall curled herself into a ball, weeping. Beatrice detected a thin stream of urine creeping out from under the poor woman's tattered skirt. Two attendants mounted the scaffold and led her away. Unable to walk, she had to be carried down the steps. Beatrice watched as they dragged her over to the pyre across from the rack and tied her to the stake with ropes. Her eyes glazed, her body limp and unresistant, Trisha Hall seemed to be in a trance.

Beatrice scanned the darkness for Simon. Where are you? she thought. There's no time left.

When the men had finished their grim work, Trisha Hall looked over at Beatrice. The two women smiled weakly at each other. Beatrice began to recite the Twenty-third Psalm. Trisha Hall joined in.

"The Lord is my shepherd, I shall not want.
He maketh me to lie down in green pastures:
He leadeth me beside the still waters.
He restoreth my soul.
He leadeth me in the paths of righteousness
For his name's sake.

Yea, though I walk through the valley of the shadow of death, I will fear no evil: for thou art with me . . ."

They said the comforting words with tears in their eyes. Gradually, a calm came over both of them as they prepared to meet their fate.

Desmond Crowley, still on top of the scaffold, raised his arms up to the sky and clasped his hands in prayer. The seated men bowed their heads.

"Merciful God," Crowley said. "We, your humble servants, do now deliver unto You two more chattels of hell. Grant us grace that we may continue Your great work on earth and fight against the forces of Satan. Amen."

"Amen," the men murmured.

"We shall proceed," Crowley said. "In the name of Defensores Fidei, tell us where you have hidden the copy of the grimoire, Witch!" Crowley shouted, pointing a finger at Beatrice.

"There is no copy!" Beatrice said.

Crowley nodded to the hooded man, who gave the crank on the pulley a sharp turn. Beatrice felt unutterable pain shoot through her body as the machine stretched her out.

"Where is the copy?"

"There is . . . no copy," Beatrice said weakly.

Crowley nodded again to the hooded man. The crank was turned again, yanking the sockets of her shoulders and hips with gruesome ferocity. Beatrice felt white-hot pain.

"Once more, we put to you the Question: Where is the copy?"

"No . . . copy," Beatrice gasped in agony.

"You are stubborn, Witch," Crowley said. He paused. She knew what he was thinking—another pull would snap her and make her useless to him. "Your refusal means your friend will pay the price."

Slowly, he raised his huge right arm to the heavens, in a kind of salute, and held it there for a long moment, his face twitching with rage. Beatrice remained silent.

"Proceed!" he bellowed, snapping his arm down in front of him in a commanding gesture.

An attendant lowered a torch and lit the outer edge of Patricia Hall's pyre. The kindling ignited in small, crackling flames as wisps of smoke arose like diaphanous snakes and swirled into the air. Trisha's eyes widened in disbelief. "No! No!" she yelled. Gasping and screaming, she thrashed from side to side in an effort to free herself and avoid the steadily encroaching fire.

"Stop! Stop it!" Beatrice yelled. "I'll tell you what you want to know!"

"Tell us now," Crowley said without emotion. "There is still time."

"I memorized the access code!" she blurted.

Crowley's expression flashed in triumph.

"Out!" he commanded.

Attendants rushed forward with large wooden buckets of water and doused the flames. There was a hissing sound as the fire died down in thick clouds of gray smoke. Trisha's screams became small whimpers of relief.

"Now, Witch," he said. "You will tell us what you know."

"Can't tell you . . . ," Beatrice said with effort. "Have to write it down."

Crowley nodded to the attendant, who slackened the pulley. Beatrice exhaled fiercely as the pain abated. The hooded man unbound her and lifted her off the rack. Her legs buckled as she tried to walk. The man clasped her right arm and wrapped it over his shoulder, dragging her toward the scaffold. Gradually, she found her footing and her strength. Shrugging the attendant off at the foot of the structure, Beatrice held on to the rickety wooden railing and made her way up the steps of the scaffold alone.

She reached the top, where she stood with her legs apart, arms crossed in front of her, facing Crowley in a defiant posture.

"The brazen witch has a fine memory," Crowley said. "Now, perhaps, she will share it with us."

Beatrice began to play for time. Although there seemed to be no hope left, she felt coolheaded. Furtively, she looked around the scaffold to ascertain if there was anything—any weapon or object—she could use against Crowley if the opportunity presented itself. Her eyes fell upon one of the blazing oil lamps nearby.

"I must have your word—" she began.

"You must have nothing from us!" Crowley interrupted her scornfully.

"I'll write down the code for you. I will," she continued. "But I must have your word that you will let us both go. Both of us."

Crowley squinted at her, then turned away. "It is a brazen witch indeed," he said in a scornful aside to the assembly.

Muted laughter rippled through the audience.

"We cannot let you go, Witch, for you would surely betray us."

"If we're going to die anyway, why should I give you the code?"

"You will not die. You will be spared. . . . Death by the fire is . . . uncomfortable. Ask your friend what she would prefer," Crowley said with mock civility. "We promise you will not die. That is our only promise."

Play for time, play for time. That's all Beatrice could think of.

"I have your word you won't kill us?"

"My word as a Christian."

"But you won't let us go. That's a helluva deal," Beatrice said sarcastically.

"Unfortunately, it is the only one we have to offer you. Our patience is ending."

"I need a pen and some paper," she said at last.

Crowley sighed, looking out at the audience. "Do any of you Learned Gentlemen have a pen?" he asked with mock civility.

Signor Antonelli raised his hand. Fishing inside his soutane, the old man retrieved a fat black fountain pen and held it up. Crowley dispatched an attendant to fetch it. Antonelli handed him the pen. He ran up to the scaffold and, bowing slightly, presented it to Crowley.

"Your old friend and Presenter, Giuseppe Antonelli, has come up with the instrument of your salvation," Crowley said, giving the pen to Beatrice. She unscrewed the cap, noticing the heavy pen's thick, pointy tip, which gleamed in the firelight like a tiny gold spear.

"Now . . . write down the code here, in the frontispiece of the great and good *Malleus.*" Crowley opened the book.

Beatrice began to write the list of names from the grimoire, as Crowley peered over her right shoulder.

"And take care, Witch," he warned her. "If you should try to trick us in any way—if these names be not the exact code—then we promise you and your friend a death that is far more excruciating than mere fire. . . . You will both suffer as slow and as painful an end as any ever devised by your master, the Lord of Hell."

Beatrice knew she was buying time and that was the most important thing. She paused for a moment, calculating that Crowley would need a day or two to check out the code. Someone would have to go to Zurich and present the list to the bank. By that time,

Simon was sure to come to their rescue. But what if they managed to spirit her and Trisha away to a place where Simon couldn't find them? Keeping the real code to herself was her only chance. That way they would have to keep her alive.

"Continue," he said.

"I'm thinking," she replied. "I want to get it just right."

She resumed writing, feeling wafts of Crowley's hot stale breath on the back of her neck as he leaned over her. She completed the list, writing the last three names—"Tetragrammaton, Tiros, Tremendum"—exactly the way they appeared in the grimoire, but *not* the way Borzamo had edited them, to constitute the true access code. Then she stepped aside. Crowley walked up to the lectern, devouring the still-damp list with his eyes. He recited the names aloud, like a catechism. Finishing, he drew himself up to his full height and, raising his clasped hands to the heavens, gave thanks to Almighty God.

"Thy will be done!" he boomed.

"Amen!" echoed the assembly.

"Satisfied?" Beatrice said.

"Is this the true code? You have not tricked us, Witch?"

"It's the one I memorized," she said, lying.

"We shall find out soon enough...." He looked at her contemptuously. "And should you have given us a false code, this is what will happen to you.... Light the pyre!" he ordered the attendant at the foot of the scaffold.

"No!" Beatrice screamed. "What are you doing!"

"I do not make pacts with witches!"

The attendant obeyed, walking to the stake and burrowing his torch deep into the pyre, close to Trisha, where the wood was still dry. The fire flared up with a fury. Even the damp kindling around the outer edges began to smoke. Trisha screamed and thrashed as the flames ignited her dress. Beatrice could hardly believe her eyes.

"You maniac!" she yelled.

Gripping the pen in her fist, Beatrice lunged forward and attempted to stab Crowley's right eye. He ducked and the point of the pen missed its mark, but it made a deep gash in his forehead. Blood spurted out, blinding him. He emitted an agonized shriek and clutched his face in pain.

The men let out a collective gasp and sprang to their feet. One of the guards ran up to the scaffold. With a madwoman's strength,

Beatrice pivoted behind Crowley, flung her left arm around his neck, and raised the pen up, ready to puncture his jugular. But the guard was too quick for her. He grabbed her wrist before the pen hit home. Cruelly wrenching her arm behind her back, he held her fast. The pen fell to the platform.

"Don't kill her . . . don't kill her," Crowley moaned, as a rivulet of blood mixed with black ink poured over his face, down his neck to the collar of his soutane.

Trisha's screams were choked off as she lost consciousness. Her skin turned black. A sickly smell like roasting pork filled the air. Beatrice crumpled, sobbing uncontrollably, while the guard held her in a viselike grip.

Crowley leaned over and wiped his face with the hem of his soutane. An attendant bandaged the wound with a handkerchief. Crowley's blood-smeared face looked demonic.

"You wretched, blasphemous witch!" he roared in a glistening rage.

"You're a monster," Beatrice whimpered. "A monster. . . ."

After a time, one of the guards poked at Patricia Hall's charred corpse with a stick. The crescent moon shone brightly, cutting like a sickle into the black sky. A gentle breeze swirled the putrid smoke heavenward.

"She's dead!" he reported.

"Amen!" Crowley cried. "Bring up the witnesses against the witch! Not the woman . . ."

Beatrice held her breath as Stephen and Diaz were led up to the scaffold with their hands tied behind their backs. Two attendants led Stephen to one of the chairs, untied his hands, and sat him down. Lashing his arms and legs to the chair with ropes, they removed his hood. They did the same to Diaz. Then one of the attendants scurried down from the scaffold and ran up again, holding two rope collars with attached wooden bars. He handed one to his confederate, who placed it around Stephen's neck. The other attendant placed the duplicate device around Diaz's neck. Both Stephen's and Diaz's heads drooped forward. They seemed unaware of what was going on. The attendants then stood at attention behind their captives, awaiting Crowley's orders.

"Are you familiar with the term 'garroting'?" Crowley said to Beatrice.

"Oh my God. . . ." She quivered. "You can't. . . ."

"I see that you are," he said, relishing her reaction. "The Spaniards used it somewhat excessively during the Inquisition. . . . Such an effective method for getting the truth out of heretics, but equally effective for executing them—and less prolonged than the fire."

"No, please. . . . I beg of you. . . ." She groaned.

"Don't worry. We do not enjoy seeing *men* suffer," he said pointedly. "We prefer authenticity whenever possible, but we shall be quick. . . . Proceed."

Beatrice stood by helplessly. There was no way to save them. If she told Crowley she had given him a false code, he would wind up betraying her anyway, as he had just demonstrated. Simon was her only hope, but she now feared that he had either deserted her or been captured. Her only consolation was that they would never get their hands on Göring's fortune.

She watched in horror as the two attendants began twisting the wooden bars, causing the ropes to knot and tighten around the victims' necks. Beatrice saw the congregants lean forward, craning their necks to get a better view. She looked at Stephen as the rope cut into his flesh. His face bulged, turning a ghastly shade of purple. His eyes swelled up in their sockets like two tiny inflating balloons, and his tongue protruded from his mouth grotesquely as he gasped for air. She looked over at Diaz, who was kicking and squirming in agony, clawing at the arms of the chair, desperate to free himself.

Beatrice squeezed her eyes shut, unable to endure the terrible sight any longer. This was hell, she thought: the unimaginably horrific become real, the unendurable coming to pass. In a few minutes, it was over. The attendants untied the bodies and carried them down the scaffold, off into the night. The company of men seemed to treat the murders as if they were nothing more than a theatrical spectacle, a piece of Grand Guignol to amuse them on a Saturday night.

"Now, Witch," Crowley said, "you see the possibilities awaiting you if you have lied to us about the code. . . . Take her away! We can no longer bear the sight of her!" he ordered, with a dismissive wave of his hand.

23

NCE AGAIN, BEATRICE DESCENDED THE STEPS OF the underground prison. The guards locked her into her manacles and departed. She lay still and stared vacantly at the wall where Trisha Hall had been chained. The crimes she had just witnessed were beyond comprehension. Images of Trisha's charred remains, Diaz's clawing hands, Stephen's agonized face, and the satanic figure of Crowley flashed through her mind in a dizzying, stupefying reel. She was too shocked to move, too shocked even to weep. . . . And what would they do to her, once they found out she had given them the wrong code? Crowley's words promising her "a death that is far more excruciating than mere fire . . . as slow and as painful an end as any ever devised by your master, the Lord of Hell," echoed in her mind. Wretched and stunned, she lay on the cold stone floor, awaiting her fate like a chained dog.

Mercifully, she drifted into sleep. She was awakened some time later by footsteps. The cell was filled with soft morning light. She looked up and saw a hooded figure in a black soutane. He held a small black bundle. Thinking him one of the guards, Beatrice recoiled instinctively and screamed, "Get away! Get away from me!"

"Quiet! Quiet!" the figure admonished her, dropping the bundle and removing his hood.

"Simon!" Beatrice cried. "Oh, Simon!"

He rushed to her side and held her close. "Oh, my love, my love. . . . You're safe. . . . Thank God you're safe," he whispered, caressing her hair and her face.

"Do you know what they've done?" she asked, weeping. "They've killed them all—Trisha, Diaz, even my darling Stephen. . . . Horrible deaths . . . horrible. Oh, Simon . . ."

"Forgive me, Beatrice—I failed you. But I won't fail you now. We have no time to lose. . . . The keys. Pray they didn't find the keys and the file. I hid them here."

Simon got up and began rummaging around the pile of wood where he had hidden himself. In no time, he retrieved the circle of keys and the file and held them up triumphantly. Returning, he grabbed her right wrist. "Which one are you, you little devil?" he said, trying several keys in the lock.

"Tell me what happened," Beatrice said as he worked.

"I tried to follow you after they took you away, but one of the guards spotted me. I knew him and pretended I was looking for my father, but he saw the gun and didn't believe me. He took me back to the Bungalow at gunpoint and told me I had to wait there with him—that my father was 'occupied.' Occupied!" Simon repeated derisively. "We sat staring at each other in that room. I pleaded with him. I threatened him, but he just stared at me and told me I had to wait. He'd put my gun on the table next to him. I knew time was running out, so I just lunged for it. . . ."

Beatrice could see that Simon was now breathing with difficulty.

"There! That's it!" he cried as the lock sprung open.

He unlocked her other manacle, moving oddly and with effort. Then she saw the dark stain on the left side of his soutane.

"Simon, you're wounded!" she said with alarm.

"It's nothing. . . . A bullet grazed me."

"Oh, Simon!"

"It's just a flesh wound. I'll be all right. Don't worry about that now. . . . Are you strong enough to run for it if we have to?"

"What choice do I have?" Beatrice said, her spirits lifting. She scrambled to her feet.

Simon grabbed up the small bundle from the floor and shook it out. It was a black soutane, wrapped around a black hood. "Put these on," he ordered her.

Beatrice slid the soutane over her clothes. Simon helped her button up.

"And this."

She slipped the hood over her head, adjusting it so she could see through the eye slits.

"Now I'm one of them," she said facetiously.

"Let's hope they think so."

Simon put his own hood back on, took Beatrice's hand, and led her gently up the steps of the cellar to the mouth of the entrance. She was weak with shock and fatigue and faltered once or twice, but Simon urged her on. Just before they stepped into the open air, he stopped.

"Now listen to me closely," he began. "Fold your hands in front of you. We'll walk together side by side along the path to a clearing. When we reach the clearing, just follow my lead and continue walking across it toward the woods. Whatever you do, don't run. When we get to the woods, I'll give you the signal. Then run like hell. Run straight. In about a quarter of a mile, you'll see the barbed wire. I filed out a section last night when I sneaked in. You can just get through. A few yards after that, you'll reach the main road. You understand?"

"Yes." She nodded.

"Are you all right? Are you able to make it?"

"Yes," Beatrice replied with resolve.

He gripped her shoulders. "Don't talk. Don't look back. And above all, don't stop for anything. Promise me."

"I promise," she said solemnly.

Simon and Beatrice stepped out into a cold, pale dawn. Beatrice noticed that the green leaves of the large shade trees were flecked with yellow and red, signs of the approaching autumn. The tranquil grounds, whose idyllic beauty was heightened by the soft warbling of birds and the mild rustling of nature, belied the terrible secret of the place. As they walked along the path, Beatrice was alert for any people. Her heart beat fearfully.

Presently, they reached a large clearing. Sparkling rays of early-morning sunshine cut sharply through the trees in the dense woods up ahead. Beatrice lifted her soutane slightly to facilitate her steps as she trod over the rough, grassy terrain, moist with dew. The ground was studded with rocks, and Simon stumbled. Beatrice stopped to wait for him.

"Keep going!" he exhorted her. "Don't stop!"

Reluctantly, she marched on ahead and continued for a few moments, until she could no longer detect his footsteps behind her. Ignoring her promise to him, she glanced over her shoulder. He was some distance away now, struggling to keep up, clutching at his wounded side with his hand. Moving slowly, as if in great pain, he flicked his other hand out in front of him, desperately motioning her to keep going.

Finally reaching the woods, Beatrice breathed a long sigh of relief. She felt safer navigating through the tall clumps of trees. Simon was very far behind her now, and she had no idea where to go. She stood still for a moment, waiting for him to catch up. Turning around, she saw him staggering toward her.

"It's no use," he gasped, collapsing on the ground in front of her. "I'm hopeless. You've got to go on alone. . . ."

Beatrice fell to her knees and cradled his head in her hands. "Simon, my dearest . . . I can't leave you here like this."

She saw his hand becoming bloody as he pressed it deep against the wound in his side. It was obviously much more than a graze. She winced in pain for him and hugged him closer.

"Go, Beatrice. I order you to go! They'll find me, but my father won't harm me. Get help if you can, but I don't know if you can trust the Milbern police."

"I'll have to trust them, Simon. I'll just have to."

"Go, then. Go!"

"But I don't know where to go!"

"Go directly east. Follow the sun. You'll come to the fencing soon enough. Here," he said, hiking up his soutane and extracting the file from his pocket. "Take this. If you can't find the opening I made, you'll have to file through the barbed wire somewhere else. Now go!"

She paused, agonizing over whether or not to leave him.

"You're no use to me here," he said sternly. "Bring help. Go!"

Beatrice leaned down and gave him a gentle kiss on the mouth. "God bless you and keep you, Simon Lovelock."

"You too, my love. You too."

Beatrice got up and headed on without looking back. Gripping the file, she walked quickly, toward the sun, as Simon had directed her. Finally, she came to the imposing barbed-wire fencing. The wires were thick and intertwined, studded with thorny spikes. She saw that it would be impossible to climb over, and knew that filing through the twisted metal cords would take a long time. Removing her hood and soutane, and tossing them on the ground, she ran frantically to the right, searching for the opening Simon had said he'd made. No luck. She doubled back and ran in the other direction.

Suddenly, she spied the opening at the bottom of the fencing. She lay on her stomach and dragged herself through the jagged aperture, gripping the grass and undergrowth to pull herself forward, wondering briefly how Simon had managed it. She used all her strength to keep going as spikes from the barbed wire grazed the flesh on her bare arms and legs. When she got through and stood up on the other side, she dusted herself off. Her scratched arms and legs were bleeding slightly, but she was free! Pushing the thickets of bushes aside, she ran straight ahead until she reached a ribbon of gray road. The exhilaration she felt infused her with a new burst of energy.

She walked for a while. Then she heard a car approaching from behind. What if the driver was someone from the Duarte Institute? Then she thought of Simon, bleeding in the woods. She had to get help—and quickly. She decided to take a chance and try to flag the car down. She stood in the middle of the road, waving her hands. The big old station wagon slowed to a halt. The driver, a middle-aged woman, rolled down the window and peered out. Beatrice ran up to her.

"Help me!" she cried.

"You poor child!" the woman exclaimed, gazing at Beatrice's arms and legs in horror. "You're all cut up! What on earth's happened to you?"

"Will you take me to the police?"

"Yes, yes, get in," the woman replied.

Beatrice ran around to the other side of the car as the woman leaned over and pushed open the door. She slid into the passenger's seat and slammed the door. "Please hurry!" she begged.

The woman, who was dressed in riding clothes, gunned the motor, and they sped off down the road.

. . .

Forrest Whiting, chief of the Milbern police, tapped a pencil on the legal pad on his desk, as Beatrice, struggling to maintain her composure, recounted her nightmare journey through the Duarte Institute and the hellish events she had witnessed there during the previous twenty-four hours. Two young police officers stood flanking her, and she noticed Whiting flashing them incredulous looks as she relived the grisly, improbable-sounding tale.

"So you see," she said in conclusion, "I didn't know whether to come here or not—whether you might be part of it or not. But because Simon's in such danger and he might even be dying, I had to take the chance."

Whiting, a stolid, silver-haired man with an amiable expression, raised his eyebrows, leaned forward, and looked at her, perplexed. "What do you mean when you say I might be 'part of it'?" he asked her seriously.

"It's a vast conspiracy, you see," she explained. "I know it sounds crazy, but it's true. You wouldn't believe the men who are involved in this—"

"This. . . . Inquisition," he said, interrupting her.

"Yes! That's exactly what it is. Father Morton, Phil Burgoyne—"

"Phil Burgoyne, the talk-show guy on TV?"

"Yes. . . . I know it sounds mad. They're all very important, highly placed people. But they're all part of it. They're all torturers and murderers!"

"And you say Desmond Crowley is the head of it. The, uh— what'd you call him?"

"The Grand Inquisitor."

"Right," he said, making a note on the pad. "The Grand Inquisitor. . . . Deacon, how do you spell 'inquisitor'?"

One of the officers let out a slight guffaw but quickly covered his mouth when Whiting glanced at him disapprovingly.

"I-n-q-u-i-s-i-t-o-r," the officer called Deacon replied, deadpan.

Finishing his notation, Whiting sighed, leaned back in his chair, and toyed with the pencil, rolling it between his thumb and index finger.

"Well, now, Miss O'Connell," he began slowly, "I feel obliged to tell you that I know Professor Crowley personally. Not well, of course. But he's lived up here for years. He's a real solid citizen—

well thought of by folks. I know he's connected with the institute and he does a lot of work there." He started to stroke his cheek absently with the pencil eraser.

"What you have to understand," he continued, "is that the Duarte Institute is kind of a feather in our caps, so to speak. Interesting people come from all over the world to visit it. There's a lot of prestige attached to it. And they do a good deal of business in the town. They're a nice bunch of people. Pay their bills on time, keep to themselves—"

"I don't care what they appear to be. I'm telling you what they *are,*" she cried emphatically. "They're murderers, torturers! They burn women and kill innocent men! They tied me up to a rack and stretched me out until I thought my bones were going to rip out of their sockets! I watched a woman burn at the stake! I watched while they strangled my ex-husband and a friend of mine! And how do you think I got this way? Who do you think did this to me? Just look at me!"

"Whoa! Slow down. . . . Just calm down," Whiting said, motioning to Deacon to bring her a drink of water.

The burly officer filled a paper cup from a water cooler in the corner and handed it to Beatrice. She drank it down in two gulps.

"I'm sorry," she said, recovering. "Just come with me and see for yourselves. That's all I'm asking."

"Well, you have to lodge a formal complaint."

"I am. I am lodging a formal complaint," she said, thinking to herself how ludicrously understated those words sounded given the atrocities she had witnessed. "But informally, I beg of you, just come with me now."

"I still think we oughta get you to a doctor," Whiting said.

"No! We've got to go there *now,* while there's still time. Please, I'm begging you!"

Whiting tossed his pencil on the desk and threw up his hands in a gesture of resignation. "Okay," he sighed. "I'll take you on over there. Deacon, order us a car."

The police car turned into the entrance to the Duarte Institute and headed up the winding trail. The two young officers were sitting up front. Beatrice was in the back seat, next to Chief Whiting. She felt herself growing increasingly agitated as they reached the white gravel road leading to the high wooden fence surrounding the property.

What if they're in on it? she thought as they waited at the closed metal gate.

She remembered the last time she had seen that gate and the sprawling farm beyond. She had been with Stephen. The thought of him pierced her heart, and she fought back an overwhelming urge to cry. But there was no time for that now, she told herself. She had to keep calm and think of Simon, who she prayed was still alive. . . .

The gate clicked open, and they drove on through, cruising slowly past the imposing nineteenth-century barn with its gleaming copper roof and cow weather vane, past the bucolic pastures and grazing animals, into the wooded grounds on the road leading to The Bungalow.

"You know, I'd forgotten . . . this is some spread they have here," Chief Whiting remarked admiringly, staring out the window. "They must have two, three thousand acres. Oh, to be a rich man," he added wistfully.

"Hey, get a load of that little guy in the bushes," Deacon said with amusement, pointing to the stone Pan peeking out of the trees.

Finally, pulling around the circular driveway, the car stopped in front of the huge limestone Bungalow. The officer driving the car got out and stretched. Deacon opened Beatrice's door and helped her out. She was beginning to feel the effects of hunger and exhaustion as much as shock. As Whiting, the two officers, and Beatrice mounted the steps to the entrance, the double doors swung open. Father Morton appeared, looking fresh and alert. The sight of the portly cleric so repelled Beatrice that she reeled slightly. Officer Deacon took her arm and steadied her as she glared at Morton.

"Murderer!" she cried.

Morton seemed taken aback for a moment. Then an expression of distress swept over his face. He reached out a sympathetic hand. "Dear Miss O'Connell. . . . What on earth has happened to you, my child?"

"Keep away from me, you bastard!" Stepping back, she clutched at the protective arm of the officer.

"I don't understand," he said, looking at Chief Whiting in bewilderment. "I'm Father Morton. What is all this about?"

"I'm Forrest Whiting, chief of the Milbern police, Father. . . ."

"I'm pleased to meet you, Chief Whiting," Morton said, offering his hand.

Whiting cleared his throat. "We need to come in and talk to you, if we may."

"Yes, of course. Please do come in," Morton said solicitously, ushering them inside.

He led them through the large entrance hall to the pristine white dining room where Beatrice and Stephen had lunched with him during their visit. Morton planted himself in a wooden armchair at the head of the refectory table and motioned the others to be seated on the benches. Folding his hands on the table and leaning in with a look of great concern, he addressed the chief of police.

"Now," Morton said, "what exactly is going on here?"

"Well, that's kinda what we want to ask you," Chief Whiting replied.

Father Morton's face gathered a look of astonishment as Whiting repeated Beatrice's grisly tale. Beatrice, unable to contain herself during Whiting's cool account, interrupted once or twice to amplify certain events. When Whiting had finished, Father Morton rested his elbows on the table, propped up his chin with the tips of his fingers, and considered for a long moment.

"I'm afraid I'm really at a loss for words," he said, shaking his head from side to side, with wide, disbelieving eyes. "Is this some sort of bizarre joke?"

"It's no joke, you murderer!" Beatrice shot back. "I wish to hell it was."

He pinned her with his eyes. "What on God's earth has led you to dream up these terrible, terrible accusations, Beatrice? I can't even begin to fathom it. You have a very macabre imagination, my dear."

"Cut the shit, Morton!" Beatrice cried. "Where's that murderer Desmond Crowley?"

"I have no idea where Mr. Crowley is at the present time. In his own house, I would suppose. He doesn't live at the institute, you know."

"What about Antonelli and Monahan and Burgoyne?" she said.

"I don't know."

"They're not here?"

"No."

"They weren't here last night?"

"No. Not that I know of."

"Oh, for Christ's sake!" Beatrice cried. "You know they were here! You were all here, relishing the sight of people being burned and strangled at your Inquisition!"

Morton turned helplessly to Chief Whiting. "I have no idea how to react to this insanity," he said, with concern. "If the child didn't seem quite so distraught, I would have to laugh."

"Well, listen," Whiting said, "you mind if we have a look around? You can order me to go and get a search warrant—"

"No, no, no—that's not at all necessary," Father Morton replied. "Be my guest. Look anywhere you wish. The grounds and the buildings are all open to you. I'll accompany you myself."

Father Morton took them on a tour of the property. Not one of the large, open fields he led them to contained the slightest evidence of charred wood, scorched earth, or any of the apparatus connected with the ghastly ceremony—the scaffold, stake, rack, and benches. There must be another field, she told Chief Whiting—one that Morton wasn't showing them. Whiting followed his own route around the grounds, but a thorough search turned up nothing.

A moment of hope surged up in Beatrice when she spied a golf cart loaded with firewood parked some distance off the road on familiar terrain. She demanded they stop the car. Beatrice got out and ran over to the little black cart. It was parked in front of the root cellar! Her first thought was of Simon. Maybe he was down there, chained up, as she and Trisha had been. But whether he was down there or not, she would now have her proof, she thought triumphantly: let the murderer Morton explain the two sets of manacles bolted to the floor!

She careened down the cellar stairs and bumped smack into a young man in a black suit, carrying a stack of logs. The man fell backward and teetered on the edge of the steps. He regained his balance, however, managing to hold on to the bundle.

"Oh, pardon me!" he exclaimed politely.

"Pardon you, my ass!" she cried, pushing past him.

He looked at her impassively, continued on up the steps, and disappeared outside.

Reaching the bottom of the stairs, Beatrice looked around the dank chamber. It was the same place, all right, she said to herself, recognizing only too well the configuration of the room and the stacks of logs and kindling behind which Simon had hidden the night of the Inquisition. But the manacles and chains were gone. She flew to the wall to which she had been chained and ran her hands over it in disbelief. There were no signs of any bolts or chisel marks ever having defiled the stone. Angry and frustrated, she cried out like a madwoman, "Bastards! Bastards! Bastards!" thumping her fist against the wall.

After a time, she became exhausted. Looking up, she saw Father Morton, Chief Whiting, and Officer Deacon standing on the cellar steps, staring down at her pityingly.

"This is the place—I swear it. . . . This is where they chained us up. . . . Trisha was right over there." She pointed feebly to the other side of the cellar. "But it's all gone—the manacles, the chains, everything. . . ." She looked at Chief Whiting. "They're diabolical, don't you see? . . . Don't you see that?" she pleaded. "God knows what they've done with Simon. . . . God knows how they managed to cover up the fires. . . . They've just gotten rid of all the evidence, but it happened. It really happened. You've got to believe me!"

Whiting and Deacon glanced at each other. Beatrice saw the young officer roll his eyes heavenward. "Oh, you must believe me!" she sobbed weakly. "You *must* believe me!"

"There, there, my child, this is all nothing more than a delusion—a hideous dream. You must look to God and have faith that He will help you in this most terrible hour of need," Father Morton said sanctimoniously, his arms outstretched to console her.

The sight of Morton's bulky frame and simpering countenance moving toward her filled Beatrice with such revulsion that an unexpected rush of strength galvanized her. She charged across the room and flew at him.

"Where's Simon!" she screamed, attempting to claw his face. "What have you done with Simon!"

The surprised cleric retreated and ducked his head, trying as gently as possible to fend off her attack. Whiting and Officer Deacon ran down the steps and came to his aid. Together, they pulled Beatrice off the beleaguered priest and held her tight. Father Morton straightened his collar and smoothed back his hair as they restrained her.

"The poor child needs help," he said to Whiting. "We must get her to a clinic."

Turning his head slightly, he surreptitiously flashed Beatrice a knowing sneer. She spit at him.

"Hold on there, young woman!" Whiting rebuked her. "That's enough, now!"

"God bless you, my dear, dear child," Morton said. His feigned compassion and look of deep solicitude confirmed him as the undisputed victor.

The situation was futile. Beatrice realized how insane she must appear to the outside world. Who would ever believe me? She could hardly believe herself when she raved on about a vast conspiracy and the horrific events she had witnessed. Whiting clearly wasn't one of them, but she knew he wasn't taking her seriously. Would anyone ever take her word against the eminent and upstanding Father Morton, pastor of Saint Xavier's? she thought disconsolately. She was all alone now, in mortal danger.

Her mind raced. If Simon wasn't dead, he was doubtless no longer at the institute; most likely, he was being hidden somewhere else, she reasoned. And Crowley was probably on his way to Zurich. Her one consolation was that the false code she had given Crowley would ensure his failure to acquire Göring's vast fortune and use it to finance his terrible cause. She knew the moment had come to change gears if she was going to try and get the money herself and somehow save Simon—provided he was still alive.

After completing a thorough search of the grounds and buildings, they drove back to The Bungalow to drop off Father Morton. Beatrice and the two police officers waited in the idling car as Chief Whiting and the priest stood on the steps, conferring in hushed tones. Beatrice saw Whiting glance in her direction once or twice, while Morton shook his head sadly. Though they were out of her hearing range, what the two men were saying to each other was painfully clear to Beatrice: she was hysterical, deranged, in dire need of help, poor child. She could just imagine the sympathetic offers of assistance Morton was proffering on her behalf under the guise of great concern.

"Don't hesitate to call upon me if there's anything I can do. I'm very fond of the dear child, and she's been through a great ordeal, what with the death of her father and all," she heard Morton say to Whiting as the two men shook hands. His words made her cringe.

Whiting returned to the car and slammed the door hard.

"Okay, let's get out of here," he said with an aggravated sigh. He turned to Beatrice. "You satisfied?"

Implementing her new tactic, she nodded. "I'm sorry to have caused you all so much trouble," she said meekly.

"Listen, I know you don't believe it, but that guy is on your side, okay?"

"He is?" Beatrice said, wide-eyed.

"He sure as hell is. He just now told me about your dad and the terrible thing that happened to him. He said there was no telling how it had affected you—how a trauma like that would affect anyone. . . . Listen, I have a daughter myself, and if something like that happened to me, she'd go bananas."

Beatrice swallowed hard and, ever mindful of her new goal, gathered her wits about her.

"Yes," she said, lowering her eyes. "I think you're right. My father's murder has unhinged me a little, I suppose. I loved him so much, you see."

"I know, but you can't go around making nutty accusations against distinguished people."

"I'm sorry," she said.

Chief Whiting ordered Deacon to take them to the Milbern Clinic, where Beatrice was examined by an attending physician. Her new attitude, which was calm and contrite, convinced the young doctor, who treated her cuts and questioned her that there was no need to hold her for observation. She washed up and combed her hair before leaving the clinic.

Taking pity on her, Whiting gave her an old raincoat from the station house to cover her stinking clothes and drove her to the bus station. There, he bought her a ticket back to New York.

"We all go through rough times in this life," he said, pressing the ticket into her hand. "You've had more than your share, what with your dad and all. But you have to understand, we live in a world where innocent folks can get into a lot of trouble if people start slinging mud at them. It's a damn dangerous thing to do, and I hope you've learned your lesson."

"Oh, I have, Chief Whiting," Beatrice said with feigned sincerity. "I really have."

His expression mellowed. "Go home now. Get some rest."

"Thank you," she said. "I can't tell you how much I appreciate this. . . . You know, I think the thing that most shocks me today in the world is—" She stopped, feeling a lump in her throat.

"Is what?" he asked.

"Kindness," she replied in earnest, for she was truly grateful to him for helping her. "And you're a very kind man."

The compliment seemed to both touch him and make him uneasy.

"Well, now, you better not get yourself into any more trouble, Miss O'Connell," he said gruffly, pointing a finger at her. "Next time, people may not be so lenient."

24

EATRICE SAT ALONE NEAR THE BACK OF THE half-empty Greyhound bus as it barreled down the thruway toward Manhattan. Whiting had unexpectedly handed her a ten-dollar bill as she was boarding.

"In case of emergency," he had said with a wink. He walked away before she could thank him.

She felt utterly drained. Aimlessly folding and unfolding the bill in her hands, she contemplated her next move. She knew she couldn't go to the state police; her recent experience with the law had taught her the foolishness of such an effort. And besides, Detective Monahan, a key conspirator, would certainly manage to discredit her. And God help her if he maneuvered her into custody on some false pretext; she'd surely be done for then.

She thought briefly about going to the FBI. But how likely were they to take her word against so eminent a group as the board of directors of the Duarte Institute? Even if she did succeed in convincing them to look into the disappearances of Stephen, Luis Diaz, and Simon, they would require time. And time was one thing she didn't have. Simon's life was at stake; so was her own.

Beatrice leaned back and closed her eyes. She tried desperately to fight off the fatigue that was fast enveloping her. Lulled by the hum of the engine and the steady motion of the bus, however, she could no longer help herself, and she soon fell sound asleep.

She awakened to see the familiar Manhattan skyline looming in the distance. The bus made its way through the outskirts of the city, cutting in and out of the burgeoning traffic. They would be arriving at the bus terminal soon. Feeling somewhat refreshed from her nap, Beatrice sat up and once again concentrated on formulating a plan.

Simon was paramount in her mind. Was he still alive? And if so, where had they taken him? How could she get to him? She knew she had no chance of saving him all by herself. The members of Defensores Fidei were too powerful for her, and there were too many of them in high, unexpected places. So she had to get to Zurich as soon as possible and tap into the money. Göring's vast fortune would give her the means to hire protection while she launched her own investigation.

Glancing down the center aisle, she noticed a thin young man in black, looking back at her impassively. He was nondescript, except for his skin, which was pockmarked. As their eyes met, he quickly faced front. A little arrow of fear pierced her heart.

Beatrice had to assume they were hunting for her. That meant she could not safely return to her house or go to Stephen's apartment. It was a mark of how isolated she had become in the last few years that she could not think of a single person she really trusted and in whom she could safely confide her story without fear of ridicule. No—her so-called friends would think her mad, she thought with amused disdain. Poor Beatrice, so unhinged over her father's death. They would try to persuade her to go directly to a shrink or enroll in some therapy group where she might "share" her paranoia with like-minded loonies.

Then, suddenly, it hit her. There was one person in the world who might believe her—a person she barely knew but who, more than anyone she could think of, was likely to be receptive to her chilling tale: the old Santeria *madrina*. Who better than a witch to help a witch? she thought. By the time the bus pulled into the terminal, Beatrice had made up her mind. She would go to Sister Marleu and seek her help.

After the bus had come to a halt, Beatrice remained seated until all the other passengers had filed out—especially the young man in the black suit. When the last person had disembarked, Beatrice made her way down the aisle. Stepping off the bus, she looked around the bustling, gritty station, scanning the crowd for his pock-marked face. He was nowhere in sight, and she wondered if her imagination had got the better of her after all. He was probably just another passenger, she thought, as she climbed the steps leading to the exit.

Outside the building, she hailed a taxi. It was close to five o'clock, and the rush hour traffic was heavy going uptown. Beatrice fiddled with the ten-dollar bill as she watched the cab meter click away. She knew she was taking a big risk going to a woman she barely knew, but there seemed to be no alternative. Where else could she go without fear they would be lying in wait for her?

The cab pulled up in front of Sister Marleu's shop in Spanish Harlem.

"You better watch yourself in this neighborhood, honey," the cabbie said as Beatrice handed him the fare. She noticed that he locked all his doors before speeding away from the curb.

Beatrice descended the familiar short flight of stairs, only to discover that the front door of the tiny shop was locked. A small handwritten sign reading *Cerrado* hung on the knob.

"Closed! Goddammit," she cursed under her breath. She started pounding on the door, on the off chance that Sister Marleu was inside but simply not open for business. "Oh, please, Sister, *please* be there!" she said frantically to herself.

There was no response. Beatrice ran up the steps, out onto the street once more, and dashed into the convenience store next door. A woman behind the counter was arranging packs of cigarettes in a display.

"Sister Marleu," Beatrice said breathlessly. "Is she away?"

The woman looked up at her blankly. "*Qué?*"

"Sister Marleu, next door. Is she away? ... Sister Marloo," Beatrice reiterated.

"Ah, Marloo! *Sí, sí. Al lado. Al lado.*" She pointed.

"I know she's next door," Beatrice said, exasperated at her inability to communicate with the woman. "Is she there? Does she live there?"

"*Qué?*" the woman said, grimacing.

Just then, a fresh-faced teenage girl with her hair in rollers came forward from the back of the store, carrying two Coke bottles, a bag of corn chips, and a box of detergent. She put the items on the counter and pulled out some money.

"Hi," Beatrice said.

The girl looked Beatrice up and down. "Hi."

The woman behind the counter began ringing up the purchases.

"Do you speak Spanish?"

"Yeah," the girl said, shifting her weight from one leg to the other as she waited for her change.

"Could you do me a favor and ask her if she knows whether Sister Marleu lives next door in her shop?"

"Yeah, sure." The girl turned to the woman behind the counter. "*Quiere saber si Sister Marloo vive al lado? En la tienda?*"

"*Sí, sí. Ella vive ahí,*" the woman said as she placed the items in a bag.

"Yeah, she does," the girl said.

"Could you ask her if she's there now? The shop is closed."

"*Está ahí ahora?*"

The woman shrugged. "*Qué se yo?*"

"She says, 'How would I know?' "

"Oh," Beatrice said, deflated.

"*Casi siempre está ahí. Escondiéndose,*" the woman volunteered.

The girl looked amused.

"What did she say?" Beatrice asked.

"She says almost always she's there, hiding."

"Thanks very much. I appreciate your help."

"Okay," the girl said. Taking her change and the bag, she walked out of the shop.

"*Gracias,*" Beatrice said to the woman.

"*De nada,*" the woman replied, going back to sort out the cigarettes.

Back on the street, Beatrice decided to try her luck once more. As she approached the little shop, she spied the man she had seen on the bus. He stood across the street, looking right and left. She ran down the small flight of steps and hid in the doorway.

Christ, she thought, her heart pounding furiously. He followed me. He *is* one of them!

She pounded on the door again. There was still no answer. Sneaking up the steps, Beatrice peered out onto the street. Now the man was nowhere in sight. However, she couldn't see clearly on either side, so she decided it was best not to make a run for it just yet. Huddling down against the door, she waited, scratching on it reflexively in fear. Then, unexpectedly, the door to the little shop swung open and the curtain of red beads rustled. Parting the strings and holding them up to either side with her hands, Sister Marleu stepped forward, the reddish light of the shop glowing behind her. She gazed at Beatrice.

"What do you want?" Marleu said.

"Oh, Sister Marleu, thank God!" Beatrice cried with relief. "Do you remember me? I'm Beatrice O'Connell. I came here with Luis Diaz one day."

Sister Marleu's tight mouth broke into a wide grin. "Oh, yes," she purred. "Sister remembers you very well."

"I'm being followed. Can I come inside?" Beatrice asked urgently.

"Come in," Sister Marleu said, holding the curtain aside so Beatrice could pass through.

Marleu shut the door behind them. Once again, Beatrice found herself standing in the magical little place, filled with jars, bottles, and amulets, lit by all sizes of red and white candles.

"Welcome again," Sister Marleu said.

The short, plump woman cocked her head to one side and leaned in so close that Beatrice could feel Marleu's breath on her face. Marleu looked deeply into her eyes.

"You have trouble," she said. "Big trouble . . ."

"That's true."

"Sister Marleu understands. You have changed."

"Yes, that's true too."

"Sister Marleu likes you better now. Now you have met your wolf and you are friends with him."

"I'm worried about this man who's following me," Beatrice said. "I think he's going to try to kidnap me, or kill me. And if he asks next door, he's going to realize I'm here."

"Do not worry about him," Marleu said, waving her hand.

"Whoever he is, he is a goat in the lion's den. . . . Come, sit down with me."

Marleu guided Beatrice to a chair near the back of the shop and sat down, facing her.

"Now, tell me why you have come to Sister Marleu, wolf woman."

"Your friend Luis Diaz is dead," Beatrice began slowly. Marleu's eyes flickered. "I saw him murdered with my own eyes. He was strangled horribly, like in the Inquisition. . . . Sister, during the past two days, I've seen things no one would believe—my ex-husband strangled, a woman burned at the stake, appalling carnage. And a group of evil men—very important men, but woman-haters and murderers nonetheless—watching it all, planning it all, with glee. They call themselves Defenders of the Faith and think of themselves as saviors, but they are evil. Evil!

"And the problem is that this is all so incredible that no one—not even decent, honorable people—can possibly believe me. I know I sound mad, but there's a terrible conspiracy in this country, against women. These people think we're all witches, and they're out to punish us and murder us for being who we are."

"For communing with the wolf, maybe?" Sister Marleu said.

"Exactly. You understand. It's all about our sexuality. . . . They have a book called *The Witches' Hammer,* which they're using to plot our destruction. And I believe this book has poisoned the view of women in the Catholic Church and elsewhere down to this day—"

Sister Marleu suddenly raised her index finger to her mouth. "Shhh!" she cautioned. "Someone is coming."

"That's him! I bet it's him!" Beatrice whispered in alarm.

"Stay still," Sister Marleu said calmly.

Beatrice tensed as she heard the front door creak open. A few seconds passed, and then she saw the barrel of a gun poke through the strands of the red bead curtain, gently pushing them to one side. She glanced at Sister Marleu, who was staring intently at the gun, her black eyes shining in the candlelight. The gun pushed the beaded strands farther apart until the figure of a man was visible in the entrance. Beatrice didn't dare breathe. The man slid slowly into the room, holding the gun out in front of him. Having entered, he blinked once or twice, trying to accustom his eyes to the sparkle of the myriad candles.

"Beatrice," he called out in an oddly high and eerie voice. "I know you're in here. You can't escape from us. . . ."

With that, he saw Sister Marleu, who stood up from her chair with a defiant look on her face. Swinging the gleaming black snake-like braids of her hair from side to side, she let out a demonic howl. He aimed his gun at her, squinting through the candlelight.

"No!" Beatrice screamed, leaping in front of her, pushing her down to the floor. Beatrice expected a shot, but instead she heard a soft whooshing sound, followed by a raspy gurgle. A cold silence gripped the air as Beatrice lay on top of Sister Marleu, paralyzed with fear. Sister Marleu started to chuckle softly and pushed Beatrice aside. The plump little woman struggled to her feet and leaned down, extending her hand to Beatrice, who was still too frightened to move.

"You are a brave woman," Sister Marleu said. "Sister is grateful."

When Beatrice stood up, she looked over at the curtain, where the man had been standing. He was on the floor, his head turned to one side, lying in the growing pool of blood that streamed from his throat. His eyes glazed, his mouth opening and closing in rhythmic spasms, he resembled a dying fish gulping for air. Two squat young men with round, chocolate-colored faces reminiscent of Sister Marleu's were standing at the foot of the body. They wore rolled-up shirtsleeves and jeans, and each held a commando knife. The blade of one knife was bloody.

"Meet my sons, Alfredo and Manuel," Sister Marleu said proudly, flashing the brilliant, toothy grin Beatrice remembered from their first meeting. "My sons look after me. With the businesses that are run up here, they have to know how."

"*El cabrón está muerto, Mamá. Viva Chango!*" one of the young men said.

"What does that mean?" Beatrice asked, stupefied.

"It means 'The goat is dead, praise to Chango,'" Sister Marleu replied. "Come now, wolf woman. Sister will make you some tea, and you will tell Sister how she can help you."

Marleu guided Beatrice along a narrow corridor off the back of the shop, into a small room that looked like a combination parlor, kitchen, and herbary. Dried plants and herbs, in sheafs bound neatly with colored strings, were piled together inside the gaping mouth of a cumbersome oak rolltop desk. A big black kettle and two large copper pots simmered on the gas burners of an old-fashioned black stove. Resting on a table next to the stove were several bottles containing murky liquids of varying hues and consistencies, along with a collection of ladles, measuring cups, and spoons. A row of glass jars filled with colored powders lined the sill of a calico-curtained window that faced out onto a brick wall. Marleu instructed Beatrice to sit down on a commodious tufted armchair in one corner while she prepared them tea.

Beatrice watched the little woman snip a variety of herbs into a china teapot and pour hot water over them, after which she added a teaspoon of greenish powder from one of the jars and a shot of brown liquid from a bottle. Then she lifted up the pot in both hands, jiggled it around so the water sloshed from side to side, and put it down again, letting the brew steep for a minute or two. Pouring two cupfuls, she handed one to Beatrice.

Beatrice, who was still extremely unnerved by the recent episode, took a cautious sip, prepared to be revolted. God knows what's in here, she thought as an aromatic liquid filled her mouth. Much to her surprise, the concoction tasted sweet and delicious. After a few more swallows, Beatrice felt a soothing warmth sweep over her.

"This is wonderful tea," Beatrice said, as Sister Marleu refilled her cup. "But I don't recognize the flavor. What's in it?"

"Tranquillity and energy . . . mixed," Marleu said, playfully rubbing the thumb and index finger of her left hand together in a circular motion.

"Is this where you make the potions for your shop?" Beatrice inquired.

"This is where dreams come true. . . . Nightmares too," Marleu responded. "You are in search of a nightmare, wolf woman."

"It's more like a nightmare's in search of me," Beatrice said. "And there's no hope of it ending unless I get your help. Even then. . . ."

"So—tell Marloo your desire."

Beatrice explained the situation in detail, while Marleu stared at her intently. As she spoke, she felt the woman was somehow penetrating her mind, curling around it like a snake.

"So you see," Beatrice said in conclusion, "I need protection so I can go home and get my passport and credit cards. I know they're watching the house, and they'll grab me if I show up there. I don't dare go there alone."

"You must not go home," Marleu warned her.

"But I have to. I *have* to get to Zurich," Beatrice said emphatically.

Marleu held up her hand. "You will tell Marleu where your house is and where to find your things. Marleu will send someone."

"But I don't want to put someone else in danger."

"Marleu knows. But you must not go there," she said, squinting at Beatrice. "You will write down for Marleu the address of your house and where you have put your things. Marleu will send someone good."

Beatrice decided not to argue. Marleu handed her a piece of paper and a pen. As she was writing down the information, a thought occurred to Beatrice.

"I keep my passport hidden, but not the credit cards. I wonder if Nellie took them.... Oh, well." She shrugged. "We'll find out soon enough." Beatrice handed Marleu the paper. "We keep a spare key in the garden, under the plant stand by the back door. I hope it's still there; otherwise he'll have to break in."

Sister Marleu left the room, and Beatrice drifted off to sleep. She awakened with a start when Marleu returned. The room was dark, and she had no idea how much time had passed.

"It is done. Now we must wait.... Here." Marleu handed Beatrice a beat-up brown wallet.

Beatrice looked up at her blankly. "What's this?"

"It is from the pocket of your friend."

Feelings of distaste did not prevent Beatrice from opening the billfold eagerly to examine its contents. Not surprisingly, there was no identification—nothing to mark this would-be assassin if he got caught or died in the act, Beatrice thought. There was only a hundred fifty–odd dollars in cash, the receipt for the bus ticket, and a thin scrap of yellow paper with the numbers "011411507113" scrawled across it.

Beatrice sat in the chair, fingering the slip of paper as she absently watched Marleu brewing her potions at the stove. What could the numbers mean? A bank account? A lottery number?

"Where do you come from, Sister Marleu?" Beatrice said, in the midst of her ruminations.

"Marleu does not answer stupid questions," she snapped, as she added powders to one of the simmering pots on the stove.

Beatrice smiled. Diaz had been right: this little woman had real power, though Beatrice couldn't quite put her finger on what constituted it. True, she was a forceful presence in an exotic setting, and she knew how to play her *madrina* role for all it was worth. But there was something more—something indefinable and uncalculated. The fact was, Marleu had a potent aura of mystery about her, which prevailed, oddly enough, despite her unmistakable theatrics, not because of them. If there really was such a thing, Beatrice thought, this strange little woman was surely a witch.

Beatrice curled up in the armchair and examined the numbers once more. Then it hit her! Why hadn't she thought of it immediately?

"Sister Marleu, can I use your phone?"

Marleu, engrossed in her preparations, grunted an assent. Beatrice picked up the receiver of the touch-tone phone nearby and slowly punched out the numbers. She waited, holding her breath. Then the phone started ringing—a staccato double ring, familiar to Beatrice.

"Baur-au-Lac Hotel. *Guten Tag*," a cheery female operator's voice said.

"Do you speak English?" Beatrice said.

"Yes."

"Where am I calling?"

"You are calling the Baur-au-Lac Hotel in Zurich, Switzerland, madame. How may I help you?" Her tone was most obliging.

"Uh—Mr. Desmond Crowley, please," Beatrice said slowly.

"One moment. I will connect you."

After several short rings, Beatrice heard someone pick up the phone.

"Yes . . . ?" said a groggy voice. Beatrice waited, not daring to speak. "Hello . . . ? Who . . . who is this?"

"Simon!" she cried, recognizing the weak voice. "Simon! It's Beatrice! Are you all right?"

"Beatrice . . . How . . . how did you find us?"

"Never mind that now," she said urgently. "Are you all right?"

She could hear him breathing heavily, struggling to speak. "Yes. . . . No. . . . Where are you?"

"I'm in New York. They tried to get me, but I'm safe."

"Thank. . . . God." He sighed.

"Simon, what's happening to you? Why are you there with him?"

"Can't. . . . can't talk long. . . . You. . . . you gave him the wrong code."

"Yes, I know. Why has he brought you there?" she pressed him.

"Committed. . . . Taking me to Davos tomorrow . . . to a clinic."

"A clinic—what for?"

"Going to give me shock treatments. . . ."

"Dear God! Where in Davos? What clinic, Simon? . . . Simon? Are you there?. . . Simon!"

"Dr. Friedrich. . . . Wilhelm Friedrich."

"Simon, I'm on my way. Don't give up, whatever you do."

"Too late. . . . He's got me."

"No, Simon, no! Hang on!" She heard a commotion at the other end of the line. It sounded as if the phone had dropped. "Simon? Are you there?" There was a long silence. "Simon, I'm on my way! . . . Simon!"

"Who is this? . . . Who is this!" she heard another voice say. She knew instantly it was Crowley and hung up.

"Trouble?" Sister Marleu inquired.

"Big trouble, I'm afraid. I've got to get to Switzerland as fast as I can. Crowley's going to try and fix Simon so he'll forget."

"You will," Marleu replied laconically.

Beatrice ruminated on a plan of action while Sister Marleu went about her work, carefully funneling exact portions of the finished brew into little glass vials and sealing them shut with cork stoppers. It began to dawn on Beatrice that she would now have to try and kill Desmond Crowley if she could possibly get to him. That was the only sure way to prevent him from incapacitating Simon and eventually killing her. She felt strongly that Defensores Fidei would quickly crumble without Crowley's leadership. And besides, he had been responsible for countless gruesome deaths—including her father's. She therefore reasoned that she wouldn't be killing Crowley so much as executing him—carrying out a just sentence on a demonic criminal. But how? How could she kill him? What means could she use?

Some time later, the two women heard voices in the front of the shop. Marleu left the room and soon returned, holding Beatrice's passport out in front of her.

"You got it!" Beatrice cried, delighted. "Was there any trouble?"

"There is always trouble, as you know," Marleu said.

"What happened?" Beatrice asked, alarmed.

"Never mind. It is over."

"No one was hurt?"

"No," Marleu assured her.

"What about my credit cards?"

Marleu shook her head. "You were right. They were not there."

"Christ," Beatrice sighed. "Now what? How am I going to get there without money?"

Marleu ambled over to the desk and stooped down, extracting a key from the pocket of her shift. Unlocking the bottom drawer, she pulled it all the way out, brought it over to Beatrice, and placed it on her lap. Beatrice looked inside and saw that it was filled with cash—bundles of used hundreds, fifties, and twenties, bound with rubber bands.

Her eyes widened. "Jesus, there's a fortune here."

"Take it," Marleu said.

"I don't need all of it."

"You will need more than you think," Marleu said, fetching a plastic bag from a cupboard. She held the bag open for Beatrice, who started dumping the bricks of cash inside.

"Where did you get all this money? From the shop?"

"The believers are generous," Marleu said.

"Some believers must be drug dealers," Beatrice joked.

Marleu did not smile. When Beatrice had finished, Marleu replaced the empty drawer in its niche.

"I don't know how to thank you," Beatrice said. "I'll pay you back. I promise."

"You are right," Marleu said. "You will." Her tone was vaguely ominous. "But that is not all, wolf woman."

"What do you mean?"

"You must take something else with you as well."

Beatrice looked at her, uncomprehending. "What?"

"A weapon."

"Yes, I've been thinking about that. But I can't sneak a gun on the plane, much as I'd like to. I don't know how to shoot one, anyway. And I'm squeamish about knives," she said, shuddering, as she thought back to the recent spectacle in the front of the shop. "I don't think I could use one effectively."

"Marleu sees many things. Marleu sees the future. You will need a weapon."

"You see that in my future, do you?"

"I do."

"What sort of weapon?"

"Woman's weapon."

"What's that?"

"Poison."

It wasn't a bad idea. She might just find an opportunity to poison Crowley at that. It was certainly worth a shot.

"What kind of poison?" Beatrice asked, intrigued.

"The deadly kind." Marleu grinned. "Marleu will fix it for you—in a syringe with a needle. You will see."

"It has to be quick and untraceable."

Marleu nodded. "Do not worry. Marleu has a special recipe—from my island."

"And do me a favor, will you?" Beatrice said.

"What is that?"

"Make it painful."

BEATRICE NOW SET ABOUT MAKING RESERVA- tions. Much to her chagrin, she discovered that she could not get a flight to Zurich until the next evening. She couldn't afford to wait. There was only one solution: the Concorde. She called British Airways. The Concorde departed from Kennedy at 8:45 the next morning and arrived in London at 5:25 P.M. local time. A connecting Swissair flight at 7:15 P.M. would get her to Switzerland at 9:50 P.M. The agent said he could arrange for a car to meet her at the Zurich airport and take her to Davos that night. It was expensive, but Beatrice wasn't counting costs—Simon's life and a billion dollars were at stake. Marleu had been right: she did need more money than she had thought. Would the woman's other predictions come true as well?

"Have the driver meet me under the name 'Dante,' " she told the airline agent, knowing she couldn't be too careful when it came to Crowley and his minions. The choice of the name was deliberate. If I'm to go through another circle of hell, I'd rather do it as a poet than a saint, she thought, referring to the masterpiece after which she was named.

Sister Marleu supplied Beatrice with a small suitcase and some warmer clothes. Beatrice tried to get some sleep in the parlor, but she was too keyed up. Early the next morning, carrying the suitcase, in which she had secreted the hypodermic syringe and the little vial of poison Sister Marleu had prepared for her, she took a cab to Kennedy Airport and boarded the sleek supersonic jet. She was surprised at the cramped seats and the noise, but the food was delicious and the service extremely accommodating. She settled into her seat, fascinated by the little screen in the front of the cabin that displayed a digital readout of the Mach speed of the aircraft as it soared through the sound barrier.

The Concorde landed at Heathrow on schedule, and her Swissair connection left promptly at 7:45 P.M., landing in Zurich two hours later. Clearing immigration, Beatrice walked out into the main terminal and spotted a man in a black chauffeur's suit and cap, holding up a placard inscribed DANTE. After changing some of Sister Marleu's money, she approached him and introduced herself.

"I'm Ms. Dante," she said.

The driver, a glum but courteous older man, bowed slightly, took the carry-on bag from her hand, and escorted her to a roomy black sedan parked nearby. He opened the door for her, and she climbed into the back seat. Things do function like clockwork here, she thought with some satisfaction. He placed her bag in the trunk, got into the driver's seat, and started the car.

"We are going to Davos, yes?" he said, glancing at her in the rearview mirror.

"Yes." She nodded. "How long will it take?"

"*Bitte?*" he asked, uncomprehending.

"Davos. . . . What time will we arrive in Davos?" Beatrice said slowly, pointing to her watch.

"Three hours. But maybe more, maybe less."

Scattered lights from distant towns and villages twinkled across the horizon as the car traveled through the crisp Alpine night. They wound their way up into the dense black mountains, where the road narrowed significantly. Beatrice asked the driver if he knew of a good hotel in Davos.

"Yes," he grunted, without further elaboration.

"Take me there, please."

It was close to one in the morning when they reached the dark, sleeping village. The car pulled up in front of a cozy hotel with a gingerbread facade, just off the main street.

"Schweizerhof," the driver announced.

Beatrice got out and stretched, filling her lungs with the fresh, clean mountain air. The driver went around to the trunk and pulled out her suitcase, handing it to her. She paid him in cash. He thanked her and got back in the car, yawning, to head on his way. Beatrice entered the small hotel.

The lobby of the Schweizerhof was decorated with sturdy, unpretentious furniture and a few touches of folksy bric-a-brac—a Swiss horn, some cow harnesses, and, in a high recessed space on the back wall of the enclosed reception area, a row of colorful antique beer steins. The sleepy concierge checked Beatrice in. Once again, she used the name Dante, saying she would pay in cash.

"Do you know of a Dr. Wilhelm Friedrich?" she asked the concierge.

"Dr. Friedrich, *ja.*" The man nodded.

He reached to the right of the front desk, where the keys of unoccupied rooms dangled on little hooks above cubicles for mail. Two keys remained, and he plucked one down, holding it for a moment.

"Second floor. Very quiet, but no view. It's all right?" he asked tentatively.

"That's fine, thanks."

Satisfied, he handed her the key.

"There are many tourists in Davos just now. . . . A big conference. All the hotels are nearly filled."

"Where is Dr. Friedrich?" Beatrice asked as she followed him into a small elevator at the other end of the lobby.

"He has a private clinic. Very expensive."

"And where is the clinic?"

"Above the village." The concierge pointed his index finger upward. "You must take the *Seilbahn.*"

"Can I go tonight?"

He smiled and shook his head. "No, no. Closed. Seven o'clock tomorrow it will start running again."

The elevator stopped, and the concierge led her down a narrow corridor to her room. Thanking him, she went inside and immediately drew herself a hot bath. It was close to two in the morning by the time she fell into bed, exhausted.

. . .

Beatrice awakened at seven, went downstairs, and had a quick breakfast. Getting directions at the desk, she headed for Dr. Friedrich's clinic immediately. The neat little village of Davos was picturesque and compact. Everything was within walking distance. Beatrice hurried past the decorative shops on the main street. She noticed a pretty church and a small café next door, where people were already sitting outside, drinking coffee and reading the newspapers. What a lovely, pleasant town, she thought. It was difficult to imagine that in the midst of this fairy-tale setting, Simon might—at this very moment—be undergoing a shock treatment to wipe out his memory and his will. Reaching her destination, she bought a ticket and waited.

Gradually, the little station filled up with tourists, hikers, and locals. After about twenty minutes, a clanging bell heralded the arrival of the *Seilbahn*. Beatrice walked toward the platform with the other passengers. A steel gate barred them from going outside right away. In the near distance, she saw a large square car, with windows running the length of the sides, gliding down the mountain on heavy steel cables, its white metal exterior gleaming in the morning sunshine. Roughly nestling into the station to a steady accompaniment of clanking noises, the bulky conveyance came to a halt. The doors slid open and a few people got out. When the last of them had disembarked, the steel gate swung open to allow the new passengers to get on.

Taking her cue from those around her, Beatrice shoved her way onto the spacious but seatless bus and grabbed hold of one of the leather straps hanging from the ceiling. In a few minutes, the automatic doors slammed shut. The car shuddered slightly, clanking as it disengaged from its harbor. Suddenly, they were airborne.

As they traveled up the mountain, Beatrice pressed her nose against one of the large picture windows and admired the breathtaking view. The majestic, verdant, snow-capped Alps were all around them, studded with thick shawls of pine trees.

After about fifteen minutes, they reached the top. The doors slid open, and the eager crowd piled out and quickly dispersed, showing scant regard for courtesy. Beatrice emerged from the little station and looked around. Immediately to her left was a restaurant perched atop one of the slopes. Some distance ahead of the restaurant, up a gently sloping hill, was a tall gate made of thin wrought-iron bars shaped like arrows, pointing aloft. Beatrice walked up and, poking her nose through the bars, saw a sprawling two-story building in the style of a chalet, that looked like a luxury hotel. A huge veranda, facing out over the mountains and furnished with comfortable wooden deck chairs and accompanying low round tables, ran the length of the structure. Beatrice assumed that this was Dr. Friedrich's clinic, though no sign was posted. The gate was locked, and there was no buzzer.

She walked back down the hill and went inside the restaurant to inquire. A fresh-faced young man, dressed in lederhosen, knee socks, and a Tyrolean hat with a feather, was polishing glasses in front of the bar. He looked sexless in the cunning little folk outfit.

"Bitte," Beatrice said. "Do you speak English?"

"Ja, a little." The young man had a thick Swiss-German accent, and his voice was unusually high-pitched. "But I am sorry, but we are closed."

"I just want to ask you a question. Is that Dr. Friedrich's clinic up there behind the gate?"

"Ja."

"How do I get in?"

"For this you must have the appointment."

"I see."

"Ja, you must have the appointment or they do not let you inside. When you have the appointment, then they are always sending someone down here to meet you."

"Have you ever been inside?"

The young man laughed. *"Nein!* It is for the very rich people. Foreigners most."

The young man fumbled and dropped the glass he was holding. It didn't break, but when he leaned down to pick it up, his hat fell off, revealing a long blond ponytail. Beatrice realized that he was not a young man at all! She stared in amazement as the girl straightened up, stuffed her hair back into her hat, and continued on about her business.

"Is that the costume of the restaurant?" Beatrice asked her.

"Ja." The young woman nodded. "All of the boys, they wear the lederhosen, and the girls, they wear the dirndls. But my brother is sick, so I am taking his position for two days. This was the only costume. You understand?"

"Yes, thank you."

Outside, Beatrice took another look around. She concluded that it would be next to impossible to sneak into the clinic and try to find Simon, much less get him out. And she had to assume that Dr. Wilhelm Friedrich—whoever he was—was a member of Defensores Fidei. Riding back down in the *Seilbahn*, she decided she would have to take the bull by the horns and confront Crowley head-on. But how? Where? The minute he saw her, he would certainly attempt to grab her and try to get the code, either by using Simon or by other, physically painful means.

As Beatrice walked back to her hotel, the image of the young woman wearing lederhosen kept flashing through her mind. Then she passed a shop window that had a similar outfit on display. She began to wonder. . . . What if she dressed up like a boy and engineered an encounter with Crowley in a public place? It was an outside chance, but it was the only one she had.

Beatrice went into the shop and tried on the entire ensemble—socks, breeches, and shirt. She stuffed her hair into a hat and pulled it down low over her brow. Then she stepped back and studied herself closely in the dressing room mirror. The wide-legged, loose-fitting short pants covered her thighs, and the thick high socks successfully hid her delicate ankles and shins. Only her knees peeked out. The wide white shirtsleeves covered her arms, so there was no problem there. The bib of the shorts hid her breasts. She really could pass for a boy, she thought. Pulling the hat's curved brim down low over her brow, she was quite pleased with herself. She might just be able to get away with it.

She paid the amused proprietor, collected her purchases, and headed back to her hotel. The concierge greeted her at the front desk.

"*Guten Tag*," he said cheerfully. "Did you find the clinic?"

"Yes, thank you. Tell me, can you arrange for a car and chauffeur to take me to Zurich this morning?" she asked, as he handed her the key to her room.

"To Zurich?" He rubbed his chin and thought for a moment. "You can take the train, you know."

"No, I need a car and chauffeur. Can you arrange it?"

"*Ja, ja*, no problem. But it costs much, because he needs to make a round trip."

"That's fine," Beatrice said. "Just arrange it, please."

"*Ja*, I am doing that immediately," he said, writing a note to himself. "Er—what time?"

"You know the little café by the church just down the road here?"

"Meyer's, *ja?*"

"I want the car to wait for me there, directly in front of the café, at eleven sharp."

"*Ja*, okay," he said with an obliging smile.

"And would you get me the telephone number of the Friedrich clinic?"

"*Ja*, no problem. . . . A beautiful day, no?"

"We'll see," Beatrice said as she headed toward the elevator.

"Mr. Desmond Crowley, please. . . ." Beatrice gripped the receiver tight as her call was being transferred. He's there, she thought excitedly. He's there. . . .

"Hello?"

At the sound of the voice, she hesitated.

"Hello?" the voice said again, irritated.

"Professor Crowley?" she began. There was no response. "This is Beatrice O'Connell speaking. I would like to talk to you."

"Where are you, Witch?" he asked slowly.

The sound of his voice rattled her.

"Never mind that just now," she continued deliberately. "I have a proposal I want to make to you."

"Go on."

She swallowed hard. Her mouth was dry. "I know you've been to the bank and discovered that the code I gave you was inaccurate. . . . I also know that you have your son with you against his will."

"Shut your foul mouth, Witch!"

"Wait—listen to me." She paused. She could hear Crowley breathing in fury at the other end of the line. "You want the code. I want Simon. . . . Are you willing to trade Simon for the code?"

There was a long silence.

"That depends on your offer, Witch."

"But you would consider it?"

"Tell me your offer."

She took a deep breath. "Okay, here it is," she went on, choosing her words carefully. "I'm here in Davos. . . . Meet me at eleven o'clock at the little café next to the church on the main street—*with Simon*," she said emphatically. "I'll have a car waiting there, and the three of us will drive to Zurich in time to get to the bank this afternoon. I'll go with you myself and give you the correct code so you can get the money. Then I'll take Simon home with me."

Another long silence ensued, during which Beatrice bit her thumbnail to the quick. "Go for it," she said anxiously to herself. "Please go for it. . . ."

"If this is a trick, Witch, you will pay dearly," Crowley said at last.

"It's not a trick," she answered calmly. "It's a valid offer. Do you accept? It's the only way you're ever going to get that money."

Another pause and then, "Eleven o'clock. Sharp!" he snapped. There was a click.

Beatrice put down the phone slowly. She was trembling all over. "I've done it," she said to herself. "He went for it." Now, she thought, there's not a moment to lose. She called down to the front desk, and asked the concierge to prepare her bill. Springing up from the bed, she opened her suitcase and removed the hypodermic and the vial of poison. She put the little bottle on the table, gently removed the cork, and filled the syringe with the venomous yellow liquid. When the vial was empty, she extracted the needle and gently pushed the plunger up until a couple of drops of poison dribbled down the point. Replacing the plastic cap on the tip of the needle, she gingerly put the little weapon on the bed. She would get rid of the vial when she went outside, she thought. Then she ripped open the bundle of clothes and began to dress.

A short time later, Beatrice, wearing sunglasses, dressed in her new outfit, and armed with the syringe in her pocket, went downstairs to the lobby, carrying her suitcase and coat. The concierge came out from his office.

"*Guten Tag,*" he said, and addressed her in German.

It was obvious that he didn't recognize her. His response when she removed her hat and sunglasses was heartening.

"Ach!" he cried. "I thought you were a village boy!"

"Did you really?" she asked.

"*Ja,* surely. The girls, they wear dirndls, not lederhosen," he said with a wink. "You have bought the wrong costume."

"American girls are different," Beatrice said. "The car is all arranged?"

"*Ja*—eleven o'clock at Meyer's café. The driver, he is a tall man with a beard. The car is green."

"He may have to wait."

"*Ja, ja,* I told him. No problem."

Beatrice handed him her coat and suitcase.

"Could you give these to the driver, please? Tell him to put them in the car."

"Certainly. . . . Here is your bill."

Beatrice paid him in cash, tucked her hair back into her hat, put on her sunglasses, and started out.

"You are going to fool all the people of Davos," the concierge said with a laugh.

She turned and glanced over her shoulder as she opened the lobby door. "Just one. . . . I hope."

When Beatrice arrived at the *Seilbahn*, it was just past ten o'clock. Riding up the mountain in the crowded car, she ignored the view, concentrating instead on the syringe in her pocket and the mission at hand. She was going to commit murder, she thought—calculated, cold-blooded murder. The planning of it seemed simple compared to the actual act itself. Could she go through with it? When the time came and the opportunity arose, could she really jab Crowley with that needle and pump the deadly poison into his bloodstream, without fear of the consequences—or, worse, fear of her own conscience? She steeled herself for the act, knowing deep in her heart that it was either him or her. She reminded herself that it was an execution, not a murder. "I must do it, I must not hesitate," she repeated over and over to herself like a litany, "for my father, for Stephen, for Diaz, for Simon, for Trisha and all the other women, for the world, and, finally, for me."

By the time she got off the *Seilbahn*, Beatrice had convinced herself that she was an avenging angel. She held firmly to that thought as she sat at a table outside the restaurant, staring at the gate of the clinic.

Time dragged slowly. The cable car came and went. Beatrice watched the passengers make their way in and out of the small station. She kept glancing at the clock on the wall. It was growing closer to eleven, the appointed hour. She began to fear that Crowley and Simon had left before she got there. But no, that wasn't possible, she thought. They would have needed more time to get ready.

She knew she would have to make her move on the *Seilbahn*. It would be too dangerous to try and jab Crowley in the café or on the street. He might recognize her before she got the chance; besides, she would have to be certain no one was watching. Her one hope was that Crowley wouldn't be looking for a man. He was not a man hunter, she thought sardonically. No—risky as it was, her only chance was to attempt his murder on the crowded cable car, just before they reached the station.

Suddenly, three men emerged from the clinic. Beatrice slumped in her chair, and pulled her hat low over her brow, eyeing them as they walked down toward the gate. She immediately recognized Crowley and Simon, but not the third man, who was wearing a dapper tweed jacket, tan melton trousers, and a loden-green felt hat. Oh Christ, she thought, who the hell is *he?* And what if he comes with them? Then her plan would be completely foiled. The third man unlocked the gate and held it open for Crowley and Simon to pass through.

Crowley gripped Simon's arm, guiding him down the sloping hill toward the station. Simon, who looked frighteningly pale and thin, was having some difficulty walking. Dammit! He *is* going with them, Beatrice thought, as the third man—a stocky, sandy-haired fellow with rugged, Nordic features and a leathery, sportsman's complexion, trailed them jauntily, sucking on a pipe that he had briefly stopped to light.

They halted almost directly in front of Beatrice. The stranger put his hand on Crowley's shoulder, and they exchanged a few hushed words while Simon stood by, staring vacantly into space. At one point, the pair broke into laughter and raised their voices slightly. Though she still couldn't make out what they were saying, Beatrice thought she heard Crowley address the man as "Wilhelm." Was this Dr. Wilhelm Friedrich? she wondered in a panic. If it was, he might well be accompanying them to Zurich in order to look after Simon.

Then, to her profound relief, Crowley and the third man shook hands. Beatrice watched as the man turned and headed up the hill toward the clinic. Crowley pulled Simon forward into the station. Beatrice got up from her chair and followed at a discreet distance. She watched Crowley purchase two tickets and move onto the platform, waiting for the incoming car. Concealing herself behind a small group of boisterous German tourists with cameras, she held her breath as the *Seilbahn* cruised into the landing dock and came to a halt. The incoming passengers disembarked, and the gate opened. The crowd moved forward.

Inside the nearly full car, Beatrice stood with her back toward Crowley and Simon, who were off to one side. Simon was leaning against the window, looking as if he might pass out. Crowley whispered in his ear as the *Seilbahn* started gliding down the mountain.

As they descended, Beatrice edged her way closer to Crowley, who seemed entranced by the view. Examining the suit he was wearing, Beatrice decided not to take the chance of trying to stab him through the material. She would have to go for the bare skin at the back of his neck when no one was paying attention.

After about fifteen minutes, the little station loomed ahead. Beatrice was very near to Crowley now—almost within striking distance. Carefully pulling the syringe out of her pocket, she removed the protective plastic cap and positioned the hypodermic between the third and index fingers of her right hand, pressing lightly on the pump with her thumb. She kept it low and out of sight. When she felt the familiar shudder of the car making contact with the tracks, she moved in. She was standing right next to him now.

Without warning, he pivoted and gazed at her. She froze as he briefly looked her up and down. But the blank expression on his face told her he did not recognize her. He blinked and stared past her, seemingly preoccupied. The cable car came to a halt, and the doors slid open. People started pushing forward. Crowley held back a bit to avoid the crush, taking Simon's arm. As he was navigating Simon through the crowd, Beatrice drew herself in close behind him, raised up her right hand, and stabbed the back of his neck, simultaneously pushing in the pump with her thumb.

Crowley emitted a little cry of pain and slapped the back of his neck. Flailing, he whirled around and knocked Beatrice's hat and sunglasses askew. As Beatrice backed away, their eyes made contact.

"Witch!" he exploded, lunging for her.

Grabbing her throat, he pulled her down and rolled over on top of her, his great bulk making it impossible for her to move. Beatrice struggled to get out from under him as his mammoth hand squeezed her trachea.

"You cannot win, Witch!" he whispered, glaring at her. "The Inquisition is eternal!"

Furiously wrenching her head from side to side, Beatrice

gasped for air. She felt his grip loosen. Then Crowley's hand fell from her throat as he began to heave. Beatrice managed to scurry out from under him.

"He's having a heart attack! He's having a heart attack!" she screamed, scrambling to her feet.

Crowley lurched onto his side, his body contorting in ferocious spasms. With his tongue grossly protruding from his mouth, his face swelled up and turned a purplish blue. By now, several of the passengers had turned around. Suddenly, his eyes widened, bulged out of their sockets for an instant, then shut. He went limp. A commotion began. As people stooped down to come to Crowley's aid, Beatrice grabbed hold of Simon's arm and pulled him off the cable car.

"Come on, Simon," she panted. "We've got to get out of here!"

"Beatrice, is it really you?" He looked utterly bewildered. Stopping for a moment, he tried to bring her into focus.

"It's really me," she said, dragging him onward.

"What's happening . . . ? Where's my father?"

"Dead, Simon. He's had a heart attack. Now let's get the hell out of here!"

"I love you, Beatrice."

"I love you, Simon. Come on!"

They hurried out of the station and into the street. Beatrice propped him up as they walked the short distance to the café next to the church. The green car was waiting out front, as promised. Beatrice shoved Simon into the back seat and got in next to him.

"Zurich," she said to the driver. "As fast as you can."

"*Jawohl!*" he said, gunning the engine. They sped on their way.

26

HE FOLLOWING MORNING, BEATRICE WAS STAND-
ing in front of a dung-colored six-story 1920's
building on the Bahnhofstrasse in Zurich. The
discreet gold plaque near the entrance read:
UNITED SWISS BANK.

She walked into the foyer and told the re-
ceptionist she had come for her appointment
with Carl Haemmerli, the bank's president. Presently, Herr
Haemmerli, a tall, silver-haired man, impeccably dressed, came
down personally to meet her. Speaking English with only the
faintest trace of an accent, he was extremely correct in his manner.
He accompanied her to an old-fashioned elevator. They got in. He
pushed the large white button, and the brass gate clicked shut.

At the top floor, Herr Haemmerli escorted Beatrice into his
spare office, where they sat down.

"Now," Haemmerli began, "will you give me the name or
number under which the account is to be accessed?"

Beatrice opened her purse and handed him a slip of paper. "I'm not sure this is exactly right," she said. "I memorized the list once and never had a chance to look at it again."

Haemmerli regarded her. "I am sure you understand that it must be exactly right," he said. "Particularly with an account of this size." He made no mention of Crowley's attempt to get at the funds. The Swiss banker's legendary discretion, she thought.

Beatrice stared at Haemmerli as he opened the piece of paper. On it was written:

Alpha et Omega, Acorib, Agle, Amaymon, Bamulahe, Bayemon, Beelzebut, Egym, Enga, Englabis, Imagnon, Ingodum, Ipreto, Madael, Magoa, Meraye, Obu, Ogia, Oriston, Penaton, Perchiram, Phaton, Ramath, Rissasoris, Rubiphaton, Satan, Satiel, Septentrion, Tetragrammaton, Tremendum.

She had omitted the name Tiros, the name Borzamo had crossed out. Haemmerli got up from his chair. "Excuse me," he said. "I will not be a moment."

The code may not be right, Beatrice said to herself—not for the first time. Though she had consciously given Crowley a wrong code, she wasn't altogether certain she knew the right one. She didn't entirely trust her memory, particularly not after all she had been through. But what if it is the right code? Then Göring's fortune would be hers, she thought.

Her first priority was to get Simon well. The wound on his side was healing. The doctors at the clinic had damaged him—but only slightly. In the car on the way back from Davos, he had told her about the single shock treatment Friedrich had given him. She was confident she had rescued him in time.

Dear, dear Simon, she thought, remembering their conversation the previous night in the hotel. He had thanked her for saving his life and told her again that he loved her.

"But I know that you could never love me," he had said shyly.

"Why not?" she had asked him.

"I know how I appear to the world. I'm an ugly, nervous man, and I've lived under the shadow of evil. And then there's my obsession with my books...."

"You're my true and faithful knight," she had said, gripping his hand.

"Am I?"

"Sans peur et sans reproche, as the troubadours sang."

At that moment, Simon had closed his weary eyes and said, "None of my precious books contains a story stranger than this one." His sweetness had brought tears to her eyes.

She resolved never to tell Simon the truth about his father. She would allow him to think Crowley's death was due to natural causes. And indeed, that was how the *International Herald Tribune* had reported the incident that very morning. FATAL HEART ATTACK STRIKES AMERICAN PROFESSOR ON CABLE CAR read the small headline buried in the middle of the paper. She could never confess that she was guilty of murder—not even to Simon. It was a secret she would take to her grave. . . . Well, on second thought, maybe not. Maybe one day she would confide in him, if they grew very close. But that was in the future. She had more pressing things to think about.

Now that his father was dead, Simon would have no fear of telling all that he knew. Between them, she and Simon could get the FBI to launch an investigation. In the meantime, she would hire enough protection for them both in case Defensores Fidei got any ideas about revenge. Somehow, she doubted that they would. Insane causes need an insane leader, she thought, and their leader was dead. Nevertheless, she vowed to use her resources to bring Father Morton, Signor Antonelli, Detective Monahan, and the whole lot of them to justice.

Having got those essential things out of the way, she would move on to her real objective. She had known for some time how she would spend the millions if they became hers. And now, silently, she repeated her resolve: *I'll donate the money to every cause that the Nazis and Defensores Fidei would detest. It'll be history's most expensive joke—the haters financing a war against hatred.*

It was not long before Herr Haemmerli entered the room. He stood before her and handed back the paper that bore the names. Beatrice held her breath.

"Miss O'Connell," he said in a crisp, businesslike tone, on his face a banker's tight smile. "Please come this way. I would like to explain to you the services we offer our clients."